NORWICH GOLD

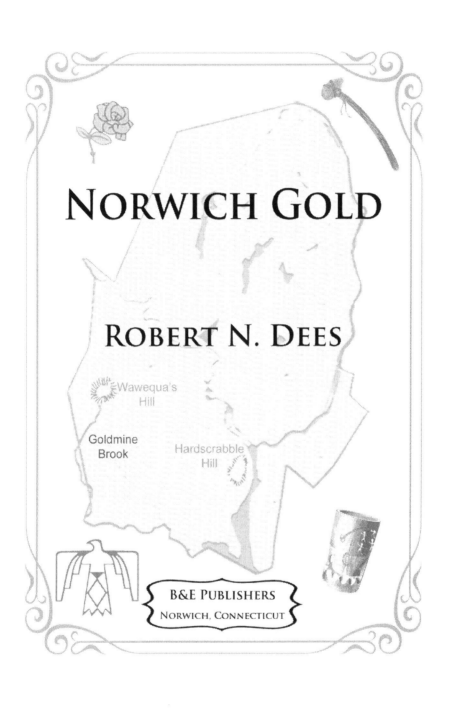

Norwich Gold

Robert N. Dees

B&E Publishers
Norwich, Connecticut

NORWICH GOLD

By Robert N. Dees
Copyright © 2023 by B&E Publishers
Norwich, Connecticut
All Rights Reserved

Library of Congress Control Number: 2023911411
ISBN: 979-8-9885630-1-3
Printed in the United States of America

No part of this book may be reproduced or stored in a retrieval system or transmitted in any form or by any means, electronic, mechanical, photocopying, recording, or otherwise, without permission from the publisher.

The story and events portrayed in this novel are works of fiction that flowed from the author's imagination. However, most places and business enterprises described in the book existed during the period. The author attempted to accurately portray all locations and business enterprises except for the Wawecus Hill Gold, Silver, and Nickel Mining Company.

Some characters portrayed were real and resided in Norwich, Connecticut, in the 1858-1859 time period. All Native American groups and characters depicted in this novel are entirely fictional. All dialogue for all characters is imaginary. Names of all fictional characters are a product of the author's imagination, and any resemblance to any living person is purely coincidental.

To Ellen
My soul mate, dedicated wife, best friend, and companion who supports me, our family, friends, and community in countless ways

Forward

A few years ago, while exploring Norwich, Connecticut's rich history, I noticed the name of a brook near the southwestern town boundary, Goldmine Brook. Why would it occur to anyone in Norwich to choose such a name?

The brook empties into Trading Cove Brook, which feeds Trading Cove Pond, and eventually empties into the Thames River. However, if you follow Goldmine Brook northward, you'll notice this winding body of water extends more than two miles. Its headwaters are in a meadow near the base of Wawecus Hill.

After some research, I learned that a group of men from Rhode Island organized the Wawecus Hill Gold, Silver, and Nickel Mining Company in 1851. They planned to mine gold and other precious minerals. Jesse Fillmore, the company's president and largest stakeholder, organized the company with a capital of $500,000 ($18,600,000 in 2023 dollars).

The 1859 Bicentennial Jubilee celebration of the founding of Norwich highlighted in this novel was indeed one of the town's most memorable, spectacular events.

All the geographical locations discussed in this historical fiction novel are real, and all the business enterprises mentioned were active during the period. Many characters were also real and lived in Norwich during the time frame.

The story and all dialogue in this novel are entirely fictional.

Bob Dees

Cast Of Characters

1676 Fictional Characters
Wawequa – Lucas's brother & leader of a Quinebaugan village on Wawequa's Hill
Tantuk – Wawequa's son, who made Quinebaugan tools and weapons

1850s Fictional Characters
Bowie – Pocawansett instrument man on Corey's survey team
Brynn Dunham – John Dunham's daughter; Lydia's friend
Corey Pallaton – Pocawansett leader and regional land developer
Crockett – Pocawansett bookkeeper on Corey's survey team
Dexter – Brynn Dunham's Norwichtown terrier
Elena Pallaton – Corey Pallaton's wife and company accountant
Faith Mathews – Travis Mathews's mother
Jeremy Pallawotuk – Corey Pallaton's survey team chief
Jonathan Mathews – Travis Mathews's father
Lydia Stedman – An adventurous newspaper reporter
Maisie Finnegan – A young Scottish immigrant
Rachel Flowers – Quinebaugan Medicine Woman
Travis Q. Mathews – Young man who discovers gold
White Eagle – Quinebaugan sage who lives at Kachina Rock

1850s Real Characters
Aaron Stevens – First Congregational Church choir director
Amos W. Prentice – A former mayor of Norwich
Caroline Jameson Stedman – Lydia Stedman's mother
C.C. Brand – Owner of a factory that makes whaling guns
Emeline & Isabella Norton – Henry B. Norton's twin daughters
Fidelia Foster Hyde – Senator Lafayette Sabine Foster's sister
Francis A. Perkins – Treasurer of the Norwich Savings Society

General William Williams – Norwich businessman, militia leader, church leader, and philanthropist

Harriet Peck Williams – William's wife & generous donor

Henry Bill – Publisher of Bibles and a Norwich land developer

Henry Norton – Owner of Norwich-based steamboat company

Henry F. Walling – Norwich cartographer in the mid-1850s

Hiram P. Arms – Minister of First Congregational Church

James D. Mowry – Owner of Norwich rifle production company

John Dunham – Former postmaster and mayor of Norwich

John W. Stedman – Lydia Stedman's father, publisher of the Aurora newspaper, and current Norwich postmaster

Lucius W. Carroll – Owner/operator of a wholesale goods store

Lucy Apply Mathewson – Shareholder in the mining company

Mary Dunham – John Dunham's wife, Brynn Dunham's mother

William A. Buckingham – Governor of the State of Connecticut

TABLE OF CONTENTS

Prologue 1
1: Gold! 7
2: Goldmine Brook 13
3: Pow Wow 22
4: Travis Mathews 35
5: Wawecus Hill Gold, Silver, and Nickel Mining Company 40
6: Snakes 48
7: Get Things Rollin' 57
8: Brynn 61
9: Advertisement 68
10: Lydia Steps Forward 75
11: Church With The Stedmans 82
12: Treasure Hunt 88
13: New London County Fair 100
14: Fund the Company 112
15: Building Supplies 119
16: Mathews Family Heritage 124
17: Company Progress 133
18: Jubilee Organizational Meeting 143
19: Social Mixer ~ The Ladies 154
20: Social Mixer ~ The Gentlemen 163
21: Social Mixer ~ The Dance 175
22: Dinner at the Wauregan 189
23: Seven Cents 197
24: Gold Fever 206
25: Corey's Fortress 213
26: Recital 221
27: Crossroads 228
28: Consequences 232
29: Friends Helping Friends 238

30: Barrel Bonfire 248
31: Company Meeting 256
32: Defamation 272
33: Disbelief 277
34: Social Justice 280
35: Jubilee Planning 289
36: Pesikutes Ridge 300
37: Faith Mathews & Rachel Flowers 306
38: Aquilablanca 313
39: Wawequa 322
40: Laypetea 331
41: Bursting Balloons 348
42: Liquidation 355
43: Goodbye, Miss Porter 360
44: Pixie, Dixie, and Velvet 369
45: Lucas's Chair 382
46: Final Planning 388
47: Jubilee Procession 396
48: Jubilee Dinner 403
49: Jubilee Ball 416
50: Revelation 430
51: Recovery 438
52: Dunham Family Picnic 442
53: Green Corn Festival...454
Afterward 470
About the Author 471
References 472
Illustration Acknowledgements 472

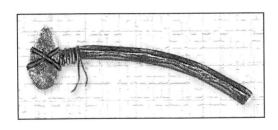

PROLOGUE
WAWEQUA'S HILL
AUGUST 1676

Tantuk wondered how it would feel to be bitten by a snake. Once long ago, as a young boy, he had watched in amazement when a serpent struck his father. After his face tightened, a copious stream of sweat began rolling off both sides of his forehead. Moments later, he knelt on one knee, and Tantuk saw how Wawequa's breathing quickened as his entire body began to shake. When he looked closer, tiny droplets of blood exited from two small holes on his father's forearm.

Tantuk's mother's sudden, eerie scream broke his trance when she ordered, "Lie down, don't move."

She began to firmly knead his forearm, just above the bite, encouraging the venom/blood concoction to exit his body through holes created by the fangs. Finally, after several minutes, which seemed like an eternity to Tantuk, his father's breathing slowly returned to normal. Tantuk's mother calmed, and life as they knew it continued.

Tantuk could hardly believe that the bite from a single snake could cause such a reaction. However, in the weeks following the incident, Tantuk noticed that his father seemed almost invincible. Somehow, the snake venom had transformed Wawequa into a stronger, even more influential leader.

After that day, the thought of snakes never bothered Tantuk. On the contrary, he felt drawn to them. Sometimes, after his mother's squirrel traps imprisoned unsuspecting mice, Tantuk fed the rodents to his reptilian friends. He liked hearing the sound of the rattles at the end of the serpent's body as the mice slowly made their way down the snake's gullet.

~~~~~

Today, Tantuk's memory was crystal clear. He felt as though the events of his life had occurred only yesterday. Tantuk was most thankful for the many skills his mother taught him as a young boy. At an early age, he learned the art of grinding parched corn into yokeag from her. They used the majority of the coarse, dry powder to feed their family immediately. He liked the feel of grinding kernels of corn and transforming them into a more easily edible form that would sustain his family throughout the long winter when food was scarce.

Tantuk later learned to use a much larger, more substantial mortar and pestle than the one needed for corn. He used these tools to separate veins of gold from sharp, irregular-shaped, translucent rocks that he had found on the hillside. Finally, after many attempts, he learned how to press the precious, golden flakes onto the rounded stone tip of a small tomahawk he had made.

His mother had also shown him how to decorate tools used by the Quinebaugan. In addition to being the wife of Wawequa, the leader of their local community here on Wawequa's Hill, she was an accomplished artisan. She had lovingly shown Tantuk how to make an ink-like substance that she used to inscribe Quinebaugan history onto the tools of their daily lives.

Tantuk became the tribe's most respected artisan, like his mother before him. He used sharpened rocks as knives to carve totems into cherry tree branches and fashioned unique totems for his young friends. His personal totem was the rattlesnake.

Tantuk's most cherished possession as a boy was the golden-tipped tomahawk he fashioned from a small, curved branch and a rounded rock. The handle bore the shape of a rattlesnake, and he felt invincible when he held it. He became powerful, just like his father!

In the prime of his life, Tantuk had the honor of decorating the Quinebaugan symbol of power and dominance in New London County. It was his finest work! He gilded the mortal stone on his father's tomahawk and adorned its handle with his rattlesnake totem.

Quinebaugans told the story of Wawequa's tomahawk thousands of times because it was an essential piece of their tribal history.

~~~~~

Today was a day of change, a day of transition, and a day of transformation. Tantuk's parents had already become one with *Munduyahweh,* the Creator of Mother Earth and all life. All of his brethren who had lived here on Wawequa's Hill had moved to other areas, and now Tantuk was alone.

Today, he only heard the sound of voices of ancestors from the distant past and the murmur of the brook below.

Today's Hoopanoag Sachem Metawando, a.k.a. *Prince Philip,* and the Pocawansett Sachem Pallatonomo were again causing trouble in New London County. They had joined to fight the English and many Quinebaugan warriors. However, Prince Philip was rapidly losing the war. Only yesterday, Tantuk learned that sixty-five Pocawansett refugees had arrived in Norwich after surrendering their arms. The town's authorities ceded a large tract of land, here on Wawequa's Hill, to the now-homeless Pocawansett. Norwich's *act of generosity* donated Tantuk's native homeland to people who despised him and everything he had ever stood for.

Tantuk gently placed his large, beautifully decorated mortar and pestle inside the rock-lined opening on the side of the hill. Next to it, he carefully placed the small golden-tipped tomahawk from his childhood. He needed to feel the power embedded in his tomahawk for one final moment. Just as he wrapped his fingers around the weapon, he felt the presence of his ancestors. Then, one after another, after another, he felt the poisonous fangs sink deeply into his arm.

Tantuk experienced renewed strength, peace, and tranquility as his parents' spirit entered his soul. He loved this spot. He was satisfied with his abundant life here in his Quinebaugan homeland.

182 YEARS LATER ...

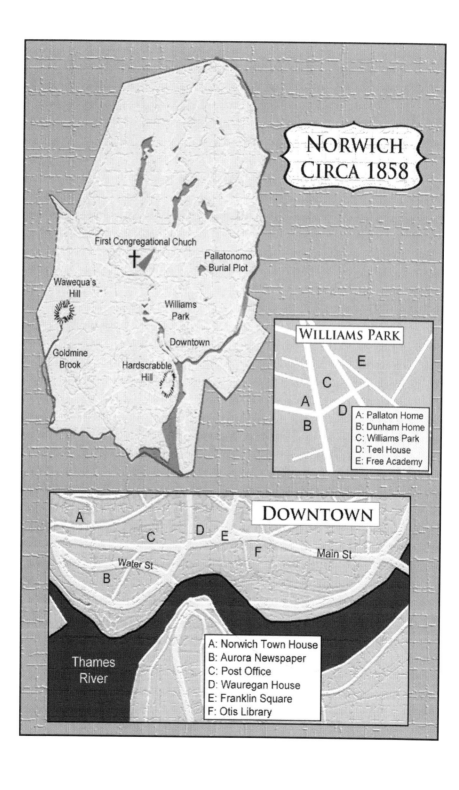

1: GOLD!
WAWECUS HILL
MONDAY, AUGUST 16, 1858

"For the third time, Gimpy, I said back up!" Jeremy snapped at him.

"I heard you the first time, arsehole!" Travis snarled. He enjoyed this part-time job but didn't care much for his fellow survey party members. Nevertheless, Travis, or Gimpy as they called him, desperately tried to position the rod precisely on the edge of the precipice. He knew the party needed accurate rod placements along the area's perimeter so they could later draw a reliable map for future home lots.

Jeremy, nicknamed Bear, Bowie, Crockett, and Travis, had been contending with uneven terrain, overgrown vegetation filled with poison ivy, downed tree limbs, tall grass, goldenrod, ragweed, bittersweet, and snakes for several days.

The party needed a clear, safe pathway through the brush to access the site. So their instrument man, Bowie, enthusiastically slashed his way through the bramble using a 24-inch Jim Bowie knife. And, their bookkeeper, Crockett, protected the party from snakes with a pair of Smith & Wesson revolvers.

Travis thought Bowie and Crockett enjoyed using their weapons more than necessary. Travis had nothing against knives.

He had a strong emotional connection to the Damascus steel-bladed knife that his father had given him. He used the whale bone-handled, four-inch-long knife often for countless small, routine tasks. However, it was a mere toy compared to Bowie's gigantic blade.

It had been a hot, sweltering, uncomfortable mid-September afternoon, and Travis's eyes watered profusely. He'd been sneezing all day due to the abundance of ragweed pollen. Then, standing near the outer edge of the flat survey area, Travis heard a noisy brook just below the steep, rocky hillside. For a brief moment, he mulled how good it would feel to dunk his face and hands into the cool water. The rustic view of the valley below and the lush countryside filled with mountain laurels gave him a sense of belonging. He thought, *"This area is my native homeland."*

But his focus wasn't on the trees or the brook today. Instead, it was on ensuring he didn't accidentally step on a snake or off the steep hillside. Travis wasn't afraid of snakes; he simply didn't want to harm one by stepping on them.

He took one small step backward and balanced himself on the loose rocks at the edge while holding the survey rod.

Travis yelled to the instrument man, "Okay, take the reading. I'm at the edge!"

A moment later, a breeze picked up, and a large cluster of ragweed pollen drifted into Travis's nose. He couldn't stop it. His nose twitched, and a thunderous sneeze erupted from the core of his chest. As Travis felt his footing give way, he desperately tried to regain balance by thrusting the rod into the rocks. But the stones only cracked open and provided no support. He didn't even have time to yell or make a sound.

Travis desperately tried to regain his balance. But he was born with his left leg slightly shorter than the other and had always had trouble balancing. All survey party members noticed and joked about his slight, ever-present limp. These Pocawansett teenagers were merciless to Travis, a native Quinebaugan.

As the rod dropped from his grasp, Travis tumbled down the hillside. He felt his knees crash against several rocks along the way down. Several rhododendrons, forsythia, and other shrubs whipped and thrashed him up one side and down the other. Finally, Travis's excruciating journey ended when his leg struck the trunk of one of the large maple trees at the bottom of the hill.

For a moment, he lay there in a daze. Then, he wondered, "What the hell just happened? Where am I?"

His head was still spinning, and he saw multiple tiny, bright pinpoints of light seemingly emanating from the back of his eyeballs. Then, as Travis finally gathered his wits, he remembered. He had taken one backward step too many.

After a quick survey of his damaged body, he knew he would eventually be okay, except for his left ankle and left arm. His forearm was bleeding slightly after being scraped by several rocks on the trip down. Travis stood up slowly and gingerly made his way over the brook. He knew his arm needed to be cleaned and dressed as well as possible.

As he immersed his hands and arms into the cool, refreshing water, the late afternoon sun shimmered off the surface of the brook. But it was more than just a shimmer, he thought. And it wasn't just reflecting off the surface. Instead, the points of light seemed to radiate from rocks on the bottom of the stream's bed.

He thought, "I must have a concussion because I'm seeing things that aren't real."

Travis reached deep into the water with his extraordinarily long right arm and picked up a rounded, translucent rock. As he lifted the mineral above his head, he saw the setting sun's rays reflect off small deposits within its body. What a stunning display of glory!

It was amazing! As he studied the rock, he saw several thick veins of a mineral that looked like gold snaking through the quartz rock.

Travis's heart pounded deep within his chest. Could it be gold? It sure looked like it. He placed the promising stone into the pocket of his trousers and returned up the hill.

The others had scampered to the hill's edge by this time. They wanted to see the result of Travis's fall.

Jeremy, the survey party's leader, yelled to Travis, "Heh! Are you all right down there?"

Travis replied. "Yeah, I'm okay. I'm on my way up."

He knew the climb would be challenging due to his aching body, but there was no choice. His turned ankle made each step more painful than the one before, and his arms still stung from the forsythia thrashing. The loose rocks, the steep incline, and the long shadows from the tall maple trees made it even more challenging.

Before cresting the hill, loose rocks gave way beneath his boots. Once again, the slide and tumble down the hillside punished Travis. However, this time, it was more of a roll than a total collapse. He repeatedly flopped from his stomach to his side, to his back. And this time, seemingly with divine intervention, his downward journey ended only halfway down the hillside. His body finally stopped when he landed beside a rock outcropping just above a grass-covered mound.

NORWICH GOLD

He thought the mound's shape was unnatural but could not determine what it was in the near darkness. Nevertheless, he placed his hand on the rise to balance himself and stood. Travis felt three long, slender, thin rocks beneath his palm. A sudden, odd sensation rushed through his aching body.

Then he suddenly realized, "They are *not* rocks; they are bones! They feel like the remains of someone's fingers."

For a moment, he couldn't trust what his eyes clearly saw. He knew that his brain was still foggy. However, Travis also knew his initial feelings and thoughts were correct when he looked closer. They were indeed bones. He didn't understand why his entire being felt enlightened and invigorated when his hand contacted the skeleton's fingers.

By the time Travis reached the top, the sun had drifted just below the horizon, and the other guys were beginning to pack it up for the day.

Travis called out, "Heh, Bear! Come look at this."

Jeremy yelled back. "What is it? Hurry up. I've got to report to Mr. Pallaton before dark."

Travis walked over to Jeremy, showed him the chunk of gold-laced quartz, and replied, "I think it's gold."

Jeremy stared at the mineral for what seemed an eternity. Then, he looked and Travis and said, "Gimpy, where did you find this?"

Travis pointed to the brook below.

After thinking a moment, Jeremy motioned for Crockett and Bowie to join him. He showed them the gold-laced rock and said, "Looks like Gimpy may have found something of value."

He looked at his companions, smiled, and said, "Good thing Gimpy fell off the cliff. Maybe he's good for something other than holding our rods!"

They laughed, and the trio instantly rushed to the stream, fumbling and stumbling in gleeful excitement to search for more gold. These young men had constantly struggled for survival for most of their lives, and now, the hope of instant wealth filled their hearts with greed.

Darkness fell after twenty minutes of searching the brook, forcing the boys to discontinue their quest.

Jeremy said, "I'll give this rock to Mr. Pallaton tonight. Then, let's meet at the office tomorrow morning at sunrise and devise a plan to find more gold."

2: GOLDMINE BROOK
AT BASE OF WAWECUS HILL
TUESDAY, AUGUST 17, 1858

At six feet four inches tall, Travis was significantly taller, stronger, and stockier than most twenty-year-olds. Additionally, he had dark, golden eyes, jet-black eyebrows, thick black hair, and a prominent snake-shaped birthmark above his left eye. Everyone noticed Travis's birthmark; some friends even kidded him about it. But he liked the way it looked. It made him feel special.

Travis was a proud member of the Quinebaugan tribe and loved living among his friends in Lucasville. However, he yearned for adventure on the high sea and to visit exotic lands firsthand. His father's endless seafaring stories had mesmerized him.

So, after years of daydreaming, Travis hit upon a plan. He would become a navigator on one of General Williams's whaling ships. It was a natural progression for Travis because he had already become familiar with several tools of the maritime trade, such as whaling guns, at his regular, full-time job.

Several months ago, Travis had also volunteered as a part-time apprentice surveyor to implement his plan. He worked at Mr. Henry Walling's cartography office in downtown Norwich because he wanted to learn to use a sextant. Travis knew that

Walling used the precision measuring instrument for mapping and that ship navigators used sextants to pinpoint their ship's position at sea. If Travis could learn to use one skillfully, he would be able to earn his dream job as a ship's navigator.

Corey Pallaton entered Walling's office two weeks ago, looking for help. The youngest, least experienced teen, who had served as his survey team's rodman, had recently been struck by yellow fever. The steamship *Commonwealth* employed the lad as a part-time steward when his services were not required on the survey team. The ship regularly transported passengers to and from New York City and Norwich. Unfortunately, the Pocawansett steward died several days after one of the New York passengers infected him and many others aboard one of the voyages.

Since Walling's survey team was currently between jobs, he suggested that Corey hire Travis for the housing project. He highly recommended Travis, saying he was a rookie surveyor who aspired to learn more.

Pallaton instantly hired him. He knew it would be difficult for Travis to fit in with his survey team because the other three team members were also members of the Pocawansett tribe. Travis was of Quinebaugan descent, not Pocawansett. The team was still mourning the loss of their lifelong brother, and Travis would be an obvious outsider. The others would feel little need to be friendly because they needed a whipping boy to help relieve the pain of their loss. Corey also knew making fun of Travis's appearance would be easy.

Unfortunately, Travis's several peculiar physical features left him vulnerable to teenage boys' scorn. In addition to his limp, Travis's upper torso was much longer than expected, and his arms were extremely long. As a result, for most of his adolescent life, other boys teased him constantly. They mercilessly reminded him of his limp and spindly, peculiar stature.

However, Travis's long arms came in handy for his job as a rodman. He could easily reach out and place a rod firmly on the ground farther than almost anyone. It made for quick, more accurate readings. However, as boys will be boys, Travis was always the first to be anointed with an unwelcome nickname.

Bear, whose real name was Jeremy Pallawotuk, had a noble nickname that Pocawansetts held in high esteem. Bears symbolized authority, strength, courage, and authority in the Pocawansett culture.

Jeremy had nicknamed Travis, *Gimpy*. Travis hated the name and despised Jeremy for pinning it on him.

~~~~~

This morning, Travis had not traveled from Hardscrabble Hill with the other survey team members. He hoped that circumstances would never again force him to ride with them. Instead, he had ridden in comfort and companionship with his beloved horse today. Moshup was his best friend, primary transportation, companion, and responsibility.

Travis enjoyed tending to Moshup. The horse required a never-ending supply of food, water, and grooming, but the benefits of friendship far outweighed all the labor that Travis happily supplied.

This morning's ride had been an enjoyable, relaxing outing. Unlike yesterday afternoon's extreme heat and high humidity, today's air was clean, brisk, and almost autumn-like. Travis wanted to find out if Wawecus Hill concealed any more secrets.

After giving Moshup a long swig from the brook, Travis treated him to a ripe apple he'd picked along the way. The trees were laden with fruit at this time of year, and he loved sharing nature's bounty with Moshup.

He questioned himself, "Should I search for gold or check out the boney fingers before the others arrive?"

After deciding to search the brook, he noticed its shallow water flowing over a bed of promising rocks and minerals. However, the view of this morning's stream was unlike yesterday's shimmering beauty resulting from the late afternoon, sinking sun. Since a host of red maple trees shaded the western slope of the hillside, Travis knew it would be difficult to find even a speck of gold at this time of day.

The rocky banks of the brook were overgrown with thick-stemmed cattails and tall grass. The vegetation throughout the flat, wooded area near the stream was thick. The densely wooded area was similar to that found above the hillside they had recently surveyed.

For an instant, he wondered if anyone had ever lived in this spot, then thought, "Of course they did. I found bones on the side of the hill. What was I thinking?"

"Let's see if I can find the rest of Mr. Boney Fingers," he chuckled at his new nickname for the skeletal remains.

As Travis fought through the brush to the base of the hill, he spotted the small outcropping and grassy mound. In the morning's clear daylight, he recognized the giant mountain laurel shrub hovering over what appeared to be an indentation in the outcropping.

As he was about to investigate, Travis heard the creaking, squeaking wheels of the company's buckboard wagon. He knew they would soon trudge through the last hundred yards of vegetation on foot to join him.

NORWICH GOLD

~~~~~

Travis greeted the approaching group, "Good morning, Mr. Pallaton!"

Bowie used his machete-like knife to clear a path for them. Crockett carried the tripod and sextant case, and both Jeremy and Mr. Pallaton brought several survey books and large rolls of maps. They unhitched the horse from the wagon and carried the rest of the equipment and provisions to the worksite.

Corey greeted him, "Good morning Travis. We're a little late because getting the wagon through the brush took quite a while. I need you to get over here and help carry our equipment."

Corey looked around and added, "That's a fine-looking horse you've got there. He's huge!"

Travis replied, patting Moshup's back, "Yes. Moshup is strong, steady, and reliable."

Corey replied with a grin, "Well, Moshup may be a good packhorse, but Lightning, here," he said, motioning to his horse, "could outrun him in his sleep."

Everyone smiled, and Corey continued, "Travis, would you unload Lightning, give him a drink, and tie him up next to Moshup?"

Travis nodded with a slight smirk, "Sure."

He knew Corey was very proud of his prize racehorse, whose duties included pulling the buckboard wagon and carrying supplies for the survey party.

After a quick look around the brook and surrounding area, Corey held out the gold-laced rock Travis found the day before and asked, "Exactly where did you find this rock?"

Travis directed them to the spot, pointed to the brook, and said. "After rolling down the hill, I came here to clean the blood off my arm. When I saw a reflection off the bottom rocks, I picked it up. I knew the guys were packing up for the day, so I had no time to search for anymore."

Corey smiled, nodding at Jeremy, and continued, "After Bear brought this mineral to me last night. I tested it for gold content, and I'm happy to report that the sparkle Travis noticed is indeed a vein of gold."

Corey instructed, gesturing to the brook, "Okay, boys, get in there and see what you can find."

Travis and the other three young men stepped into the shallow stream and carefully inspected many of the rocks on the bottom of the brook. Unfortunately, the sun wasn't striking the creek from the same angle as yesterday. As a result, it wasn't easy to see differences between one rock and another. Nevertheless, they all found several nuggets that appeared to contain gold. Finally, after an hour of searching, they handed Corey several handfuls of hopeful treasures.

Pallaton carefully tested every stone. After several minutes, he slowly looked up from his task to the others. Finally, he triumphantly proclaimed, "Four of the rocks tested positive. So we may have just found ourselves a fortune!"

"For now, do not share news of our discovery with anyone. Our treasure will be a secret until I decide how we can best proceed."

He added, "We need to search this entire area with a fine-tooth comb to see what's here. It will be a lot of hard work, but I am sure you are up for it. But, first, we must organize and make a rough map of the area."

"I estimate this area is about five acres. I want you to do a quick survey today and identify boundaries for about twenty lots.

First, form small lots on both sides of the brook, and as you get further away from the water, make them larger."

Corey stopped for a moment, looked directly at Jeremy, and thoughtfully said, "Once you've drawn an outline map of the area, I want you to pinpoint the location of every stone we find that appears to contain gold. This *Found Gold* map will help guide us in our search for more gold and help keep track of how much we've found."

Gesturing to the entire group, he said, "Everyone, whenever you find anything, be sure to report where and how much you find directly to Bear."

He returned his attention to Jeremy and said, "I need you to show me an updated *Found Gold* map at the end of every week. Will you do that for me?"

Jeremy looked at Corey solemnly and replied, "Yes, Sir. I will."

Corey nodded. Pointing to a flat area about forty feet from the brook, he said, "Okay, as far as site layout is concerned. We'll need one large lot here."

"We'll build a field office and set up the machinery for processing the gold there."

Corey stopped momentarily and stood erect, and his tone suddenly became solemn.

He addressed everyone, saying, "My fellow tribesmen, we are *not* simply standing on a wooded lot near the base of Wawecus Hill. We are *not* simply looking at a babbling brook on the outskirts of Norwich."

"We have discovered **Goldmine Brook!** From this day forward, this stream will be known as Goldmine Brook. The brook is ours. It is on our land! The gold we find in and around this brook will help reunite our people!"

"Okay, boys. Let's get to it!"

Even though Travis was not Pocawansett, Corey's words exhilarated him, and he could hardly wait to begin prospecting. He felt everyone's enthusiasm and wanted to find more gold.

~~~~~

The party fought through the thicket all morning and into the early afternoon. They took careful measurements throughout the five-acre area. It was arduous work. Travis's boots were soaked and covered with mud from standing in and around the brook. It appeared to Travis that Bowie's knife was slashing slower and slower. He looked tired.

Jeremy supplied Corey with an updated list of the measured coordinates every hour. As the day progressed, Corey's preliminary map began taking shape. Jeremy defined and marked twenty-four lots on the map by the end of the day.

Corey called everyone together and said, "Gather around."

While studying the newly drawn map, he said, "I'll create a new company to oversee this gold field. The company will exercise its mineral rights on twenty lots, and we'll erect a field office and processing facility on the remaining four."

Corey announced, "Bear, Bowie, and Crockett, for your dedicated service and loyalty to me, I offer you unlimited mineral rights for one lot of your choosing! I appreciate all that you've done for me through the years. Please study this map carefully and choose any lot you wish."

The young men were stunned. Their faces glowed with pride. Each of them picked a promising lot adjacent to the brook.

Travis saw the happiness on their faces but felt like an outsider.

Corey stood beside the map and proclaimed, "Travis, I know you haven't been with us very long, but I want to reward you too. Come over here."

Corey pointed at the edges of the map, "You may choose any of these five lots. The new company will own the land, but anything you find there will be yours to keep."

Travis was happy that Corey had recognized him but disappointed that none of the offered lots were in prime areas near the water's edge. But, he understood Mr. Pallaton's reasoning.

Then Travis turned his attention from the map and visually scanned the landscape of five offered areas. The lot in the farthest corner of the map included the small mound where he had discovered the bones.

He thought, "Well, if I don't find any gold, perhaps I'll find the rest of Mr. Boney Fingers."

Travis replied, pointing to the lot, which included the mound, "I'll take that one."

The others grinned, and Jeremy said, "That's an unexpected choice. Good luck with that, Gimpy."

3: Pow Wow
Sachem's Plain
Friday, August 20, 1858

It was a warm, clear evening, and a full moon illuminated Sachem's Plain and the nearby Shetucket River. A score of Pocawansett elders and dancers were assembled near the Pow Wow tent, awaiting the Grand Entry for the opening ceremony.

Only a few yards away, Jeremy Pallawotuk's heart raced as he violently kicked his feet and cracked his horsewhip. His body was working its way into a frenzy.

Crockett yelled, "Heh, Bear, you should be more careful; otherwise, you'll hit someone!"

After his concentration broke, Jeremy paused and yelled, "I'm just practicing for the Grass Dance. And I suggest you practice too because I remember how one of your pistols flew out of your hand at last year's Pow Wow!"

Crockett laughed and said, "Yeah. I remember that. But it wasn't dangerous because the gun wasn't loaded. However, it did excite a few girls in the front rows. They noticed me."

Jeremy said, "It looks like the ceremony will begin pretty soon. Have you seen Mr. Pallaton?"

Crockett replied, "No. I haven't."

Jeremy looked northward to the nearby hillside where one of the Pocawansett's greatest warriors and most celebrated sachems was buried. Upon closer inspection, he saw a tall man, with his head bent slightly, standing near the Pallatonomo monument.

Jeremy reverently joined Corey. He knew the tribe's Medicine Man was mentally preparing for the Pow Wow and said, "They're about to begin."

Corey turned slowly toward Jeremy and said, "Yes. The time has come to honor our forefathers, tradition, and heritage. But, unfortunately, our dwindling numbers and declining quality of life threaten our very existence. So, this evening, you and I must do everything possible to restore our tribe's former glory."

Jeremy replied, "Yes. I am encouraged that our discovery of gold will provide relief for our brothers and their families."

Corey said, "But reenergizing our tribe will require much more than money. We also need strong leadership. Elena and I tried to bear a child for several years but were unsuccessful. As a direct descendant of Pocawansett Sachem Pallatonomo, I had hoped to continue my bloodline through a son. Unfortunately, Elena failed us because she is barren. However, I love her anyway because she has tried to fulfill her duty."

"Jeremy, since you were a child, I've taught you everything I know and am proud of you. I'm proud of how you lead our tribesmen and your pure Pocawansett royal bloodline. I'm also proud of your physical strength and wisdom. I think of you as my only son."

Jeremy bowed his head slightly and said, "Thank you, Corey. Since the day my father was lost at sea, you've nurtured me and provided for my mother. I will be in your debt forever."

Corey responded, "You and your mother are dear to my heart. I dream you will someday become our next Medicine Man and perhaps even Sachem."

Jeremy nodded and remained silent.

After pausing, Corey continued, "It is time for us to lead our brethren."

~~~~~

Elena Pallaton heard the voices of her nearby sisters and brothers and the popping embers beneath the mammoth cast iron pot before her. She was acutely aware of the aroma of the sweet corn concoction wafting through the air. Elena tended the flames of the fire, centered in the Pow Wow arena, gently stroking the bottom of the tribe's simmering evening meal with a 24-inch long cast iron spoon. Tonight, she would cook the feast perfectly. The slight hunger pang in Elena's stomach only heightened her anticipation of the upcoming evening.

After filling her lungs with the scent of her succotash for one last check, she smiled and thought, "This may be my best batch ever."

Knowing the Grand Entry was about to begin, Elena looked around for a place to sit. The elders and dancers were still outside the tent, and thirty or so tribe members, plus several invited guests, sat inside. Elena knew almost everyone but spotted a young woman with long, curly red hair sitting alone. To Elena, she appeared out of place.

She wondered who this girl might be, so Elena approached her and said, "May I join you?"

The young woman smiled shyly and replied, "Sure. Please sit."

Elena sat and, after introducing herself, said, "I haven't seen you before. Are you friends with someone in our tribe?"

The girl timidly replied, "Yes. My name is Maisie Finnegan. I'm friends with Bear, Bowie, and Crockett. They are Pocawansett surveyors who work for Mr. Pallaton."

Elena threw back her head, chuckled, and replied, "Yes. I know them all quite well because Mr. Pallaton is my husband."

Maisie replied, "Oh. What a surprise! I want to tell you that those fellows deeply respect your husband. I'm so happy to meet you!"

She continued, "I've been looking forward to Pow Wow for quite a while. Crockett told me this annual event is fun, full of interesting stories, exciting, and offers lots of good food."

Elena replied, "Yes. The Pow Wow is all that and more. It's my favorite event of our fall festival of the Harvest Moon."

She continued, "I'm a member of the Hoopanoag tribe and a direct descendant of Massasoit, the Great Sachem who befriended Roger Williams 200 years ago. I've attended both Hoopanoag and Pocawansett Pow Wows my entire life. You might be interested in the fact that I met Corey at a Pow Wow when I was seventeen. My heartbeat quickened as I watched him dance around the Pow Wow fire pit. I fell in love with him instantly."

"But I also loved the Pow Wows for the vast array of Native American food. My mother was our tribe's succotash chef. For years, I helped her harvest ears of sweet corn and prepared her secret recipe of Hoopanoag *msickquatash*, called *sohquttahhash* by the Pocawansett and succotash by the English. My mother's recipe included corn, lima beans, yellow cherry tomatoes, and one secret ingredient, which gave her succotash a unique consistency, appearance, and taste."

"My mother planted several okra seeds specifically for the event in the back of her garden every year. She knew her recipe differed from the *msíckquatash* that her ancestors served the Pilgrims during the first Thanksgiving, but she believed her dish tasted even better. The okra made hers both tastier and contained more life-sustaining nutrients."

Elena continued, "Two hundred years earlier, soon after the European immigrants arrived in Rhode Island, my ancestors fed succotash to the starving English. However, they did not share their recipes with the English. Instead, they kept them as a cherished, guarded part of their culture, which they selectively passed down from generation to generation."

Elena said, "Oh, you must excuse me. I'm so sorry for dominating the conversation. I sometimes obsess over my succotash, and I can't help that I love sharing stories. Please tell me about yourself. By the way, I think your red hair is beautiful."

Maisie blushed and said, "Thank you for your compliment. I can hardly wait to taste your succotash."

She continued, "My father was Irish, and my mother was Scottish. We boarded a ship for Boston about fifteen years ago because of the terrible potato famine in Scotland and England. I was just a toddler, but my mother later told me the famine decimated our town. Unfortunately, my father became mortally ill during the voyage due to scurvy and perished."

Maisie continued, "After a few months of not finding work in Boston, my mother found safe passage on a ship from Boston to Chelsea Harbor. Luckily, she found work in the cloth factory here in Greeneville. Unfortunately, she could barely buy enough food for us, so I started working at the Germania Lodge in Norwich a couple of years ago. In fact, that's how I met Crockett, Bowie, and Bear. They visit the tavern almost every weekend."

Elena smiled and said, "Yes. They are good surveyors, land developers, builders, and workers. And, they need to blow off a little steam now and then."

Maisie smiled broadly, giggled, and replied, "Yes, they do. That Crockett, he sometimes gets a little rowdy!"

Elena said, "I'm particularly excited for this year's Pow Wow because it includes the Pocawansetts and Hoopanoags living in the area. The Europeans and the Quinebaugan tribe displaced the Pocawansetts from Rhode Island. But many years later, we reestablished a small, combined Pocawansett & Hoopanoag community here in New London County. So most all of my friends are here this evening."

Maisie looked around and saw four large Pow Wow drums just beyond the outer perimeter of the large circle. Someone had centered each drum on a spot that marked a cardinal direction: East, North, West, and South. A sole drummer sat at the West position.

Maisie said, "Look. That man is beginning to beat his drum, and I hear sounds getting louder outside the tent."

Elena smiled broadly, "Yes. The drummer is our Medicine Man. That's Corey, my husband."

Maisie exclaimed, "Oh my God. I didn't know. He is so handsome and looks very strong."

Elena brimmed with pride as she watched Corey open the Pow Wow. As he began a slow, rhythmic, powerful drum beat, the murmur of all voices was hushed. The sound of disorganized, muffled footsteps heard outside the tent soon transformed into the rhythmic resonance of an assembled parade. The Grand Entry began.

Maisie and Elena's pulse heightened as a group of aging men entered from the East. They marched lockstep into the arena to the beat of Corey's cadence. After circling the central fire pit several times, the older men took their place at the North, East, and South drums. The remaining men huddled around them.

Maisie turned to Elena and whispered, "Who are those men?"

Elena answered, "They are tribal elders and previous Pocawansett and Hoopanoag Sachems. We honor and respect them for their years of service and dedication to tribal members."

However, Elena knew today's actual tribal leadership rested upon her and her husband's shoulders. Without regard for costs, she and Corey supported every local Pocawansett and Hoopanoag member. They gladly bore responsibility for their tribe's well-being.

Next, the elders began their chant, and several young, well-muscled dancers appeared at the East entrance. Fit men dressed from the bottom of their moccasins to the top of their headdresses entered the ring. Each dancer's regalia unmistakably identified them as either a Pocawansett or a Hoopanoag. In addition, each held items that revealed their personal character traits.

One brave brandished a long, large-bladed weapon resembling a Bowie knife. Another held a revolver in each hand. A third dancer proudly displayed his four-foot horsewhip. At the whip's end, the popper loudly cracked as the young man paraded around the fire.

Maisie gasped, "Oh my God! There's Crockett. Look at him! His outfit is stunning, and he's carrying guns."

Elena said, "Oh yes. All the dancers are dressed in traditional Pocawansett or Hoopanoag regalia. The dancers' mothers, wives, and girlfriends decorated their attire with bells, shells, and feathers. By the way, Crockett's guns aren't loaded."

Elena marveled at their beautifully beaded regalia and breathtaking ability to move their toned bodies. They tossed their limbs from side to side, top to bottom, and front to back as the braves pumped their weapons into the air and yelled stern warnings. Bells seemed to be ringing inside Elena's head when suddenly, an actual bell came out of nowhere and rocketed toward her. After a glancing blow to her arm, it landed in her lap.

She chirped, "Heh, Bear. Show a little respect for your elders!"

Jeremy had kicked his leg so vigorously that one of the hastily tied ankle bells had come loose. He grinned at Elena, continued to dance, and kicked even harder to ensure everyone heard and saw his frantic movements. The bells added to the cacophony of the drums and frenzied chanting."

Maisie shuttered with excitement as Crockett whooped, hollered, and waived his guns about the central fire pit.

~~~~~

After the male dancers sat, Corey's heartbeat hastened as he watched Elena stand and lead the tribe's wives, daughters, grandmothers, sisters, and nieces in the Buckskin Dance. The other drummers followed Corey's lead as he began beating his drum faster. Everyone noticed the timbre of the elder's chants change and felt the air bursting with excitement throughout the Pow Wow tent.

Corey was mesmerized by the visual feast before him and focused on the most beautiful sight he'd ever seen. His tribe's women wore hand-crafted buckskin dresses decorated with brightly colored beads. The rhythmic sway of their hips and free-flowing hair transported his thoughts to a different time and place.

Yet, he could not take his eyes off the long ribbons that danced on Elena's shoulder blades and fell to the small of her back. When she turned and faced him, they exchanged a glance. Then, as she rotated her lithe body full circle again, the ribbons closed around her. They created the appearance of a lotus flower, closing its petals at day's end.

The Pocawansett Sachem rose, walked to the tent's center, and prayed to his tribe's deity, saying, *"Catanyahweh*, we offer our thanks to you for this opportunity to celebrate this year's bountiful harvest and to join with our Hoopanoag brethren. We pray for unity between our tribes and the good people of Norwich. We ask for your blessings upon our people and the food before us. *Hear me, Catanyahweh!"*

The women and children formed a food line at the back of the tent. Everyone enjoyed the vast array of freshly cooked meats, vegetables, and apples, but Elena's succotash was almost everyone's favorite dish.

Corey's fellow brethren enjoyed the food and reconnected with one another. Finally, however, Corey's thoughts turned to his personal Pocawansett ancestral roots. When he finished eating, he stood, and the audience's attention turned toward him. The chattering throughout the room quieted to complete silence.

"Our most honored Sachems, elders, family, and friends, it warms my heart to share this sacred event with you! Our Pow Wow is a time to meld together, celebrate our heritage, dine together, and remember our ancestors. I am grateful that we can collectively become one through shared touch, taste, smell, and sound this evening. I now urge you to focus on your ability to hear and truly listen to the wise words of our tribe's Story Teller."

"Our ancestors have passed the sacred duty of Story Teller down through maternal bloodline for generations, and the time has come again for this year's tale. So please welcome our most esteemed Story Teller, my wife, Elena Pallaton."

~~~~~

She rose and began to pace around the fire pit slowly. Elena looked directly into the eyes of her audience and connected with them at a visceral level. She knew this story well. *She knew all the stories well.* Her mother had carefully repeated them to her in great detail.

The tips of her mouth turned down, and her smile transformed into a solemn stare. Then, after circling the pit several more times, Elena pointed to the east.

She commanded, "Everyone, please turn your attention to the stone monument on the hillside."

"The bones of one of our most powerful warriors and sachems lie there. His spirit ascended to *Catanyahweh* upon his tragic death, but it is here with us today. *We* are his brethren! *We* are his people! *We* have survived, and *We* will prosper!"

She began the story.

"In 1643, Pallatonomo, a powerful Pocawansett sachem, worked diligently to form a consolidated Native American alliance of several tribes in this area. He planned to negotiate and work with the English using a unified Native American voice. Unfortunately, the Quinebaugan leaders refused to join the alliance. Ultimately, Lucas claimed that Pallatonomo had sent an assassin after him."

"Outraged at this lie, Pallatonomo led a force of more than 900 warriors and planned to attack the Quinebaugan here in

Norwich. After Lucas pretended to offer a peaceful parlay, the Quinebaugan warriors mercilessly shot thousands of arrows into the kill zone and murdered many of our Pocawansett warriors. Both the English and the Quinebaugans killed many innocent people. However, Pallatonomo was captured and taken prisoner by Lucas. It was the largest battle between two Native American nations in history."

"Shortly after that, Pallatonomo was escorted to Hartford by Lucas and several of his trusted warriors. The two sachems pleaded their case to the English authorities. After a quick deliberation, the English court decided that the situation was purely a Native American affair. Accordingly, they gave the Quinebaugan Sachem Lucas an unjust license to deal with Pallatonomo as he saw fit."

She paused momentarily, folded her arms, and tears welled in her eyes, and said, "Everyone, you must always remember the words I am about to speak. You must remember how the Quinebaugans stripped our tribe of our beloved sachem."

"Lucas ordered his brother, Wawequa, to execute Pallatonomo on this very spot we sit tonight. Lucas and his Quinebaugan murderers stood by and watched as Wawequa approached Pallatonomo, brandishing a tomahawk. They saw his tomahawk's long, curved handle and smooth gilded stone. Someone had even carved the symbol of a snake into its handle. Then, in a single stroke, Wawequa's golden-tipped tomahawk swiftly found its target, and Pallatonomo's head cracked open like a melon."

She paused for a moment and then continued.

"With this vile action, the Hoopanoag and Pocawansett hope of fair negotiation and peace with the English instantly became a faded dream."

"Wawequa raised his tomahawk once again. He proclaimed, *Let the world know, both now and forevermore, that we, the Quinebaugan, will always be strong, and this land will always be our homeland!*"

Elena paused and slowly walked around the fire several times. She raised her fist. The only sound to be heard was the crackling embers.

"He was wrong! We are *not* a defeated people! We survived those vicious atrocities, and we are *here*. We are *now. This is our homeland!*"

The assembly broke into a cacophony of yells, whistles, whoops, and screams, and Elena sat.

~~~~~

Corey rose his six-foot-two-inch frame, thick legs, and broad shoulders. He hoisted a Springfield rifle above his head and looked directly at members of his tribe.

As his wife had done moments earlier, Corey circled the fire pit slowly and said, "As you all know, we now own land on Wawecus Hill and will soon build a new, modern community for our displaced Pocawansett and Hoopanoag brethren. I've already begun to map home lots for all of you."

"I have a monumental announcement this evening. We are now at a critical crossroads in our tribe's history. We discovered gold on our land this past week!"

He continued, "Justice has been served. We'll use the gold we find to build and help pay for homes for you on Wawecus Hill. No one will ever be able to infiltrate our sacred homeland again!"

Now, as he paced around the pit, he was no longer looking into the eyes of his brethren. Instead, he solely concentrated his focus on the fire. He stopped, knelt, and gently placed the rifle on the ground before the fire pit. Then, as everyone watched in anticipation, their Medicine Man reached into one of the leather bags tied to his waist and raised his fist. When he tossed a handful of gunpowder into the fire, everyone gasped at the eruption of billowing black smoke and a cacophony of loud popping.

Corey carefully reached into the other leather bag with both hands. Then, once again, he lifted his outstretched arms above his head. This time, however, the symbol was not a Springfield rifle or gunpowder. Instead, it was a five-foot-long snake with fangs glistening on one end and rattles vibrating on the other.

"This is Pocawansett and Hoopanoag homeland! Justice is ours! We, the true people, will fulfill our destiny. No one will subjugate us ever again!"

He turned, facing the fire, and walked toward the pit holding the rattlesnake barely above its hungry flames. When the writhing ceased, Corey tossed the snake's lifeless body into the embers, turned away, and walked out the west exit of the arena.

The fire pit's flames dimmed the moment after Corey's exit, and every Pow Wow member shrieked when a lightning bolt struck just outside the tent. A moment later, a sudden peal of thunder shook their very core.

Then, when the Pocawansetts and Hoopanoags looked to the nearby hillside, a second bolt illuminated Pallatonomo's gravesite. No one understood how these events could occur on a calm, clear evening like tonight. However, they *knew* that the spirit of Pallatonomo had spoken!

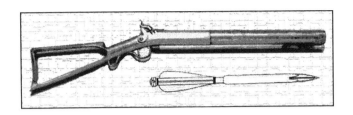

4: Travis Mathews
Downtown Norwich
C.C. Brand Whaling Gun Factory
Monday, August 23, 1858

Travis stood at his well-lighted work table and carefully inspected every component of the virgin whaling gun before him. Finally, he called out, "Father. I can't see inside the breech. Did you check it for cracks?"

Jonathan Mathews replied, "Of course I did. You don't need to worry because I'm sure the gun is solid."

Travis replied, "Well, I want to be sure. And besides that, *you're* not the person testing it for the first time. I still remember the gun barrel that blew up in my face last year!"

Jon replied, "We fired the guy who forged that barrel because he ignored too many details. But I know you pay close attention to detail, so I'm sure you'll be fine."

Travis knew this barrel would be okay because he had personally forged it. And, after last year's catastrophe, the gun shop's owner, Mr. C.C. Brand, charged Travis with added responsibilities. He gave Travis the jobs of quality assurance inspector and forging gun barrels in addition to his current job as a weapon tester. However, his father also double-checked all barrels before the first test fire nowadays.

Travis rolled clumps of bee's wax into two small balls and stuffed them deep into his ears. Then, he lifted the gun and carried it to the makeshift firing range on the far side of the assembly area.

Afterward, he yelled loudly, "Fire in the hole!"

Travis aimed at the target thirty feet away and slowly squeezed the trigger. The loud *boom* shook the entire workshop and every other business within a one-block radius.

When the small puff of smoke cleared, both Jon and Travis smiled at one another and examined the results. The lance landed squarely in the target's bulls-eye.

Jon said, "Looks good."

Travis said, "Yes, but the trigger pull is light. No one would want this thing to fire by herself."

Tightening the trigger tension, Jon replied, "Okay, I'll take care of it."

Travis and Jon's concern for safety was well-founded because the whaling gun was powerful and dangerous. Its ammunition wasn't anything like a standard rim-fired cartridge revolver. Instead, it fired a specialty harpoon-like round recently designed, developed, and patented by the owner and operator of this shop, Mr. Christopher C. Brand.

The bomb-lance looked like a shortened version of a standard harpoon, but there were significant differences. The bomb-lance could be fired from a whaling gun by a marksman perched in a whaling boat. The whaling gun / bomb-lance combination was more accurate and killed faster than any standard harpoon.

Two simultaneous actions were set into motion when a hunter pulled the trigger of a whaling gun. In addition to the harpoon-like lance taking flight, an internal fuze began to burn.

Precisely five seconds after launch, the lance's tip exploded deep inside a whale's body. The whaling community loved the gun because it was safer and dealt a more deadly blow to their prey.

~~~~~

Mr. Brand called to them from the upstairs salesroom, "Jonathan, Travis. General Williams is here. Bring up the gun and the lances."

When they reached the top of the stairs, they saw Mr. Brand and General William Williams Jr. standing near the display case, engaged in a lively discussion. Jon respected them profoundly and looked forward to showing them the new gun.

Jonathan had worked on one of General Williams's whaling ships as a harpooner for many years before joining C.C. Brand. Like many other Quinebaugan tribesmen in the 1840s, Jon earned his livelihood as a whaler. Even as a young lad, he was an expert marksman. Jon could throw a harpoon for twenty yards and strike his prey with uncanny precision. So when Williams purchased one of the first-ever whaling guns, it was only natural that Jon became his preferred gunman.

Williams greeted Jon and Travis, "Jon, it's so good to see you again! How are you, Faith, and Travis doing?"

Williams genuinely enjoyed the company of the Mathews family. He met them many years ago while teaching Sunday school to Quinebaugan children in Lucasville. He taught young Travis tenets of the Christian faith. Jonathan's family had always been friendly with Williams and his wife, Harriet.

Jon replied while nodding at Travis, "We are all doing well, Sir. Thank you for asking."

Williams replied, "Travis. You've grown up! I can hardly believe you're so tall. The last time I saw you, you were still chasing fireflies!"

Travis smiled and replied, "Yes, Sir, it has been a while. I still attend services with my friends at the Quinebaugan church. Our congregation is small but faithful and united."

Williams responded, "Well, I am happy to hear that."

Jonathan turned to Williams, saying, "The word around town is that your last expedition was quite successful. My wife loved the soap and perfume I bought from a local store last week. The shop's owner told me your ship's captain procured them while in France. So I want to thank you for finding such fine fragrances and bringing them here to Norwich."

Williams paused, thought for a moment, pursed his lips, and said, "Well, I'm happy I could help you make Faith clean, cozy, comfortable, and *very happy*."

Everyone burst out in laughter.

Williams continued, "Let me see that gun."

He gingerly took the gun from Jonathan and inspected it closely. C.C. Brand's design for his whaling gun focused on power and weight minimization. Its 1.25" diameter steel barrel provided for a deadly bomb-lance, while a cast iron, hollowed-out, short stock minimized its weight.

Brand produced several whaling gun models. This particular gun could fire two types of lances: Oliver Allen's patented lance and C.C. Brand's much more effective 1856 patented bomb-lance. Everything about the gun looked perfect.

Williams asked, "This is a beauty! But, has it been test-fired?"

Travis piped up, "Yes, sir, she is smooth as silk fabric from the West Indies, and she's also got quite a kick. But, unfortunately, I could only test her with an older model, less powerful lance."

Williams replied, "Of course, I'm sure the big boys will do their job just fine. How many bomb lances do you have in stock? I need at least twenty."

Travis snickered, "I personally made two dozen, and I can guarantee they will fly true, hit their mark, and help make you a rich man."

Williams replied, "I'm sure you're right on all three accounts. So I'll take all twenty-four."

As Travis lugged crates filled with lances out to Williams's horse-drawn carriage waiting outside, Williams asked, "By the way, I've heard through the grapevine that you're learning to use a sextant. Is that true? I may need a good navigator for one of my ships someday."

Travis replied, "Yes, sir. I am. I work part-time on a land survey team on Wawecus Hill and as a cartographer's apprentice for Mr. Henry Walling. I frequently dream of working for you on one of your ocean-bound ships, so I'm learning all I can about using navigational instruments and making maps. Please keep me in mind for any of your future voyages."

General Williams thought and said, "I will indeed. I'm proud you're growing into such a fine young man. You are on the right path."

Travis wholeheartedly agreed.

5: WAWECUS HILL GOLD, SILVER, AND NICKEL MINING COMPANY
HARDSCRABBLE HILL
COMPANY OFFICE
FRIDAY, AUGUST 26, 1858

Corey's office enjoyed a panoramic view of the valley below. Perched in a prominent location atop Hardscrabble Hill, Corey sat and contemplated the bustling city of Norwich, the Thames River, Chelsea Harbor, steamboats, and steam-powered locomotives transporting passengers and freight.

This morning he thought about the coming changes to Norwich. Only last week, a group of missionary women from the Second Congregational Church approached him and Elena. They were scouting for a building to house a new Sabbath School near their company office. The terrain for this section of Norwich, West Chelsea, was rugged, and its inhabitants had long endured many difficulties; thus, the name *Hardscrabble Hill*.

However, these kind, thoughtful missionaries sought to improve the area's environment and reputation. They had already established several Sabbath Schools in Norwich's West Side, and now they planned to enhance the standard of living on the hill.

He and Elena discussed their plans and embraced their efforts. Elena suggested they rename Hardscrabble Hill to

Mount Pleasant. She noted that words such as *hardscrabble* evoked feelings of strife and difficulty, while a name such as Mount Pleasant would be more attractive. The missionaries agreed and told Corey and Elena they would change the hill's name at the future school's dedication ceremony.

He knew changes in his personal life were coming as well. Corey was proud of his accomplishments as he sat at his large oak desk overlooking Chelsea Harbor. As he focused his attention past the river to the exquisite homes on Laurel Hill, Corey remembered the many months of hard work he and his crew had toiled to transform the forested hill into a lush, vibrant suburb. As a result, many wealthy Norwich entrepreneurs now thrived in the neighborhood.

With his recent discovery of gold, Corey now had an opportunity to develop Wawecus Hill for his tribe. The well-being of his brethren was embedded in Corey's soul. Even his office decorations reminded him daily of his heritage. Corey's clients often asked about the significance of a framed painting of an old Pocawansett wigwam, a bronze statue of a Pocawansett warrior, a Hoopanoag dream-catcher, and specimens of his firearm collection.

Corey also displayed a modern Springfield rifled musket prominently behind his desk. He was friends with several firearms manufacturers in Norwich, but his favorite gun maker was Mr. James Mowry. Mowry's Greeneville-based shop produced precisely machined barrels for several types of rifles. Corey considered Mowry's recently designed prototype Springfield rifled-musket a work of art. So, he was ecstatic when Mowry agreed to sell him the prototype.

Corey shouted to his wife in the front room, "Elena, could you fetch me another cup of coffee?"

Elena responded, "Sure, it will take me a few minutes because I'll have to make a fresh pot."

Their task for today was to organize the new company. The office was a modern, two-room house they had converted into commercial space. On a typical morning, Elena would greet potential new home buyers in the front room with a friendly face, a fresh cup of coffee, and a handful of sales brochures. The simmering pot of coffee, which hung in the fireplace, added a welcoming aroma to the office.

Handing Corey a cup of coffee, she asked, "What do you think we should call the company? Perhaps we should name it the Norwich Gold Company or the Wawecus Hill Gold Corporation?"

Corey thought and said, "Well, when prospectors adventured west to California, Arizona, and New Mexico to search for gold a few years back, they often found silver and nickel in the same area as gold. Unfortunately, we haven't found any silver or nickel in the brook yet. But who knows what we may find? What would you think about naming it the Wawecus Hill Gold and Silver Company?"

Elena responded, "I agree, but we can do better. We'll likely find gold, silver, *and nickel.* Therefore, I vote for the Wawecus Hill Gold, Silver, and Nickel Mining Company."

Corey grinned at her, tapped his coffee cup to hers, and exclaimed, Wawecus Hill Gold, Silver, and Nickel Mining Company it is."

~~~~~

They heard the cracking and popping of Jeremy's horsewhip outside. As the wagon neared the building, Corey and Elena saw the company's buckboard wagon and Corey's horse, Lightning, trudging up the hill. The path to their office atop Hardscrabble Hill was steep and somewhat arduous, but the view of the harbor below was well worth the effort.

Jeremy put away his whip, hitched Lighting to the post before Corey's office, gave him a drink, grabbed several maps, and entered the building.

Jeremy opened the door and greeted them in the front room, "Good morning, Mr. and Mrs. Pallaton!"

Corey asked, "And, good morning to you too, Bear. How was the ride up?"

Jeremy answered, "The air is crisp and clean, and Lightning is pretty frisky this morning. I think he's getting anxious about the race."

Corey asked, "Yes, Lightning loves the fair and winning the race too. Have you been able to do any practice runs yet?"

"No. We haven't. We've both been too busy working at Goldmine Brook. But I'm taking him to the fairground for a test run this weekend. I cleaned and lubricated the sulky yesterday. But, quite frankly, I'm a little worried about him."

Jeremy continued, "Just because we won the last three years doesn't mean it will be easy this year. I've seen a few young studs running that look pretty good. Lightning is getting a bit long in the tooth, but I'm sure he can pull it out. I may have to push him harder than usual."

Corey thoroughly enjoyed watching Jeremy and Lightning run in the annual harness race at the New London County Agricultural Fair. He especially liked that his horse, with his protégé at the helm, usually won. Every time they won, Corey felt a slight sense of retribution because the fairground location was on the very spot where his ancestor, the great Pocawansett Sachem Pallatonomo, was defeated by Lucas 200 years earlier.

Jeremy confidently stated, "Don't worry, Mr. Pallaton. We'll win it again for you."

He continued, "I've got the updated plans for the proposed mineral plots and the *Found Gold* map. It took us a while to fight our way through the brush. But I believe we've developed a good layout and an accurate set of plans."

At that moment, Elena greeted the morning's first customers and offered them a seat and a cup of coffee. Next, Corey motioned Jeremy into his office and said, "Come into my office and show me what you've got."

Jeremy laid several maps out flat onto Corey's desk. He pointed at one and said, "Look. We've placed most plots along the brook here. Off to the side, I outlined a large, flat area that I want to use for the field office. The rest of the plots aren't near the brook, but maybe we'll find something of value. Eventually, we could also blast into the hillside to create a mine shaft if needed."

After studying the maps, Corey said, "You've done a fine job. The plots appear in the right locations, and you've sized them properly. So we'll go with this layout."

He continued, "Elena and I have put a lot of thought into forming the new company. We'll call it the Wawecus Hill Gold, Silver, and Nickel Mining Company. I'm drawing up the registration papers now, and we need to file them with the city and state as soon as possible."

"This company will be extraordinary because we'll use most of its profits to benefit the Native Americans here in Norwich. We will use the profits to build homes for our people."

Corey continued, "As discussed last week, you and the rest of the survey team are free to prospect for minerals on your plots during weekends. But, while on company time, you'll only search for gold, silver, and nickel in the brook and on company plots. We'll also hire a man to operate an ore-grinding machine for mineral recovery. Then, I'll sell the gold on the open market."

"You, Elena, and I will operate the company; however, shareholders will own the company. We'll sell shares of stock to local businesses and people. They will provide us with funds to build the company and pay us to operate it, but they will be silent partners. Of course, we'll have to give them a portion of the profits, but we'll be able to use most of the funds to invest in our tribe's well-being."

Corey continued, "Elena and I have also considered who will serve as company officers. I will be the president, and Elena will be the treasurer, bookkeeper, and accountant. She will also be responsible for sales and advertising."

"Jeremy, you've worked loyally by my side for many years, and I appreciate all you've done for our tribe. Elena and I want you to serve as vice president of the company. You will run the field office and process the ore at the Goldmine Brook site. Are you willing to accept these responsibilities?"

The offer temporarily surprised Jeremy. Then, as tears of pride welled in his eyes, he said, "Yes, sir. It would be an honor. I will always do whatever it takes to help further our heritage and serve you."

Corey responded, "The job won't be easy and will require much hard work, but I know we can make it happen."

Jeremy nodded, and Corey continued, "Okay, Bear, I need you to prepare the area for the rock crusher and field office. Then, once you lay out the exact locations for the office and equipment, mark them on the map, and get it back to me."

"I need to finish putting the company organization package together for the bank and the town officials. The bank must see the layout and proof of gold to get our loan. Also, the town will need to see the boundaries of the mineral plots. I need these jobs complete by next week so we can file the maps, get the bank loan, start advertising, and spread the word."

Jeremy looked hard at Corey and said, "That's too much work for only one week! I don't know if that's possible. The guys are already overworked, and they'll be pissed."

"Yes, but you and I both know they can do it."

Corey added, "I want to look at the most recent *Found Gold* map. Show it to me."

Jeremy rolled out the map, pointed to it, and said, "As you can see, I've added the location of many landmarks, such as Goldmine Brook, the extent of Wawecus Hill, and the proposed office. Here's where Gimpy found the first gold rock in the brook."

He said, "While we were clearing, we kept an eye out for sparklers or other promising rocks. The brush is pretty thick, and we didn't find anything more in the areas around the brook. We looked pretty hard. Most of the gold must be in the brook itself. Who knows? We'll see."

After a moment, Jeremy said, "I just wanted to let you know that the Pow Wow got me fired up. I liked Elena's history lesson and the taste of her succotash too. Was that snake that you threw into the fire real? Did you really cook him alive? It sure looked that way."

Corey's smile turned into a solemn stare, "When it comes to those who oppose us, I don't fool around. Didn't you see the snake's rattles shaking? Didn't you see his body squirming? Yes. He was real, and I have several more of his brothers at home!"

Jeremy replied, "Good, I hate those damn snakes! I almost got bit several times while working on Laurel Hill last year. The slimy bastards all deserve to die!"

6: SNAKES
GOLDMINE BROOK
AT THE BASE OF WAWECUS HILL
SATURDAY, AUGUST 27, 1858

Today, Jeremy had the difficult task of motivating his team to finish clearing and mapping the area designated for the future field office and mineral processing equipment. He'd been able to fend off Corey for over a week but knew that he had to finalize the map today. Corey needed it immediately to complete the company organization package.

Jeremy's problems began this morning when the team encountered a snake nest while clearing the brush. Throughout Norwich, and especially the outlying areas such as Wawecus Hill, many feared the presence of timber rattlesnakes. Anticipating this potential problem, Corey had provided the survey party with a pair of .22 caliber revolvers from Horace Smith and Daniel B. Wesson. The guns, designed, fabricated, and sold in Norwich, featured their recently patented 'Number One' cartridge that revolutionized the firearm industry. The weapons were ideally suited for protecting the team from snakes and other varmints.

When Crockett saw the snakes, he yelled, "Look out, guys! I'll take care of them."

Travis watched as Crockett frantically yanked out the six shooters and began firing. The first two bullets found their mark, and the blacksnakes died quickly. However, since the remaining four snakes in the nest were alerted, they escaped, and the last four bullets missed.

When the snakes reared their heads again, Travis yelled, *"Stop!! They're only blacksnakes!"*

But, unfortunately, his words fell on deaf ears because Crockett's memory of a rattlesnake bite during a previous job on Laurel Hill was fresh in his mind. So, as far as Crockett was concerned, any snake, poisonous or not, should be killed.

Travis saw the crazed look in Crockett's eyes as his fingers fumbled while reloading the Smith & Wessons. By that time, snakes from three other nearby nests had awakened. They seemed to be everywhere.

Travis stared in horror as Bowie drew his machete-like knife and began chopping away. After Bowie stooped to finish the last of the snakes, he saw Crockett pointing the loaded Smith & Wessons in his direction.

Bowie yelled at Crockett, "Stop! I've got this covered! Don't point your damn guns at me!"

Bowie gleefully finished the job, and Travis cried out, "What the hell are you guys doing? Those snakes can't hurt you because they're only blacksnakes. You're just a bunch of cowards!"

Crockett and Bowie stopped in their tracks and glared at Travis.

Crocket stepped toward Travis, guns in hand, and said, "Who the hell do you think *you* are trying to boss me around?"

At that point, Jeremy stepped between the others and said, "Calm down, guys. We've gotta get this job done today. Relax."

The entire team had been on edge since the incident, and Jeremy only wanted to finish marking the map and deliver it to Corey's office. However, he was still nervous for his and the group's safety. Jeremy knew they would likely run across more snakes because warm rocks attracted rattlers on hillsides such as Wawecus Hill. He also knew Norwich had a well-documented history of problems with timber rattlesnakes.

At one of the Pow Wows several years ago, Jeremy had listened to Elena Pallaton tell the tale of Simon Huntington IV. The Pocawansett Storyteller intended all her stories to teach lessons, but this story struck a twinge of fear int his young heart.

DEACON SIMON HUNTINGTON IV

In the year 1700, the town of Norwich purchased the home lot of Deacon Samuel Huntington III. The town wanted to build a parsonage for Mr. John Woodward, the recently ordained minister of the First Congregational Church. However, the church leaders decided to set aside a portion of the plot as a community burial place. The one-and-a-half area later became known as the Old Norwichtown Cemetery.

Just a few years later, in 1707, Simon Huntington IV, the son of Simon Huntington III, was mowing the lot's meadow when a timber rattlesnake bit him. It was a hot July afternoon, and due to his strenuous exercise, the snake's venom quickly inflamed Simon's blood. The poison worked quickly. His body became swollen, his flesh turned purple, and he died within a few hours.

Simon Huntington IV was only twenty-one years old. His body became the third body interred at the cemetery. Simon's family buried his body only a few yards from his grandfather, Deacon Simon Huntington Jr., whose body was the first to be interred at the cemetery.

NORWICH GOLD

To alleviate Norwich's snake infestation, in 1700, the town selectmen approved a law authorizing the town clerk to pay a bounty for any rattlesnake killed within the town's boundary. As a result, from 1700 to 1739, the town compensated snake hunters for more than 1400 rattlers. The hunters had to produce a tail and at least one bone joint to prove their kills.

Unfortunately, the bounty paid did not solve the problem immediately because any would-be snake hunter would have needed to kill about thirty snakes daily to earn a decent salary. As a result, the town raised the reward three times before enough young hunters were willing to take such an enormous risk. Thus, by 1735, a mercenary could almost earn a full day's wages by killing a single rattlesnake.

Over time, the increased financial incentive solved the problem near the town's population center. But, the infestation persisted near the outer city limits.

Young men like Crockett and Bowie were happy to earn bounty pay during their recreational weekend hunts.

~~~~~

It was late afternoon, and Jeremy knew his time had run out. Corey would be furious if he didn't receive the completed map before sundown. So, Jeremy yelled to the team, "Okay, fellas, get me the coordinates of the corners of the office, and we'll be done for the day."

Jeremy called everyone together after recording the coordinates in the survey book and drawing the shape of the future field office on the map. He hurried them along and announced, "Let's pack it up and get going. Good work, everyone."

After loading the company's buckboard wagon, Jeremy, Crockett, and Bowie jumped aboard and began their hour-long return journey to Norwich proper. Jeremy would drop Crockett and Bowie off at their homes before meeting with Corey at his office on Hardscrabble Hill.

Travis was glad to see them leave. He walked to where Moshup stood and said, "Alright, Boy, here's a nice juicy apple. We have a couple of hours to do some more interesting work!"

Travis had been itching to prospect for gold on his plot all day. So, when he finally had the chance, he made his way past the area designated for the future office building to his plot. Unfortunately, the thick undergrowth was still covering his plot.

He cut away brush and inspected many rocks for veins of gold for nearly an hour. Unfortunately, Travis was not successful, but he believed a future, more thorough check would yield better results. While catching his breath and taking a short break, he gazed at the mound where he'd found the human finger bones earlier.

"Okay, Mr. Boney Fingers, let's see if I can find the rest of you now."

He went to the back of his plot, where the mound and outcropping were situated. The outcropping was located only a few feet above the flats of the valley. At first glance, it appeared to be a natural extension of the hillside.

Travis stopped at the mound and cleaned out small rocks beside the finger bones. Then, as he uncovered more and more of the hand, he could see the remnants of a complete left arm.

It wasn't only an arm. It was clear to Travis that he had stumbled upon an entire skeleton. He thought to himself, "Who could this be? Why is this skeleton here in this particular spot?"

The moment he touched one of the bones, Travis felt a zing of white-hot energy flow through his hand, arm, shoulder, and neck. The heat settled into his forehead and his birthmark. It felt as though his snake-shaped birthmark was on fire! Although he was dazed, his curiosity needed to be satisfied.

Travis turned his attention to the stone-covered outcropping above and studied its unnatural arrangement. It appeared as though someone had deliberately arranged the rocks to hide or protect something. Travis noticed each stone stacked neatly upon another as he removed the rocks. The cairn appeared to mark an entrance to an opening in the hillside.

Travis worked for several minutes carefully, removing a combination of hard-packed dirt and successively smaller and smaller rocks. Finally, reaching about a foot into the hillside, he felt the perfectly flat face of a small object. Travis pulled it out and saw a two-piece, lidded box that someone had carved from stone. He estimated its dimensions to be four inches long, two inches wide, and two inches tall. He couldn't imagine why anyone would have taken so much care and effort to craft such a small box.

However, he soon received the answer. It appeared as though the lid had been securely cemented to the body of the box using a mixture of finely ground quartz crystals and dirt. Therefore, he couldn't remove the cover easily using his fingers alone. So, Travis searched the area and quickly found a small, stiff stick he used to clean the seal. When he finally broke the weather-proof seal and pried the lid off, he found a stash of pure gold flakes.

He grinned from ear to ear! The flakes appeared as though someone had stored them only days earlier. The sparkling gold before him convinced Travis that his ancestors had found and processed gold here on Wawecus Hill.

He could only imagine what other artifacts he might find. He turned his attention back to the hole in the hillside. The site was quickly emerging as a small cavern.

Upon excavating deeper into the hole, he removed a single, larger stone that seemed to protect a larger object behind. Travis heard the rattle, but it was too late. A pain shot up his right arm and throughout his entire torso. It felt like a bolt of lightning. His body lurched backward, and he landed on his back.

Travis saw the timber rattlesnake quickly slither away, and he almost panicked because he wondered if more snakes were in the nest. Suddenly, Travis remembered he was alone and was several miles from home. The excruciating pain and shortness of breath quickly shot gruesome thoughts through his brain.

As he lay there awaiting the worst, Travis wondered if perhaps, by some miracle, someone would rescue him. His outlook brightened briefly when he remembered last week's newspaper article about another snake attack on Wawecus Hill.

WAWECUS HILL SNAKES

A party of laborers was out on the hill at work, and one of them was employed at some distance from the others. His companions were suddenly alarmed by his cries and shrieks for help. They ran to his assistance and found him rolling on the ground with several black snakes on his body. He stated after his rescue that these reptiles came upon him out of a thicket with such fury as to put it out of his power to defend himself. They wound about his legs, lashed them together, bound up his arms, and were near his throat when his friends came to his assistance.

However, Travis knew that Jeremy and the others would not return today. No one would rescue him. His right forearm was throbbing, his heart raced wildly, and he knew his life was in *Munduyahweh's* hands.

He closed his eyes, placed the palm of his left hand over his wounded forearm, and remembered that he was a child of the Quinebaugan divine spirit, *Munduyahweh*. He prayed for a gift of healing energy to save him. Within minutes, the pain subsided, and his heart returned to its normal rhythm. He gave thanks to *Munduyahweh* and wondered why he was allowed to survive.

As Travis gathered his thoughts, he remembered getting poisoned in his early youth. He recalled waking up after the incident with his mother and grandmother by his bedside chanting ancient Quinebaugan prayers. He was very sick for a day but recovered with no ill effects.

His discussion last week with his mother about the recent newspaper article had prompted her to tell him that he probably had lifetime immunity to snake venom. The poison he drank and recovered from as a young boy was from timber rattlesnakes.

He thought to himself, "She was right!"

After a few more minutes, his breathing finally returned to normal, and the pain disappeared.

His curiosity compelled him to continue his search. The snake must have made its home inside the small, safe space behind the large rock. The idea that the snake had been guarding something else leaped into his imagination.

He bent down closer, checked the area for any remaining snakes, and peeked behind where the last rock had been. The opening now extended about a foot into the hillside. With the sun beginning to drift below the horizon, all that Travis could make out was a stick protruding from the back. Before reaching into the cavern again, he took a second look to ensure there weren't more snakes.

There weren't any. When Travis grabbed the stick and pulled it out, he instantly realized it wasn't a stick at all. Instead, it was the handle of a small tomahawk. Travis had never held a tomahawk. However, he had grown up gazing at a tomahawk featured in the artwork displayed inside his family's living room. The painting was a portrait of Lucas's brother, Wawequa, holding a long-curved tomahawk over the head of the slain Pocawansett Sachem, Pallatonomo. However, the weapon Travis had just found was much smaller than the one in the artwork.

This bone-handled tomahawk was only six inches long and sported the body of a snake carved along its entire length. Its head was a single, smooth, rounded stone gilded in gold! When he held the tomahawk at arm's length, the setting sun reflected beams of gold into his eyes.

Travis felt a sense of empowerment unlike any he'd ever known. Once again, he felt an intense, pulsing sensation emanating from his birthmark and sensed the spirits of his ancestors flow throughout his body.

Yet, he still didn't comprehend his feelings and wondered what was happening to him.

7: Get Things Rollin'
Hardscrabble Hill
Company Office
Saturday, August 27, 1858

From the front of the office, Elena shouted, "Corey, could you come to take a look at this ad? I've been working on it for a while and think it's in good shape. I like how it looks."

Corey replied, "Sure."

He stood from his desk and stepped into the front room of their company's office, where Elena was designing the company's first newspaper advertisement.

She was anxious to please him and hoped he would be impressed. They had worked well together while running their real estate business and now were on the cusp of a new, much more lucrative venture.

Their first business served the community by developing land and building stylish homes on Laurel Hill. But, this new enterprise would benefit a significantly different clientele. The Wawecus Hill Gold, Silver, and Nickel Mining Company would be a privately held company that sold stock to investors. Elena knew that she needed to instill confidence in locals so they could feel safe buying shares of a new company that had yet to produce anything of value.

Corey studied it carefully. After a minute, he said, "This ad breathes life into the company! It will spark great interest, and potential investors will want to learn more."

"You should work on the graphics more. I suggest you replace the gold bars with gold nuggets. You've still got time to work on it. We don't need to submit the ad just yet because I want the state to approve the company incorporation packet before we run it."

Elena responded, "Okay, I'll redo the graphics. I considered using nuggets instead of bars. But, it didn't make a great difference to me."

~~~~~

Jeremy entered the front door of the company office and said, "Hello, Corey. Good afternoon to you, too, Mrs. Pallaton."

Corey questioned, "Hi, Jeremy. How did you and the crew make out this week?"

"We did well. Getting through the brush to lay in the coordinates for the office was tough, but we got it done. Here's the updated map showing the mineral rights plots, the office, and the placement of the ore processing equipment."

Corey carefully studied the map and responded, "This all looks good. I see you've also identified and located Goldmine Brook. We'll likely find most of the gold and silver near the stream."

"I approve your layout. We've got enough documentation now to get the company rolling."

"Jeremy, I want you to submit this map to the records office at the Town House on Monday morning. We need to stake our mineral rights claim for each plot. The town already has the map showing boundaries of our entire Wawecus Hill lands, but I want to ensure that we have sole mineral rights in the Goldmine Brook area."

"Also, I want to get this map and the company incorporation package filed and approved by the state as soon as possible. I need to apply for a loan to pay for the remaining land clearing, the field office construction, the employee payroll, and the ore processing equipment. We'll need quick approval from Norwich and the State of Connecticut because I've already scheduled a loan appointment at the Norwich Savings Society."

Showing Jeremy the ad, Corey continued. "I want this advertisement submitted to the Aurora newspaper. When you see Travis, tell him to pick it up from Elena. We'll advertise the company to everyone in New London County. Since Travis and his family are well-known here in town, he'll be a good one to help spread the word."

Jeremy responded. "Okay. I'll tell him to do it."

Corey replied, "Have him submit it as soon as possible. I have a good feeling about the Wawecus Hill Gold, Silver, and Nickel Mining Company. We'll be able to make a real difference in the daily lives of our Pocawansett and Hoopanoag brethren. And, perhaps some of the local business and Norwich citizens will also make a little money."

"At the moment, we need to get the word out to everyone. The more people we can encourage to invest in the company, the better off everyone will be."

As Elena left Corey's office, she said, "Corey, we need to get home before it gets too late. I'll collect our things."

~~~~~

Jeremy's face tightened, and he quietly said to Corey, "Every day, while we broke for lunch, Crockett, Bowie, and I searched for more gold in the brook. But, unfortunately, we couldn't find any."

Corey said, "Don't worry. We'll find more. Once we get the loan and sell a few company shares, we'll have plenty of time and money to scour the entire area carefully."

"Don't alarm Elena. She worries too much already. When we find a mother lode of gold, silver, or nickel, she and everyone else will be ecstatic."

8: BRYNN
DOWNTOWN: CORNER OF CHURCH & COURT STREETS
NORWICH TOWN HOUSE RECORDS OFFICE
MONDAY, AUGUST 29, 1858

It was yet another mundane Monday morning in the Norwich Town House Records Office, and Brynn Dunham was bored. She had filed all the outstanding records from last week's transactions and had little more to do than sit at her desk, gaze over the counter, and wait for someone to enter with a new request.

The Town Clerk entrusted Brynn to run his office on Mondays due to low traffic, her abilities as a competent assistant, and her family ties. Brynn had learned to file birth and death certificates, marriage certificates, and official documents from her father, John Dunham. During previous years, Mr. Dunham had served as the town clerk, the mayor, and the postmaster. The Dunhams were a highly respected family in Norwich.

However, activity at the Courthouse and Town House, built thirty years earlier, had not always been slow or without incident. For example, after abolitionist Henry B. Stanton gave an anti-slavery speech inside the courthouse, an angry mob stoned the building, broke windows, and seriously injured one of the local peace officers. Even though issues associated with slavery were becoming more heated throughout the country, Brynn did not expect any powerful speeches or angry mobs today.

She believed today would be more interesting than most Mondays because her best and most loyal companion, Dexter, had accompanied her to the office. He always gave her undivided attention, watched for her safety, and listened.

Dexter, Brynn's Norwichtown Terrier, sat across from her, guarding the front door. He was full of energy and eager to please.

He adored Brynn, in part because she made him feel needed. Since Brynn was an only child, she confided in him constantly, asked his opinion on almost every matter, and played fetch with him for hours. And sometimes she even sang with him.

Since no customers were in the office this morning, Brynn decided to rehearse for next week's anthem at the First Congregational Church. She and her friends in the choir were learning the recently published hymn, 'Nearer, My God to Thee,' by Sarah Flower Adams. The music was composed only two years earlier by Lowell Mason. She began,

NEARER MY GOD TO THEE

Nearer, my God, to thee, nearer to Thee!
E'en though it be a cross that raiseth me,
Still, all my song shall be,
Nearer, my God, to Thee;
Nearer, my God, to thee, nearer to Thee!

As she began the next line, Dexter started singing with her by howling at the top of his lungs.

Dexter sang along happily, "*Yaooowl, Yaooowl, Yaooowl.*"

After Brynn finished the hymn, the front door suddenly swung open, flinging Dexter's entire body across the office floor.

Brynn glared, yelled, and pointed at the entering young man, "Hey, be careful! Watch what you're doing!"

Jeremy quickly crossed the room and dropped a pile of maps on the counter.

Then Dexter barked several times and growled at the intruder but didn't attack.

Jeremy quipped, "Is this the Town's records office or a dog pound?? Tell your dog to shut up!"

But, just as his words landed, he looked at Brynn and instantly felt remorse. Then, momentarily stunned, he said, "I'm sorry, I didn't mean to yell. It's just that I didn't see the dog next to the door."

It was as if he had seen an angel. The large, soft curls of Brynn's thick blonde hair flowed over her shoulders, and the fire in her sea-blue eyes seared through him. She was gorgeous! A tight-fitting blouse accented her voluptuous frame.

Jeremy guessed her to be seventeen or eighteen.

Yes, her finger pointed at him at that particular moment, but he sensed her deep love for Dexter. He saw Brynn's passion and hoped she might someday direct it toward him in a more favorable venue.

Trying to deflect his earlier statement, he asked, "Will you please forgive me? Is this the Town House's records office?"

Brynn answered curtly, "Does this look like the fire department? Or does it look like the mayor's office? *Yes*, of course, it's the records office! So what do you want?"

Jeremy began, "My name is Jeremy Pallawotuk. I am the vice president of the Wawecus Gold, Silver, and Nickel Mining Company. I'm here to submit several updated maps in the

Wawecus Hill area of Norwich. My company bought the land a couple of months ago, and we now need to claim its mineral rights and file maps of individual land plots."

Jeremy felt empowered by his own words.

Unfazed, Brynn replied, "I've never heard of such a company. So, whose name is on the deed for the land?"

Jeremy said, trying to impress Brynn, "Oh, that would be Mr. Corey Pallaton. He's my partner."

Brynn professionally replied, "Okay, I'll pull the maps, deeds, and other records for the area and review it. So please sit, and I'll be with you shortly."

She turned and walked toward the rear of the office where the maps were stored. As Jeremy watched her walk away, his heart throbbed so hard that he could hardly breathe. Her hips slowly moved from side to side in a slow, rhythmic motion, and his knees felt weak.

He sat in the lone straight-back wooden chair and waited.

Brynn quickly overcame her initial anger as she searched for the maps. But she was in no hurry to cater to his desires.

She thought, "How did this guy become the vice president of a gold mining company? I've never heard of any gold mine in Norwich. Have they truly discovered gold, silver, or nickel here? He is quite handsome. He is not too tall or hairy. But he is a little rough around the edges."

Brynn was not attracted to men with beards or mustaches. She was a passionate young woman and liked that Jeremy was confident and appeared sturdy, agile, and successful as a businessman.

She thought, "Stop thinking about him and focus on the documents."

NORWICH GOLD

~~~~~

After ten minutes, Jeremy began to tap his shoe on the wooden floor, and Dexter stared at him intently. Jeremy stared back at him, stuck out his tongue, and hissed. Jeremy didn't care much for dogs, snakes, or horses. He considered animals as beasts of burden who should obey orders and fulfill his needs. His family never had pets, and he felt none the worse for it.

Dexter growled softly, and Jeremy responded in a low voice, "Shut up, mutt."

Jeremy impatiently called out, "Excuse me, Miss. Are you finding the maps okay?"

Brynn replied, "Oh yes. I'll be just a minute."

However, she thought, "Maybe five more minutes more. And that's if you're lucky."

After another ten minutes, she reappeared at the counter with maps, deeds, and other documents associated with the property.

She began, "Okay, Did you say your name was Mr. Pallawotuk?"

He answered, "Yes. Jeremy Pallawotuk. But my friends call me Bear. So please feel free to call me Bear."

She replied, "Okay, Mr. Pallawotuk. I have the records associated with the land in question, and I don't see your name on any of the deeds, maps, or forms. Nor do I see any records with the name Wawecus Hill Gold, Silver, and Mining Company. So, are you sure these are the documents you want?"

He answered sternly, "Oh, you misunderstand me. We are just now in the process of forming the company."

Then, holding up a thick, fifty-page document, he said, "This document describes our company and contains an application for its incorporation. After the Town Clerk or his attorneys review it, Mr. Pallaton will become president, and I'll be the vice president."

Brynn replied, "I'll pass it on to the town clerk tomorrow. He'll review it and submit it to the State for approval. That is if it's all in order."

Brynn smiled at him coyly, placed her hands on her hips, and taunted him, "And, is there anything else you desire?"

After regaining his composure, Jeremy replied, "I also need you to update the maps and file our claim for mineral rights."

He placed his maps on her desk and added, "These updated maps show the location of Goldmine Brook and our mineral rights plots."

Jeremy could not avert his eyes when she bent down to study one of the new maps. The line of tiny pearl buttons along the top of her blouse drew his immediate attention to the cleavage formed by her healthy breasts. She looked up quickly, caught him staring, and answered, "I've never heard of Goldmine Brook. Is that brook misnamed on your map?"

Brynn loved the power she wielded over young men such as Jeremy.

Now beginning to lose his patience, he said, "*No. It is not a mistake.* It's the new name of our brook. That is what I'm trying to tell you. I am holding a new map with newly discovered and identified areas. We have found gold in the brook and will sell shares in the new company!"

Brynn felt exhilarated. She had known it wasn't a mistake and knew precisely what he wanted. This young man had a fire within him, which stirred her deeply.

Goading him more, she said, "Okay. I see now. What proof of your so-called discovery do you have?"

Jeremy reached deep into his pocket and slowly wiggled his hand to and fro as if searching for something. Finally, after six seconds of fumbling, she looked down at the wiggling hand in his pocket.

She smiled at him, laughed loudly, and teased him, "It doesn't look like you've got much down there, Mister."

However, Jeremy knew he could top her comment. He pulled out a quartz rock that glimmered with veins of gold. It was an exquisite specimen that clearly had great value.

He said, "I found this in Goldmine Brook last week, and there are many more like it."

She smiled again, thinking, "There may be more to this man than I first thought."

She smiled and said, "I'll get these maps and documents to the Town Clerk. I'll make sure they're filed appropriately."

Walking to the door, he turned around and said, "By the way, what is your name? You never said."

"My name is Brynn Dunham. You may call me Brynn."

He said, "Brynn, Norwich will host the New London County Fair at the East Great Plain Fairground this weekend. I will be competing in the harness race on Friday afternoon."

He placed a ticket on the counter. "Here's a VIP visitor ticket to the fair and a ticket for the surrey ride as well."

After pausing thoughtfully, he placed a second set of tickets on the counter and said, "If you'd like to bring one of your girlfriends, here are tickets for her also. There are many exciting things to see at the fair. You'll have lots of fun!"

He continued, "By the way, I've won the race for the last three years and would like to see you cheer me to victory."

Brynn wondered what the surrey ride and the fair were all about and said, "We'll see."

THE NORWICH AURORA

9: Advertisement
Downtown Norwich
Norwich Aurora Office: Water Street
Friday, September 3, 1858

Lydia Stedman was writing her weekly column for Sunday's issue of the Norwich Aurora newspaper. She typically reserved the column for announcing local social events and discussing the recent buzz of activity around town. But this week was different; she could no longer contain her views on the issue of slavery. So Lydia planned to publicize one of her political opinions in the Aurora.

It was a scathing editorial focused on the President of the United States, James Buchanan. He was a Democrat from the northern state of Pennsylvania, but his views on slavery often sympathized with the southern states. He had become a *doughface*. His views on slavery were pliable and moldable, allowing others of stronger minds to control him. Everyone viewed him as a puppet, and Lydia thought his actions were totally unacceptable.

She was only seventeen, but Lydia had already formed strong opinions of how people should treat one another. Like her father and most other Norwichians, she was a Democrat who staunchly opposed slavery. In later years, her father, Mr. John W. Stedman, would serve on Norwich's Committee of Seven, which promoted the enlistment of soldiers into the Union Army.

Printing and publishing in Norwich was a competitive endeavor in the 1850s. Mr. Stedman purchased the Norwich

Aurora newspaper when it was a defunct, failed enterprise. It had taken him ten years to pay off the loan needed to buy the printing office and newspaper business. But, as a hard-working, thoughtful, enterprising family, he and Lydia turned the printing facility into a flourishing, profitable business. They published the Norwich Aurora newspaper and printed wedding invitations, business cards, tickets, show cards, books, and pamphlets.

Publishing the weekly Aurora was by far Stedman's most challenging task. John and Lydia read national, regional, and local news daily to keep up-to-date on current events. They both authored the newspaper, but John primarily focused on local politics, business, and production.

Lydia was a curious reporter, editor, and graphic artist. In addition to writing articles for the newspaper, she was responsible for interacting with customers, creating artwork for advertisements and admission tickets, and maintaining her weekly social column.

Today, she was alone at her desk and focused on the job at hand. So Lydia was startled when the bell, attached to the front door, dinged. She saw a tall, handsome young man with jet-black hair and a slight limp enter the office.

She said, "I'll be with you in a moment. Please have a seat."

Travis removed his bag and sank into an overstuffed, dark blue velvet chair. It was his first time in any printing facility, and he was fascinated by the press, which occupied the middle section of the office. It employed a series of massive gears, multiple rollers, and large sheets of paper to print newspapers, invitations, or flyers.

While he waited, he wondered how anyone could design such a complicated machine and how the petite young woman at the desk could possibly operate it.

Travis was familiar with the simple process of pouring molten metal into a mold used at the whaling gun factory. He'd also watched his father tediously create small parts for trigger assemblies. But Travis never imagined publishers needed such a large, intricate, beastly-looking machine to produce newspapers.

He noticed the back of her long, thick, black hair while she wrote at the desk. She repeatedly dipped her twelve-inch long, white-feather quill pen into a crystal ink well. It seemed to take forever. Finally, after several minutes passed, he called out, "Hello, back there, I'm still here."

She answered, "Yes, I know. I'll be there in just a minute. I'm finishing an article."

Lydia carefully put the pen down, stood, and walked toward him. She smiled politely, looked him directly in the eye, and said, "What can I do for you?"

Travis instantly felt her warm, inviting presence. As she walked to join him, he noticed her slight limp. However, it didn't turn him away; instead, it drew her to him. The black-striped, reddish-brown feather Lydia wore in her hair projected an air of confidence. She couldn't have been any more than four feet tall. But her athletically toned figure, tiny waist, and delicate hands stopped his heart momentarily.

He began. "My name is Travis Mathews, and I work for the Wawecus Hill Gold, Silver, and Nickel Mining Company. I want to place an advertisement for the company in the Aurora."

She asked, "What kind of ad do you have in mind?"

Travis opened his brown leather messenger bag and pulled out the drawing Elena had given him. After handing it to her, he said, "Here it is. How does this look to you?"

After reading and digesting the ad, she responded, "Well, are you sure this is accurate? I've read many things about Norwich during the past several years but never heard of anyone mining gold, silver, or nickel. And I've never heard of the Wawecus Hill Gold, Silver, and Nickel Mining Company either."

Travis responded, "That's why we want to place the advertisement. My boss is incorporating the company at this very moment. Its owner, Mr. Corey Pallaton, filed paperwork with the City of Norwich to officially incorporate the company yesterday.

Today, he and the company's vice president are applying for a loan at the bank. They need to purchase mining equipment to build a field office at the base of Wawecus Hill. We found gold there a few weeks ago."

He paused and then said, "Actually, I discovered the gold. I rolled down a hill, almost fell into the brook, and found a quartz rock laced with gold."

He smiled and sheepishly added, "I'm sometimes a bit clumsy."

Lydia sensed his comfortable, open manner as she listened to him. However, she couldn't help but notice the large, pronounced birthmark that ran from the corner of his left eye to his ear. She thought it unusual because the mark almost looked like a snake. Yet, something very natural and down-to-earth about Travis resonated with her.

Thinking of her own limp, she responded, "Well, don't feel too bad. Nobody's perfect."

A large grin overcame her face, and she continued, "That is quite an interesting story. I hope that it all works out for you. The ad looks interesting. I see here that shares are now available for sale to the public. How is that going to work?"

Travis replied, "I'm not exactly sure. I only know they plan to sell shares of company stock and then share the profits with the shareholders. I work for these guys part-time, and they haven't clued me in on details."

He continued, "I'm the rodman on their land survey party, but my regular job is at C.C. Brand's whaling gun company on the other side of town. I make castings for whaling guns and test-fire the completed products. Mr. Brand's guns are much safer for harpooners than the old whaling guns."

Travis stopped talking and asked himself, "Why am I babbling on about myself? What is it about her that makes me so talkative?"

Lydia said, "How often do you want to run this ad? It will cost 50¢ weekly, and we can start running it next weekend."

"Oh no. Mr. Pallaton wants to run it in this coming Sunday's edition because it must be published well before the Jubilee planning meeting. He knows many wealthy Norwichians will attend the meeting and wants to get everyone talking about his company before then. So the ad must run immediately and at least every Sunday for four weeks."

As she turned her large, beautiful, dark brown eyes downward, Lydia replied, "The deadline for this weekend's edition has passed, and I've already begun setting the type for it. I'm sorry, I can't get it in for Sunday."

He asked, "What is your name?"

She answered, "Lydia. Lydia Stedman."

"Lydia, please. I really need this. Mr. Pallaton is counting on me to get the ad published, and he will rake me over coals if it's not run. Is there anything I can do to help you meet your deadline?"

She responded, "I know about the upcoming Jubilee planning meeting because General Williams invited my father and me to attend. Everyone knows that next year's Jubilee will be a grand event. One like Norwich has never seen. My father plans to be a member of several organizing committees, and I'll publish newspaper articles to keep the public abreast of the planning progress."

Continuing, she said, "You are right. The fact that someone discovered gold in Norwich will be a popular topic, and I suspect everyone at the meeting will be interested. Maybe a few people will even want to become shareholders. You're right. The public needs to see this ad before the meeting."

She smiled and added, "I'll have to work several extra hours to get the ad in. But, for you, Mr. Mathews, I'll do it. You're going to owe me a favor, though."

The tone of her playful voice was comforting to him. Lydia seemed reasonable, and there was just something about her that made him feel at home. Maybe it was how she looked at him. Or perhaps it was her confident manner. He wasn't sure. But Travis was grateful for her willingness to spend extra time to run the ad for him this coming weekend.

He pulled two silver dollars from his pocket and handed them to her. "Thank you. I promise that I'll make this up to you. You can count on me. You'll see."

Travis grinned at her with a smile that spanned from one ear to the other. He hadn't ever been romantically involved but was interested in girls. However, he was keenly aware that they had always noticed his limp, gangly frame and prominent birthmark. Travis didn't want anyone to feel sorry for him.

He was especially pleased that Lydia had not stared at his gait, nor had she asked details of how he stumbled and fell down Wawecus Hill.

He said, "By the way, the feather in your hair is quite beautiful. Is it from a red-tailed hawk?"

Lydia answered, "Why, yes, it is. You must know your birds well. Thank you for noticing."

10: LYDIA STEPS FORWARD
DOWNTOWN NORWICH
NORWICH AURORA OFFICE: WATER STREET
TUESDAY, SEPTEMBER 7, 1858

Lydia's father, John W. Stedman, was a Democrat who upheld most of the tenets of his party's beliefs. His newspaper often published editorials that politically opposed Norwich's other newspaper, the Norwich Courier. But, today, he might agree with the Courier. He had difficulty deciding how to word the content for his column in the upcoming Sunday issue.

After reading the news on his office's telegraph machine this morning, he learned Mr. Jefferson Davis, the secretary of war for the former President of the United States Franklin Pierce, addressed the Democratic Gubernatorial Convention in Boston last evening. Even though Mr. Davis was very well-spoken and admired by many, Stedman opposed his views.

During his nomination speech of Erasmus Beach for governor of Massachusetts, Davis defended slavery and charged that every state had the right to choose its position on slavery. He criticized abolitionists and painted them as bent on destroying the country. Davis said, "The political agitator, like the vampire, fans the victim to which he clings but to destroy."

John asked Lydia, "Have you read this yet?"

Lydia replied, "Yes. However, I think that Davis is wrong. I believe freedom is a God-given right to everyone, and no state or government has the right to enslave anyone."

John replied, "I agree with you. I'm concerned that the issue of slavery is tearing our country apart. Most Norwichians oppose slavery, but there are still a few holdouts. I am trying to convince these so-called moderates to understand our point of view."

He continued, "I'll finish writing the editorial. But we need to make a final decision as to which other newsworthy articles you could write for Sunday's issue. Perhaps we could run an article that publicizes the Jubilee and the upcoming Jubilee organizational meeting and social. There are a lot of folks who will be interested in this. What do you think?"

Lydia replied, "I completely agree with that. I'll compose the first draft for you by tomorrow."

"I believe we should also write something about the new gold mining company. The advertisement we've been running for them has aroused great interest. But, so far, the company has only mentioned they're selling shares. They haven't announced much about the discovery. So I'm wondering how much gold they've found."

She continued, "The young man who submitted the advertisement for the gold mining company also works for the C.C. Brand Whaling Gun Company. He told me that Mr. Brand's new patent for the bomb-lance is making it safer for Norwich's whalers who risk their lives for us."

She continued, "Many people in New England are interested and want to learn more about the whaling industry. The industry provides daily staples such as candles, soap, margarine, and many other products. Norwichians should recognize our local whalers for the dangerous work they do for us."

Lydia asked, "What would you think about running a public interest story about the new bomb-lance or the status of the gold company?"

John thought for a moment and said, "I agree with you. I am also interested in learning about the bomb-lance and the gold mine. When I saw the advertisement for the gold company, I wanted to hear more about it. Those folks in California made a bundle of money on gold a few years back. So perhaps Norwich is also poised on the edge of a Golden Era."

"I think it best for you to find that young man and see what you can learn from him.

Lydia was quite pleased with herself. The conversation had progressed precisely how she had hoped. Since the moment Travis placed the mining company ad, she had been thinking of how to arrange a *necessary meeting* with the tall young man with the unique birthmark.

~~~~~

That afternoon, the city of Norwich was abuzz with activity. Lydia looked forward to seeing Travis again and learning more about his discovery of gold. She wasn't too excited about writing the whaling gun/bomb-lance story but knew that writing public interest stories was sometimes required of a reporter.

Today, her mother was using the Stedman family carriage, so Lydia hired a horse and buggy to make the trip from the Aurora office to the whaling gun shop. When they entered Franklin Square, Lydia couldn't help but notice the congestion of shoppers on foot and horse-drawn carriages. Horses and people seemed to be everywhere.

As they passed the Wauregan House, a prominent hotel in downtown Norwich, Lydia noted to the driver, "Downtown is pretty busy today. With all this traffic, it will take us thirty minutes to get to the other side of town."

The driver replied, "Nowadays, so many people travel from one place to another. It causes a lot of congestion, just like you see today. You should see Franklin Square in the morning. All the mill workers here in town need a ride to Greeneville. People have speculated that town leaders will build a horse-drawn railway from downtown to Greeneville. That would speed things up and reduce congestion."

Lydia replied, "What is a horse-drawn railway?"

He answered, "If they build it, horses will pull large passenger wagons that roll along parallel steel rails. The roadway would extend northward about two and a half miles from downtown to Greeneville."

She replied, "Sounds like a good idea to me."

Lydia paid the fare and included a generous tip when they arrived at the whaling gun factory.

She smiled and added, "Thanks for the ride. Please feel free to give your horse an extra apple for me. He earned it. I love horses because they are loyal, hard-working, and strong."

Lydia was excited as she stood at the showroom entrance because she knew she was about to learn more about Travis. But, at the moment, she could only see two middle-aged men in the store. Travis was not visible.

The man himself, the owner of the whaling gun factory, Mr. Christopher C. Brand, greeted Lydia at the door. "Good afternoon, Miss. May I help you?"

She smiled as she gestured with a wave around a collection of guns on display and said, "I do surely hope so. But, as you might guess, *I am not here to buy a gun*, Sir."

She continued, "My name is Lydia Stedman. I am the Aurora newspaper reporter and work with my father, Mr. John Stedman. Perhaps you know of him; he publishes the Aurora and is Norwich's postmaster."

Christopher Brand replied, "Why yes, Miss Stedman. I am aware of his service to the community, and I am also aware of the interesting articles that you've written in the Aurora. Only last week did I read your exposé about President Buchanan. I agree with your opinion. He is a *doughface*. What can I do for you?"

Knowing Mr. Brand would be most interested in the public learning about whaling guns, Lydia began, "Last week, I spoke with one of your employees about your guns and your new bomb-lance. I believe his name is Travis Mathews."

She continued, "He told me your gun and bomb-lance patented designs make it safer for the whalers. I had hoped to speak with him to learn more about the gun so I could write an article in the paper about how it has benefitted the whalers and our community."

Another man, who had overheard the conversation, stepped forward and said, "Miss Stedman, I am Travis's father, Jonathan. He told me he met you at the newspaper office the other day when he placed the ad for the gold mining company."

She nodded politely to him and said, "Yes. I'm pleased to meet you, Mr. Mathews,"

He continued, "Travis isn't here this afternoon. He's out working with the survey party today. Those Pocawansetts have convinced him that there's a ton of gold out there. I'm not so sure. But, I *can* tell you a lot about the whaling gun and the bomb-lance."

Jonathan continued, "You may or may not know, but my family is Quinebaugan. We come from a long line of Quinebaugans and are proud of our tradition. For years, many of the remaining Quinebaugan men in Norwich became whalers. I was very young when I became a harpooneer on one of General William Williams's whaling vessels. Hundreds of years ago, our ancestors shot bows and arrows, and my job was to throw and shoot harpoons."

He grinned and added, "So, I'd say, what goes around, comes around."

"It was an exciting time of my life that I'll always cherish. My friends and I visited many foreign ports and enjoyed exotic experiences we never thought possible. Unfortunately, however, the act of harpooning a whale is hazardous."

When he paused, Lydia responded, "I have learned a little about the whaling industry based in New London, but please tell me more about how you support them here in Norwich."

Jonathan continued his discourse, "Whaling is dangerous, hard work. I have personally witnessed several friends being tossed out of our small whaling boat while trying to land a harpoon. So when Mr. Brand created this new kind of whaling gun, I was lucky enough to be chosen as the gunman on our vessel. Using this gun, I learned to shoot harpoons from the whaling boat rather than throwing them by hand. It was a great leap forward."

"The problem, of course, was that the gun kicks something terrible. After a year of firing it, my shoulder bone cracked, and I decided to retire. I am indebted to Mr. Brand for letting me work with him here using the new design. I helped him develop the idea of the bomb-lance."

Mathews held up a long spear-like object and said, "After this *bomb-tipped* lance lands deep into the body of a whale, it blows up and instantly kills the whale. It makes our work easier, is safer, and is a more humane way of ending a whale's life."

He continued, "Whaling boats based in New London often search for whales in northern seas partially covered in ice. An injured, harpooned whale can drag a small whaling boat under the ice to certain death in cold region hunts. The risk of this occurring is significantly reduced since a bomb lance kills the whale much faster. The bomb-lance saves whalers' lives."

Jonathan asked, "Is that enough information for your article?"

Lydia answered, "Why, yes, it is. It sounds gruesome, but I thank you very much for your explanation. I was unaware of the importance of your gun and bomb-lance. I will pass this on to the readers of the Aurora in this week's issue."

She added, "I'd still like to speak with Travis about the gold discovery. Could you let him know for me?"

Jonathan responded, "I'll let him know that you stopped by. I'm sure he'll be happy to tell you all about it. Where may I say that he can find you? Should he stop by the Aurora office?"

After pausing momentarily, she said, "I'll be singing in the choir at the First Congregational Church on the green this Sunday. Could you let him know I'd like to discuss this with him after church?"

Lydia was disappointed that she hadn't seen or spoken with Travis but had no doubt that he would come looking for her.

Jonathan chuckled to himself, "An interview about Travis's job after church on Sunday??? It sounds more likely that a few sparks are flying between them."

11: Church With The Stedmans
Norwichtown
First Congregational Church
Sunday, September 12, 1858

Travis was anxious to attend a service at the Congregational church. He wasn't sure what to expect but believed it would be different from his home church. Travis grew up in the Quinebaugan church in Lucasville while fellowshipping with his family and friends. He always felt their love and kindness. Members of the congregation instinctively trusted and loved one another. Travis was proud that everyone trusted him.

During church services, the congregation sang hymns and listened to stories of how Jesus was the Savior to underprivileged people. Travis had early, fond memories of General Williams attending their church each week to teach him and his buddies at Sunday school. The General taught the parables of Jesus in his own unique style. But, it seemed to Travis that he only told stories about ocean-going adventures.

Travis laughed as he remembered the General's version of the parable of how Christ had walked across the ocean, reached below the waves, and pulled out a whale to feed the poor, hungry people back home. He also loved how Jesus taught the hungry people how to fend for themselves rather than ask for handouts. General Williams told how Christ showed his disciples how to set the sails on a modern-day whaling ship, navigate the ocean, and fish for whales by accurately throwing their harpoons. Perhaps this was why Travis wanted to become a ship's navigator.

Travis loved the Quinebaugan church and now wanted to get acquainted with the people of the First Congregational Church on Norwichtown Green. Specifically, he was eager to become more acquainted with Lydia. So when he, his horse, and gig carriage pulled up to the church, Travis couldn't help but notice the beauty of the colorful foliage provided by maple and oak trees surrounding the church. The trees gracefully framed the church, its congregation socializing on the lawn, and its bell calling out from the belfry.

As Travis entered the scene, a tall, distinguished man and his wife approached him. She was a dignified woman with a light complexion and curly blond hair. The man reached out to shake Travis's hand and said, "Good morning. You must be Travis Mathews. I'm John Stedman, and this is my wife, Caroline. Lydia told us that we might expect you here today."

Travis shook Stedman's hand and said, "Yes. Good morning. I'm Travis. It is nice to meet you, too."

He thought, "These people seem to be very nice. I wouldn't mind becoming a part of this community."

The cordial introduction made Travis feel at home. But he was surprised because Lydia's parents' physical appearance was nothing like hers. Instead, they were much taller than he expected. Also, Lydia's skin tone was much darker than theirs.

Mrs. Stedman smiled and spoke up, "Church will begin in just a few moments. We should make our way inside. Lydia is with her friends in the choir. They do so love singing."

After being ushered to their seats, Travis gazed around the church. The furnishings and pews were simple yet elegant. What made this church notable was not the building. Instead, it was the congregation, the choir, and the minister. Reverend Hiram P. Arms sat beside a plain wooden podium, with the all-female choir to his left. Lydia sat in the front row, wedged between her best friends, Brynn Dunham and Emeline Norton.

After Reverend Arms welcomed everyone, the entire church sang the hymn, 'Fairest Lord Jesus', a cappella. The words of the melody stirred him at a deep level.

FAIREST LORD JESUS

Fairest Lord Jesus, Ruler of all nature,
O Thou of God and man the Son,
Thee will I cherish; Thee will I honor,
Thou, my soul's glory, joy, and crown.

Beautiful Savior! Lord of all the nations!
Son of God and Son of Man!
Glory and honor, praise, adoration,
Now and forever more be Thine.

Lydia's voice transported him to a higher realm as the choir sang.

The hymn reminded him of Jesus's lessons and how he had learned them as a boy. The words of the melody rang true to Travis. He also believed everyone should honor those who help others.

The congregation sat in rapt attention as Reverend Arms began the sermon. Today's discourse focused on diversity and willingness to accept those who appear different from themselves. He spoke of the British Pastor John Fawcett, who grew up as an orphan. Upon establishing a devoted congregation as minister to a small, local church, a large, posh church in London offered Fawcett their pulpit. However, he refused the job in favor of staying with his loyal flock in a poor, downtrodden neighborhood.

As the sermon progressed, Reverend Arms discussed the subject of the cruel treatment of enslaved people by plantation owners in the South and other underprivileged people throughout the world. The reverend said that the people of Norwich should not only think along the lines of global and national boundaries. Instead, they should also think and act locally. They should be more accepting of local underprivileged people, for instance, the Quinebaugans in Lucasville.

Travis instantly felt very uncomfortable as all eyes turned to him. It was obvious to everyone in the congregation that Travis was the only Quinebaugan in attendance. He was a first-time visitor to the church and didn't want them to feel sorry for him. Travis had never considered himself underprivileged. On the contrary, he was proud of his heritage and worked hard to support himself and his family.

As the reverend continued to preach, Travis felt everyone's eyes bearing down upon him. He understood the minister meant well. However, Travis was still uncomfortable with being the focus of attention.

As the service ended, everyone rose and sang 'Blest Be the Tie That Binds.' The hymn was written by the good Pastor John Fawcett, whom Reverend Arms had spoken of earlier. By now, Travis had no desire to be *bound* to this church in any manner whatsoever. He only wanted out of the building and to speak with Lydia.

Outside on the lawn, Mr. Stedman spoke to Travis. He said, "Thank you for joining us today. I hope that you felt welcome. We'd love to have you join us again."

Stedman wanted to ask Travis to elaborate on his discovery of gold but thought it better not to bring up the issue in this setting.

Before Travis could reply, Lydia emerged from the church's front door. She called out, "Hi, Travis. It's good to see you."

Relieved, Travis said, "Hello. It's nice to see you too."

She said, "Did you enjoy the service?"

He responded, "I liked hearing the hymns. They reminded me of the music played in my church. You and the rest of the choir sounded joyful. But I must say I am happy to be outside now. It is such a beautiful day."

Travis continued, "My father told me you stopped by our shop this past week looking for me."

Lydia replied, "Yes, today is a gorgeous day. I love the colors of the fall leaves. And, yes, I did stop by your office. I'm writing an article about how Mr. Brand's whale lance is helping to make it safer for local whalers. Your father told me he is a retired whaler and how the new lance works."

She continued, "However, I hoped to see you and hear more about the gold mining company. Since running the ad, we've received hundreds of inquiries. So far, I've had to refer all the questions to Mr. Pallaton."

Travis perked up. These were the words that he'd hoped to hear Lydia say. He said, "Mr. Pallaton gave me the mineral rights to one of the plots at Goldmine Brook, and I'm going out there this afternoon. Would you like to join me for a picnic and an adventure? I want to see if I can find any more golden nuggets."

Lydia looked at her father and said, "That sounds like an interesting adventure. I'd love to get some fresh air. Father, is it okay with you for me to go?"

John Stedman smiled and said, "Yes, you may go, but I urge you to be very careful. The rattlesnakes are still active on the ledges near Wawecus Hill. The recent weather has warmed the rocks, and the snakes love it."

Travis joined in, "That won't be a problem, sir. I know how to deal with snakes. I'll protect your daughter."

Lydia said, "Thank you, Father. I need to change clothes and pack a picnic lunch for us. Travis, please follow us home. We live just down the street."

12: TREASURE HUNT
NORWICHTOWN
STEDMAN FAMILY RESIDENCE
SUNDAY, SEPTEMBER 12, 1858

Lydia bounded out from the Stedman's home, bearing a large picnic basket under one arm and an apple in hand. After handing Travis the basket, she marveled at his horse. He was a giant draft horse with well-developed muscular legs, a sleek, shiny black coat, and large black eyes. He looked to be the most impressive animal that she'd ever seen.

Lydia approached him slowly, allowed him to smell the back of her hand, and offered him the apple. Then, after gently stroking under the horse's chin, she softly said, "You're such a good boy."

With his nostrils open and relaxed, he responded with a low neigh and cheerfully ate the apple.

Travis helped Lydia into the carriage, took the reins, and gently called to Moshup, "Let's go, boy."

After Travis made a short clicking sound with his tongue, he turned to Lydia and said, "I can see that he likes you."

Lydia remarked, "Yes, I think he does. Your horse is handsome and looks strong as well. What's his name?"

Travis answered curtly, "Moshup."

Lydia turned the left corner of her mouth upwards, tilted her head, looked directly at Travis, smiled, and said, "Well. That is a very odd name. How did you come up with it?"

Travis laughed aloud, responding, "His name was not *my* creation. My mother named him after a mythical Native American giant named Moshup. He lived near the Quinebaugan settlement of Shantok and also on the coastline of New London County. Moshup had a peaceful, calm, gentle disposition and taught the Quinebaugan how to lead balanced lives."

He continued, "When my parents gifted him to me, my mother told me the folklore surrounding him. Since he was so large and powerful, she suggested naming him Moshup. I thought it to be a great idea. I love Moshup. He's my best friend, and I trust him."

Travis paused, glanced at Lydia, grinned broadly, and added, "I've got a little secret I'll share with you. But, you *must promise* never to share it with anyone."

She laughed and said, "Oh, Mr. Mathews. I absolutely can keep a secret. Let's hear it!"

He smiled again and said, "My mother nicknamed me Mooshi because I was much taller and larger than the other boys. She'd say, 'Heh Mooshi, flex your muscles and take out the trash. Or, Heh Mooshi, reach up there with your long arms and clean out the spider web on the ceiling."

He continued, "I guess that Mooshi isn't so bad. People have called me a lot worse names lately."

Lydia now smiled from ear to ear and said, "Don't worry, Mooshi, your secret is safe with me."

~~~~~

When Travis and Lydia reached the base of Wawecus Hill, they heard the comforting sound of a trickling brook, smelled the crisp forest air, and felt the bright, warm sunshine.

After stepping down from the carriage, Travis said, "This looks like a good spot. What do you think?"

Lydia answered, "Looks great to me! So, is your plot nearby? Are we going to eat first or begin our search?"

Travis laughed, helped Lydia from the carriage, and said, "If it's okay with you, I'd like to eat first. There's plenty of time for prospecting. I'll grab the picnic basket, and you can spread the tablecloth."

Lydia opened the discussion as they began their picnic lunch of fried chicken, carrots, homemade dill pickles, fresh fruit, and berries, "It is so peaceful out here. I've only heard about Wawecus Hill from others at the newspaper office. Most of the talk about this area is focused on rattlesnakes attacking people. It's a shame because the natural beauty here is quite comforting."

Travis responded, "I agree. However, I think most people's preconceived notions of the place are unfair. Yes, it is rustic, overgrown, and there are snakes, but the area has a great deal of charm."

Pointing to the nearby stream, Lydia asked, "Is that the stream you're calling Goldmine Brook?"

He answered, "Yes, Mr. Pallaton named the brook after I found the gold-laced rock in it. That's a story in itself."

She smiled and responded, "Well? You know I want to hear that one."

He pointed to the top of Wawecus Hill and began, "It's a little embarrassing, but here goes. I was standing on the top of the ledge there. Unfortunately, I lost my balance, and when I sneezed, I began rolling down the hill. After getting thrashed by several bushes on the way down, I finally landed here."

Then he pointed at a large, nearby irregular-shaped rock and continued, "I cracked my head open on this rock."

"After I got up and cleaned the blood off my face using water from the brook, I saw a glimmer of gold shining up from the bottom. So when I picked up the rock causing the reflection, I couldn't help but think that the gold-colored vein might be real gold."

He continued, "When Mr. Pallaton tested it and determined it *was indeed gold*, I wasn't surprised."

Lydia looked at him and said, "Wow! That is quite a story. Did you look for any more rocks in the brook?"

He answered, "The entire survey party searched for a while, but it was getting dark, and there wasn't much time. But, the next day, after Mr. Pallaton inspected the site, he gave members of our survey party mineral rights on plots of our choosing."

He had Lydia's full attention. Finally, she questioned, "Okay, so where's your plot?"

They trudged through the brush, about fifty feet toward the base of the hill, and said, "It's here!"

Lydia looked perplexed and said, "Why on God's green earth did you choose here instead of over there, near the brook?"

Travis replied, "Well, Mr. Pallaton let me choose a plot, but he limited my choice to areas far from the brook."

Then, he paused, smiled playfully, and said, "I have a surprise for you that I'll share later."

She answered, "Well, I'm not much on surprises, Mister! Can you at least give me a hint?"

He chuckled and said, "Nope, no hints for you. But I would like us to search my plot and see if we can find any gold. I'm not too optimistic, but you never know what we might find."

Travis trekked back through the brush to where they had hitched Moshup and packed away the picnic basket. After feeding Moshup the leftover carrots and apples, he grabbed a shovel, a pickax, and a machete and returned to his plot, where Lydia patiently awaited.

Travis said, "Okay, the plot is about thirty feet wide by twenty feet long. I marked each of the corners of the lot with a cairn. I didn't want anyone to be able to mistake the extent of my lot."

He pointed at a neatly formed pile of large, flat, rough stones, neatly stacked, three feet high, and said, "Here's the front, left corner."

He pointed out the remaining three cairns, marking the other corners, and said, "As you can see, the front two-thirds of the lot is flat and overgrown, and the back third is clear but rocky and on the hillside."

He asked her, "Where do you think we should begin?"

She chuckled and blurted out, "Well. Of course, let's start at the beginning!"

He laughed and said, "Okay, Miss Know-It-All. We'll start here in the middle and work our way outward. Let's work together. I'll clear the brush with the machete, and you can search the exposed areas."

Lydia replied, "Okay, let's get to it. Twill be fun."

They cleared, picked, searched, dug, and hunted for promising specimens for over an hour. Finally, after searching about a fifth of Travis's plot, they found two handfuls of jagged granite rocks laced with quartz and other crystalline minerals.

Most of the stones were small, but one of the specimens grabbed their attention. It was a large rock, about the size of someone's fist, and appeared to have several veins of gold.

Travis said, "Okay, I think we've looked enough for today. We can try again later. After we get home, I'll test all the rocks for gold."

Lydia was disappointed and said, "I'm sorry we only found these few samples, but perhaps one of the veins is real gold. I do believe there's more gold in the brook."

Travis responded, "Yes, me too."

He paused and said, "I want to make good on the promise I made you."

Lydia perked up and said, "Okay, I'm listening."

Travis began, "When Mr. Pallaton offered me a choice of lots, I chose this one for an unusual reason. After tumbling down the hill and finding the rocks in the brook, I climbed back up the hill, tripped again, and rolled back down a second time."

He laughed, adding, "Yes, it's embarrassing but unfortunately true."

"This time, I landed in the back, right corner of my lot. If you look back there, you can see a small outcropping. It looks somewhat like a mound. Do you see it?"

She answered, "Yes, I do, but it looks peculiar. It seems a bit out of place. So, what's the surprise?"

He replied, "Okay. We'll go over there, and I'll show you. But I want to remind you that the warm rocks on the side of the hill could be dangerous. The last time I was there, a rattler bit me. It hurt me, but not too bad because I'm somewhat immune to snake venom."

Lydia looked at him and said, "I've never known anyone to be immune to snakes. How could that be?"

He laughed, smiled at her again, and said, "You sure have a lot of questions. It's another embarrassing story. But, I'll tell you."

As they made their way to the mound, Travis said, "When I was young, my mother and I visited my grandmother's house. My mother and her best friend, Rachel Flowers, were meeting with my grandmother. While they were meeting, I got bored and decided to explore her house. She has a million interesting things there. Everything was grand until I snuck down into the basement."

"I think my curiosity got the best of me. I was merrily exploring my grandmother's herbs and medicines, and the next thing I knew, I woke up with my grandmother, mother, and Mrs. Flowers hovering over me. Their arms and hands were flailing about, swaying to and fro and singing Quinebaugan chants. It scared the hell out of me."

"I heard them say something about releasing the rattlesnake venom from my body. My mother later told me I was probably immune to snake venom for the rest of my life."

Travis continued, "Since the fall season is upon us, the snakes are probably dormant now. But it is quite warm and sunny today, so I'm not sure how safe it is to go over there."

She scowled and said, "Okay. So let me get this straight: You've got this big surprise, but you won't show it to me because it *might be unsafe*."

Perplexed, Lydia proclaimed, "Travis. I've been curious and adventurous for my entire life and will not begin living in fear now. Let's go!"

When they reached the mound, Travis pointed to the skeletal hand he'd found earlier. He said, "Lydia, I'd like to introduce you to the one and only Mr. Boney Fingers!"

Her eyebrows lifted, and she exclaimed, "Wow! That is shocking. Do you think the entire skeleton is buried here? How do you think that he ended up here?"

He said, "Well, yes, I know for a fact that it is. And I believe he was Quinebaugan. I've got something more to show you."

Travis took a few steps up the hillside and removed the rocks he had previously used to hide the outcropping opening. Then, he reached in and pulled out the lidded, stone box partially filled with gold flakes he'd found two weeks earlier. He handed the box to Lydia and said, "What do you think of this?"

When she opened it and saw the flakes of solid gold, she exclaimed, "Amazing! This is simply amazing. Now, you've got me wondering. I've got a thousand questions. Who left this here? Why here? What was it used for? I can hardly believe it."

Travis replied, "I cannot answer all your questions, but I can answer one."

Lydia was puzzled and said, "Okay. I'll take the bait. How could you possibly answer any of those questions?"

Travis reached deeper into the small cavern and pulled out the small tomahawk he had found earlier. He held it up, showed it to her, and said, "Someone used the gold in that box to gild the head of this tomahawk."

Once again, Lydia was surprised and taken off guard. She trembled nervously, laughed, and said, "Mr. Travis Mathews, you *are* full of surprises."

She stood as tall as possible and, without thinking, hugged and politely kissed him.

It was the sweetest and most exciting feeling that Travis had ever experienced! He could hardly restrain himself from lifting her, pulling her close, and smothering her with his pent-up affection. Yet, being a gentleman, he politely said, "I am here to please you, and I'm hoping this is the first of many wonderful surprises we have in store for one another."

She smiled and replied, "Have you found anything else?"

He laughed and said, "That's not enough?"

After a moment, he said, "Actually, I've also been wondering if maybe there's anything more in the mound. I found these two things very late in the day and didn't have time to finish searching the little cavern. I think we've got enough sunlight remaining to continue searching now."

She said, "Sure, let's do it."

They returned to the site and began removing more rocks. Travis reached deep into the hole and cleared out stones and debris using his incredibly long arms. After a few minutes, he felt a smooth, unnatural surface. "

He exclaimed, "I've found something. It feels like a pot."

The object felt like the wall of a curved ceramic pot to Travis. He carefully removed the dirt to avoid breaking or damaging the artifact. Finally, after another minute, Travis safely pulled the treasure from the cavern.

Lydia declared, "It's not a pot. Instead, I think it's a mortar and pestle. I can see remnants of crude decorations on them. Unfortunately, several layers of caked-on dirt obscure most of the artwork. Someone spent a lot of time crafting these."

Travis replied, "I agree, but it's the largest mortar and pestle I've ever seen. I wonder why someone buried it here."

Lydia said, "I can hardly believe this. These must be artifacts from the first Quinebaugans in New London County. I learned bits and pieces of their heritage while writing articles for the newspaper. Wawecus Hill is named after Sachem Lucas's brother, Wawequa. He led a small community of Quinebaugans who lived here on the hill. The place was originally called Wawequa's Hill, and over time, the name morphed to Wawecus Hill."

She continued, "May I hold it?"

Travis stepped aside, and Lydia stepped forward. She said, "I wonder what purpose this mortar and pestle served. The ones used for grinding corn are much smaller. I want to take a closer look at the pestle. Maybe there are some clues."

The mortar was at least twelve inches tall, and the pestle was about ten inches long. Lydia separated the pestle from the mortar using her tiny, delicate fingers.

Reaching deep inside the mortar, she said, "I wonder if they've left anything inside it."

She suddenly screamed a cry of pain that pierced Travis's ears like the sound of pending death itself! The heavens instantly filled with black clouds, lightning flashed, and thunder reverberated around them. Suddenly, a driving, punishing sheet of rain belted them. The rain wasn't simply falling. It was sweeping horizontally in from the northeast. Then, after a minute or so, the rain suddenly abated, and the skies cleared.

Travis thought, "What the hell just happened? Where did that snake come from? How did the thunder and lightning appear and leave so quickly?"

After he watched the serpent slither away, he felt helpless. Lydia lay there in front of him in agonizing pain. Travis desperately wanted to help but had no idea how even to begin. He felt helpless. What could he do?

Upon regaining his composure, Travis realized he needed to extract the venom immediately. When he examined her inner forearm, he saw two small holes where the fangs had struck.

He ran down to the brook and gathered several cattails. After returning to her side, he broke them into short pieces. The stems were hollow, and now he could use them as stents. Travis hoped that he could use them to suck out the venom.

Lydia's breathing rate had increased dramatically, and her heart was still racing. He inserted one of the makeshift stents and began to suck. He thought it was working when he felt several drops of venom land on his tongue. Then, suddenly, his head began to reel, and he lost his balance. He was yanked away from her when his forehead began burning like the fires of hell.

His snake-shaped birthmark had sparked to life. He was dazed but knew there was little time. He fought through his pain and returned to Lydia, where he continued to suck out the remaining venom. With every drop of poison on his tongue, Travis felt the burn of Lydia's pain. Finally, he placed the palm of his right hand over her wound, closed his eyes, and allowed *Munduyahweh's* healing energy to flow through his body into hers.

Travis felt her breathing and heartbeat slow to normal. As her body relaxed, his fear for her life subsided. However, his heart sank as he realized the pain and suffering that his *adventure* had caused. He had no idea what he could do to ease her pain or how to show his deep remorse.

Finally, after ten more minutes of rest and recovery, they looked deeply into one another's eyes and remained silent.

They gathered the box of gold flakes, the tomahawk, the mortar, and the pestle and made their way over to Moshup. The skies were calm, clear, and peaceful throughout the ride home, but their thoughts were anything but tranquil.

Travis and Lydia's friendship was strong, but they both needed time to process the events that had just occurred.

13: NEW LONDON COUNTY FAIR
NORWICHTOWN
DUNHAM RESIDENCE: WASHINGTON STREET
FRIDAY, SEPTEMBER 17, 1858

Brynn lived a somewhat sheltered life. As an only child, much of her time was filled with long, lonely hours and boring activities such as clerking at the Norwich Town House records office. However, the part-time job gave her many opportunities to interact with others. Brynn needed and enjoyed the attention of others.

She spent many hours tending the family rose garden with her dog, Dexter, who also enjoyed gardening. When Dexter first arrived as a young pup at the Dunham's home, he immediately ran out to the backyard and began digging in the garden.

He helped her plant and cultivate many unique varieties of roses. The combination of copious sunlight, rain, and fertile soil helped her produce some of the most delicate roses ever seen.

Today, Brynn was excited and anxious because she had never attended the county fair in Norwich. She had only gleaned bits and pieces about its activities by overhearing her parent's conversations. However, she knew the New London County Agricultural Society sponsored the fair, and a variety of livestock, such as chickens, pigs, cows, goats, and horses, would be judged.

However, Brynn was uninterested in livestock or any other agricultural-related topics.

She hoped that her friend, Emeline Norton, would introduce her to a couple of her girlfriends while attending the fair. Brynn didn't understand why most girls her age weren't friendlier. She had no trouble attracting boys. Hopefully, she would also have the opportunity to speak with Bear and watch him win today's harness race.

Since it was a hot September afternoon, Brynn chose her wardrobe carefully. First, she decided upon a multi-buttoned, baby-blue skirt complemented by her favorite white, long-sleeved blouse. Her blouse featured a smiling-face chiffon ruffle-lace bow tie surrounded by a high-neck collar. This form-fitted casual attire accentuated her thin waist and shapely figure.

Brynn's outfit was made complete by a large-brimmed, floppy hat decorated with fresh pink roses from her garden. Brynn was a beautiful sight to behold, and she knew it. So, she thought to herself, "Mr. Bear will surely be impressed."

At noon, she walked next door to the Norton's home, where she saw Emeline and her family's elegant gig carriage. Emeline brushed the mane of a dappled mare hitched to the gig. Brynn was indeed Emeline's best friend, but the Norton family's horse, Queenie, ran a close second.

After putting the brush down, Emeline smiled and said, "Queenie and I are ready!"

Emeline Norton and Brynn Dunham had always been close friends. They lived next door to one another, had attended school together, and had sung in the church choir for many years. Today, they both looked forward to the buggy ride from the Norton's home on Washington Street to Norwich's East

Great Plain. It would give them plenty of time to catch up. The two-and-a-half-mile trip would take them about thirty minutes.

Emeline had to use a great deal of coaxing and persuasive reasoning to convince her parents to allow her to borrow the family carriage. But, in the end, she successfully made her case.

She argued that the famous aeronaut, Mr. Samuel A. King, would ascend high into the heavens, riding in a gas-filled balloon above the fairgrounds. Her parents were not convinced.

Then, Emeline almost won them over with a show of intense emotional grief. Next, she reminded her father that she couldn't attend last year's fair due to illness. And she might never again have the chance to see such an unusual sight.

One of Emeline's friends told her that an aerial trapeze artist performed an astonishing feat near the end of Mr. King's descent last year. She amazed the crowd with a series of tricks on a trapeze suspended from the bottom of the balloon. The entertainer completed the act by parachuting hundreds of feet to the ground below.

Finally, they agreed after Emeline reminded her parents they had already permitted her twin sister, Isabella, to attend the fair with her suitor, Mr. Timothy Blackstone.

Emeline was twenty years old and could be trusted to drive and protect the family's horse and gig carriage. As Brynn stepped into the gig, Emeline said, "You look great today! I love your hat."

Brynn chirped, "Thank you. It's such a beautiful day!"

She added, "I've brought you a gift. So close your eyes."

When Emeline smiled, closed her eyes, and held out her open hands, Brynn placed a petite pink rosebud in the palm of her hand. Brynn said, "This is a late-blooming rose that I've been cultivating in our greenhouse. I hope you like it."

She added, "Turn to me, and I'll pin it just below the top button of your blouse."

Emeline smiled and said, "Oh. It's lovely! Thank you so much. I love your roses."

Emeline added, "So tell me more about this young man you met at the Town House."

Brynn perked up, "Well, he's a bit cocky and brazen but quite handsome. He's slightly taller than me and has a very nice head of black hair. His name is Jeremy, but his friends call him Bear. I think that he might be part Native American. I'm not sure, but that doesn't really matter. I like him."

She added, "He's also the vice president of a new company in town that discovered gold up on Wawecus Hill last month."

Emeline interjected, "What!! No one has said anything to me about that."

Brynn said, "Oh, yes, he filed a map showing the mineral rights plots at the Town House. He even showed me a chunk of gold that he found. They're going to begin selling shares in the company pretty soon. I told my parents about it, and they are quite interested."

Emeline replied, "That is very interesting. I'll let my father know, too."

Brynn could hardly stop talking. She chattered on, "He'll drive a sulky in today's harness race. Bear and his horse, Lightning, have won the race for the past three years. I hope they win today. Isn't that exciting?"

Emeline replied, "He does sound interesting. I'm looking forward to seeing what this lad looks like."

Brynn said, "Well, there is one thing about him that I don't like. When he entered my office, he slammed Dexter across the floor and called him a mutt. I don't think he likes Dexter very much, nor do I think Dexter likes him either. Maybe they'll get better acquainted and become fond of one another over time."

Emeline replied, "Yes, maybe, but maybe not. Dexter is an excellent judge of character."

~~~~~

When they arrived at the parking area for the buggies at the fairground's entrance, Brynn clutched the girls' tickets, and her heart beat faster. She saw scores of carriages and wagons hitched to posts in an open field near the ticket booth. Many well-heeled ladies and fine-looking gentlemen were standing in line to buy tickets.

However, Emeline and Brynn bypassed the ticket line and entered the elegant 'Very Important Person' surrey marked 'VIP.' Regular visitors would walk from the parking area and ticket booth across the street to the fairgrounds, but entering the fair was much more fashionable while riding aboard the VIP surrey.

The horse-drawn surrey accommodated four adults on its two benches and two children in the front. A bright red-striped cloth awning suspended from above shaded all the passengers. It ferried young ladies and elites along Surrey Lane to the central area of the fairground. Bear's VIP visitor passes and tickets for the surrey made Brynn feel special!

Emeline and Brynn saw several vendors selling specialty foods as they neared the main fairground. Smoke rose from the coals of a heated kettle full of freshly cooked caramel. The smell was divine! Brynn had seen apples on a stick covered with caramel but had never eaten one. Perhaps today would be the day.

When the surrey entered the main fairground, Brynn and Emeline saw it. In the middle of the field, a dozen or so men surrounded what appeared to be a large wicker basket. Each man was holding a rope attached to a huge cloth balloon. As they watched, the balloon slowly grew larger and larger.

Brynn could not contain her emotions. Without a thought, she pointed and said loudly enough for everyone in the surrey to hear, "Look at that balloon! It seems to be growing. How are they making that happen?"

The surrey driver answered, "If you look just to the right of the balloon's basket, you'll see several large steel containers. Do you see them?"

Emeline and Brynn both looked around and spied the containers.

Brynn answered for the two of them, "Yes, we see them."

The surrey driver continued, "Each container was filled with town gas yesterday at the Norwich Gas Light Company plant. They produce lighter-than-air town gas using coal. The gas can lift the balloons higher than the old-fashioned hot air balloons. Furthermore, filling a balloon with town gas is easier than hot air. Look over there. You can see the hoses inflating the balloon now."

They stepped down out of the surrey to get a closer view. When they looked near the bottom of the basket, they saw where someone had connected the hoses to the balloon. Then, just as the balloon finished filling, a man and a woman dressed in brightly colored costumes hopped into the basket. Brynn saw the balloon's name, *Queen of the Air*, proudly displayed across its midsection.

After the balloon ascended twenty feet, the aeronaut disconnected and threw out all the ropes that tethered the craft to the ground. Everyone cheered and shouted with excitement.

Brynn said, "Emeline, that woman must be the trapeze artist!"

The balloon continued rising for several minutes, and everyone saw a rope ladder unfurl from the bottom of the basket. All watched as a slender, fit woman climbed out of the raft and began the long descent down the ladder. Brynn knew that she was about to thrill the crowd.

Everyone gasped when a strong gust of wind suddenly kicked up, and the balloon began to shake and quiver. Then, the balloon started trembling sideways, in a northerly direction. Emeline, Brynn, and almost everyone else around them lost their breath as they saw the trapeze artist thrashing about while dangling from the rope ladder.

Brynn screamed, *"Oh my God! No! Get back in the basket!"*

As several more, less violent wind gusts rose and fell, the aerialist eventually returned to safety. However, the fair visitors could barely see the balloon or the two people in the basket by now. They had drifted far away.

The observers all wondered about the fate of the balloon and its passengers. But, over time, a steady, gentle breeze replaced the gusts, and everyone's anxiety was relieved.

Before the crowd surrounding the center of the field disbursed, a man bearing a large cone-shaped megaphone appeared. He slowly spun in a circle so that all could hear and announced, "Ladies and Gentlemen. I am certain that Mr. King, his lovely assistant, and the *Queen of the Air* will land safely. They are professionals, and they frequently face dangers such as this."

He said, "The annual harness race will commence in one hour. So, gentlemen, please attend to your horses and make ready your sulkies."

~~~~~

After the excitement, Brynn and Emeline only wanted to stroll around, explore what the fair offered, and calm their nerves. So Emeline told Brynn, "Let's look at the racehorses."

Brynn responded, "Sure. Let's see what foods they have, and after that, I want to see the horses too. Maybe we could find Jeremy."

At its core, the New London County Fair was a genuine agricultural fair. Brynn saw a collage of blue, red, and white ribbons hanging from the winning animals' necks. However, she didn't know how the judges could see differences between the chickens, pigs, sheep, or goats. They all looked the same to her. But she didn't really care. Brynn only wanted to ensure that her trendy skirt and blouse did not get soiled.

Emeline pointed to one of the food exhibitions and said, "Look over there. Someone has an ice cream cone!"

Brynn had eaten ice cream before, but only as a special treat at one of the shops in downtown Norwich.

They made their way to the ice cream stand, and Emeline noticed that a well-muscled man was turning a long crank attached to a small barrel full of ice. Curiously, she asked the man, "What are you doing?"

He smiled, "Step right up, young ladies, and behold my ice cream maker! On May 30 of this year, Mr. William Young patented and produced this machine. They call it the Johnson Patent Ice-Cream Freezer. Norwich is one of the first cities to see it in action!"

He continued, "Today, I'm making a batch of vanilla caramel ice cream. I'll use fresh cream from one of the cows you see across the way and fresh caramel from the vendor in the booth next to me. And, yes, he is the gentleman who makes the caramel apples. Would either of you like to purchase a scoop?"

Emeline could not resist the lure of fresh vanilla caramel ice cream, and Brynn's curiosity about the caramel apples also had to be satisfied. So they shared their delights with one another and felt that today was one of the best of their lives.

~~~~~

The harness race was about to begin, and Jeremy, like Brynn, was excited. But he was excited and nervous for different reasons. This year's field of competitors included several young studs that he knew to be fast and strong. Unlike most harness races that only allowed horses of a given age, this county fair's race was open to horses of all ages and genders. Jeremy was perplexed at why the fair organizers would allow mares to run. However, he didn't believe they had any chance of winning.

Three years ago, he and Lightning won the fair's race for the first time. At that time, Lightning was a powerful two-year-old in the prime of his life. He still had the fire of a competitive racer burning inside his belly, but years of pulling the company's heavy-laden buckboard wagon and service as a beast of burden had taken its toll. Jeremy was worried.

Observers situated themselves along the perimeter of the oval-shaped, makeshift track. Even though the population of Norwich was little less than 14,000, it seemed to Jeremy that the entire town had come to witness the event. Spectators were everywhere, and he and Lightning were the focus of many.

Jeremy couldn't help but notice several groups of men exchanging fistfuls of silver dollars in heated debate. They were obviously betting on the race, and he knew that Corey would be the first in line to wager a large sum.

But, most of all, Jeremy was concerned about one young lady in particular. *She, the girl of his dreams,* was standing at the finishing line wearing a baby blue skirt, a tight blouse, and a big floppy hat decorated with pink roses. Her long blonde hair fluttered in the breeze, and Jeremy's juices flowed.

Most New England harness races required three round trips around a quarter-mile track. But today's race demanded a full mile, four complete laps. The shorter three-quarter-mile races favored the older horses because they could muster a great deal of speed for a short period. The full-mile races were more suited to younger horses with more stamina.

The race began as the eight competitors trotted side-by-side around the track. They ran at uniform speed as they rounded the final bend and headed toward the starting line. The starting officials aligned the horses so none were ahead or behind the others.

As the sulkies passed the starting line, Jeremy thought, "We'll stay in the middle of the pack for the first three laps and then pour it on during the fourth."

He saw Brynn waving, smiling, and cheering for him. He had to win!

By the end of the first lap, he felt good about things. He and Lightning were in fourth place and running about three lengths behind the leader, a tall young gelding with a shimmering black coat. He and his driver were dressed in black silks with white numbers. Before the race, Jeremy observed the pair as they pranced in front of the spectators. He was concerned about this horse because it looked like he had plenty of youth, stamina, and willpower to win.

He wasn't concerned about any of the other horses. One of the horses, a mare, was running in seventh place, about six lengths back. Her name was Dig for Diamonds.

Jeremy thought, "What a stupid name for a horse."

The horse was dapple gray and appeared to be malnourished. She and her driver were decked out in pink silks with a large red number 1 planted in the center. It was almost laughable.

Jeremy's position within the pack was unchanged during the second lap. It seemed to him that the other drivers might also be using his strategy. Then, nearing the end of the third lap, Jeremy felt Lightning's strength begin to fade. The lead black gelding had already dropped back into third place and started to tire.

Jeremy snapped the popper near Lightning's ear as they began the final lap. Lightning responded by picking up the pace, but Jeremy could see small jets of white foam forming around the edges of his mouth. Nevertheless, they edged into second place ahead of another tired horse.

Halfway through the last lap, Jeremy was gaining on the lead horse. They were only one length behind. He could hear the crowd screaming and hollering. He'd never heard such applause in all the races he'd run! His confidence was increasing by the moment. The crowd's enthusiasm for him propelled his faith for a sure win.

Just as he and the lead horse rounded the final turn, headed toward the finish line, he saw a flash of glory. It was Dig for Diamonds! Dig had suddenly sparked alive and passed everyone in no time. She ran as though her life depended on the outcome, and Jeremy couldn't believe it. He suddenly realized that the crowd wasn't cheering for him. Instead, they were cheering for Dig for Diamonds!

Dig was now in first, and Jeremy was close behind in second. Jeremy had no intention of losing, especially to a mare. He began slapping Lightning with the whip, and now the foam spewing from Lightning's mouth had become a steady stream. His entire mane was slathered in a sea of foam. For the last 200 feet of the race, Jeremy whipped him repeatedly to no avail. Lightning could not run any faster. Instead, he began to slow. The only feeling left inside Lightning was the searing pain from Jeremy's ruthless beating.

Dig for Diamonds easily won the race by two lengths. As Jeremy and Lightning passed the finish line in fourth place, he saw tears in Brynn's eyes. He knew they were not tears of joy. Instead, they were tears of sorrow for the beating that Lightning had just received.

14: FUND THE COMPANY
DOWNTOWN NORWICH
NORWICH SAVINGS SOCIETY: MAIN STREET
FRIDAY, OCTOBER 1, 1858

The Norwich Savings Society was incorporated in May 1825 and was Connecticut's second-oldest savings bank. The conservative institution instilled a spirit of thrift and commonsense investing for businesses and individuals. Today, Mr. Francis A. Perkins, the bank's treasurer and secretary, sat across from Corey Pallaton and Jeremy Pallawotuk.

Corey knew the seventy-four-year-old banker to be a wise man with a well-cultivated, open mind. He was a conservative civic and spiritual leader who had served a two-year term as the mayor of Norwich twenty-five years earlier. Corey could have chosen to do business with several banks in Norwich. However, he wanted to receive his loan from Francis Perkins because he knew potential investors would trust any company associated with Mr. Perkins and Norwich Savings Society.

As young Jeremy gazed out Mr. Perkins's second-floor office window, he saw the hustle and bustle of downtown. He noticed a well-to-do family stepping down from an elegant horse-drawn carriage across the street at the recently opened Wauregan House. Perhaps they were visitors from New York who had sailed on the Norwich & New London Steamboat Company's passenger ship, *Commonwealth*. The family likely sailed on the 1,000-passenger sidewheel steamer to Allyn's Point and then rode on the Norwich & Worcester Railroad's Company passenger train to complete the trip to Norwich. Jeremy wanted to visit Boston and New York someday, and he knew that his position as the vice president of the Wawecus Hill Gold, Silver, and Nickel Mining Company could be his ticket.

Perkins offered his hand to Corey and said, "Welcome, Corey. It's nice to see you again."

After pausing, he continued, "I don't believe I've met your companion."

After shaking hands, Corey replied, "Yes, it is good to see you again, too, Mr. Perkins. This is Mr. Jeremy Pallawotuk. He and I have worked together for many years, and now I've asked him to become a trusted officer of my new company."

After Perkins shook Jeremy's hand, he said, "It is nice to meet you young man, and I hope this fine autumn morning finds you and Corey well. My wife, Abby, and I took a carriage ride to the top of Hardscrabble Hill this past weekend and enjoyed a picnic lunch and the beautiful scenery. We saw several small sailing craft docked in Chelsea Harbor and the splendor of Norwich's fall foliage. Corey, isn't your office in the neighborhood of Hardscrabble Hill?"

Corey replied, "Why yes, it is. It's atop the hill, next to where local boys burn barrel bonfires every Thanksgiving. We love it there. We're able to enjoy the scenery year-round. This past weekend, my wife, Elena, and I visited there to hang the sign for our new company."

Mr. Perkins responded, "I heard rumblings that you're starting a new business. Please tell me about it."

Corey began, "As you know, I've been clearing land and building houses in Norwich for the past few years. Several weeks ago, my survey crew cleared lots for a new subdivision near Wawecus Hill. We intend to build low-cost homes for displaced Native Americans in southern New England."

Corey continued, stretching the truth, saying, "During the process, we discovered a sizable cache of minerals laced with gold and silver at the base of the hill. Shortly after that, we laid out several precious mineral plots along a stream that runs through the area. We named it Goldmine Brook."

Corey said, "Over the past week, Jeremy and I formed a new company focusing on unearthing, processing, and selling precious minerals. Its name is the Wawecus Hill Gold, Silver, and Nickel Mining Company. I'm the president, and Jeremy is the vice president. We've filed papers to incorporate the company and expect approval within the week."

"You may have seen our advertisement in the Norwich Aurora to sell shares of company stock. We plan to share company profits with shareholders and, of course, with our displaced Native American brethren."

Corey continued his pitch, "However, we need financial support to help build the business and mining operations infrastructure. We'll need funds to build an operations office at the goldfield, buy mineral processing equipment, purchase office equipment, and pay employees."

Jeremy unrolled a detailed map of their goldfield from his portfolio and said, "May I show you our map?"

Perkins sat forward, leaning on his desk, and nodded.

Jeremy pointed at the map, "Here, you see the upper ledge of Wawecus Hill."

"Just below the hill lies the headwaters of Goldmine Brook. Most of the gold and silver we've found thus far is in or near the brook. So, we plan to build the field office in this flat area slightly east of the brook. And, just to the south, a rock crusher will grind the gold-laced minerals down to coarse particles. Later, we'll refine the mixture into a pure gold and silver powder."

Corey resumed command of the briefing, saying, "We'll need two strong, secure safes to store the recovered gold, silver, and nickel. We'll maintain one safe at the site and the other at a secure, off-site location."

"Mr. Perkins, I've invited you and the Norwich Savings Society to join us in this endeavor because of your many years of highly respected service. Our new company will help further Norwich's reputation as a great place to conduct business. Would you be interested in joining us to make this once-in-a-lifetime opportunity a reality?"

Perkins questioned, "Well, Mr. Pallaton, this is quite an opportunity. Can you share your detailed business plan with me? How large of a loan do you require?"

Corey motioned to Jeremy to hand their business plan to Perkins. After several minutes of careful review, Perkins said, "Your plan is ambitious and costly, and the proposed startup costs are higher than most new businesses I've funded in the past."

Perkins added, "I deduce that the whole premise of your business depends on the quantity of gold, silver, and nickel you can recover. Do you have proof of your gold discovery?"

Corey smiled again and motioned to Jeremy, who reached into his pocket. He pulled out the large quartz rock laden with gold Travis had found in the brook and handed it to Corey.

Holding up the rock, Corey lied again, saying, "This is one of the many specimens we've found."

Francis Perkins sat motionless momentarily, considering his next course of action.

Perkins began, "Mr. Pallaton, I believe you have stumbled upon a great opportunity, and I sincerely desire you and your company to succeed. But the actual amount of gold and other minerals on Wawecus Hill concerns me. Please remember, I have a fiduciary responsibility to the bank and must proceed in their best interest."

"However, with that said, I feel good about you and your company. Therefore, I can offer you a 5% interest rate loan. What collateral can you offer to secure the loan?"

Pallaton had feared this might be the case but had planned for the possibility.

He responded, "I'm sure we'll find more gold than anyone can imagine, and our company will be profitable. As you know, I live in a beautiful home next to Williams Park at the corner of Washington Street and Sachem Avenue. Our home is mortgage-free and worth far more than any funds needed to cover this loan. I would consider offering it as collateral if you could offer a lower interest rate."

Pallaton continued, "The 5% rate you offer is slightly higher than I expected. Could you do a little better?"

Perkins thought, "Okay, would a 4½% rate work for you?"

Pallaton replied, "Yes, that is most generous of you."

Once again, Francis Perkins extended his hand to Corey and said, "Mr. Pallaton, it is good doing business with you. I'll need to speak with the bank president for approval of a large loan like this, but I'm sure I can convince him to agree to it. It will take several days to draw up the papers and establish a line of credit for you."

Corey said, "Okay. Thank you. The end of next week will be fine."

Perkins added, "By the way, are you aware of the upcoming Bicentennial Jubilee? Norwich was founded in 1659, and we are planning to celebrate the 200th anniversary of the event next fall. The Jubilee will be a fabulous celebration! It will be the largest event ever held in Norwich."

"The first planning meeting was held last week at General William Williams's house, and the second meeting will occur three weeks from now. We'll organize committees to oversee the Jubilee at the planning meeting."

"General and Mrs. Williams will also host a social gathering for many prominent Norwichians later in the evening. We want to get as many people involved in the Jubilee planning as possible. Lucius Carroll, I, and many others will attend. Lucius is a vice president of our bank's board of directors and will undoubtedly be interested in learning about your company."

"I pray that you and Jeremy can attend the planning meeting."

Perkins smiled, turned his attention to Jeremy, and said, "Oh, yes. I almost forgot. Please invite your wives and, or girlfriends to the social."

Corey responded, "Yes, Jeremy and I would be pleased to attend the meeting. Of course, we'd also like to participate in the Jubilee planning. And I'm sure my wife would love to attend the social, too."

Corey turned to Jeremy and questioned, "What do you think, Jeremy?"

Jeremy didn't quite know what to say. He didn't have a wife and knew that Brynn was highly disappointed in him. He replied,

"Well, I'm not married, but I would thoroughly enjoy attending the social."

Corey quickly interceded, "We'll all certainly attend. Perhaps you could introduce me to Mr. Carroll at the meeting? I'd love to tell him more about our company."

Perkins responded, "You're in luck because he is downstairs waiting to speak with me on another bank matter. I'll introduce him to you on your way out. Lucius owns a wholesale goods store down the street that sells various equipment needed to operate businesses like yours. Perhaps you could purchase your company supplies and production equipment from him. He is always looking for new ways to further business enterprise in Norwich."

Corey responded, "Thank you, Mr. Perkins. I will do that."

After being introduced to Lucius Carroll, Corey and Jeremy exited the bank's front door. Corey told Jeremy, "I want you to prepare a list of everything we need, get down to Carroll's store, and buy it all as soon as the line of credit gets approved. Be sure the safes are strong."

Corey added, "Also, I want you to begin laying out a site for a model home on one of the best lots we surveyed on Wawecus Hill. While at Carroll's store, also buy windows and paint for the model home."

Jeremy replied, "Should I use the line of credit to pay for the house materials?"

Corey answered firmly, "Yes, of course. We'll have enough money to build twenty houses."

15: BUILDING SUPPLIES
DOWNTOWN NORWICH
LUCIUS CARROLL'S WHOLESALE STORE
FRIDAY, OCTOBER 8, 1858

Jeremy needed to buy building materials, gold processing equipment, and safes for the company. But he wasn't quite sure where to begin. How much lumber would be needed to build the office and the model home? What other mineral processing equipment would he need besides several panning sieves and a rock crusher?

However, Corey had given explicit directions for the two safes. Both needed to be fire and burglar-proof because Corey planned to temporarily use the field office container to store a week's supply of processed gold. It needed to be secure but only required to be of medium size.

The requirements for the company's primary safe were quite different. Corey had decided to have it installed in his home on Washington Street. It needed to be large enough to prevent any would-be thief from moving or breaking into it. And it had to be large enough to hold the entire cache of the company's processed gold, silver, and nickel. It also needed to be fireproof.

Once Jeremy purchased the safe, how would he transport the safe to Corey's home once he bought it? He was sure he would need someone to help him load and unload it on the wagon. But who would help him, and how would they do it?

Jeremy's first stop would be at Mr. Lucius Carroll's wholesale store near the end of Main Street. Hopefully, Mr. Carroll could help him make buying decisions.

It was early morning, and Jeremy had ridden into town on the company's buckboard wagon with Corey's horse, Lightning, leading the way. Since the county fair race, Lightning had changed. Jeremy's mean streak had broken Lightning's spirit.

As he hitched Lightning to the post just outside Carroll's store, Jeremy could see Mr. Carroll through the window of his establishment. Carroll opened the door and said, "Hello, Mr. Pallawotuk. I didn't expect to see you soon, but I'm glad to see you."

Jeremy replied, "Yes. Good morning. I'm happy to see you too. After taking care of the horse, I'll be right in."

He entered the store a minute later, and a small, yapping terrier met him. Jeremy almost stepped on him but kicked him away at the last moment. Then, he thought, "Why do people put up with these pesky little dogs?"

Carroll responded, "Oh, I'm sorry, don't mind Izzy. She's a great watchdog but gets a little excited when shoppers first arrive."

Changing the conversation, he added, "That is a fine-looking horse you've got there. He looks strong and healthy."

"Yes, sir. He is Mr. Pallaton's horse. He's healthy and can still pull the wagon just fine. I think that Mr. Pallaton will keep him for at least another year. We'll see how he fares as he gets older."

Mr. Carroll motioned, "Come in and let me show you around. You've probably never seen a store like this. We are a wholesale outfit that only sells to businesses like yours. Mostly, we support the cotton and wool dyeing companies up in Greeneville."

Carroll pointed at his fully stocked shelves and said, "The cans here contain fabric dye, mixed paint, and other chemicals. We also sell spindles and other spare parts needed for their looms. In addition, I procure large equipment and specialty materials for the cotton mills from my external vendors. Over here, on the counter, I maintain several catalogs where we can find almost any type of manufacturing equipment that you might need. Can you tell me more about your business, and perhaps I can better serve you."

Jeremy retold the story of how they discovered gold, formed the company, and now how the company was selling shares and building the onsite office. And why he needed panning sieves, office chairs, tables, a desk, a coal-fired heater, and two safes.

Carroll said, "We should be able to find everything on your list. Our store carries a large selection of office furniture, supplies, and coal-fired stoves. If we don't have a particular item on the showroom floor, I can always order it for you from one of our catalogs."

Motioning Jeremy toward the catalogs, Carroll continued, "Okay. Finding a sieve supplier for panning gold is easy. When the '49ers struck gold in California a few years back, many young entrepreneurs began making prospecting supplies and are happy to support enterprising young men like yourself."

Turning the pages of one of the catalogs, Carroll added, "You'll need more than just sieves. This catalog also offers picks, axes, shovels, and rock-crushing equipment. This wholesaler has priced all of his equipment fairly."

Jeremy thought to himself that the prices were irrelevant. Then, after choosing everything that he believed his team would need, he said, "Can you get these to me by the end of the week?"

Handing Jeremy another sales pamphlet, Carroll said, "Yes, I can have these items ready for you on time. But let's shop for the safes before placing your order. I have a small one here in the store that, I believe, will suit your needs. You can take it today, but we'll have to order any larger one from the Hall Safe and Lock Company in Cincinnati."

Jeremy studied the Hall catalog. He could hardly believe the size and solidity of these monster safes. Then, using a measured, commanding voice, he said, "This 1849 Fire and Burglar Proof model is exactly what we need. Order it for us. How long will it take to get it here?"

Carroll responded. "It will take four to six weeks. This model is one of their largest and most expensive, so the manufacturers only keep one or two on hand. I'll ask them how many they have in stock at the moment. They'll transport it to New York City on the Buffalo & Erie Railroad. Then, they will load it on a horse-drawn wagon and bound for Norwich."

"You are in luck. Hall's Company delivers and installs their safe for you. However, you'll need to ensure that the floor, where the safe will stand, is strong enough to support the weight. Where do you want it delivered?"

Under his breath, Jeremy uttered a great sigh of relief, knowing that he wouldn't have to deal with this arduous task.

He said, "We'll place it inside Mr. Pallaton's drawing room at his private residence. I'll let him know about the foundation requirements."

Jeremy paused momentarily and said, "We also need building materials for a model home. Our company plans to provide housing on Wawecus Hill for many of our displaced Native American brethren. Do you sell interior and exterior paint, and could you support local Native Americans by offering a discounted price?"

Carroll smiled and replied, "I can provide you as much paint as you need and will happily discount the price by 20%. I'd be proud to support your families."

He added, "I've seen your company's ads in the Aurora seeking investors. Your organization sounds like a fine company. I plan to support your efforts and will invest in your endeavors."

Jeremy responded. "Thank you. You won't be sorry."

He continued, "It is good doing business with you. But, unfortunately, I've got to be on my way. Before returning to Goldmine Brook, I must visit Central Wharf to purchase several other supplies."

CHAHNAMEED

16: MATHEWS FAMILY HERITAGE
LUCASVILLE
MATHEWS FAMILY RESIDENCE
MONDAY, OCTOBER 18, 1858

Tonight, Travis finally had the opportunity to study the Quinebaugan artifacts more closely. His curiosity demanded that he examine the relics in greater detail to decide what to do with them. So Travis gathered them, carefully carried them down to the basement of the Mathews's home, and placed them on a workbench. He, his father, and his mother regularly used this sturdy wooden workbench. They had positioned a shelf lined with candles so they could work during evening hours.

Tonight, the tomahawk first drew Travis's attention. He used a small, soft, moist brush to clean the handle. After that, Travis exercised much more caution as he neared the tomahawk's head. Clearly, someone had gilded its head in gold, but several layers of caked-on debris had built up over the years. As he cleared the dirt, the tomahawk's head shimmered brilliantly in the candlelight. It was stunning!

However, Travis couldn't think of a plausible explanation for why the tomahawk was so small. He knew it was too large to be a baby's toy yet too small to fit into a grown man's hand. Also, due to its gilded head, it certainly had not been used as a tool.

Finally, he wondered why someone had carved the shape of a snake's body into its handle.

When Travis turned his attention to the mortar and pestle, the memory of Lydia's snake bite erupted into his brain. He couldn't forget the pain he saw in her face and his fear for her life. He questioned several aspects of the incident, "How did the snake burrow its way inside the mortar? How did the fierce rain, thunder, and lightning storm suddenly appear after her snakebite? Was it simply a coincidence that a snake had also bitten him while unearthing the tomahawk?"

Travis thought the series of events unnatural because he remembered several Quinebaugan legends his mother had told him as a youth. The combination of all these events convinced him these relics were *extraordinary*. So, he planned to use great caution while handling them.

After meticulously cleaning all the surfaces of mortar and pestle, he studied them carefully. The cylindrically shaped granite mortar was about a foot tall. Its diameter was about six inches at its base and ten inches at its top. Travis had seen his mother use a mortar and pestle to grind corn for several delicious recipes, but hers was much smaller.

The primitive decorations that adorned its entire outer surface were unexpected. Travis saw that an artisan had smoothed the granite face, covered it with a primer, and then decorated it with pictographs. To Travis, the graphics looked to be a series of small child-like stick figures, several snakes, two hammer-shaped tools, a crude chair, a simple Quinebaugan dwelling, and several other objects. One of the hammers was small, and the other was quite large, with a curved handle.

Travis then removed the pestle housed in the mortar. It looked about ten inches long, with a smooth, rounded head.

This pestle was much larger than any he'd ever seen. In addition, he noticed several tiny glimmers of gold embedded in its head. It looked like residue from a mixture of crushed rock and gold.

Travis's heart began to beat wildly, and he could barely control his emotions. Then, finally, it dawned on him that the tools were for not grinding corn. Instead, the mortar and pestle formed a hand-operated rock grinder!

When he examined the bottom of the mortar more closely, he saw tiny grains of golden-colored material embedded in its base. Finally, he thought, "Someone used these tools to grind and extract gold from rocks on Wawecus Hill."

He surmised, "Perhaps I could use these tools."

Travis retrieved the gold-laced rock he and Lydia had found earlier and placed it in the mortar. After a few attempts to grind it into smaller pieces, he could see that the stone needed to be much smaller before the mortar and pestle could work their magic.

So, he placed the rock on a small burlap bag, gathered its corners, and smashed it with a hammer. He knew this method of reducing the stone to a manageable size wasn't ideal, but for today, it worked just fine.

He then collected several fragments, placed them in the mortar, grabbed the pestle, and began grinding. Finally, he could see that the process was working. After several minutes, Travis examined the finely ground particles and noticed two different shades and textures of golden minerals.

He thought, "Some of the powder must be real gold, and some must be fool's gold."

Travis heard the basement door open as he began grinding the next batch.

His mother appeared and said, "What on Earth are you doing? What have you got there?"

Travis's heart sank because he didn't want to keep secrets from his mother. Her love and trust in him as an honest, transparent son was the glue that bound them together.

He hesitated to share his Quinebaugan treasures with her but knew the time had come to reveal all. So, finally, he showed her the artifacts and told her how, when, and where he and Lydia had found them.

Faith was astonished when he informed her that snakes had bitten them both at the moment of their discoveries. She asked, "Are you okay? Is Lydia okay?"

Travis replied, "I'm fine. And I think she's okay, too. But Lydia hasn't been too friendly lately. I think she's disappointed that I put her into such a dangerous situation."

She said, "I wish you would have told me about your discoveries sooner. I believe you've uncovered something of great value because these artifacts link us to our Quinebaugan heritage."

After looking the artifacts over, she added, "We need to return them to the tribe immediately. But, first, I want to tell you some things about your ancestors."

Faith began, "When Lucas was the Sachem of our people, most of the tribe lived here in Lucasville. His cabin stood about a mile from our house. But, there was a second, smaller Quinebaugan settlement. Their leader was Lucas's brother, Wawequa, and they lived on Wawequa's hill, known today as Wawecus Hill. Like many Quinebaugan in Lucasville, the community on Wawequa's Hill was mostly comprised of farmers. But it is believed that Quinebaugan artisans and craftsmen on Wawequa's Hill made tools and weapons for the entire tribe."

She suggested, "Look at this small tomahawk. I believe it is a symbol."

"Its head is gilded. The tribe probably used this symbolic tomahawk during rituals to remind them of the Quinebaugan triumph over the aggressive Pocawansetts after Wawequa used it to execute their leader, Pallatonomo. He was a major threat to our people."

"The snake that coils around its handle probably symbolizes the healing effect that Wawequa and his weapon brought to our people. After Pallatonomo's death, the Quinebaugan enjoyed many years of peace and harmony."

She continued, "I must tell you a few things about your lineage. Firstly, you come from a long line of Quinebaugan royalty. My full name is Faith *Wawequa* Mathews. You, my mother, and I are all direct descendants of Wawequa. Secondly, you and your father are direct descendants of Lucas. So, Travis, your bloodlines are pure, and your heart is true Quinebaugan."

Travis was surprised. He'd always been proud to be a Quinebaugan. But, the newly gained knowledge of *royal blood running through his veins* gave him a profound feeling of gratitude and responsibility. His extraordinary height, abnormal strength, and unique birthmark differed from both his Quinebaugan and English friends. Travis had always trusted his basic instincts but now better understood why.

His mother continued to reveal more of his family ties to Quinebaugan tradition, saying, "Rachel Flowers is destined to become our tribal ceremonial leader. She and I are always learning and recording more of our cultural traditions."

"I want you to think back to the day you were poisoned at your grandmother's house. A miracle occurred that day! Rachel and I met with your grandmother. She has shared her knowledge of herbal healing, legends, traditions, and prophecies with Rachel and me for many years."

"While we were meeting, you quietly snuck down into the basement and got into trouble. You ate several dried herbs and drank a vial of rattlesnake venom. We were in the process of converting the toxin into an antivenom, but you got to it before we had a chance to process it."

"I know that you've always believed that a snake bit you. But, no, there were no snake bites. You drank snake venom. The vial contained enough poison to kill three grown men. We brought you upstairs and sang the old chants while you cried out in agony. *Munduyahweh* listened to our prayers and granted you a renewed life."

"As we sang, your birthmark glowed a bright reddish-purple color, and your forehead inflamed. It appeared as though the venom energized a spirit within you."

"That poison should have killed you, but it eventually made you stronger. I believe the tomahawk's coiled snake handle symbolizes its healing ability."

Faith reached out to Travis, touched the snake-shaped birthmark above his left eye, and said, "I believe *Munduyahweh* granted you a divine gift. It is the gift of healing. Someday, you will likely become a healer of some sort. Perhaps a medical doctor, or perhaps even our tribe's Medicine Man."

Her words touched Travis at a gut level. When he thought back to when the snakes bit him and Lydia, he remembered the feeling of energy rising from the earth through his body. He did not understand the sensation then, but her words rang true. Somehow, *Munduyahweh's* energy healed him.

She turned her attention back to the mortar and pestle. Clearly, someone used them to complete the process of extracting gold. But she thought, "But why would they decorate the tools?"

She said, Travis, look at these drawings of snakes, tomahawks, small stick figures, a horse, and other symbols. The tomahawks seemed to stand out from the other objects to me. I believe that someone has placed them in positions of prominence."

She continued, "See how one tomahawk is very small, and the other is large. You've found the small one."

Travis added, "I believe the pictographs tell us an untold Quinebaugan story, myth, or prophecy. Perhaps there are more buried artifacts. Perhaps they are a map of some sort. But, unfortunately, I don't have any good answers. So what do you think?"

She knew that *Munduyahweh* had called Travis to serve the Quinebaugan tribe but couldn't be sure what that calling might be.

Pausing momentarily, she said, "I need to tell you another story."

TALE OF CHAHNAMEED'S WIFE

Many years ago, there was a beautiful, inquisitive, young, adventurous Quinebaugan girl. She loved making beaded buckskin dresses for the women in our tribe.

One day, she traveled to the coast of The Devil's Belt (it is called Long Island Sound today) to gather shells and feathers. She used shells to make beads for dresses and loved to wear feathers in her long black hair.

Late in the day, a man named Chahnameed paddled in from the sea. He was a fisherman and loved exploring the ocean. So when he first saw her, he stared in awe at her beauty. That very day, Chahnameed took her for his wife, and they paddled out to the island where he lived.

They lived there happily for a while, but Chahnameed often went to sea and left her alone for long periods. Finally, after a time, she decided to leave him. One day, she got into a canoe and paddled back toward the mainland, but Chahnameed saw her. He got into his canoe and furiously tried to catch her.

As his canoe drew close to hers, she quickly raised her hand to her head and pulled out a long hair from the top. She drew it through her fingers, and immediately, it became stiff like a spear. Chahnameed thought he would catch her now, and he did not see what she was doing. She balanced the hair spear in her hand and threw it straight. It hit him in the forehead, and he fell out of the canoe, sank beneath the waves, and died.

She paddled back to the mainland and returned to our tribe in Lucasville. But, she was ashamed that she had made the mistake of marrying Chahnameed. She did not want to answer questions about her misadventure for the rest of her life. She left the area alone in shame. No one knows, with any certainty, where Chahnameed's wife lives today.

Faith said, "A very old woman named White Eagle lives alone at Kachina Rock. She knows more of our tribe's history than anyone. Years ago, Lucas used this sacred spot for tribal meetings and gatherings. Many believe the tale of Chahnameed is not a simple folklore myth but instead an exaggerated true story. They say that White Eagle was Chahnameed's wife. But, to my knowledge, no one has spoken with her in several years."

"White Eagle will be able to shed light on these artifacts and will know what to do with them. You've got to take them to her and ask her for guidance."

The stories that Travis had heard as a child about White Eagle made him nervous. He thought she might be a sorceress or perhaps even a witch. So he paused momentarily and said, "Grandmother also knows a lot about our history. I'll take the objects to her instead."

Faith replied, "I disagree. These are very, very old objects. I've spoken with Grandmother many times about our traditions and legends. She told me that White Eagle knows more of matters like this than anyone."

Travis replied, "Okay, you've convinced me these artifacts are an important piece of our heritage. Lydia and I found them, and I believe we've been called to learn more. So we'll search for more relics before visiting White Eagle."

Faith replied, "I also believe you'll find more artifacts and will receive a deeper understanding of your calling. But, you should first seek out White Eagle. She can help you."

Travis thought for a moment and said, "Ok, Mother. I'll meditate and pray to *Munduyahweh* for guidance."

He knew that *Munduyahweh* would guide him and Lydia.

17: COMPANY PROGRESS
GOLDMINE BROOK
COMPANY FIELD OFFICE
SATURDAY, OCTOBER 23, 1858

Jeremy and his crew had been working their butts off since discovering gold. As he stood in front of the model home near the apex of Wawecus Hill, Jeremy felt a strong sense of pride and accomplishment. It took his team of new recruits only a week to build the foundation, walls, and roof.

Jeremy saw Corey and Lightning approaching him as he looked down the narrow dirt path that led away from the house. Lightning looked like he was on his last legs and probably needed replacing.

Jeremy was happy to see Corey because today was payday. Of course, everyone was expecting to be paid, but Jeremy was concerned. The business did not seem to be going well because, as far as he knew, Corey and Elena had only sold a few shares of company stock. However, Mr. Pallaton had not shown any concerns when they last spoke.

Jeremy said, "Good afternoon Mr. Pallaton. It is nice to see you."

Corey responded. "Hi, Bear. Good to see you, too. Let's take a look at the home."

Jeremy said, "We've got the foundation, walls, and roof almost done, but we still need to finish the floors and interior rooms. We'll have it complete and ready for a family in two or three more weeks."

After entering the future home, Jeremy gestured to the three men building the floor and said, "I hired these guys from our tribe last week. They only needed a few general instructions, and they've done all the work."

Corey stepped into a bedroom and watched as the workers quickly put down their tools, stood erect, and bowed their heads slightly. They knew and respected Corey Pallaton. He was both their employer and their tribe's Medicine Man.

Jeremy knew he did not command the same respect as Corey from his Pocawansett brethren. They did his bidding for fear of reprisal for most of his life. His physical strength and presence intimidated them all, but he lacked all the emotional aspects of authentic leadership.

After a quick inspection of the building, Corey addressed the men. "This home is the first of many we will build. It represents a new era in the history of our people, and we'll unite our families here by next summer. Keep up the good work!"

He continued, "Bear tells me, and I can see you're doing a fine job. You'll each find an additional 10% in your pay later this afternoon. Congratulations!"

Jeremy felt a sigh of relief as he and Corey made their way down the hill to the field office building site. Finally, he was sure there would be no problem meeting the payroll this week.

His team was nearing the completion of the field office. As they approached, a three-man crew was on the roof, tapping a row of red cedar shingles into place.

Jeremy said, "We'll have the office operational by the end of the day. And, like the model home construction team, these men have also worked long hours to finish it quickly."

Corey was surprised when he entered the building. He could hardly believe the progress made in such a short time. He saw Jeremy's work desk, four chairs, a gas lantern, and the small safe that Jeremy had purchased at Carroll's store.

Corey noticed a small work area in the back left corner of the office. As he approached to inspect, he saw a large stone mortar and pestle, a small metal bowl, a fluid-filled glass cylinder, and several bottles of chemicals on a work table.

"Jeremy, please tell me what you're doing here."

Jeremy said, "After one of our crew crushes the large stones outside, I bring them here to complete the process. I first grind the crushed rock into a fine powder using this stone mortar and pestle. Then I separate the gold dust from the powder and then place the powder in this metal bowl."

"The next step involves mercury and nitric acid. After I add quicksilver to the mix, it finds and attaches itself to small particles of gold. I then pour the slag and add nitric acid to the mixture to complete the separation process."

Holding a large bottle, he cautioned, "But, I've got to be careful, though, because the nitric acid could blow up if I mix the chemicals incorrectly."

Corey said, "That's pretty impressive. Where did you learn all this?"

Jeremy responded, "When I bought the sieves, picks, and shovels at Mr. Carroll's store, he explained the process and sold me the chemicals and equipment. I've successfully used the process on several samples. Look here."

Jeremy removed a small bottle from the safe and showed the partially filled container to Corey.

He said, "I'm unsure if all the powder is real gold."

Corey took the bottle, shook it, held it above his head, studied it, and said, "Don't worry, I'll test it after I return home."

Corey continued, "I like the looks of this safe, but I'm concerned that someone might ransack this office and steal it. The large safe from Cincinnati will be delivered and installed in my house by the end of next week. From now on, I want you to bring the processed gold powder to me at the end of each week. I'll store it in the heavy-duty safe in my home."

Corey walked to the desk and said, "I know you've been very busy building the model home and field office, but have you made time to search for gold?"

Jeremy responded by opening the desk drawer and unfurling the latest *Found Gold* map. He said, "Yes, I knew everyone wanted to search for gold, so, for the past week, I let them all do a little prospecting. We spent the last hour of each workday searching. Let me show you the latest map."

He pointed to the map and said, "Okay, we've only found a dozen or so rocks that may contain gold. And you should be aware that we discovered them all in the site's northern riverbed. You can see it here. I've pinpointed the exact locations."

Corey said, "Well, I thought you'd found more than that."

Jeremy responded, "Yes, I know. All the guys have brought me many rocks, and they think that most of them are full of gold. But, I haven't been completely forthright with them because I want to keep everyone optimistic."

Corey said, "Yes, you're right. And I do agree with your approach. But please keep this map up-to-date."

Jeremy nodded, and the two walked outside to join the others. Jeremy saw Travis digging a post hole for the three-rail wooden fence surrounding the site. He shouted out, "Heh, Gimpy! Go up to the home site and tell the guys to get their asses down here. Mr. Pallaton wants to talk to everyone."

Travis nodded. He hated the nickname, and his patience had worn thin.

While waiting for everyone to gather, Jeremy told Corey, "Gimpy has only been working a couple of days a week because he's got those other jobs with the gun maker and the map maker.

Then, pointing to the outhouse behind the office, he added, "But he's doing a pretty good job. He built most of the fence. Can you see the shitter up there?"

Corey nodded.

Jeremy continued, "He built that all by himself. Even though he's not one of us, we should keep him on. I'll need him to work on the survey party starting next week. I know that you want us to lay out all the home lots, build a second model home, and search for more gold, all at the same time. I want to focus on processing the gold and supervising the construction crews. So, maybe you could tell Gimpy to help survey the home lots."

Corey said, "That's not a bad idea. I'll think about it."

Everyone gathered near the rock crusher on the other side of the field office. They wondered why Bear had them asked to assemble because it was long before regular quitting time. Corey began, "It's great to see all of you and your fine work here. I want to offer my thanks to you."

He continued, "Until now, we've focused on building company infrastructure, and I know you all must be anxious to spend more time prospecting the goldfield. That time is about to begin. Next week, we'll shift our efforts to panning, digging, and finding gold. And, of course, I expect we'll also find silver and nickel."

He looked around and said, "Bowie, you'll be in charge of the prospecting party. Crockett, you'll run this crusher, and Bear will refine the crushed minerals into gold dust. Jeremy will also continue as the site supervisor. On Monday, he will give everyone specific assignments."

Corey continued, "I have a bonus for you all today. You are free to prospect in the brook for the next hour. You are welcome to keep anything you find for yourself!"

"Everyone is dismissed for the week. Have a great weekend, and be prepared to find more gold on Monday. For those of you who haven't been paid yet, please see Bear."

Travis watched as Jeremy paid the others. They were joking around and plunging into the brook in search of gold.

Crockett asked the others, "Would anyone like to join me in town tonight? The Germania Lodge will be brimming with plentiful wine, women, and song. I'm especially looking forward to seeing Maisie. She's a hot ticket!"

Bowie laughed and responded, "Oh yeah. I'll be there. You're right. Maisie is something special."

Travis didn't want any part of them.

When Corey returned to the office, Travis followed him in. He was anxious to speak with Corey because he wanted to discuss his future role in the company. So Travis said, "Mr. Pallaton, do you have a moment to speak with me?"

Pallaton replied, "Sure, Travis. What can I do for you?"

Travis started, "Thank you for letting me work on the survey team. As I mentioned last month, I plan to become a ship's navigator someday and need to learn to use navigational instruments better. While working on your survey team, I learned the job of rodman, but after discovering gold in the brook, I haven't learned much more. Bear showed me how to take and record measurements, but I'd really like to become an expert at using the instruments."

While speaking, Travis considered how much he disliked digging fence holes, building the outhouse, and serving as the lowly rodman.

He continued, "I also want to thank you again for giving me the minerals rights on that plot at the back of the goldfield. Unfortunately, I haven't had much time to explore it, but I do look forward to it."

Travis continued, "I know your team will find a lot of precious metal in the brook, and I've told my parents that I believe they should invest in the company. But I believe it is time to begin following my dream and traveling the world. So, I'm thinking about parting ways with your company."

Travis asked, "Would you tell me the role you foresee for me in the company? And, if I quit, would you allow me to hold on to the mineral rights?"

Corey took a moment and responded, "Travis, thank you for being candid about your feelings. However, I need you to understand that the primary goal for my real estate company and the mining company is to help support my tribe. I want the profits to help pay for our new housing development."

"Many years ago, my ancestors were displaced from their native homeland or slaughtered by the English and the Quinebaugan. Several years after the massacre, Norwich leaders ceded land on this very hill to help the displaced Pocawansett.

But they were so poor and scattered throughout New London County that my tribe couldn't reorganize."

"You may be unaware of this, but I am a descendant of royal Pocawansetts on both sides of my family tree. My surname, Pallaton, is a shortened version of Pallatonomo. The Quinebaugan may have murdered him, but his blood still runs in my veins today. I feel his presence every day."

"My great-grandmother, Minnetinka, was the daughter of the great Pocawansett Sachem Pallawotuk. After the Quinebaugans and the English killed both her parents, she had no choice but to marry a European. So when she married William Corey, they changed Minnetinka's name to Elizabeth Corey. Giving respect to her, my parents named me Corey."

"The English and the Quinebaugan have tried to destroy my tribal heritage for many generations. As the current Pocawansett Medicine Man, my sworn duty is to provide *medicine* to my people. Today's *medicine* will manifest itself as comfortable housing and respectable employment. I am providing both to our people here in Norwich."

He continued, "Travis, I know you are of Quinebaugan descent and are a hard-working, decent man. I bear no ill feelings toward you because of your ancestry, and I sincerely hope that you will continue in my employment."

"Winter is coming, and I want to complete laying out the boundaries of the entire housing development before the cold sets in. As you know, I've assigned Bear to oversee the mining site and home construction. As I mentioned in the meeting, the company will soon focus on prospecting for gold. But we'll also build at least one more home on the hill and complete the subdivision layout before winter."

"I want you to become our survey party chief. Bear, Bowie, and Crocket will be too busy to help you, but Bear tells me you've already learned enough to do the job. You may hire two men from Mr. Walling's office to help you. I've reviewed the preliminary map and estimate that you'll be able to complete the job in two to three weeks."

Corey continued, "I listened to your concerns about the recent jobs that Bear forced upon you. And, yes, I know that you and Jeremy aren't on the best of terms, but I am asking you to work for me for the next several weeks and help me get another Pocawansett family resettled before winter."

Corey concluded his statement, "If you're willing to do this, I'll increase your pay by 25%, and I'll allow you to retain the right to keep anything you find on your plot."

Travis was happily surprised at Corey's response. He could gain more practical experience as the survey party chief, keep the mineral rights, only work three more weeks for Corey, and receive a salary increase. He answered, saying, "Thank you for your generous consideration. I will continue working for you and will finish the survey. I am honored to help the Pocawansetts here in Norwich. Like you, I believe they deserve a fresh start."

They both heard a loud commotion outside. Apparently, someone had discovered another gold-laced rock. Then, they heard Bear shout out, "Corey. You must get out here and see what we've found."

Corey leapt up and made his way out to the others quickly. Travis was happy that someone had found something, but more importantly, he was more optimistic about his future with the company.

~~~~~

Before leaving the office, Travis thought it wise to study the preliminary site plan for the future homes. He wanted to begin planning how he would approach his new job. When he opened the drawer where Jeremy kept the maps, he couldn't help but notice the *Found Gold* map.

As he studied it, Travis was shocked. There were *only six areas marked on the map*. He could hardly believe the team had searched the site for over two months and had identified so few areas containing gold-bearing minerals. Travis had personally given Jeremy thirty or so promising specimens and watched as others gave him more than a hundred.

Travis concluded that either the samples he found were fool's gold or Jeremy was skimming. Either way, he was sure Jeremy and Corey Pallaton were misleading everyone.

18: JUBILEE ORGANIZATIONAL MEETING
NORWICHTOWN
TEEL HOUSE: BALLROOM
MONDAY, OCTOBER 25, 1858 – 3:00 PM

Today's events would afford Corey Pallaton the opportunity of a lifetime because he had good reason to intermingle with many of Norwich's most influential, wealthy leaders. He could proudly announce his discovery of gold to Norwich's elite. As he walked the two blocks from his home to the Teel House, Corey was confident he could raise more funds to benefit his Pocawansett brethren.

Like many others he would meet today, Corey and Elena resided on the fringe of Williams Park. They lived directly across the street from the monument dedicated to the Quinebaugan Sachem Lucas. The fourteen-foot tall, cold, granite obelisk was a constant, sore reminder of the atrocities bestowed upon Corey's ancestors. It repulsed Corey that the President of the United States, Andrew Jackson, had laid the monument's cornerstone twenty-five years earlier.

However, the monument now sat in the middle of John Dunham's flower garden. So it seemed fitting to Corey that the obelisk, intended as a grand memorial to Lucas, was now reduced to serve the role of a common, ordinary garden ornament.

Corey spotted Henry Bill near the front entrance of the Teel House as he walked from his home on Broadway to the afternoon meeting.

He and Henry had a mature, mutually beneficial relationship. After achieving significant success as an illustrated Bible publisher and national distributor, Henry Bill decided to invest in Norwich by developing land in the Laurel Hill section of town. Two years earlier, he'd employed Corey to clear the land and build houses for affluent local citizens. Initially, Corey and his Pocawansett Native American construction crew had no prior experience, but Mr. Bill hired them because he wanted to support the local, underprivileged company that Corey managed.

Over time, Corey learned to develop the land and build modern homes. Mr. Bill benefited handsomely from Corey's hard work and determination.

Corey smiled, tipped his hat, and said, "Good afternoon, Henry."

"Good day, Corey. It's been a while since we've spoken. I pray all is well."

Corey replied, "Yes, all is quite well. Thank you. My land development company continues to thrive, and I have news for you. I've begun a new housing project in the Wawecus Hill area. Of course, the homes won't be as fashionable as those we built on Laurel Hill. Rather, they'll provide Norwich with affordable housing for several of our lower-income families. We completed the first model home just last week, and I'd love to give you a tour of the land parcel and the model home."

Mr. Bill smiled and nodded, "I am glad to hear of your success. The residents of Laurel Hill are extremely proud of their homes, and I'm sure the community will also cherish your future homes on Wawecus Hill."

Corey continued his sales pitch. "I'd like to share other exciting developments with you. While mapping out the home lots, we discovered gold. Just below the hill, there is a stream named Goldmine Brook. We found a cache of gold-laden minerals in the brook. As a result, I created a new company, set up a field office, and began the gold refinement process. It's an exciting opportunity for me, my wife, and all my employees."

Bill responded, "That is terrific news! I've read how the discovery of gold out west brought immense prosperity to California. Since the price of gold seems to be constantly increasing, your company should do very well."

Bill continued, "As you know, my company produces and sells family Bibles featuring beautifully gilded illustrations. So, as you might expect, I need a reliable source of inexpensive, high-quality gold leaf. But, unfortunately, the gold flakes used for the drawings significantly drive production costs higher. So I'm interested in your company's endeavors and would like to visit your field office, see the homes you're building, and see Goldmine Brook firsthand."

A deep satisfaction overcame Corey, and he responded, "I can arrange that. I assure you, many people like yourself are interested in my company. We're offering shares of stock to make the ownership process easy. Perhaps you could stop by my office on Hardscrabble Hill and discuss possibilities."

Henry Bill answered, "I'd like to visit your site first, and then, if all is in order, I'll discuss it with my wife, Julia. Let's choose a date later."

Corey replied, "Okay. I'll ask Elena to coordinate with your company's secretary."

The majestic Teel House came into view at the corner of Washington Street and Broadway. It would be the meeting site for today's organizational meeting for the Norwich 200th Jubilee.

Joseph Teel built the establishment in 1790. This section of Norwich was sparsely populated at the time and was conveniently midway between the Town of Norwich and Chelsea Landing. Teel positioned his business at this ideal location to serve as a tavern and resting spot for travelers.

First known as 'Teel House – Sign of General Washington,' the three-story mansion was a popular destination frequented by locals and travelers.

Today, the Teel House was the home of General William Williams Jr. and his wife, Harriet Peck Williams. The Williams family was prosperous and wealthy. However, they had endured many emotionally devastating events. All three of their children died before their time. Their first son, William, lived for only twenty-one months. Their daughter, Bela, passed from this earth at the young age of fourteen.

Like his father, their son Thomas was a partner in the Williams and Barns whaling company based in New London. Thomas and his wife Amanda bore William and Harriet four grandchildren. However, all four died in childbirth. When Thomas died suddenly at the young age of forty, William and Harriet were left with no heirs. It was too late for Harriet and William to produce another family because William was sixty-seven years old, and Harriet was sixty. Only William, Harriet, and their servants resided in the Teel House today.

As Henry Bill and Corey Pallaton stood at the mansion's front door, Corey felt out of place. Several extravagant gig carriages, owned by others who had already arrived for the meeting, were hitched to posts outside. Their well-dressed servants were tending to the horses.

Corey's family still used the company-owned buckboard wagon for transportation. The Pallatons were financially stable but couldn't afford a luxurious carriage. So, Corey felt like an outsider. Nevertheless, he believed he and his wife deserved wealth, status, and respect from Norwich elites.

After being ushered into the house by General Williams's butler, Pallaton and Bill entered the front foyer. Corey felt that he should remove his shoes so as not to scratch the highly polished, pristine oak flooring. However, his attention quickly turned to an ornately decorated parlor on his left, a commanding staircase leading to the second floor in front of him, and the first-floor living room on his right. Finally, he saw a formal dining room entrance at the end of the center hallway. To Corey, the home and its grandeur were visual works of art.

He'd been privileged to see the inside of the Teel House only once before. Corey had accompanied Henry Bill to a business meeting with General Williams a few months earlier. Bill and Williams were financial-tied business partners. General Williams, the president of the Merchants Bank, supplied loans to Mr. Bill's company to construct Laurel Hill homes. Bill had arranged the meeting to update Williams on the project and to introduce Corey, his homebuilder.

Corey was already impressed with the Teel House, and today, after a complete tour, he was even more dazzled. After climbing the stairs to the second floor, passing the ladies' parlor and gentlemen's billiard room, they ascended to the second set of stairs to the third floor. The entire third floor was a spacious ballroom. The chamber hosted parties, social events, and business meetings for over 60 years. Today, the ballroom was filled with more than twenty of Norwich's most prominent leaders. They were here to organize the 200th Jubilee of the founding of Norwich.

The twenty-one Arrangements Committee members were seated in four rows of six metal-framed folding chairs. At the end of the front row, a petite young woman bearing a stenographer's pad sat ready to take notes. At the head of the room, General Williams, the governor of Connecticut William A. Buckingham, the mayor of Norwich Amos Prentice, and John W. Stedman sat in folding chairs behind a long oak table.

Most of the men in this room had banded together only four years earlier to incorporate the Norwich Free Academy, which stood across the street. These generous patrons of the educational system helped make Norwich the envy of many other towns in Connecticut. They all knew one another well.

Corey was impressed with the Norwich *royalty* gathered at today's meeting. But he was also curious about the folding chairs. So Corey asked Henry Bill, "Do you think it safe to sit in these chairs? I've never seen such a contraption."

Mr. Bill smiled at Corey and responded, "Yes, they're safe. John Cram of Boston patented these and began producing them three years ago. I bought several for my company's meetings too. They aren't very comfortable, but that is okay with me because I don't like long meetings."

Corey chuckled and said, "Yeah, you're right."

~~~~~

General Williams called the meeting to order. "Gentlemen, thank you for attending today. Norwich is on the cusp of entering its third century as a civilized community. The land we inhabit was purchased from the Quinebaugan tribe 199 years ago, on June 6, 1659. It is befitting that we now honor our forefathers, celebrate our present successes, and instill a sense of hope and excitement for the future."

"At last month's meeting of this body, we decided to host the 200th commemorative celebration during the first week of next September. We believe thousands of past and present Norwich residents will attend the celebration. Norwichians will remember the Jubilee as a magnificent display of our love for the city."

Williams continued, "It will be a two-day event. The first day will showcase a grand parade marching from Franklin Square to Williams Park. Upon arrival at the park, the citizens of Norwich will be seated in a large tent where speakers will remind them of Norwich's glorious heritage. Later, in the evening, various guests will deliver speeches, read poems, play music, and sing hymns."

"Another procession will occur on the second day at the Yantic Cemetery. We plan to lay the foundation for a monument dedicated to the memory of Major John Mason. Our Masonic brothers will retell the story of the friendship between Major Mason and Lucas. An evening dinner feast, followed by a formal ball, will conclude the Jubilee."

He smiled and gestured with his outstretched arm to the attendees, "As I'm sure you know, the organization and planning of the jubilee will require a focused and committed group of community leaders like yourself."

"Now, let's get down to business. In addition to the current residents of Norwich, I want to send invitations to every known former resident. We'll also send them to the governors of all thirty-two states. I also want to invite every former governor of the great state of Connecticut. Gentlemen, we need an Invitation Committee. Who among you would like to volunteer to become the chair of this prestigious committee?"

Without hesitation, the man sitting next to Williams, the governor of Connecticut, William A. Buckingham, stood and said, "I would be proud to serve in this capacity. I have many contacts but will need to enlist the aid of several of you to compose and send the invitations. Do I have any volunteers to join me in these efforts?"

Francis A. Perkins, the aging treasurer and secretary of the Norwich Savings Society rose slowly. He said, "I've been around for many years and have done favors for many people over the years. I'll happily call in a few markers for this glorious event."

Henry B. Norton, president of the Norwich and New London Steamboat Company, stood and said, "I also volunteer to serve on this committee. I look forward to helping spread the word and extending invitations to our most esteemed guests."

After he sat, Reverend Comfort D. Fillmore rose. "I am not in a position to serve on your committee because I'm not as well connected as many of you esteemed gentlemen. But my grandfather is also the great-grandfather of the former president of the United States, Millard Fillmore. Millard and I played together during our youth at several family events. I am sure I could persuade him to honor us with his presence at the Jubilee."

In jubilant agreement, everyone in the room pounded their feet loudly on the oak flooring and repeatedly said, "Here here," "Here here."

General Williams stood and said, "Thank you, Reverend, for your involvement and participation. We will also form a committee to address the issue of historical and inspirational speeches. The Committee on Speeches and Sentiments will seek speakers to prepare and deliver inspirational messages."

He continued, "Who here would be interested in leading this committee?"

John W. Stedman, Lydia's father, volunteered. Stedman stood and said, "I plan to document every detail of the Jubilee, including all the addresses. My daughter, here in the front row," he gestured toward Lydia, "will be assisting me in documenting and publishing every aspect. Based on our experience at the Aurora newspaper, we know who is best qualified to deliver the said speeches."

He continued, "My wife and I are also in close contact with the remaining 100 or so Quinebaugans who still live in the area. We'll work with them to get an accurate record of their early history in Lucasville and Norwich. Additionally, we should invite Quinebaugan leaders to attend the dedication of Major Mason's monument in Yantic Cemetery."

General Williams added, "Thank you for your support, Mr. Stedman. I know that Mr. Daniel Coit Gilman, a native of our fine town and the current librarian of Yale College, is familiar with Norwich's early history. I suggest you invite him to present a speech at the Jubilee that chronicles our long and distinguished past. The discourse should include as many facts surrounding our Quinebaugan friends, both past and present."

Almost everyone in the room nodded in agreement. Then, however, Corey's temper began to rise. He thought, "Even today, 200 years after the decimation and displacement of my ancestors, Norwich's leaders are dismissing and ignoring Pocawansett's rights to our native homeland."

~~~~~

Corey had watched and listened intently for the past hour and desperately wanted to volunteer for a committee. But, he was well aware that his qualifications for committee leadership did not compare well with the others. But, after General Williams formed the Grand Procession Committee, the Dinner Committee, and the Formal Ball Committee, Corey finally saw an opening.

General Williams selected Timothy Norton and James Mowry to head the Finance Committee. Timothy, one of the three prominent Norton brothers, was a perfect fit for the Finance Committee because he sat on the board of directors for two local banks. He was also a director of the Norwich-based Bacon Arms Company. On several occasions, Corey had spoken with Timothy about the pistols that Bacon Arms Company had produced for his personal firearms collection.

Corey was also relieved when General Williams added his friend James Mowry to the finance committee. He and Mowry attended church in Greeneville, hunted deer the past fall, and loved discussing precision-crafted firearms produced in Norwich.

Corey stood, and all heads turned slowly in his direction. Then, finally, he said, "I would be honored to also serve on the Finance Committee. I could assist Mr. Norton and Mr. Mowry as their secretary."

James Mowry stood and said, "That is a splendid idea! I believe that I also speak for Mr. Norton. We welcome your support."

Corey felt an overwhelming sense of relief. He was now a vital member of the powerful Finance Committee and, as its secretary, would have access to all funds related to the entire 200th Jubilee organization. In addition, he would have the opportunity to create a more personal relationship with many whom he could convince to buy company stock.

Soon afterward, General Williams announced, "Gentlemen, we have made excellent progress today. Please join Harriet and me this evening for our social mixer. Everyone will be able to learn more about the Jubilee. Please join us. There will be a string quartet and dancing here in this very ballroom. The activities will begin at 6:00."

He concluded, "I look forward to seeing you and your lovely wives. Thank you all!"

19: Social Mixer ~ The Ladies
Norwichtown
Teel House: Ladies Parlor
Monday, October 25, 1858 – 6:15 pm

Corey and Elena stood on the front stoop of the Teel House, anxiously awaiting to join the activities.

Elena said, "Corey, We're late. We were supposed to be here at 6:00 o'clock. I don't understand why you can't seem to ever be ready on time!"

He quipped, "You don't understand social etiquette. It's fashionable to be a few minutes late."

When the large double door swung open, a butler dressed in striped-black trousers, a formal white shirt, a low-cut black vest, a white bow tie, and white gloves ushered them in. He said, "Welcome. Please come in, and I will summon the lady of the house."

Elena whispered to Corey, "It looks like we're the last to arrive!"

Harriet Williams descended the ornately decorated French provincial-inspired staircase. She was about to greet them when the majestic six-foot tall grandfather clock, standing in the foyer, chimed and played a melody that announced the quarter-hour. The music played loudly for a full ten seconds.

Harriet said, "Good evening, Mr. and Mrs. Pallaton. It is very nice that you could join us this evening."

Elena anxiously replied, "Good evening, Mrs. Williams. Thank you for inviting us. Your clock is so beautiful and sounds wonderful as well."

Harriet smiled and replied, "Well, thank you. The General and I love this clock. It's one of our family's most cherished possessions. William's father purchased it directly from Mr. Thomas Harland and later gifted it to William. As you probably know, Mr. Harland made many fine pocket watches and heirloom clocks right here in Norwich. This model chimes on the quarter-hour and displays the day of the week."

She continued, "One feature that makes it so special is its cabinet. Mr. Harland didn't make this particular case. Instead, it was crafted by Mr. Thomas Chippendale of London and exported to Mr. Harland's shop."

Harriet gestured to the staircase and said, "Please. May I escort you to the parlors?"

Corey and Elena followed her up the staircase to the second floor. At the landing, she informed Corey, "Mr. Pallaton, the gentlemen are gathered in the billiard room on your right. I'm sure that you can make yourself comfortable there. Please excuse Elena and me while we mingle with the ladies."

Harriet and Elena entered a room filled with color, beauty, and exquisite furnishings. Harriet announced, "Ladies, may I have your attention? I want to introduce Mrs. Elena Pallaton. She and her husband have recently moved into our neighborhood, and I'd like you to all welcome her."

Harriet knew that the Pallaton family had moved in nearly two years earlier. But now, with the rumor of Pallaton's gold discovery, she wanted to create the illusion of a favorable first impression.

Elena's face flushed with embarrassment. She did not think of herself as a member of Norwich's club of elites. Instead, she self-identified as the local Pocawansett tribal storyteller and gatekeeper of tribal customs. She was not accustomed to this type of attention. Elena had worked closely with many Norwich families as the public face of the Pallaton real estate company. Still, she had never aspired to become a member of the elite inner circle of Victorian-era Norwich women.

Elena was glad she hadn't worn perfume because her skin began warming. The smell within the room was already a mixture of rose, lavender, and a concoction of other unidentifiable exotic fragrances. As she glanced around the room, she saw an unoccupied square-shaped, carved mahogany table in the center and asked, "Could we sit for a moment?"

Harried responded, "Why, certainly. Please have a seat. Would you care for an absinthe?"

Elena wasn't quite sure what absinthe was but knew it was green, alcoholic, and the drink of choice for many Victorian-era women. She answered, "Yes, please, that would be delightful."

Harriet turned her head and motioned her maid to approach. "Amanda, please bring me and Mrs. Pallaton a touch of absinthe."

Amanda nodded, "Yes, madam."

A colorful board game, decorated with several dozen lithographs and the words 'Reward of Virtue: A New Moral and Entertaining Game,' was laid out on the table. Harriet could see that Elena was curious about the game board. She said, "The General and I are striving to further the educational system here in Norwich. We often entertain and help educate the young girls who study at the Free Academy. They love to play this game."

She continued, "The game helps them learn the benefits and rewards of leading a virtuous life. It is a fun instructional game in which players navigate their pieces around the board, moving closer and closer to the inner circle. The first to reach the center can claim the 'Reward of Virtue.' Would you care to play?"

Elena thought to herself. "Why would anyone need to learn virtue from a board game? They should know it first-hand from their family. Her Hoopanoag mother, aunts, and grandmother taught her the virtues of hard work and family tradition daily."

Elena politely replied, "No, thank you. I need to save my energy for dancing later."

Elena was happy when Amanda arrived with the drinks. She wanted to drink it down in a single gulp to quell her nervous energy. But she pursed her lips and slowly savored a small sip of the licorice-flavored beverage.

Harriet said, "The General and I saw an advertisement for your company in last week's edition of the Aurora. Could you tell me more about it?"

Elena perked up and replied, "Yes, it would be my pleasure. My husband's real estate company is developing a new, affordable housing project in the Wawecus Hill section of town. After he bought the land and began clearing brush for the future home lots, his crew found several rocks laced with veins of gold. They found even more precious minerals when they sifted through the brook."

She continued, "About a month ago, we submitted maps of the area to the Norwich Town House and petitioned to form a new publicly owned company. I'm happy to say that we received final approval from the state, and we now want to share its potential value. So we are now selling shares in the company to local businesses and private citizens, like you and your husband."

Harriet responded, "As you know, my son, Thomas, died three years ago, and we have no remaining heirs. Thomas was a successful whaling merchant based in New London. Like the General and me, Thomas was very interested in the education of our youth. So I'm entertaining the idea of building a modern school focused on educating the young women of New London and Norwich. We plan to build the school in honor of Thomas, and if we can complete this dream. We'll call it the Williams Memorial Institute."

She continued, "If we invest in your company and it is successful, perhaps I could establish an institute like that on a much larger scale. I'll discuss this opportunity with my husband and will get back to you."

Elena responded, "It would be an honor for us to help enrich your philanthropic endeavors. Our office is on the top of Hardscrabble Hill. Please visit me there whenever you're ready to learn more."

Harriet stood up and said, "It has been so nice speaking with you. I must mingle."

Harriet made her way over to her neighbor, Mrs. Emeline Norton. She was standing with her twenty-year-old twin daughters, Emeline and Isabella.

Harriet said, "Emeline, it is nice to see you, Emmy, and Isabella. How have you all been?"

Mrs. Norton answered, "Our entire family has been well. Thank you for asking. Did you hear that a rail baron is courting Isabella?"

Harriet looked at Isabella. Her demeanor bestowed the essence of confidence and beauty. Isabella's milky-white cheeks, comforting smile, and large brown eyes made everyone around her feel at ease. So, Harriet was not surprised that an exceptional suitor had chosen Isabella.

Harriet smiled and replied, "No, I haven't. Please enlighten me."

Looking at Isabella, she added, "And, by the way, Isabella, you look stunning this evening."

Mrs. Norton replied, "Her suitor is Mr. Timothy Blackstone, a railroad tycoon from Chicago. He met her here in Norwich while visiting his brother Lorenzo, who is also my brother-in-law. They fell in love at first sight. I believe they are a match made in heaven. We're all hopeful for a bright future for them."

Harriet turned to Isabella and said, "I am so happy for you, Isabella."

She then turned her attention to Isabella's twin, Emeline, and said, "Emmy, is it true that you sing in the church choir?"

Emeline answered, "Yes, Ma'am, I love singing and spending time with my girlfriends in the choir, Miss Brynn Dunham and Miss Lydia Stedman. Last week, Lydia published my article about the virtues of abstinence from alcohol in her newspaper column. She is so well-informed, and I just love chatting with her. Oh, I see her sitting on the divan right now."

Emmy was squirming to make an exit. And she continued, "Mother, may I be excused to speak with them?"

Her mother answered, "Certainly. Go ahead and enjoy yourself."

Harriet thought to herself, "Emeline is so homely. I do hope that she's able to find a good man someday. But she makes things so difficult for her own well-being by always standing near that Brynn Dunham. The boys naturally focus on Brynn instead of Emmy."

~~~~~

Elena had joined her across-the-street neighbor, Brynn, and they were engaged in lively conversing on the other side of the room.

Elena said, "Brynn, it is so good to speak to you. Corey and I have seen you working in your garden during our afternoon tea. Last week, I intended to walk across the street and visit you and your mother. Please forgive me. I've simply been too busy."

Brynn smiled and said, "Yes, I've noticed you and Mr. Pallaton having tea on your porch. Your home is so lovely."

She added, "I love working in the garden. The roses have fared well this year but are almost done for the season. Roses grow so well here in Norwich. I love them!"

Brynn continued, "My parents recently learned to play a card game called 'Whist.' They seem to enjoy it and are constantly playing it with their friends. Perhaps you and Mr. Pallaton could learn to play. I know that my parents would love to become friends with you."

Elena responded, "That is a great idea. I'll look into it. But, Brynn, I've just got to say how beautiful you look this evening. Those bright red roses woven into your hair look gorgeous! Did they come from your garden?"

Brynn turned slightly away from Elena and gazed at herself in the full-length, majestic mirror in the lady's parlor. Then, she answered, "Why yes! They did. Thank you for noticing."

She thought to herself, "My buttons look great, too. Why didn't she mention them?"

Brynn admired the mirror and said, "Isn't this mirror beautiful? I've never seen one quite like it."

Elena responded, "Yes, it is lovely. Mrs. Williams told me all about it. It is what they call a *French Provincial* mirror. The white enamel paint and elegantly engraved, gilded pattern on the frame is so elegant. Harriet told me that the General purchased it for her while on a business at the French port of Marseille."

Elena continued, "Brynn, I have been itching to speak with you on another issue. As you know, Corey and I have been very busy since our survey crew discovered gold. Jeremy always asks me about you when he gives us his weekly update. He is very interested in getting to know you better."

Brynn bristled momentarily and said, "Yes, I met him at the Town House when he submitted your company's maps. He is quite handsome and confident. But, on the other hand, he's a bit too cocky. We had a date at the New London County Fair, and I think he may be a little too rough around the edges for me."

Elena questioned, "Why do you say that?"

Brynn responded, "Well, when he first entered the Town House, he kicked Dexter across the floor. And later, while racing at the fair, he whipped his horse pretty hard. And it was for no good reason because they lost the race anyway. So, I don't think he likes animals, and I'm uneasy around him."

Elena answered, "Brynn, I've known Jeremy all his life. His parents were tough on him during his youth, and I know he appears rough outside. But that is not his innate nature."

Elena continued, "He has a solid sense of loyalty, and I know he would do anything for Corey. Jeremy is also a very hard worker, so I'm certain he will help make our company profitable. Someday, Jeremy will be a very wealthy man. I hope that you decide to give him a second chance."

Brynn tilted slightly, smiled, and replied, "We'll see. I'm not so sure. Thank you for your observations."

20: SOCIAL MIXER ~ THE GENTLEMEN
NORWICHTOWN
TEEL HOUSE: BILLIARD ROOM
MONDAY, OCTOBER 25, 1858 – 6:30 PM

When Corey first entered the Billiard Room, he saw many of Norwich's wealthy business and civic leaders had cheerfully filled every corner of the room with a haze of cigar smoke. So he felt a twinge of excitement when he saw Jeremy and John Dunham playing billiards in the center of the room. He knew he and his protégé had become accepted members of Norwich's elite.

Mr. Lucius Carroll momentarily turned from his discussion with General Williams and greeted Corey at the doorway. Carroll said, "Good evening, Mr. Pallaton. It is so good to see you. I've been waiting for the opportunity to introduce you around. General Williams, this is Corey Pallaton."

Turning to Corey, Williams replied, "I believe that Henry Bill introduced us a few months back. Right? However, we didn't have a chance to get to know one another very well."

Corey said, "Yes. That is correct. Henry and I worked together to build homes on Laurel Hill. I'm now working on two new projects on Wawecus Hill."

Lucius Carroll added, "Corey is being far too modest. His new company is building modern, affordable housing for the Pocawansett tribe members. And, while laying out the home lots a couple of months ago, he found several handfuls of gold nuggets."

The statement immediately sparked Williams's attention. I've heard rumblings of someone discovering gold here in Norwich."

He continued, "Frankly, I was shocked to hear these rumors because I've lived in Norwich for more years than I remember and have never heard any mention of gold."

Corey confidently replied, "Yes, it is true; my survey team discovered gold. My company is in the early stages of building a housing development, and we've already completed the first model home. While clearing the area, we discovered gold in Goldmine Brook. So I created a company and began processing the gold and silver."

Lucius Carroll joined the conversation, saying, "Yes, our bank gave Corey's company a generous loan to help them get started. His company also purchased a full complement of building materials and office supplies from my wholesale supply store."

Carroll continued, "You should see the two safes we supplied him. The first is a regular-sized container that protects valuables safely at his field office. And the second is more like a fortress. It is four feet tall by four feet wide by three feet deep. The manufacturers built it to protect its contents from both fire and burglars. We had it transported by rail and carriage all the way from Cincinnati."

He turned to Corey, "My men delivered it to your home last week. Did they install it properly?"

Corey answered, "Yes. They did a nice job. I am now comforted that our company's assets will remain secure. I'm happy to report that the rewards of our gold processing efforts are filling the safe already!"

Corey lied through his teeth. In truth, he had only deposited a single one-ounce vial filled with gold flakes.

Corey continued, "We've decided to share our company's good fortune with the fine people in Norwich. You may have seen the advertisements that we placed in the Aurora. We're offering shares of company stock to local businesses and individuals. If you're interested in joining, please visit us on Hardscrabble Hill. We're using my real estate office building to double as a sales office for the gold company."

General Williams replied, "Thank you for the information and the invitation. That does all sound interesting, indeed. I'll speak with my wife about it."

Williams turned to Carroll and said, "Have any of your bank's creditors discussed the supply problem with southern states' cotton with you?"

Carroll replied, "It is interesting that you should ask because the answer is *yes*. Mr. William P. Greene, owner of the Falls Company cotton mill, and Mr. Moses Pierce of the Norwich Bleaching, Dyeing & Printing Company are both quite worried. The Southerners are threatening to cut off our cotton supply due to the slavery issue. They are trying to bankrupt our companies."

General Williams replied, "Yes, my colleagues at the Merchants Bank and I have reached the same conclusion. I will sail to Egypt next month to speak with suppliers there. We know the Egyptians can provide a reliable supply of superior-grade cotton. Those Southerners are both inhuman and greedy!"

Corey thought to himself how self-righteous these men were. Their forefathers had massacred and enslaved many of their ancestors. Corey could hardly stomach the pompous bastards. But he tempered his emotions and added, "I agree with you. We need to punish those sanctimonious Southern assholes!"

General Williams's African-born butler approached the three men with an opened box of Cuban cigars. General Williams said, "Gentlemen. These are fresh Don Jaime Partagás cigars from our recent voyage to Cuba. They are said to be the finest in the world. Would any of you care for one?"

The pungent odor of cigar smoke continued filling the room, and Corey began to feel his oats. So, he politely took a cigar from the box, clipped its end, lit it up, and enjoyed a long, slow draw before saying, "Thank you. This cigar is just what I needed."

Corey watched as Jeremy continued playing at the billiard table. The eleven-foot-long table was covered with green felt and featured tasseled leather pockets hanging below all four corners. Jeremy used a long stick to strike a white ball, apparently aiming at the colored balls. He saw four red balls on the table. He questioned General Williams, "What is the object of this game? I have never seen a table like this."

Williams responded, "The game is trendy in England and is gaining interest here in the United States. While in London two years ago, I learned to play and fell in love with it. I couldn't resist the urge to purchase this table, but it was quite a chore to get it here. However, it was well worth the effort."

He continued, "The game's name is 'four-ball billiards.' A player wins by being the first to score forty points. Each player has their own white ball, called a *cue ball*. And he scores one point when his cue ball knocks one of the red balls into a pocket. The rules are quite simple, but the strategy for positioning the balls is complex."

Corey responded, "The game looks interesting. However, I'm guessing it requires a good deal of skill."

Williams chuckled and answered, "Oh yes. It takes skill and considerable strategy. However, placing wagers on the game makes it much more interesting."

Williams continued, "Several men in this room are members of the fraternal order of Freemasons here in Norwich. Each month after we meet at Lucas Hall, we retire for an evening filled with conversation about current events and competitive four-ball games. You may want to consider joining our organization. In addition, we foster goodwill to many local charitable organizations."

Corey suddenly remembered the proverb, *Keep your friends close and your enemies even closer*, and replied, "Thank you. I'll consider it."

He would definitely join. Corey thought of how easy it would be to convince these men to invest in his company and how much his tribal brethren would benefit.

~~~~~

Corey drifted to the six-foot-long oak bench where his friends, James Mowry and Timothy Norton, sat. The three of them shared several common interests. Mowry designed and produced rifles that Corey loved to collect. Since moving to the Greeneville area, Corey and Elena attended the nearby Congregational Church. In addition, they became friends with James's family, who also attended services every Sunday.

Corey met Timothy while buying a pistol at Thomas Bacon's gun factory at the Yantic Falls manufacturing facility. They quickly became friends due to their shared enthusiasm for hunting deer and collecting locally produced firearms. Norton, a member of the board of the Bacon Manufacturing Company, inspired Corey to start a gun collection. As a result, Corey now owned over a hundred Norwich-produced firearms. He displayed the collection proudly in his home's drawing room. He had even purchased and proudly displayed one of Mr. C.C. Brand's powerful whaling guns.

Corey greeted them, "Hello, James and Timothy. It's great to see both of you! Have either of you been hunting this season?"

Mowry answered, "Hi, Corey. I haven't yet, but I hope to soon because the season is upon us. I've been swamped perfecting the design of the prototype rifled musket that I sold you last month. It's a sturdy, rugged rifle, but I still need to streamline the process of producing them in mass quantities. Our government may need them to teach those Southerners a lesson."

Norton smiled and chimed in, "Yeah, and maybe they'll need more pistols from the Bacon Company, too."

Corey said, "Seriously, now. I'm excited about the Jubilee. It's going to be a wonderful experience for all. Let's arrange a meeting to discuss how we'll run the Committee on Finance."

Timothy replied, "You're right. We should begin tracking costs incurred by the various committees and income from donations. I could set up an account at one of my banks."

Mowry replied, "Okay, that's a good idea. Let us know when you've got that arranged. Corey and I will monitor and direct funds accordingly."

Mowry continued, "Corey, I heard you've struck gold upon Wawecus Hill. Is that true?"

Corey responded, "Well, I wouldn't say that we have found a mother lode, but we did uncover a healthy deposit of gold-laden minerals in Goldmine Brook last month. So I set up a new company a few weeks ago."

He continued, "Our production process is now beginning to bear fruit. I started selling company shares to businesses and the general public a few weeks ago. So if the two of you are interested, please feel free to visit us at the Hardscrabble Hill office."

Both Mowry and Norton nodded their heads in agreement. Timothy said, "I will definitely buy a stake in your company. And, when I meet with my Farmers and Mechanics Bank associates next month, I'll encourage them to invest also."

~~~~~

Norwich's cartographer, Henry F. Walling, and Travis were seated near the fireplace while watching the lively billiards game before them. Henry grinned broadly and said, "The way I see it, playing billiards is like making a map. It's simply a game of geometry. All one has to do is visualize the proper angles and transform that perceived geometry into reality."

Travis chuckled and replied, "Well. I don't know about that. I've never played billiards, but it looks more complicated than simply *visualizing geometry*."

Walling replied, "You should give billiards a try. You're a quick learner and seem to be learning the art of surveying easily."

He added, "Seriously, you and I didn't get to discuss your job with Corey Pallaton. How is it going? Tell me."

Travis stiffened and said, "There are several problems. First of all, the other fellows on the survey team and I aren't getting along very well. I think they still miss the guy who worked with them before me. Also, they don't like me very much because I am Quinebaugan. They're all Pocawansett. You may find this hard to believe, but they still harbor ill feelings toward my ancestors."

Travis continued, "Since I found that gold rock, Mr. Pallaton hired several new Pocawansett employees. Jeremy and Corey are now teaching them several new trades. Unfortunately, it appears that he wants to train them to become surveyors and give them the jobs I had hoped to learn better. So, at the moment, I've cut back my hours with them and, quite frankly, am considering quitting."

Walling responded, "Don't be too disappointed because I have a new, much more interesting opportunity that I hope you're willing to help me with."

He continued, "Mr. Daniel Gilman, the Yale College librarian, has been tasked to prepare a discourse focused on the early history of Norwich. He wants to learn everything possible about Norwich's original nine-mile-square historical boundary. So he's asked me to create a map that clearly shows the entire area's past and present boundaries, geographic features, and venerable landmarks. The Jubilee organizers will use it to illustrate Norwich's history and how it has changed over the years."

Walling continued, "I'd like you to help me make the map. We can use my collection of maps to locate most of the boundaries as a baseline, but I don't have any maps showing the location of old Quinebaugan tribal sites or landmarks. When Gilman addresses the citizens of Norwich at the Jubilee, he wants to highlight the contributions of our Quinebaugan neighbors."

"I know that your parents are aware of these sites, and I hope you can tell me why they are historically significant, where to find them, and where to place them on a map. But, of course, it would require you to go out alone or with a friend and take the measurements. Afterward, I'll show you how to scale the measurements and produce a map. These skills should help further your education and help you fulfill your dream of becoming a ship's navigator."

Travis replied, "I'd be honored to work with you on this. It's a great opportunity for me. Thank you."

Walling responded, "Please stop by my office tomorrow, and we'll discuss the specifics."

Travis shook Walling's hand, saying, "Thank you very much."

Travis felt the buzz of excitement and adventure vibrate throughout his body. He knew this opportunity would propel him one step closer to his dream job. Creating such an important map would also give him more respect from his Quinebaugan brethren and members of the Norwich community.

~~~~~

Twenty-year-old Jeremy enjoyed playing four-ball billiards with fifty-eight-year-old former Norwich mayor John Dunham. The former mayor, who also happened to be Brynn's father, had played billiards for over a year. He taught Jeremy to play only an hour earlier. John beat Jeremy by fifteen points in the first game but could see that his opponent had a keen sense of position and outstanding hand-eye coordination. In addition, Jeremy appeared to be a natural player. It was abundantly clear that he was well-coordinated and possessed great physical prowess.

The second game was more competitive. Jeremy lost again, but only by five points. Jeremy was somewhat perturbed because he hated losing at anything. However, Jeremy knew his understanding and feel for the game were growing rapidly. He was sure that he could win the next round.

At that moment, a most fortuitous plan popped into Jeremy's brain. He said, "Mr. Dunham. Would you care to place a small wager on the next game?"

Dunham was surprised by the young man's confidence. However, he felt that Jeremy was a bit overly optimistic. Dunham had taken it easy on Jeremy during the last two games because he wanted to encourage the young man's interest in billiards.

He replied, "I'm not sure that's a good idea, but what do you have in mind?"

Jeremy replied, "I'd like to be candid with you, Mr. Dunham. I'm the vice president of the Wawecus Hill Gold, Silver, and Nickel Mining Company. And while prospecting our site last week, I found several golden nuggets. I'm happy to inform you that I've got one of them with me."

Jeremy pulled a chunk of quartz containing several thick veins of gold from his pocket. He said, "I'd be willing to wager this chunk of quartz-gold against one of your silver dollars."

Dunham was now even more astonished at Jeremy's assertive behavior. After thinking for a moment, he decided it was a more than generous proposition. He smiled broadly and said, "A small wager like this will make the game more interesting. You're on."

Dunham prepared the table and said, "Yes. I know it is customary for the winner of the last game to go first in the next game, but I'd like to defer that honor to you, young man."

Jeremy replied, "That is very generous of you. I'll take you up on that offer."

Jeremy positioned the cue ball and made the opening shot. One of the two red object balls dropped into the back corner pocket. He successfully pocketed three more balls before missing. The score was 4-0. Jeremy knew that he had mastered billiards and could easily win this game.

It was a race to see who could first score forty points. After fifteen minutes, the score was 38-37, with Jeremy in the lead. He only needed to pocket two more red balls to win. After Dunham missed a shot, Jeremy surveyed the balls scattered around the table.

One red ball lay near the left-front corner pocket, and the second sat in the middle. Jeremy envisioned a simple path to victory. After knocking the first ball in, his cue ball caromed off the front cushion and aligned with the red ball sitting in the middle.

Jeremy knew that he could easily sink the last remaining, victorious ball. But that was *not his intention*. He aimed and carefully hit the cue ball. It struck the red ball and rolled slowly toward the back, right corner pocket. And just as planned, it stopped short of the pocket, leaving an easy shot for Dunham. Jeremy feigned his disapproval, "Damn it! I knew I should have hit it harder."

Dunham quickly pocketed three more balls and won 40-39. Then, Dunham stood up, shook Jeremy's hand, and said, "Son, you had me worried there for a moment. But, I will say that I believe you'll become a polished billiards player someday."

Jeremy knew himself a much better player than Dunham already, but winning was not his goal today. He was now ready to complete his mission. Jeremy pulled the gold rock from his coat pocket, handed it to Dunham, and said, "Congratulations, you earned it. I do hope that I can become a more skilled player. Perhaps, someday, you could give me a few more pointers."

John Dunham replied, "You've got a real talent for this. I would enjoy working with you."

Jeremy spoke up, "Oh, by the way. I want to ask you for a favor. I met your daughter last month when I submitted our company's incorporation application at the Norwich Town House. She is a smart, attractive young lady, and I would like to get to know her better. She may have told you about me."

He continued, "She and I ran into one another again while I was racing at the New London County Fair. I'm sorry that I did not win the race, and I think she was a little disappointed in me."

He reached into his pocket, retrieved a second rock that contained even more gold than the first specimen, and said, "Would you please give this to her and tell her I am sorry? I want to make it up to her."

Jeremy hoped this peace offering would smooth things over with Brynn. He knew she was mad at him for thrashing Lightning during the race.

21: Social Mixer ~ The Dance
Norwichtown
Teel House: Ballroom
Monday, October 25, 1858 - 7:30 pm

Elena learned matters of the heart, family values, love, and respect for others from her mother's guidance and endless stories of their tribe's rich heritage and tradition. She had an inkling of Norwich social elite protocol but had never experienced its full glory firsthand. So when she entered the ballroom, she was bedazzled by the scene before her.

The Teel House's square-shaped ballroom filled the third floor. There were five massive nine-pane windows on each of its four walls, spanning from floor to ceiling and adorned with lush blue velvet drapes. Elena wanted to brush her hand against them to feel the texture.

She was most impressed by the affluence of the room's six large, ornate brass chandeliers. Each chandelier sported six arms that supported whale oil lamps. In addition, each chandelier hung from a long, braided cable that lamplighters raised or lowered to suit the occasion. Tonight, the lighting was soft and subdued. It simultaneously fostered an atmosphere of warmth and comfort.

Lively music played by a string quartet in the ballroom's back corner filled the air. Several couples had already begun to dance. Elena knew basic waltz patterns but was impressed with how the ladies glided across the floor gracefully and effortlessly.

However, the opulence of this ballroom and its Victorian-era appurtenances made her uncomfortable. Her lifestyle centered on helping others, supporting her tribe's traditions, and being an excellent wife to Corey.

Corey broke her concentration and said, "We should get better acquainted with General and Mrs. Williams."

Elena nodded, and they navigated through the crowd to the center of the ballroom's back wall, where the Williams's stood holding court.

When Corey and Elena arrived, Harriet Williams spoke up, "Aah, my dear Elena, please step closer. General, this is Mrs. Elena Pallaton and her husband, Corey. They are the fine couple that built houses on Laurel Hill."

Elena became nervous when everyone in the immediate area turned as General Williams bent his head to kiss the back of her hand.

He smiled and said, "Thank you for the introduction, Harriet. I spoke with Corey earlier in the billiard room. I familiarized him with several finer points of the game."

Corey laughed and said, "Yes, and thank you. I am looking forward to learning to play the game more respectably."

He paused momentarily, gestured to the ballroom floor, and added, "However, I must say that I'm not so sure I'll ever have the fortitude to conquer the art of ballroom dancing."

Everyone laughed, and Elena, supporting her ambitious husband, said, "Seriously, this ballroom is truly a work of art. The dancers are waltzing as if floating on a cloud."

Harriet smiled and replied, "Well, a significant amount of good old-fashioned, expert engineering skill went into the design of our ballroom floor. The floor is supported by a tuned spring system that cushions the floor as dancers twirl about. Everyone loves dancing on it."

She continued, "The ballroom has a long history. The Teel House's previous owners used it to entertain and amaze visitors for over sixty years. Before the turn of the century, the owners hosted a troupe of Italian rope dancers. From what I understand, it was a fascinating event. The troupe stretched a taut rope above the floor along its length. The performers sang, danced, and bobbed up and down on a single foot. I wish that I could have witnessed the affair."

Elena's curiosity needed to be satisfied. So she said, "Mrs. Williams, I couldn't help but notice the beautiful window dressings. I've never seen such a beautiful blue fabric."

Harriet responded, "Oh, thank you. It is the very fabric used in many European theaters for curtains and seat cushions. The J.B. Martin Velvet Company produced these curtains in Lyon, France. Mr. Martin convinced the General to buy these for me."

Harriet stepped near the curtains, motioned to Elena, and said, "Elena, please give me your hand."

After Harriet gently drew Elena's inner wrist against the velvet, Elena said, "It is so soft. I love how it feels. Thank you."

General Williams spoke up, "You may be in luck. While in Lyon, I discussed the possibility of Martin building a velvet factory in Norwich. He is entertaining the thought of expanding his business into America, so I told him of the many benefits and opportunities here in Norwich. If Mr. J.B. Martin builds a velvet factory here, you could easily purchase his fine cloth and use it to trim your home."

Corey gazed out the window, pointed to Williams Park, and said, "General, we've noticed that you occasionally train and parade soldiers in the park. Are your soldiers part of the United States military?"

Williams responded, "No, they are, and have been for many years, a Norwich-based militia. I have followed in my father's footsteps. He was a Major General who trained Norwich's militia during the revolution. Hopefully, we'll never need these troops to defend our town because there is security in strength. But, we stand ready if our nation's leaders ever need us."

Harriet said, "The General parades the soldiers around the park every month. I enjoy hearing the drums beat and watching them march."

She paused, smiled, and added, "I think they should change the park's name to Chelsea Parade instead of Williams Park. The General doesn't need any more public attention."

General Williams pointed to the park and added, "We'll use the park as the venue for next year's Jubilee. After we erect several large tents, we'll have enough room for half the population of Norwich. The activities will occur in the park in front of the Free Academy."

Harriet beamed and said, "William has done so much for our community! I love him so much. He, and many others here tonight, incorporated the Free Academy only three years ago. He's helped so many people. Did you know he even teaches Sunday school for the Quinebaugan children? He travels to their little church weekly and helps spread the gospel."

The General smiled and said, "It has been my pleasure to teach them the path of righteousness."

Corey could hardly bear any more of this frivolous conversation. It especially irked him that General Williams focused the discussion on the Quinebaugans. Finally, he said, "That is kind of you, General. In Greeneville, we have a small but growing community of Pocawansett families. Have you considered providing any help and guidance for them as well?"

General William Williams was momentarily speechless. Upon recovering, he answered, "That is a good suggestion, and I'll look into it. Perhaps you and I could explore the possibilities at a more appropriate time."

Pallaton gritted his teeth and smiled wryly, "Why, thank you. I look forward to the discussion."

Elena was deeply embarrassed for the second time this evening. She took hold of Corey's arm and announced, "I would love to try out this most elegant dance floor. My dear, would you please join me?"

Corey and Elena made their way to the dance floor while General and Mrs. Williams continued to hold court. As they danced, Elena leaned into Corey's ear, smiled, and said, "You're such an arsehole! You shouldn't have said that to the General."

~~~~~

In the back, right corner of the ballroom, near one of its four fireplaces, Lydia, Brynn, and Emeline all stood clutching ornate feather fans in one hand and their dance card in the other. They had been chatting about their choir at the Congregational Church, their attire, and one of their other favorite topics: the eligible young men of Norwich.

Emeline spoke up, "Lydia, I just wanted to thank you for making this fan. It is so fashionable! The feathers are so pretty, and I love how you wove them together."

Lydia answered, "You are most welcome. I love working with feathers. Each one is unique and has its own story to tell. I made yours with swan feathers."

Emeline was dressed in a full-length pink gown adorned with two strings of freshly picked roses. One strand outlined her shoulders, back, and chest; the other was draped in the front. Her twin sister, Isabella, had helped Emeline pick out the outfit.

Emeline hoped to share a few dances with eligible suitors this evening. Unfortunately, at the age of twenty, her chances of finding a top-tier bachelor had already begun to wane.

Lydia wore a lone white feather in her thick, jet-black hair. Unlike many young women in the room, she had chosen a dark red silk gown that fit tightly around her thin waist and small hips. Her petite frame and dark brown skin were adorned by a single, stunning piece of jewelry around her neck. It was a large oval-shaped quartz-gold pendant set in 14-karat yellow gold. The natural veins of gold embedded in the quartz formed the shape of a dragon's head.

She looked forward to reconnecting with Travis this evening. He had stopped by the Aurora newspaper office several times last month to meet with her. However, Lydia found reasons to avoid speaking with him. She had fully recovered physically from the snakebite, but her emotional recovery was still evolving.

Lydia had simply needed time to comprehend the disturbing incident. She knew that snakes frequently bit people. But when the snake inside the Quinebaugan relic bit *her*, energy flowed up from the earth, through her body, and into the heavens above.

Lydia felt as though her entire body had been used as a conduit for energy, causing a brief yet powerful thunderstorm. She needed to be at peace with her inner feelings before speaking with Travis.

Brynn's appearance, as usual, was gorgeous. Her full-length, baby blue ruffled dress was decorated with an array of buttons. Brynn loved buttons. Ten white, cloth-covered buttons were sewn on both sleeves, running from wrist to elbow. Two more rows of forty buttons each ran up the front of her gown from the floor to her neckline. Even though she was only seventeen, Brynn's long blonde hair, radiant blue eyes, and sassy smile attracted many young men.

Brynn glanced at her dance card and said, "Only one more gentleman remains on my list. Mr. Jeremy Pallawotuk. Do you remember him from the county fair? Have you seen him this evening?"

Emeline responded, "How could I forget how cruel he was to that poor horse? He was a bad loser, too. Thank goodness. No, I haven't seen him."

Brynn replied, "Well, I have been thinking about him. Just a bit, mind you."

As Emeline and Lydia watched, Brynn opened the clasp of her dainty blue silk purse and carefully pulled out a large piece of quartz with several veins of gold. She held it out and said, "Jeremy gave this to my father and asked him to give it to me. It was thoughtful of him, but I still don't like how he treats animals."

At that moment, Jeremy approached the three, bearing gifts for all. He smiled and bowed politely.

He said, "You ladies look lovely this evening! I am so glad to see you. But you looked famished. I have brought you special treats from Mrs. Williams's bakery."

Jeremy offered a generous portion of a colorful fruit cake filled with apples, cherries, pineapple, and pecans. Then, he said, "Who among you would care for a slice of fruit cake?"

Emeline loved fruit cake and could not resist the offer.

Next, Jeremy held out three cookies and said, "Miss Lydia, would you care for one of these freshly baked almond cookies? The Williams's baker also made these, especially for me."

Jeremy lied. He had lifted them from a tray in the billiard room.

Lydia did not care to accept anything from Jeremy but wanted to be polite in front of her friends. So she took a cookie and quietly said, "Thank you."

He reached deep inside his vest pocket and pulled out a wristlet corsage. It had four white rosebuds trimmed with a light blue dye. Jeremy's florist had woven tiny golden balls into the stems of each rose, and a baby blue silk ribbon hung in readiness to attach it to Brynn's wrist. The corsage was beautiful and elegant. He smiled, held out the corsage, gazed into Brynn's eyes, and said, "I have a small gift for you too."

She didn't quite know what to say or do. It was elegant and beautiful. Today, Jeremy was polite and attentive. Her skin warmed, and she felt nervous all over. Brynn's emotions often got the best of her. Many things enraged her, but many others instantly warmed her heart.

Finally, she answered, "Well, Mr. Bear, I don't like how you treated that horse, but if you promise never to hurt another animal, I'd be happy to try on that corsage. It is beautiful. Are those golden-colored balls real?"

Jeremy smiled and said, "From this moment forward, I promise to always act kindly to animals. And yes, the balls are real. I made them from gold I recovered from my mineral plot on Wawecus Hill."

He lied again. Jeremy had bought them from a whaler who had sailed on one of General Williams's whaling ships.

After attaching the corsage to her wrist, he said, "May I have this dance?"

Brynn handed Emeline her dance card and turned to Jeremy. Her heart pounded, and she politely said, "It would be my pleasure."

Lydia turned to Emeline and said, "He's a smooth one. I've got to give him that. But I'm not so sure about him, though. Could you excuse me? I need to speak with Mr. and Mrs. Bill."

Emeline smiled and said, "Sure, we can talk later."

Unfortunately, Emeline was once again left holding someone else's dance card. She knew she wasn't the most attractive girl in the room and understood her place in society. However, she was not happy with its consequences.

~~~~~

After Lydia navigated her way to the far side of the room, she joined Mr. Henry Bill and his wife, Julia. Like Lydia, Mr. and Mrs. Bill worked long, hard hours and appreciated all art forms. They had known each other for years through Lydia's part-time work as an illustrator at Mr. Bill's Bible publishing company.

As Lydia approached, Julia called out, "Lydia, you look beautiful. Please join us."

Lydia replied, "Oh, thank you. You look wonderful this evening also. How have the two of you been?"

Henry replied, "We're doing well. Thank you. Our business is booming. We can hardly produce the Bibles quickly enough to get them into the hands of our traveling salesmen. We feel blessed that we can provide such high-paying jobs to the young men of Norwich. I want to let you know that our clients adore the gilded illustrations you've created. We'd love to add more gilding to the pages, but the price of gold is rising daily."

Lydia replied, "I truly love gilding your Bible's illustrations, but lately, it's been difficult to find time to do it. With the political problems brewing in the South, writing news articles for the Aurora has kept me very busy."

She continued, "Speaking of the Aurora, I want to share some news. A few weeks ago, a young man advertised selling shares in a new company here in town. They've discovered gold out on Wawecus Hill. If I could get my hands on some of it, I'd be able to add more gilded illustrations for you."

Mr. Bill replied, "Oh yes. Corey Pallaton has already spoken with me about that. I hope that you're right. Julia and I will discuss the matter later."

Travis spotted Henry Bill, his wife, and Lydia at that moment. He had been stuck socializing with his family and his boss, Mr. Christopher C. Brand, for the last hour. Now, he was finally able to break free.

As Travis approached the group, his pulse quickened, and he overheard Mr. Bill say to Lydia, "I'd like to congratulate you on your upcoming birthday. May you always be as happy, healthy, and beautiful as you are today!"

Travis approached the group and stammered, "Miss Stedman. You look fantastic this evening! Well ... I didn't mean to say you don't always look great .... It's just that when I saw you at the newspaper office ... you looked different. Not bad, only different from tonight. You know what I mean ... It's just nice to see you. Yes, and Happy Birthday too!"

Travis was tongue-tied and wondered why he couldn't quite get the words out of his mouth.

Lydia responded, "Travis. Thank you. Well, it's not my birthday until next week, but it is nice to see you. Mr. and Mrs. Bill, this is Travis Mathews. He is the man that I spoke with you about earlier. He discovered the gold on Wawecus Hill a couple of months ago."

Henry Bill smiled and said, "Nice to meet you, Mr. Mathews. Your claim of finding gold here in Norwich is an unexpected yet happy surprise. How are you and the company doing?"

Travis answered, "It's nice to meet you too, Mr. Bill. I've seen several of your Bibles. They are beautiful works of art and an inspiration to me. I enjoy reading the scriptures and learning of the truth they teach."

He continued, "And yes, I was fortunate enough to find several rocks in Goldmine Brook that contain gold. I'm hoping to find more. Perhaps you could use the gold to illustrate your Bibles."

Julia responded, "Travis, that is so kind of you. Please do keep us in mind. Could you tell us a little more about the company?"

Travis said, "Well, yes and no. The firm's name is the Wawecus Gold, Silver, and Nickel Mining Company. They've set up an office and processing operation next to Goldmine Brook. But I don't know much more than that. I have worked on their survey team for a while now."

Henry directly questioned Travis, "Do you believe it would be wise to invest in their company?"

Travis waited a moment and continued, "I can't give you a well-informed answer about the company's future or growth potential. However, I can confidently say that some gold exists in Goldmine Brook. I'm not sure how much or how profitable the company will be. But, I am sure that all will be revealed in time."

Henry Bill smiled, looked at Julia, and said, "Thank you for your advice. If you find more gold, please let us know. We could sure use a reliable, local supply for our Bibles."

He looked at Julia and said, "However, for now, my dear, would you care to dance?"

As the Bills waltzed across the floor, Lydia turned to Travis and said, "They make such a lovely couple. Look at the way they gaze at one another. Their love fills the room."

Travis sensed it too. He said, "Yes, I think they share a beautiful love."

Then, as he gazed at Lydia's large, glistening brown eyes, a tiny tear formed in the corner of his right eye, his heart leapt, and he thought, *"She is beautiful."*

Travis began, "Lydia, I just wanted to tell you how sorry I am for the snake biting you at Goldmine Brook. I should have never taken you out to the wilderness like that. Please forgive me. My curiosity got the best of me."

Lydia winced and said, "I will admit the pain was excruciating. But I appreciate how you got the venom out of me and got me home safely. I've always been adventurous and know that things like that sometimes happen. It wasn't all your fault."

Lydia had always desired to dance gracefully, but her slightly deformed, smaller left foot made it difficult to sync with any dance partner. She couldn't help but notice that Travis's right leg was a little longer than his right, causing his limp. An idea popped into her head.

She waited, thought for a moment, and said, "Mr. Mathews, I'm not much of a dancer, and this may sound a bit forward of me. But, would you like to waltz with me?"

He'd never learned to dance and had never desired to do so. Travis disliked being the center of attention due to his ever-present limp. Even walking down any street, he could almost feel others' thoughts of his inadequacy. *No! He did not want to dance!*

But, as he looked into her eyes and sensed the warmth of her heart, he smiled and said, "I'd love to dance with you, Miss Stedman. But, please take it easy on me."

Travis held out his hand, and she gently interlaced her tiny fingers into his. Lydia gingerly stepped atop Travis's shorter left leg with her shorter, malformed foot and atop his longer right leg with her normal foot. Once embraced, Travis and Lydia balanced one another perfectly. They comfortably smiled at one another. No words were necessary.

Travis instantly felt a surge of energy shoot throughout his body. However, once on the ballroom floor, he felt extremely awkward. It was difficult for him to avoid the long swan feather perched in her hair from brushing against his throat.

Lydia sensed the problem and said, "Turn your head sideways, hold me close, and stop thinking. Feel the movement of my body, and I'll guide you through it. All you've got to do is count one … two … three. And on every beat, we'll take a step."

Travis relaxed, held her hand firmly, pulled her closer, and rested his large hand comfortably on the small of her back. He instantly felt their bodies floating over the ballroom floor like a pair of graceful butterflies. It was a sensation like none other

Travis had ever felt. His awkward gait disappeared, and the music stopped sooner than he expected.

Once they left the floor and seated themselves on a pair of folding chairs near the side window, Lydia smiled and said, "That was quite enjoyable, Mr. Mathews!"

Travis replied, "Why yes, it was. Thank you, Miss Stedman. We'll have to waltz again someday."

He continued, "I have been thinking more about our previous adventure. I've cleaned the Quinebaugan artifacts we found and want to show them to you. There is something exceptional about them that we need to discuss."

She looked at him and said, "And what would that special thing be?"

He answered, "Well, that's where you come in. I've got several ideas and want to share them with you. Would you mind joining me for dinner at the Wauregan House next week? I want to celebrate your birthday with you."

Lydia felt warm and happy all over. She smiled and said, "Why yes, Mr. Mathews. I would most certainly enjoy spending an evening with you. Could we meet on Friday?"

Travis stood erect, looked into her eyes, smiled, and said, "Miss Stedman, I look forward to joining you on Friday."

22: Dinner at the Wauregan
Downtown Norwich
Wauregan House: Corner of Union & Main
Friday, October 29, 1858

Lydia had anxiously anticipated her eighteenth birthday for the past several days. Although she celebrated her birthday with her parents yesterday, Lydia was more excited about tonight. It would be her first-ever proper date with Travis.

She now stood at the concierge station, carrying an overstuffed leather messenger bag, nervously surveying the dining room for Travis. Lydia adjusted her hair one final time.

Travis patiently awaited her arrival at a table near the dining room's back wall. When he saw her enter, his heart began to beat faster. Her clothing was neat and simple, but her hair's majestic red hawk feather accentuated Lydia's understated beauty. Her radiant smile, bright eyes, and enthusiasm for life were evident from across the room, and Travis jumped to his feet.

He joined her and said, "Here, let me take your bag."

Handing the heavy bag to him, she said, "Thank you. I appreciate that you asked me for dinner. The Wauregan House is so elegant. Tonight is my first time inside."

Travis said brightly, "Well, it is your birthday, and you deserve a special treat. Tonight is my first visit also. It's only been open a little more than two years. The atmosphere here makes me feel very grown-up."

She responded, "Yeah, I feel more grown-up, too. I'm impressed by the linen napkins, authentic silverware, silver service, and gas lighting. I've never personally seen gas lighting."

Travis looked around the room and said, "Yes, the lighting impresses me too. Someone has recently replaced all the candles and oil lamps with gas jets. Do you know when and who installed the gas lighting?"

Lydia confidently replied, "It's interesting that you would ask. I recently wrote an article in our newspaper about it."

She continued, "A few months ago, the Norwich City Gas Company installed town gas in the Wauregan House and the Chelsea Paper Mill at Greeneville. The company is testing town gas, a new type of fuel they produce from coal. They plan to eliminate the complaints of bad odor and frequent leakage that the old Norwich Gas Light Company caused. Hopefully, the new company will be able to introduce town gas to the entire city."

Travis said, "It sounds like Norwich is modernizing rapidly."

He lifted a crystal goblet filled with water and proclaimed, "Well. Here's to modernization!"

After several minutes of small talk, Lydia hesitated a thoughtful moment and surveyed the diversity of people in the room having dinner. She wasn't sure how much personal information she wanted to share. Finally, she decided and said, "I learned something yesterday that changed everything for me."

Looking puzzled, Travis replied, "What could that possibly be?"

She responded, "My parents told me they adopted me as a baby. I didn't believe it at first because they are such wonderful parents. I love them with all my heart, but after I thought about it for a while, I knew it to be true. I don't look like them, and there have been many times that I simply felt different from them. I can't explain the feeling."

Travis responded, "Did they tell you any details of your birth parents, or why they waited until now to tell you?"

Lydia answered, "Yes. They said my biological father died at sea a few months before I was born, and my mother died shortly after giving birth. That only left my grandmother to take care of me. But the care I needed as a baby was far too much for her. Since the Stedmans had unsuccessfully tried to conceive a baby for several years, it was natural that my biological grandmother would ask them to care for me."

She continued, "My parents said that my grandmother's only condition was that they tell me of my adoption on my eighteenth birthday."

Travis questioned, "How do you feel about it?"

Lydia answered, "Well. Quite frankly, I don't know. However, I do know that I feel different today than a few days ago. Thank you for listening."

Travis reached into his bag and pulled out a gift-wrapped package. He said, "I've brought you a small birthday gift."

She accepted the package, smiled, and said, "Hmm … I can't imagine what it might be. It doesn't weigh much and is about a foot long and six inches wide. Could it be a silk scarf? Or, perhaps a dainty pair of silk gloves?"

Travis smiled and said, "No, and no. Just open the package."

Lydia opened it, found a dozen pristine white feathers, and said, "Travis, these are gorgeous! I can use them to make pens, wear them in my hair, or make a feather fan. I love them. Thank you. Where did you find these swan feathers?"

Travis was hoping that she would ask.

He answered, "Well, I didn't exactly find them. I had to battle for them. Have you ever tried plucking feathers from a live, full-grown swan?"

Travis could barely contain his laughter, "Well, I now have that unusual experience safely under my belt. As you know, I live in Lucasville, near Trading Cove Brook. Since I saw you writing with the white feather quill pen at your office, I've been watching a family of swans who live at the brook. I stopped by the cove several times, hoping that some of its feathers might have fallen to the ground. But, no. That didn't happen. Since your birthday was nearing, my time ran out last week. So, I had to step up my game."

"I waded into the brook and tried to befriend one of them. He had very nice, long, handsome feathers. I threw out small chunks of bread and slowly lured him into my grasp. Yes, I was successful. I plucked out one after another but paid a steep price. I learned that a grown swan has powerful wings. I could hardly believe how much of a fight he put up for just a few feathers."

Lydia smiled and said, "Oh, Mooshi! You're my hero. Thank you."

She kidded, "Oh, by the way. I've planned to make two more fans, one for Brynn and one for Emmy. Can you bring me two more dozen feathers by the end of this week?"

They both broke out in laughter.

After reviewing the menu, Lydia asked, "The aroma here is tantalizing and makes me quite hungry. Have you decided what you want for dinner?"

Travis said, "Hmmm. I'm going to try something I've never eaten. I'll order the lamb."

Lydia replied, "Okay. Well, the menu says *mutton*, not *lamb*. I think mutton tastes gamier than lamb."

Travis chuckled and replied, "Well, that's not a problem. I'm GAME for it!"

Lydia laughed again and said, "Very punny, Mr. Mathews."

They both ordered roast mutton, succotash, pickled beets, and custard pie.

Afterward, Travis reached into his bag and pulled out the Quinebaugan artifacts. He said, "I brought the mortar and pestle we found last month. I want to discuss them with you."

Remembering her last encounter with the objects, she said, "I presume you've removed any snakes from them?"

He replied, "Yes, you can rest assured. I cleaned the objects inside and out. Of course, I still feel bad about your getting bitten by the snake. But perhaps there is a silver lining. I discovered several exciting things about the artifacts. For example, the pestle has a thin coating of gold residue."

He handed her the pestle and said, "Look at this. Based on the residue, the mortar's large dimensions, and thick granite walls, I'm certain that my ancestors used it to grind gold-laden stones into a powder."

He pulled a stone box from his bag under the table and said, "Here is the lidded box containing golden flakes I showed you last month."

Travis pulled out a modern box from the bag and said, "I have another gift for you. Last week, I used these tools to grind down all the rocks that you and I found. Then, I separated the quartz from the gold. So what you see inside this box are the golden remnants."

He continued, "I'm not sure if it's real or fool's gold, but I thought we could compare the particles in the two boxes to help decide. Also, since you use gold flakes for Mr. Bill's Bibles, I thought you might know if the ground powder is real gold."

Lydia studied their contents carefully and said, "I'm not sure. It's hard to tell in this lighting, but we may be lucky. I have one of the illustrations I'm working on here in my bag. Let's compare the gold in my illustration to the gold-colored powder."

After she unfurled the partially finished illustration of Daniel battling in the lion's den, Travis said, "Lydia, your artistry is exquisite! You are truly a gifted artist. I could not create anything like this in a hundred years."

She answered, "Why, thank you. Let's compare the gold."

After a moment, she said, "I can't tell by simply looking at it. The textures and colors are too similar in this light. I'll have to try using it. I know that real gold is much more pliable than fool's gold. Also, I don't think fool's gold will stick to a page properly. I'll let you know how it turns out."

~~~~~

After finishing the mutton and custard pie, Lydia said, "I loved the pie and the beets, but the taste of mutton is a bit too strong for me. It's also a little tough. I'll probably try the veal fillet next time. Did you like yours?"

He answered, "Yes, I loved it."

Travis continued, "I've been thinking a lot about the decorations on the mortar and pestle and believe they're more than simple, unrelated pictographs. I believe they are a map of some sort. Look here."

He pointed at the outside wall of the mortar and said, "See how these stick figures of children are surrounding this dwelling.

The dwelling looks to depict an old Quinebaugan wigwam. And see how wavy lines are running near the wigwam? The hut may be Lucas's Cabin, and the water may be Moshup's Spring. Both of these landmarks are near my home."

He added, "I think the map may point to buried Quinebaugan artifacts."

Lydia studied the decorations more and replied, "Yes, maybe. But there are several other symbols as well. I see one that looks somewhat like a large chair, a small tomahawk, a large tomahawk, and many snakes. They look like rattlesnakes to me."

Travis replied, "Well, we found a small tomahawk and snakes. I think this map will help us find the other objects."

Travis continued, "I showed these to my mother. She is well-versed in Quinebaugan tradition, folklore, and prophecies and believes it is a map. But, she told me I should take all of these items to the person with the most knowledge of Quinebaugan traditions. It's an old woman who lives out at Kachina Rock, and her name is White Eagle."

Lydia looked at him intently and said, "I've heard of her, and I've also heard of Kachina Rock. That's where Lucas, and several sachems after him, held meetings. I think your mother is right. We should take the artifacts to White Eagle."

Travis said, "I agree. But we should do our homework first before bothering her. I believe that we can find more artifacts on our own."

Lydia replied, "What do you have in mind?"

Travis said, "As you know, I work for Mr. Walling at his cartography office in downtown. He has been tasked to create a 200th Jubilee Commemorative map. The map will pinpoint the locations of early, historically significant sites in and around

Norwich. He has given me the job of exploring, finding, and recording the locations of the sites. "

He said, "After discussing the matter with several members of my tribe, I assembled a list of places we should identify on the Jubilee map. I thought you and I could search for more artifacts while mapping these places. Perhaps we can meet White Eagle in person after searching the sites. What do you think of the plan?"

Lydia flashed a smile and said, "That is an excellent idea! I always love a good adventure. Also, I have been thinking about how I could donate to the Jubilee personally. If it is okay with Mr. Walling, I'd like to volunteer to gild his commemorative map. I'll decorate the map with both historical Norwich and traditional Quinebaugan symbols. I'll use some of the gold that we find."

Travis flashed a smile, took her hand, and kissed it. He said, "I look forward to it!"

23: SEVEN CENTS
NORWICH / LUCASVILLE TOWN LINE
SATURDAY, NOVEMBER 6, 1858

Travis and Lydia looked forward to today's adventure. It was a cool, crisp morning, and they hoped to discover more Quinebaugan artifacts while mapping two old Quinebaugan sites.

Travis said, "I'm happy Mr. Walling agreed to let you illustrate and gild the 200th Jubilee map. He's willing to pay you, but I told him you wanted to donate your time. I think it is generous of you to donate your time and effort. I'm sure the people of Norwich and the Quinebaugan tribe will cherish the map for generations."

Lydia responded, "Oh, it's my pleasure. I'll enjoy doing it. Can you show me the preliminary map that you've drawn? I'd like to see where we are now and where we're going."

Travis gently pulled the leads in and said, "Whoa, Moshup. Easy now, boy."

As the carriage slowed to a stop, he said, "The map is in the back luggage box. I'll get it."

But before Moshup stopped, Lydia jumped out, ran around to the back of the carriage, and playfully said, "You're a little slow on the trigger. You need to move faster than that, Mister."

Travis laughed and said, "Yeah, I guess so. But you'd better be careful opening that box. You may find a rattlesnake nestled up next to the map."

Lydia smiled and replied, "Very funny. But, if I find any snakes, there will be consequences. So *you* had better hope there aren't any."

After finding no snakes and retrieving the map, Lydia handed it to Travis.

He pointed to it and said, "Okay, now. Let me see. We're right here on Quinebaugan Road, heading south toward New London. Nowadays, everyone calls it the Norwich / New London Turnpike, but the Quinebaugans still call it Quinebaugan Road. So, we'll pass through the toll gate and continue down the road that leads past my home and Fort Shantok. Our first stop will be at Lucas's cabin."

Lydia said, "Did you know this toll road was the first turnpike in New England and the second in the entire United States?"

Travis answered, "No, I did not. Tell me about it."

Lydia replied, "In 1791, the Connecticut Legislature authorized a company to build the road and erect a tollgate. Since then, the turnpike company has collected tolls to recoup their start-up costs and pay for routine maintenance."

Travis said, "That is interesting. After all that time, you'd think the road would be paid for by now. But they still charge four cents for carriages and one cent for each passenger. We'll be passing through the gate soon. I can see it up ahead, but there seems to be a problem. The four carriages in front of us aren't moving."

Lydia said, "Yes, I see that. The last thing I expected was a traffic jam. What's going on?"

Travis replied, "I know the gatekeeper. He reminds me of Billy Goat Gruff. He lives in the house next to the gate and thrives on giving people a hard time. Since many travelers are unaware of the fee, they don't carry any money. Let's walk ahead to find out what he's up to today."

Travis and Lydia descended from the carriage and strode toward the toll gate. As they neared the entrance, they saw the toll collector holding a long, wooden cane and standing beside an old carriage.

The gatekeeper began pounding on the carriage with his cane and said, "All of you. Step down from your carriage. The cost of entering Norwich on this road is seven cents. Four cents for the carriage and one cent for each of the three of you. Who plans to pay?"

A young African-American man, his wife, and his daughter stepped out. The man said, "Sir, my family and I are coming from Virginia. Mr. James L. Smith, a cobbler in Norwich, has offered me a job as his assistant. The journey here has been long and treacherous, and I'm sorry to say that we don't have any money left. It has cost us everything we had to make it this far. But I promise to pay you the toll in a few days. So, when I receive my first wages from Mr. Smith, I'll come here and pay you."

The gatekeeper sneered at the man and smashed his cane against the side of the carriage again. He looked intently at the man, his wife, and his young daughter and said, "Okay, Mister, I'll agree to that. But I'm going to need you to put up collateral. I can see that your daughter is wearing a handsome pair of shoes. I assume that you made them. In any case, I've also got a daughter who needs a pair of sturdy shoes, just like those. So, you hand over the shoes, and I'll let you pass."

Travis overheard the final verbal exchange and stepped between the gatekeeper and the black family. He said, "Good Sir, don't you think that is a rather unfair trade? We're only talking about seven cents here. The shoes are worth at least twenty-five cents."

The gatekeeper pointed at the traveler and replied, "This man is probably lying. He probably doesn't have a job offer, and I don't trust him. So he either pays or goes back to where he came from."

Travis reached into his pocket, counted out seven cents, and handed it over. Then, he said, "You should be ashamed of yourself!"

The traveler turned to Travis and said, "Thank you, Sir. I promise to pay you back. My family and I will be staying with Mr. Smith. He lives on Oak Street, and his shoe shop is on Franklin Street. Please stop by there after next week, and I'll repay you. By the way, what is your name?"

Travis replied, "I'm Travis Mathews, and this is my friend Lydia Stedman. And you're welcome. I'm glad that we could be of assistance."

After Travis and Lydia returned to their carriage, Lydia whispered, "I know of Mr. James L. Smith, the cobbler on Franklin Street. My father takes our family's shoes to him for repair. Mr. Smith was also a conductor of the Underground Railroad, accommodating the relocation of formerly enslaved people in the South. Many families traveled from Southern states to various towns in Connecticut."

She continued, "Several migrant families remained in Norwich and formed a vibrant community on Jail Hill, near downtown. My father told me that Mr. Smith was born on a

Virginia plantation and used the Underground Railroad himself to relocate to Norwich twenty years ago."

She added, "That was kind of you to pay his fare."

Travis smiled and nodded in acknowledgment.

~~~~~

After their carriage arrived at the gate, they paid their toll without further incident and continued south on the turnpike.

Travis said, "Several years ago, my family and I took a walk in the woods over by Moshup's Spring. I don't remember much about the place, but I remember seeing the remnants of Lucas's cabin. My mother told me Lucas lived in a wooden cabin with his wife and three sons. Unfortunately, all that remains now is a broken-down stone foundation. However, I'm pretty sure that we can find it. I want to place its exact location on the map and for us to search it carefully for any more artifacts."

They rode south, past Reverend Oakham's old house, the Quinebaugan church, and school, and found the dirt road that led to Quinebaugan Hill. After driving another ten minutes, Travis noticed a brook and said, "Ahh, that's it. This is the base of Moshup's Spring. Lucas built his cabin nearby this spring for a reliable fresh water supply. I remember that his cabin is on the eastern side of Quinebaugan Hill."

He continued, "My mother told me people used to come here from miles around to drink from the spring. Many still say this spring water makes one strong and healthy. So let's have a drink and fill our canteens, and then we can follow the spring up the hill."

They trudged through the undergrowth up the incline and found a group of rocks arranged roughly in a 10' x 10' square near the apex. Travis exclaimed, "Yes. We've found it."

He added, "Just think, Lucas touched these very rocks, and the view we now see is the same one he saw 200 years ago."

Without thinking, Travis lifted Lydia into his arms and hugged her. They briefly gazed into one another's eyes, and Travis felt the passion. He instinctively pulled her closer and kissed her cheek quickly. Next, he swung her around in a complete circle before gently returning her feet to the ground. Travis thought to himself, "I love being with this woman!"

He told her, "I'm so happy to share this moment with you. I can almost feel Lucas's presence."

Lydia smiled and said, "I feel it too. I can hardly explain it. I'm not even Quinebaugan, yet I sense a powerful spirit here. I feel like we've been drawn here for a purpose."

She wanted to say, "I feel *your* presence too, and it feels good."

But, she thought it better to stay mum.

Travis said, "Yes, I agree with you. Well now. Let's break out the survey equipment and record our exact location."

After descending the hill and giving Moshup a couple of carrots, they pulled the instruments from the back of the carriage. Travis set the legs of Mr. Walling's sturdy tripod on the ground and leveled its base. He then carefully removed a large, precision measurement instrument from its case.

After attaching it to the tripod and leveling it, Travis said, "This is a theodolite. We'll use it to measure both the horizontal and vertical angles. We'll use the center of the road as our base point."

He continued, "I need you to grab the survey rod and the 100-foot-long steel measuring tape. We'll work our way up the hill by taking measurements at several intermediate legs. The first step is to place the rod about 100 feet from the cabin foundation and set it on the ground. Next, I'll use the theodolite to take horizontal and vertical measurements. Then, we'll measure the distance between you and me using the tape. After recording all the measurements, we'll move on to the next leg. It's really not very complicated."

He finished by saying, "Are you ready?"

Lydia gathered up the rod and tape and began the procedure. She said, "Oddly, this is kinda fun. But, there had better not be any snakes."

Travis chuckled and said, "Well, that might be an issue if it were summertime. But, all the rattlers are hibernating now."

Travis took meticulous notes for every measurement and every leg of the survey. Then, after reaching the hilltop, they repeated the process to pinpoint the corners of Lucas's cabin precisely.

Lydia sat down, pulled out the cork of her canteen, took a sip, and said, "It's break time. Here, have a drink."

Travis replied, "Thanks. There's nothing like a cool drink of fresh water after a little exercise."

He drank and said, "Since we're at Moshup's Spring, I'd like to tell you more about Moshup. As I told you earlier, he was a giant who walked on land and sea. He lived on both Martha's Vineyard and in Shantok for many years. Moshup was so tall that the distance between his footsteps was measured in miles, not inches. And he was so heavy that his steps left mammoth footprints embedded in rocks throughout New London County."

Travis pointed to the spring near the foundation and said, "Do you know why they call this Moshup's Spring?"

She grinned, thought momentarily, and said, "My teachers must have forgotten to cover that topic. So, no, I don't know. But, I'm guessing that you're about to tell me."

Travis chuckled and said, "No. I wouldn't be so sure about that because I won't tell you. Rather, I'm going to *show* you why."

Lydia said, "Are you kidding me again?"

Travis replied, "No, of course not. My mother showed me this a long time ago."

They walked about fifty feet away from the foundation and stood on the side of the spring. Lydia looked at Travis and said, "Okay, what am I looking at?"

He said, "Check out the top of that large boulder. Do you see anything odd about it?"

Lydia replied, "Why, yes, it resembles a large footprint. So, let me guess, that's one of Moshup's footprints?"

He answered, "Yes, that is correct. There's also one in Devil's Hopyard in Moodus, Connecticut, and one in Old Lyme, Connecticut."

She said, "Thank you for showing me! I love it. When I decorate the 200th Jubilee map, I'll be sure to include an illustration of Moshup's footprint."

Travis replied, "That's a great idea. Now, let's do more exploring. Maybe we can find a Quinebaugan artifact or two. I'm thinking back to the drawings on the mortar and pestle. We saw pictographs of children and a horse, among other things. Maybe the artisan left us a message regarding Lucas's children and horses. Perhaps he hid something away in his cabin's foundation. What do you think about that idea?"

Lydia replied, "It's plausible, and you may be right. Let's check it out."

They returned to the foundation and carefully searched between and under the loose rocks.

Lydia cried out, "Travis, come look at this. I've found several arrowheads."

Travis said, "Lucas, or possibly one of his sons, probably used these arrowheads for hunting or protecting his family. They're precious. Where did you find them?"

She responded, "Someone partially buried them between these two large boulders. Let's look to see if there's anything else in there."

They explored the entire foundation for another hour, searching between and under as many rocks as possible. There were no more to be found.

Lydia said on their return trip home, "I'm pleased we found those arrowheads. I'll draw several pictures of arrowheads on the Jubilee map."

She added, "Someday, we'll have to return these arrowheads to Quinebaugan elders."

Travis replied, "Yes, we will. But I expect we'll uncover more than a handful of arrowheads."

As they passed through the tollgate, Travis said, "Tomorrow, I'll use the measurements that we recorded today and begin pinpointing Lucas's cabin and Moshup's Spring on the official map."

24: Gold Fever
Hardscrabble Hill
Company Office
Wednesday, November 10, 1858

It was mid-afternoon, and Elena was so busy that she had no time for lunch. One after another, Norwich's residents had poured into the company's office to learn more about the new mining operation. The public's response to the advertisement in the newspaper and their social networking efforts at the Jubilee meeting was overwhelming. As a result, Elena sold more than 100 shares to businesses and individuals in the past week.

She and Corey were surprised at the large number of private buyers. The price of one share was $25.00, more than a week's wage for most people. Thus far, Norwich's ordinary, everyday working people had purchased over half the shares. Elena sold many more to businesses and Norwich's wealthy elite.

A young man sat across the room from Elena, patiently waiting for his turn to meet with her.

Elena explained to her current customer, an elderly lady from Greeneville, "No, I'm sorry, I can only sell full shares. We don't offer half-shares. Yes, I know the price seems expensive, but the possible rewards far outweigh any risk you would incur."

The lady said, "Oh, yes. I understand. My husband and I are retired now and can only afford to risk $10.00 of our savings.

We got so excited when we saw your ad in the paper. We've been looking for a good investment for quite some time now, and your company looks promising."

Elena replied, "I've spoken with several people in your situation this past week. One woman asked me to help her find someone willing to share ownership of a single share. Perhaps you could speak with her and agree to a partnership. Would you like me to give you her name?"

The lady responded, "Thank you, Mrs. Pallaton. I would like that. That is a great idea."

Elena was happy that she was in a position to help this woman. She always tried to create win-win agreements that benefitted both parties in all client interactions. Elena wrote down the name, handed it to the lady, and said, "I look forward to seeing you again soon."

The young man stood up just as the older woman left the office. Elena motioned to him and said, "Please, have a seat."

But, before he reached Elena's desk, the bell hanging just above the front door dinged, and Mrs. Harriet Peck Williams, Brynn Dunham, and her beloved dog, Dexter, entered.

Mrs. Williams said, "Good afternoon, Elena."

Elena was pleasantly surprised. She and Corey had hoped to form stronger ties with General and Mrs. Williams, but she was amazed their friendships could blossom so quickly. She said, "Hello, Mrs. Williams and Brynn. I'm so happy to see you both."

"Oh my goodness! I see you've brought your little buddy with you. He is so handsome. I just love dogs."

She added, "I'll be free to speak with you after caring for this gentleman. Please have a seat."

Elena asked the young man, "How can I help you?"

He answered, "Like the woman before me, I also read your advertisement in the paper, and I just wanted to come by to learn a few more details. I overheard you tell the lady the price is $25.00 per share. I'm okay with that. But could you tell me how much gold they've found thus far? If I buy a share, I wonder how much it might eventually be worth."

He added, "My idea is to buy one share now and another next year. Then, after my fiancé and I marry, we will sell the shares to help pay for a new home. What's your opinion of my plan?"

Elena had listened to many financial situations similar to this during the past two weeks. And she was confident that the shares would grow in value. She hadn't personally seen any recently processed gold, but Corey frequently assured her their workers on Wawecus Hill were finding more precious minerals every day.

She replied to the young man, "I don't want to set your expectations too high, but I believe the value of our stock will double by this time next year. Moreover, our company is so sure of its success that we promise to buy back any shares from the original owners. However, you must maintain ownership of the shares for at least twelve months."

She continued, "As far as the quantity of gold found thus far is concerned, I'll just say this. There's plenty enough to go around for everyone."

He stood up, offered to shake hands, and said, "Thank you, Mrs. Pallaton. I'll discuss this with my fiancé, and we'll get back to you."

~~~~~

Elena was still hungry due to the lack of time to eat lunch but was enthused to see Mrs. Williams and Brynn. She walked toward the fireplace, reached for the tea kettle, and said, "May I offer you a touch of tea and perhaps biscuits and jam?"

The ladies rose, and Mrs. Williams replied, "Thank you, Elena. That is very thoughtful of you. Brynn and I have been shopping all morning and haven't had time to sit down and relax. I'd like my tea with just a pinch of sugar."

Elena was relieved to hear it and said, "And you, Brynn? Would you or your little friend there care for anything?"

Brynn answered, "Yes, thank you. I would love to try one of your biscuits. And I'm sure Dexter would appreciate a drink of water."

She continued, "Some mornings, I enjoy taking a walk around Williams Park with Dexter. So many times, when we pass by your home, I catch the scent of freshly baked biscuits. Thank you so much for sharing them."

Elena deeply desired to become better friends with Brynn's influential parents. She replied, "You are so welcome. Someday, I'd like to get together with you, your mother, and Dexter. Perhaps we could discuss gardening, play a board game, and have afternoon tea."

Brynn answered, "That would be grand. My mother had hoped to meet with you here today and discuss business. Unfortunately, my father needed her today to help handle a minor social incident in town. As you know, my father is the treasurer of the Norwich Savings Band and sometimes relies on her to help with delicate financial matters involving women. She asked me to ride with Mrs. Williams and act on her behalf."

She added, "I'll let my mother know you also enjoy board games."

After chatting for a few minutes, Mrs. Williams said, "We should probably talk business before it gets too late. The

General and I will entertain Mayor Prentice and his wife this evening. They want to discuss more plans for the Jubilee. So, Brynn, why don't you go first? The terms of my business will most likely be more complicated than yours."

Brynn replied, "Thank you."

Turning to Elena, she said, "My parents are very excited about your company and want to support you. They've discussed the company's promises at length, and you've convinced them that you, Mr. Pallaton, and Jeremy are on the right track. They want to invest now. Rather heavily, I might add. They will purchase more shares as progress continues. They'd like to start with four shares. The cost for that is $100?"

Elena replied, "Yes, that is correct."

Brynn reached into her purse and proffered five $20 gold double eagle coins. She said, "When you fill out the stock certificate, please show my father as the owner."

Elena said, "Yes, certainly. I'll bring the paperwork to your home this evening so he can sign it. Will he be home tonight?"

Brynn responded, "Yes, he'll be there and happy to see you. He and my mother discuss your company almost every night. My family believes your efforts will benefit Norwich in many ways. Thank you."

Elena answered, "Yes. We think so too. And, now, Mrs. Williams, what can I do for you?"

Harriet answered, "Please, call me Harriet. *Mrs. Williams* sounds so formal. Since our husbands and I spoke at the Jubilee planning meeting, the General and I have discussed your mining company in great detail. We see it as an answer to one of our prayers."

She continued, "Our son Thomas died three years ago, and we have no surviving children. It has been unfortunate for us, but it does open the door of opportunity to help others in need. As my husband and I enter the twilight years of our lives, we've been actively searching for ways to help future generations through monetary donations. We plan to make a large donation to the Norwich Free Academy next year and hope to use the profits from our investment in your company to build a modern library at the Academy."

"But we also have several other grand projects in mind. For example, I know that young girls and women in our community often need an extra educational boost to start on the right foot. They need good teachers in a safe environment. So we plan to build, open, and operate a progressive high school in New London dedicated to promoting and advancing female education."

Harriet continued, "The General and I have plenty of funds at our disposal, and we'd like to do as much as possible as soon as possible. We want to invest heavily in the Wawecus Hill Gold, Silver, and Nickel Mining Company to help accomplish this goal. We trust you and believe that you will also be able to help further this cause."

Elena could hardly believe the words. She said, "Harriet, I am so thankful we can work together to make your dream a reality. My husband and I are also working to help our fellow citizens. We're in the process of developing affordable housing on Wawecus Hill. Our dream is to help displaced Pocawansett and Hoopanoag Native Americans in New London County have a safe place they can call home. Your investment in our company will help make all our dreams come true."

Harriet said, "The General and I want to buy twenty shares. We'll bring payment here next week."

Elena felt blessed that she and Corey had the opportunity to benefit her fellow tribe members and future generations of young women. She said, "Yes, that would be fine. Corey and I will both be here every morning of next week. Please feel free to stop by at any time."

As Harriet and Brynn rose to leave, Elena said, "Brynn, Jeremy stopped by here a couple of days ago and told me that you and he are dating again. So, I presume you have forgiven him for his past transgressions?"

Brynn lit up and said, "Why yes. As you told me a couple of weeks ago, he is generous and has a good heart. He gave me a beautiful corsage and danced with me all evening at the Jubilee social."

Brynn smiled, winked, and continued, "He's an outstanding dancer and likes music. On Friday night, he'll accompany me to my choir recital. Before the recital, I'll probably see you because Jeremy plans to stop by your house to drop off the weekly supply of processed gold and the updated site map."

Elena responded, "Yes. Every Friday, Jeremy delivers it to Corey. Would the two of you like to join us for dinner?"

Brynn bashfully said, "Oh, thank you for the kind offer. But, I wouldn't want to impose on you."

Elena responded, "Not at all. We'd love to have you."

She added, "Oh, by the way, you probably shouldn't bring Dexter. Corey isn't fond of dogs."

Brynn replied, "Okay. Thank you again. We'll see you then."

25: Corey's Fortress
Norwichtown
Pallaton Residence: Washington Street
Friday, November 12, 1858

Elena opened the front door of their home to find Jeremy and Brynn. She graciously smiled and said, "Hello. Please come in."

Although Brynn lived directly across the street from the Pallatons, she'd never been inside their home. She was pleased to be escorted by Jeremy because he made her feel like a respected, legitimate adult. She had always wondered how the Pallatons had decorated their home. To Brynn, the theme of their company office felt somewhat masculine and impersonal due to Corey's displays of maps, houses, handguns, guns, and rifles. She wondered if she would see evidence of Elena's feminine touch in their home decor.

Brynn was dressed in her Norwich Free Academy choir outfit. She wore a long, flowing black skirt and a cream-colored Weddington blouse. This choir-approved outfit worn by the girls in the choir was attractive. But on Brynn, it was an exceptional display of beauty.

Brynn's undeniable femininity was displayed prominently by cloth-covered buttons on her sleeves, a ruffled lace trim falling gently over her shoulders, and an etched-in-lace stand collar.

She enjoyed singing and being friends with the other girls. But Brynn was thrilled for the opportunity to sing in this evening's highly anticipated fall choir recital. She relished the thought of bathing in the public limelight.

Elena said, "Brynn, may I take your shawl? I love how you've arranged the rosebuds in your hair."

Brynn responded coyly, "Thank you. I made rose corsages similar to this for all the girls in our choir. Each one has several pink rose buds and a hair clip. They seem to like them, and I enjoy helping them look beautiful. We're all so excited about this evening's recital."

Corey greeted them from his office, saying, "Hi, Jeremy. Hello Brynn. Thank you for coming. Could you please step into my office?"

From the moment they entered, Brynn was fascinated by the furnishings in the Pallaton home. Her parents were well-to-do, so she had visited the homes of many of Norwich's elite, but the Pallaton residence had a significantly different flair from the others. As they passed through the hallway to Corey's office, she noted several Native American-themed oil paintings. The art portrayed brightly colored woven baskets, families sitting outside their wigwams, and portraits of regal-looking tribal leaders. Two large, ornately carved, solid oak wooden doors stood at the entrance to Corey's office.

As she entered the room, Brynn felt as though she had just passed through the gates of a fortress and into the inner sanctum of a sacred space. She saw Corey's massive desk and the Hall's

Company safe behind it. Next to the safe, she marveled at the fine craftsmanship of several tom-tom drums, a large headdress adorned with bald eagle feathers, and two wooden flutes. In addition, Corey displayed more than two dozen rifles and guns on the walls.

Brynn said, "My, you have quite a large collection of guns."

Corey replied, "Yes, I'm proud of it. All the arms displayed here were manufactured here in Norwich. The rifles, six-shooters, cane guns, and even this whaling gun were made in Norwich."

Brynn said, "My friend Lydia's friend, Travis Mathews, works at the C.C. Brand Whaling Gun Factory. He probably had a hand in making that one."

Corey gazed at Brynn intently. After a lustful scan, he said, "Yes, Travis also works for me part-time."

He motioned her to a chair on the far side of the room and said, "Please, Miss Dunham, sit here while Jeremy and I conduct our business. Would you care for a drink?"

Before she could say no, he shouted, "Elena. Bring us three glasses of port wine."

Moments later, she appeared with an ornate silver serving tray carrying three hand-blown goblets half-filled with dark red wine. After she offered Brynn, her husband, and Jeremy the drinks, Elena politely said to Corey, "Don't be too long. Dinner will be served shortly."

Corey replied, "Thank you."

Elena left, and he lifted his glass, looked at Jeremy and Brynn, and said, "Cheers to all!"

Brynn felt his leering eyes and sunk into a massive leather chair. She was uncomfortable and wondered what Corey might be thinking. As he and Jeremy discussed the findings of Jeremy's field team, Brynn continued to survey the room's decorations. Then, as her head turned back to the entrance, she saw two large glass tanks, one on each side of each door. She thought it to be home to mice, hamsters, chipmunks, or perhaps even a rabbit. But as she looked closer, Brynn shrieked and jumped to her feet. Her heart missed several beats as she jumped up and ran toward Jeremy.

She cried out, "Are those rattlesnakes alive?"

Corey calmly stood and said, "Don't worry; they can't harm you. That's Mutt & Jeff in one tank and Ginger & Spice in the other. They are my pets."

He stepped out from behind the desk, walked toward her, patted her shoulder, and said, "As I said earlier, please have a seat. Jeremy and I will be done here in a few minutes."

She returned to her seat, glued her eyes on the snakes, and listened to their conversation. Brynn couldn't hear all the words, but it was clear that Corey was upset with Jeremy.

Jeremy pulled out a map, unfurled it on Corey's desk, and pointed. He said, "We've done a complete search of the brook's northern banks. Here. And we're now working on the midsection. Look. Here, here, and here are the places where we've found the most gold."

She knew Corey was angry as he said, *"That's all you've found? You need to look much harder!"*

Then Jeremy pulled a small glass bottle from his pocket and handed it to Corey. He said, "Here's the take for this past week."

Corey shook the bottle, brought it nearer his eyes, and peered at the contents. He scowled and walked past the giant safe. Brynn saw him tip one of the tom-tom drums on its side as he bent over and reached down. As Corey lifted an intricate-looking brass key from the drum's base, he told Jeremy, "You've got to do better."

After Corey unlocked and opened the safe, Brynn saw several beautifully gilded, black enameled shelves and inner drawers. She noticed the safe simultaneously embodied a sense of strength and elegance. However, she only saw four bottles inside the safe. Their size and shape were similar to the one Jeremy had just delivered.

When Corey and Jeremy rose to leave, Corey turned to Brynn, motioned to the room's decorations, and asked, "How do you like my office?"

She didn't quite know what to say because she felt the room pretentious and overbearing. Then, thinking quickly, she pointed to the sidewall and answered, "I am quite impressed with the craftsmanship on your drums and flutes. Do you play them, or are they just for decoration?"

He stepped closer, looked at her intently, and answered, "I am the Medicine Man for our tribe and beat the drums during our Pow Wows. You should join us at a Pow Wow someday."

She winced slightly and said, "Why yes, I hope Jeremy will introduce me to your tribe members. I can smell the aroma of seared beef in the air. Could it be that dinner is ready?"

Corey leered at her again, saying, "Yes, I smell a juicy steak cooking. I'm hungry."

~~~~~

Elena welcomed them to the dining room, where a hearty, New England-style dinner awaited them. They had all worked a busy week and were primed for a full dinner. Jeremy toiled at the goldfield, Corey met with several business owners to tout the company, Elena sold a record number of shares of company stock, and Brynn attended school and practiced for the recital.

After Corey blessed the food and helped himself to the largest steak, he passed the platter to Elena. He turned to Brynn and said, "We're pleased you could join us for dinner. Jeremy can attest that our typical Friday evening dinner is a simple meat and potatoes affair."

Brynn sensed Corey's lack of appreciation for his wife's fine meal and responded, "Yes, most people think of a dinner as a simple exercise in consuming food. However, if you think about it, there is much more to it. I can see that Elena has prepared and served us a delicious montage of steak, mashed potatoes, Brussels sprouts, applesauce, and biscuits this evening. I view the dinner she served as a personal expression of her exquisite culinary skills."

She continued, "Are you aware there are over 100 varieties of potatoes, 1,000 varieties of apples, and more than a hundred varieties of Brussels sprouts? She has chosen the best-tasting applesauce, the most tender potatoes for the mashed potatoes, and the freshest Brussels sprouts. You should compliment Elena's creative ability and skill in offering such a fine dinner."

Corey was taken aback at Brynn's offensive comments and took them as a personal affront. He answered, "So, Miss Dunham, it sounds like you've learned quite a bit about culinary arts. Did you learn this in a homemaking class at the Free Academy?"

Brynn was pleased to sense his displeasure but was unwilling to back down. Angrily, yet politely, she answered, "No. I'm mostly interested in gardening and have learned much from my mother. If you have looked across the street to our backyard, I'm sure you noticed our garden and greenhouse."

Brynn removed one of the many rosebuds from her hair arrangement, pointed it toward Corey, and said, "My mother and I have grown roses like this one for several years. As you may or may not know, almost all roses bloom in June or July, yet it is now November, almost Thanksgiving. So, you can see that I have learned to develop and cultivate roses in a controlled environment that extends the growing season. That is why I can provide hair corsages to the girls in our choir."

After Brynn pulled the rosebud, a single strand of her curled blond hair draped over her left eyebrow. Corey could barely contain his thoughts. He had never been taunted by a young woman such as Brynn. She had no respect for her elders. He was about to lash out when Elena came to his rescue and said, "Brynn, those are beautiful rosebuds. I'm impressed with your floral arrangement skills. What inspired you to begin growing roses?"

Brynn smiled and replied, "Emeline Norton, my next-door neighbor, and I have been close friends for our entire lives. When we were kids, we spent hours in her father's greenhouse. He grew several varieties of roses, and we used them to pretend we were princesses."

She continued, "Roses and other flowers have always made me feel special."

Elena said, "Have you ever considered learning the science of flower growth via a formal education? Perhaps you could become a florist or botanist someday."

Brynn answered, "Well, it's interesting that you should ask. Yes, I have. Miss Porter's School, a prominent finishing school for girls in Farmington, Connecticut, has accepted me into their program. In addition to primary study areas, such as reading, writing, and arithmetic, Miss Porter's School offers several focus areas, such as botany. So, I'll learn everything possible about growing and cultivating plants. And upon graduation, I plan to open a new florist shop in Norwich."

Elena remarked, "I've heard of the school. Several girls in our tribe applied for admission. However, the school only accepted one. But she couldn't enroll because her parents couldn't afford the tuition."

Brynn answered, "Yes. Unfortunately, I'm all too familiar with that problem. I'd hoped to become a student there last year. But, the cost was too expensive for my parents. However, now they will be able to pay the tuition, room, and board using profits from your company's stock. My family and I are so thankful that you discovered the gold and have opened the company to private citizens."

Elena responded, "Oh, Brynn, I'm so happy for you. And I'm so happy that we're able to help you. Corey tells me that the company is doing extraordinarily well."

By the end of dinner, Brynn felt much better about her parents' investment. Mrs. Pallaton had eased her worries and concerns. Elena had such a pleasant manner, and Brynn knew she could trust her. So, as they were finishing dinner, Brynn smiled and said to Elena, "Thank you very much for dinner. And your applesauce was the best I've ever had. I also think that you chose your apples wisely."

After seeing how Corey spoke to Jeremy, dismissed his wife, and how he had looked at her, Brynn did not trust Corey.

26: RECITAL
NORWICHTOWN
NORWICH FREE ACADEMY: BROADWAY
FRIDAY, NOVEMBER 12, 1858

After Brynn and Jeremy finished dinner, they left the Pallaton's home and strolled through Williams Park to the entrance of the Norwich Free Academy. It was a short walk, but Jeremy and Brynn were happy to be outside in the fresh air and on their way to the choir recital. Brynn was looking forward to performing, and Jeremy was pleased to be alone with her.

He wrapped Brynn's shawl tighter around her shoulders and asked, "Are you looking forward to the recital?"

She answered, "Well, of course. We've been practicing for the past eight weeks and are now ready to show everyone what we can do. I'm sure my parents are already there. They'll most likely be in the front row."

Jeremy said, "I've never been in the building. So, I'm looking forward to seeing it and hearing from you."

Brynn replied, "You're not alone. The good citizens of our city opened the Free Academy only four years ago. I'm a member of their third class of students. Norwich is lucky to have such an exceptional school."

She continued, "Generous gifts from local citizens entirely bore the cost of the school. Lydia Stedman and Emeline

Norton's fathers were incorporators who donated substantial sums. As the name suggests, the school is tuition-free and was founded on removing political pressures and serving every student, cost-free, regardless of race, gender, or class. Reverend John P. Gulliver formulated the whole idea for the school. This evening, he will present the opening prayer. If you'd like, I can introduce you."

Jeremy had zero interest in meeting the good Reverend. He was here for Brynn. He politely said, "No, thank you, but I'd like to meet your mother. I already met your father at the Jubilee planning meeting. I want to get to know him better."

She replied, "My mother wants to meet you also. Father was impressed at how quickly you learned to play billiards. You made a good first impression on him."

As they entered, Jeremy felt as though he were passing through the gates of city hall. The school had decorated the walls with portraits of several original donors and a massive landscape featuring Norwich's bustling harbor and lush countryside. The Free Academy boasted six classrooms downstairs, an upstairs teacher's lounge, three upstairs classrooms, and a dual-purpose meeting room/auditorium upstairs. Brynn had earlier informed Jeremy that the distinguished architect, Mr. W.T. Hallett designed the Norwich Free Academy building.

Brynn escorted Jeremy to the upstairs auditorium and spotted her parents in the front row. She said, "Mother, I'd like you to meet Mr. Jeremy Pallawotuk. He's the vice president of the Wawecus Hill Gold, Silver, and Nickel Mining Company. And, Father, I believe you two have already met."

She looked around quickly and continued, "I'm sorry, but I must join the choir now. I'm sure you have much to discuss before the recital begins."

With that, Brynn hurried off. Mr. Dunham shook Jeremy's hand and said, "It's good to see you again, Jeremy. Brynn has told us many good things about you and your company. However, I'm surprised at how young you are to be the company's vice president. You didn't mention your company to me the other night."

Jeremy was slightly insulted and replied, "It's nice to see you again. Others have brought that to my attention as well. I am twenty years old but have worked closely with Mr. Pallaton my entire life. Before the mining company, I was his construction crew chief for homes we built on Laurel Hill."

He did not appreciate Dunham's remark about his age and continued, "I know you were the mayor of Norwich ten years ago, published a newspaper, was the town's postmaster, and was the treasurer of one of our local banks back then. Your resume is quite impressive; however, Brynn tells me that you spend much of your time tending to your family's rose garden nowadays. Do you find it difficult leading a less active life now?"

At first impression, Mr. Dunham thought Jeremy to be brusque and offensive. But, on second thought, perhaps the issue of age bothered Jeremy. He answered, "Why yes, our entire family enjoys cultivating roses."

Jeremy changed the course of the conversation, saying, "Brynn tells me you've invested in our company. I want to let you know that we're on a progressive, positive track. Mr. Pallaton runs the finances for the company, but I supervise all field operations. I also own the mineral rights to one of the more promising plots."

Brynn's mother joined in to cool the conversation and said, "I saw the corsage with the golden balls you gave Brynn at the Jubilee social. She said you found, processed, and made the jewelry yourself."

Jeremy lied again and replied, "Oh yes, that's just one of my many creations. I'm working on a golden hair clip for her now, but please don't tell her. I want it to be a surprise."

As the choir entered the auditorium, Caroline responded, "My lips are sealed. I'm sure she'll love it. We're hoping to finance a portion of her future education using profits from your company. Before the recital begins, would you please update us on your progress?"

Jeremy grinned broadly and said, "Well, Mr. Pallaton and I are keeping the successes of our company under wraps. We've told no one how well we're doing. Corey hasn't even told his wife. But I'll give you a hint. You will be pleased, and I suggest you continue on your path to prosperity."

The choir and its director settled in, and Jeremy's heart began to pound. Brynn was seated in the front row, the center of attention. He noticed that she appeared nervous.

Reverend Gulliver was seated to the left and behind a wooden podium. He rose, greeted the audience, offered the invocation, and said, "Now, I'd like to introduce the Free Acacdemy's most esteemed choir director."

He paused, chuckled aloud, and said, "Yes, I'm sure you're all aware, he's also the First Congregational Church's choir director. But he joined us to direct the Free Academy's extraordinary choir this evening. So, please join me in welcoming the righteous Aaron Stevens."

The audience applauded Mr. Stevens as he stood to begin the recital. Stevens motioned the choir and the audience to rise, saying, "Everyone, please stand and join us in singing the 'Star Spangled Banner.'"

Everyone loved the anthem because it evoked intense patriotism and unity among Americans. As a result, many believed it should become the United States national anthem. Instead, tonight, it simply signaled the beginning of the recital.

Throughout the evening, the choir sang one song after another, and the choir's friends and families were incredibly proud.

Later, Mr. Stevens turned to the audience and announced, "Everyone, I want you to know that the choir, which stands before you, is the most talented I've ever directed. But, of course, that is not to say that my church choir is not talented."

He stopped as everyone laughed politely and continued, "The ushers are now passing out music sheets. Please, everyone, take a moment to stop and consider everything you are grateful for. Thanksgiving Day is approaching, and I want you to join our choir in this hymn of thanksgiving. Please stand."

The audience stood and began singing:

ALL CREATURES OF OUR GOD & KING

All creatures of our God and King,
Lift up your voice, and with us sing,
Alleluia! Alleluia!
Thou burning sun with golden beam,
Thou silver moon with softer gleam,
Alleluia! Alleluia!

The moment evoked a feeling of peace, harmony, and goodwill among all.

After the recital, John, Caroline, Brynn, and Jeremy returned to the Dunham residence. Brynn asked Caroline, "Mother. Is it okay for Jeremy and me to chat briefly outside?"

Caroline replied, "Sure, we'll be right here inside."

Brynn took Jeremy by the hand and led him to the backyard. She said, "This has been such an enjoyable evening. Thank you for joining me at dinner and listening to the recital."

Once again, Jeremy's heart was pounding. The air was cool, but he was warm. He looked around and said, "You've got a very nice garden here. Do you grow both vegetables and roses?"

She looked at him, smiled, reached to the top of her hair, and removed a rosebud. Then, she said, "I do grow vegetables, but I like rosebuds the best."

Brynn stepped near him, almost into his arms, slowly brought one of the buds to his nose, and said, "How do you like the scent of this one?"

Jeremy was mesmerized. He wanted to breathe all of her into him. He stepped closer, and just as he leaned in to kiss her, Brynn laughed lightly and pulled away from him quickly. She tousled her head so that her beautiful golden hair flowed freely down her shoulders and breasts. But Brynn didn't stop there. She skipped over to the rope and wooden chair swing, sat down, and commanded, "Swing me."

Jeremy immediately answered her call. He came up behind her and began pushing the swing back and forth at a slow, rhythmic pace. After a minute, Jeremy felt his body stiffen all over. He stopped the swing and came up close behind her. He caught the scent of her perfume as he gently kissed the back of her neck just below her left ear.

Brynn leaned back, turned her head toward him, and whispered, "Don't you think it's a bit cold out here? I want to show you the roses in my greenhouse."

As they entered the greenhouse, the scent of fresh flowers, heated perfume, and Brynn's Weddington blouse overcame Jeremy. He placed his hands on her waist and pulled her close. He felt her soft body and firm breasts as he kissed her repeatedly. He wanted her, not only a taste. He wanted all of her, right here and right now.

As he began to massage her breasts gently, he felt Brynn squirm. But, he was not to be denied. Jeremy slid both hands into her hair and pressed her head to the back of the greenhouse. Then, as he pressed himself against her and placed his hand under her skirt, he began working his way to nirvana.

Brynn tried to pull away and said, "Jeremy, you need to slow things down. I'm not ready for this."

Jeremy pressed on. Using his left hand, he held her hands behind her back and touched her intimately with his free hand.

Brynn winced and loudly said, "No. Not yet. Stop. Please."

At that moment, Brynn's dog, Dexter, rushed out of the house and began yapping loudly. When he reached them, he growled and began gnawing at Jeremy's pant leg.

Jeremy couldn't believe that she had teased him and led him on. He was stunned. He scowled at Brynn, saying, "Keep your damn dog away from me!"

She yelled back, "Keep your frigging hands off me!"

27: Crossroads
Hardscrabble Hill
Company Office
Monday, November 15, 1858

Since childhood, Travis had dreamed of exploring the world and sailing the seven seas. So today, as he looked over Chelsea Landing and watched sailors load cargo on majestic ships, he couldn't help but think of his good fortune. His life as a whaling ship's navigator would soon begin. His future was bright due to his recently developed skills and a burgeoning friendship with Lydia.

He'd heard that General Williams and his partner, Captain Acor Barns, were funding a whaling expedition for the coming spring. Since Travis had learned to use precise measuring instruments from Corey and developed map drawing skills from Mr. Walling, he now had sufficient knowledge and experience to apply for the job. His life was at a crossroads.

Travis had mixed feelings as he neared the mining company's office. He was proud to have mapped the home lots for Corey's housing project but still planned to quit working for him. Travis felt pride while speaking with his friends and neighbors because he sensed their growing respect for him. He wanted to answer the call of adventure, but, on the other hand, he desired to deepen his relationship with Lydia.

When Travis entered the office, he was surprised that he didn't see Elena at the front desk and that Corey's back office door was closed. However, he heard voices from Corey's office and recognized Jeremy's light-colored leather jacket hanging near the front door. It seemed odd for Jeremy to meet with Corey so early on a Monday morning. Jeremy should be at the work site.

Travis could only understand bits and pieces of the conversation. However, he was sure they were discussing Jeremy's map of the Goldmine Brook area. To Travis, it sounded like they were updating Corey's copy of a map. The whole conversation had an ominous tone because it sounded like the search for gold was not going well.

Then Travis heard footsteps coming his way, and Jeremy said, "Good idea. We'll expand the search."

Just as Jeremy opened the door to leave Corey's office, Travis heard Corey say, "Don't tell Elena. And be sure to stop by Carroll's store this afternoon and purchase the barrels of black powder we discussed. Bring them here, and we'll store them at the site until needed. I don't want to arouse anyone's attention."

As he left Corey's office, Travis saw Jeremy rolling up a map and said, "Good morning, Jeremy. What brings you here?"

When Jeremy saw Travis sitting in the front office area, he paused, scowled, and said, "Heh, Gimpy. The better question is, 'What brings *you* here?' You should be at the site."

Travis stiffened and said, "You'll hear about it soon enough. I'm moving on."

Corey emerged from his office and said, "What's this I hear about you moving on?"

When Travis entered Corey's personal office, he saw Corey place a map into the top drawer of his desk and said, "Good morning, Mr. Pallaton. Well, that's what I came here to discuss."

He continued, "I want to thank you again for the opportunity to lead the survey team for your housing site. We finished the layout this past Friday. Here's the final map."

Travis unrolled his map on Corey's desk and pointed to it, saying, "Okay, you can see the outline for the twenty home lots here. They are all laid out on level one-acre lots. They have ready access to fresh water from Goldmine Brook, and I positioned them far from the rocky slopes where the rattlesnakes reside."

After Corey studied the map, he said, "You've done a good job Travis, and you should be proud of yourself."

Travis replied, "Thank you. As you and I discussed several weeks ago, I'm ready to change the direction of my life. I'll continue to work at Mr. Brand's whaling gun factory and for Mr. Walling's mapmaking company until spring. After that, I plan to become a navigator for General Williams's next whaling expedition."

Corey responded, "You'll do well. As I mentioned, you may still retain your mining rights on the plot I gave you."

Travis replied, "Thank you. I've searched my site carefully and have found a few stones that appear to contain gold. I was surprised there wasn't more. Has Jeremy found much?"

Corey answered, "Jeremy's group recently found a large cache of gold in and around the brook. He was just here to give me an update. I keep the official company map that shows where and how much gold we've found here in the office. It helps guide our exploration efforts."

Travis said, "I heard you mention something about barrels of black powder to Jeremy. Will you be blasting the area?"

He smiled and said, "Well, I'm certainly considering it. We're thinking about blasting into the hillside. We are a *mining* company, after all. It may be time to start building a mine shaft."

He continued, "We'll do the best job possible for our shareholders. We've already sold hundreds of shares, and our primary goal is to keep our shareholders happy."

As Travis left the office and climbed into Moshup's saddle, he thought, "Last month, Corey announced that his main goal was to make money for the company to donate to his tribe's affordable housing project."

However, Travis knew keeping shareholders happy was *not the same as making money for them.*

Travis thought it odd that the only two people who knew how much gold truly existed were Corey and Jeremy. He also wondered why they needed to blast since they had already found such an abundant supply of gold.

28: CONSEQUENCES
DOWNTOWN NORWICH
AURORA NEWSPAPER OFFICE: WATER STREET
TUESDAY, NOVEMBER 16, 1858

Lydia sat at her desk, concentrating on every brush stroke. She'd finished writing her weekly column for the Aurora and was now gilding a drawing for one of Mr. Henry Bill's illustrated Bibles.

Travis entered the office and said, "Hi, Lydia. We need to talk."

She looked up from her desk and responded, "Hello, Travis. I'm happy you stopped by. I've got something to show you."

Travis skipped over to her desk and said, "Wow! That's an amazing drawing. I've never seen an illustration like that in any Bible. What is it?"

Lydia looked up and grinned. She said, "Well, of course, you haven't. Mr. Bill's Bibles are unique, unlike any other. He makes them special by employing me to add hundreds of illustrations to help readers understand the stories. For example, this drawing shows Nisroch tending to the Tree of Life."

Now Travis smiled and said, "Okay. You've got my interest; tell me the story."

She began, "The tale teaches us about consequences. It's told in the book of 2 Kings, Chapter 19. Nisroch was a low-level angel who tended the Tree of Life in the Garden of Eden. This drawing shows Nisroch watering the tree. You can see a watering bucket in one hand and a pine cone in the other."

NISROCH

The King of Assyria, Sennacherib, and his army worshiped Nisroch. But, after they ransacked one city after another, the King and Nisroch believed they were more powerful than God himself.

As a result, Nisroch fell from grace and became Hell's Master of Cuisine. He became the personal chef of Beelzebub, the God of Gluttony.

Sennacherib and his army continued to attack others mercilessly. But, after King Sennacherib's army murdered many of God's people in Jerusalem, God sent an angel to restore balance. The angel killed 185,000 of Sennacherib's soldiers in a single evening.

After his devastating defeat in Jerusalem, King Sennacherib returned home. Soon after that, while worshiping Nisroch, he was murdered by two of his sons. A third son then took control of his kingdom. The price Sennacherib paid for killing God's people and worshipping a false god was death.

Lydia finished her story by saying, "I believe this story teaches us that severe consequences are the just reward for hurting other people."

Travis nodded his head in agreement. He smiled and said, "I agree. Thank you for relaying the story. I'm not planning on hurting anyone, and I'm certainly not going to cross you!."

She laughed and said, "You'd better not feed me to the snakes again because when I'm angry, bad things can happen."

Travis chuckled and continued, "By the way, your artwork is beautiful. How's the gold leaf that we found working out?"

Her right eyebrow rose, and Lydia answered, "That's what I wanted to share with you because it isn't working very well. I've tried to apply it to the drawing but can't get it to adhere to the page properly. Some of it is acceptable, but most is not. Its properties are unlike any gold I've ever used, so I believe most is fool's gold."

Travis nodded again and said, "I think you're right. Yesterday, when I went to the mining company's office to resign, I overheard portions of a discussion between Corey and Jeremy. It sounded like they'd only found a small amount of real gold. As a result, they are buying barrels of gunpowder. Corey told me they might begin blasting so they can build a mine shaft. They need to blast because they're not finding enough using conventional means. That's the only plausible reason I can think of."

The full weight of Travis's statement struck her. She gasped, "So, are they announcing this development to their investors? My parents bought a large number of shares in the company. Do you think Corey will find much more gold? Do you think investors will be able to get their money back? You've got me worried now."

Travis shook his head and said, "I know Corey won't share the information publicly. I heard him tell Jeremy to keep Elena in the dark. Since he's not telling Elena everything, I'm sure he's not telling anyone. So, I don't see how it will be possible for him to return any money to shareholders. I'm guessing that Corey believes they will find more gold when he blasts into the side of Wawecus Hill. Unfortunately, I think he's wrong."

Lydia replied, "Yes, I agree. We need to find out how much gold they've truly found, and if they're misleading everyone, we must do something about it."

Travis replied, "Yes. We do. But we must find indisputable evidence to prove his claim of abundant gold is false. Because if we try to expose him without evidence, he will tell everyone that we are liars. Unfortunately, most people will believe him instead of us because Corey has become a powerful, well-respected member of Norwich's elite class."

He continued, "I've thought about this for a while and realize it is difficult to prove that something doesn't exist. After all, someone could always say, *'Oh, you are wrong. The gold does exist. You simply don't see it at the moment. Perhaps it has been sold, or given away, or donated.'* Anyone with a vested interest would believe a lie such as this."

She scowled for a moment and said, "Yes. I see what you mean. Running an exposé in the Aurora would not convince anyone either. We've got to think of something else."

Travis said, "I have an idea, but it's risky."

Lydia perked up and said, "Okay, let's hear it."

He said, "Corey and Jeremy work together as a team. Jeremy maintains a map showing the exact location and quantity of gold and fool's gold that his team finds. Jeremy takes the map and the week's supply of processed gold to Corey's home every Friday. Then, Corey updated his copy of the map and placed the gold in his safe."

"Corey also keeps an updated copy of their *Found Gold* map in the company office on Hardscrabble Hill. I know this because I overheard Corey and Jeremy updating the map while they were in his office."

Travis continued, "We need to see how much gold they actually have. There's no way we could break into Corey's safe. But we could easily see the map in the company's office on Hardscrabble Hill. If the map shows nothing, we would take the map and publish a copy in the Aurora. But, if the map shows a reasonable amount of gold, we'd leave it there and go along our merry way."

Travis questioned, "How's that sound so far?"

Lydia grinned and said, "Well, Mr. Mathews, I think you've got a fine idea. The only problem is how to do it. I've been in the mining company's office, and it's a little scary. Corey's got guns in there. If he catches us, there will be severe consequences. Do you remember the story of severe consequences I told you earlier?"

She continued, "Furthermore, breaking in unnoticed would be difficult. The Hardscrabble Hill neighborhood is tranquil during the evening, and someone would likely notice us."

Now Travis grinned and said, "Yes, it is usually quiet there, and people probably would usually notice. But, no one would see us if there were a diversion."

Lydia looked confused and said, "That is a tall order, but I'm guessing you've got something in mind."

Travis smiled and exclaimed, "Of course I do. Happy Thanksgiving!! Every year, on Thanksgiving evening, the boys of Norwich set a barrel bonfire ablaze on Hardscrabble Hill. Last year, the bonfire was located very near Corey's office."

He continued, "When I was at the office yesterday, I saw where someone stored a dozen wooden barrels for next week's bonfire. Hundreds of people will be watching the bonfire on Thanksgiving evening. The whole area will be like a carnival, and I could easily sneak into the office and look at the map while you stand guard."

Lydia grinned from ear to ear and said, "That's a great idea! I'm sure that will work."

She stiffened and added, "I respect the lessons of the Old Testament because I know our forefathers passed them down to us for good reasons. There must be consequences for one's actions. If Corey is lying to everyone, he should pay for his transgressions."

29: FRIENDS HELPING FRIENDS
NORWICHTOWN
DUNHAM FAMILY RESIDENCE: WASHINGTON STREET
SATURDAY, NOVEMBER 20, 1858

Mary opened the front door of John Dunham's home and said, "Good afternoon, Mr. Stevens. Please come in. Miss Brynn and the girls are waiting for the others to arrive in the music room. Would you care to visit Mr. Dunham in the parlor while waiting?"

Aaron Stevens, the choir director of the First Congregational Church, stepped in and said, "Thank you. Yes, please show me to the parlor."

Mary led him down the center hallway and ushered him into a handsomely decorated room. Several arrowhead collections and a few Quinebaugan Native American-themed paintings adorned the walls. As the focus of attention, Dunham had placed several crude stone tools on a square oak table in the center of the room. The room's decor instantly made Stevens feel comfortable.

When he entered, Dunham stood and said, "Welcome, Aaron. It's good to see you. Brynn tells me that the choir's upcoming Christmas cantata is shaping up nicely."

Stevens replied, "Yes, it is, and thank you for allowing us to rehearse here. I hope that it's not an inconvenience."

Dunham answered, "Oh, not at all. We were happy to oblige when Brynn told me you needed a place to rehearse because of today's Thanksgiving bazaar at the church. Earlier this morning, my wife and Brynn stopped by the bazaar and brought home an assortment of cookies and loaves of bread. My family will surely appreciate them at next week's Thanksgiving dinner."

Aaron answered, "Thank you for supporting us. Our church will donate all the proceeds from the bazaar to the Norwich Almshouse. They help families in need year-round. The church supports the Almshouse in every way possible."

John Dunham's face lit up, and he said, "Yes. It's a wonderful organization. So many people need a helping hand during difficult periods of their life. The cause of their problem is usually by no fault of their own. For example, our two maids, Mary and Alvina, once lived in the Almshouse with their mother."

He continued, "Many visitors believe that we have enslaved Mary and Alvina, but nothing could be further from the truth. Their mother, Esther Rogers, is a full-blooded Pocawansett woman married to a formerly enslaved African American named Prince Beaumont. Esther and her husband lived peacefully for several years, but the marriage ended in a bitter divorce. As a result, she and her two daughters were abandoned and had no place to call home other than the Almshouse."

John Dunham continued, "As you know, several years ago, I served as mayor of Norwich. One day, during a professional visit to the Almshouse, I was introduced to Miss Rogers and her daughters. After I told my wife of their dire circumstances, she suggested a solution that would benefit everyone involved."

"Miss Rogers now lives with and works for General and Mrs. Williams. She tends to their home, and Mary and Alvina live here. Mary is our cook and helps in the garden. Her sister, Alvina, is our seamstress and keeps the house clean. They are like family to us. We have saved them from poverty, and they have helped our family in countless ways."

Aaron Stevens listened intently to every word the former mayor spoke. He'd heard of several other *live-in* situations similar to this in Norwich. He was skeptical. He thought, "Maybe those women are free, but perhaps they are not."

Stevens said, "My family staunchly opposes slavery. I'm glad that you're helping these young women. Hopefully, they will find a responsible young man someday and have their own family."

Dunham replied, "That is indeed my heart's deepest desire. Since their mother is a full-blooded Pocawansett, they and their mother are involved in many of their tribe's activities here in Norwich. I hope they will meet someone there and enjoy a free and abundant life. However, I pay Mary and Alvina a fair wage for their work."

Stevens replied, "That is a good plan. I hope the best for all of you. Family matters can certainly become difficult and muddied. I'm always concerned about the future and well-being of my son, Dwight. After moving to Norwich, Dwight worked for a local sawmill for a while. But, he was always getting into scuffles with his co-workers. I think Dwight was bored. He didn't seem to fit in with others. So, when he was sixteen, about ten years ago, he joined the Army. He wanted to fight against the transgressions of General Santa Anna out in New Mexico."

He continued, "In the last letter Dwight sent me, he said he'd joined up with an abolitionist named John Brown. Dwight is now his chief military aide. They are somewhere out in Kansas trying to free slaves. I'm happy that he believes in freedom for all, but I'm concerned for his safety."

Dunham replied, "Yes, I understand your concerns. I worry about Brynn every day now. She is a beautiful, open-minded young woman who is very emotional and sometimes too flirtatious. Nowadays, there are far too many ways for a girl to get into trouble."

Mary entered the room and said, "All the girls but Miss Emeline Norton are present. Would you like to begin rehearsal?"

Stevens replied, "It's still early. We can wait for her."

Mary replied, "Yes, sir. I'll let them know. Is there anything that I can bring you while you wait?"

Dunham answered, "Yes. Please bring us a pot of tea and a few cookies from this morning's bazaar."

As Mary left the room, Stevens looked around and said, "John, I can't help but notice your Quinebaugan decorations. For some reason, they seem to make me feel at home."

Dunham grinned and said, "Several gentlemen have told me the same thing. And there is a good reason for your feelings. I've made this room a tribute to the Quinebaugan tribe because they previously owned the land below this very room. So the arrowheads and tools you see here have remained in this exact location for more than 200 years."

He continued, "Major Ebenezer Whiting first built this house in 1790. He ran a distillery in Norwich and was an officer in the Revolutionary War. He was also a great-great-grandson of Governor William Bradford of the *Mayflower*. While digging the foundation, Major Whiting found the skeleton of a large Quinebaugan Native American, many arrowheads, and several crude stone tools. The Quinebaugans most likely used these tools to scrape and clean leather hides. Major Whiting preserved the artifacts, and they've been here since then."

Dunham finished by saying, "I'm quite proud of the collection."

Stevens nodded and replied, "You should be."

~~~~~

Brynn's membership in the First Congregational Church choir allowed her to become friends with several girls her age. She enjoyed choir practice and relished the choir's camaraderie.

Today, as usual, Brynn was the center of attention. Lydia Stedman questioned, "Brynn, your blouse is so pretty. I don't think I've ever seen a blouse with so many beautiful buttons. Did you make it?"

Brynn beamed and replied, "It is interesting that you'd ask. As you know, I love buttons. Our family's seamstress, Miss Alvina, showed me how to make them last year. It isn't that difficult once you learn how."

She continued, "Miss Alvina makes clothes for my mother and me. She's very talented. Last month, my father bought us a new sewing machine, and Miss Alvina used it to make the blouse I'm wearing."

She pointed to the corner of the room and said, "The machine is over there, in the corner."

The girls turned and gazed at the contraption, and Lydia said, "Oh. I read about this sewing machine just a few weeks ago. The Greenman & True Manufacturing Company, here in Norwich, fabricated the machine. Mr. Cyrus B. True is the inventor, and Mr. Jared F. Greenman is the businessman. They began producing the machines and opened their office on the Central

Wharf only three months ago. The article mentioned something unique about the machine but did not elaborate."

Brynn jumped in and said, "Alvina will know. Wait a moment, and I'll ask her to come and explain."

Brynn stuck her head out the door and shouted, "Alvina. Please come join us."

When she entered, Brynn said, "Everyone, this is Alvina. She lives here with us and is our seamstress."

Turning to Alvina, she said, "The girls wonder what is so special about this machine. Could you enlighten us?"

Alvina smiled and said, "Thank you, Miss Brynn. I'd be happy to. This machine incorporates a patent from two years ago, which better bonds two pieces of fabric. It uses two strands of thread, one from the top portion of the machine and the other from the bottom, to make a lockstitch. This machine locks the two threads together and connects the two pieces of cloth much stronger than most hand stitches."

The girls applauded, and Brynn was proud of Alvina's display of her knowledge. Brynn said, "Thank you, Alvina. That was most interesting."

After Alvina left the music room, one of the choir girls said, "Brynn. She is the most well-educated slave that I've ever seen. You must be happy to have her."

Brynn was taken aback, "*No. No. No.* Alvina is not enslaved. Yes, her skin is dark, but she's no slave. Alvina is half Pocawansett and half African American. After her parents divorced, she needed a place to live, and my parents offered her a job here. My family supplies room and board, and Alvina sews and cleans our house. It is a convenient arrangement that works for all."

The irritated girl responded, "Sounds good in theory, but it sounds like slavery to me."

Brynn's temper flared, and she said, "You don't understand!"

At that moment, Emeline Norton and Aaron Stevens entered the room. Mr. Stevens said, "Good afternoon, everyone. First, I'd like to thank Miss Norton for finally gracing us with her presence."

Emeline blushed, the girls giggled, and Mr. Stevens continued, "Seriously, I'd like to thank you all for such a wonderful performance at last week's Free Academy recital. You sounded and looked great. I was proud of you. The audience could hear and see all the effort that you put forth."

He continued, "Tomorrow, our featured song will be 'All Creatures of Our God and King.' As a warm-up, we'll rehearse it first. But today's practice will focus on next month's Christmas cantata. I've collected several traditional hymns that everyone knows and loves and a couple of beautiful new melodies."

He said, "Let's start by learning the new Christmas hymn, 'O Holy Night.'"

Mr. Stevens sat at the piano, played, and sang it for them. After waiting a moment, he said, "I love this hymn. It sounds heavenly and has an interesting history as well. Near the end of 1843, in a small French town, there was a church whose organ had recently been renovated. To celebrate the newly renovated organ, the parish priest persuaded a local poet, Placide Cappeau, to write a Christmas poem. Soon afterward, a French composer, Adolphe Adam, added music to the poem. However, after they played the hymn, the French government learned that the poet was a socialist, so they banned it. The English translation of 'O

Holy Night' was only written three years ago by Mr. John S. Dwight of Boston, Massachusetts."

The choir gleefully learned the new Christmas hymn for the next hour and relearned several traditional melodies. By the end of their rehearsal, Brynn, Lydia, Emeline, and the rest of the choir felt more connected through the music. In addition, they knew the church's congregation would appreciate the Christmas cantata.

After Alvina served tea and cookies, the girls chattered about the new hymn, the upcoming Thanksgiving Day events, and Brynn's new sewing machine. The girls were all experts in the fine art of embroidery and were anxious to learn how to sew using a machine. There was a feeling of optimism and good cheer among all.

As the choir girls left Dunham's home, Lydia motioned Brynn aside and said, "If you've got a moment, I'd like to speak with you privately."

They returned to the music room, and Brynn questioned, "What's on your mind?"

Lydia smiled and said, "Well, it is a delicate matter, but I want to share a few things I've learned about Jeremy."

Brynn's skin immediately prickled. She had mixed feelings for Jeremy. Brynn felt drawn to him, yet she was intimidated by him. He was three years older, had much more experience than her, and was significantly more confident. She knew that many boys and young men were attracted to her. But, somehow, it seemed as though Jeremy was different. She had a deep, primal attraction to him.

Brynn bristled and said, "What do you think you've learned about him?"

Lydia responded, "As you know, I've gilded illustrations for Mr. Henry Bill's bibles for a while now. I tried using some of the gold powder Travis found near Goldmine Brook a few days ago. Unfortunately, I couldn't get it to stick to the paper correctly, and it has a different color than my regular gold flakes. I'm almost sure the material is iron pyrite, not real gold."

Brynn responded, "How was the gold extracted from the stones? Maybe it wasn't processed correctly."

Lydia answered, "Travis broke up the rocks with a mallet and ground the gold-colored material into powder."

Brynn said, "Well, I'm sure he doesn't have much experience processing gold. Jeremy is an expert. What does this have to do with Bear?"

Lydia answered, "Travis has worked with Jeremy at the Goldmine Brook site for several months. He is sure that Jeremy's team of miners hasn't found much real gold. He thinks that almost all of it is fool's gold. Nevertheless, Jeremy and Corey are telling everyone they've found large quantities of precious minerals and that everyone should buy shares in the company. I believe your parents have even bought shares. I'm just trying to warn you. You're a good friend, and I want to help you."

Brynn answered, "Lydia, you've been my friend for years, and you should know by now that I don't need your help. Jeremy is honest and hard-working, and I don't need your advice."

Lydia answered, "Brynn, please. I'm only trying to help. Please remember, he kicked at Dexter, whipped his horse during the race, and only last week, and you told me how he pressed you against the garden house's shed. I'm worried about you. I don't trust him."

Brynn said, "Well, it wasn't completely his fault. I like him a lot and might have teased him a bit too much that night. He responded like any other healthy young man. When I told him no, he stopped. In fact, the next day, he brought me a new silk handkerchief and apologized profusely. Jeremy told me that my perfume and beauty got the best of him. He promised to behave in a more gentlemanly fashion in the future."

Lydia responded, "Well, I hope so. I cherish your friendship. Please don't let Jeremy come between us."

Brynn hugged her and said, "Lydia, I know you've got my best interests at heart, but please, back off. I know what I'm doing."

30: BARREL BONFIRE
HARDSCRABBLE HILL
THURSDAY, NOVEMBER 25, 1858
THANKSGIVING EVENING

Travis felt time stand still as he held Lydia close and gazed at Chelsea Harbor and the valley below. He remembered the past, was anxious for today's present, and considered their future as a couple.

He said, "This has been the best Thanksgiving ever. Your parents were so kind to invite me for dessert this afternoon. And I loved your mother's mincemeat pie. I must admit that it was a first for me. Before today, I didn't realize there's no meat in a mincemeat pie."

Lydia giggled and said, "Well, for your information, many years ago, cooks made them with chopped venison or beef. But they stopped using real meat a long time ago. Today, bakers use apples, figs, or prunes as the primary ingredients. My mother's special recipe includes walnuts. Many uninformed people are missing out on this baked delight!"

As darkness enveloped the valley below, Travis felt the warmth of Lydia's body and the crowd's anticipation. More than a hundred people gathered for the event. The group stood before them, ready to experience another Thanksgiving barrel bonfire celebration.

Over the past several weeks, Travis watched as boys around town collected empty barrels, long wooden poles, and tar. He knew and understood the thoughts of those teenagers because, when he was younger, he, too, had been a bonfire boy. It was great fun stacking dozens of barrels, slathering them with tar, standing them on end, and finally lighting them up. He thought, "It would surely be fun to be a kid for just one more night."

Travis said, "Look. Look over to Laurel Hill. The boys have lit the first bonfire."

She replied, "They just fired up another one on Lucas Hill. This is so exciting! Last year, they only had two bonfires here on Hardscrabble Hill. They've added a third this year, and it will be the largest illumination the town has ever seen."

Travis's anticipation grew as the boys finished arranging the tinder around the base of the farthest pole from them. He was anxious for the celebration to begin so he and Lydia could initiate their plan. It would be risky, but Travis knew they would determine if Jeremy and Corey had misled everyone by night's end.

With their backs to the office, Travis and Lydia saw the nearest pole about fifty feet away, stacked with barrels. He knew he could quickly slip unnoticed into the office when the crowd turned its attention to the bonfires.

Everyone cheered gleefully as the boys set the first and second sets of barrels ablaze. Then, several bystanders donned their masks. The boys now surrounded the pole directly in front of them. Travis heard the crackling tinder, smelled the smoke, and saw the stack of barrels spark to life. By now, several hundred on-lookers had congregated.

Lydia said, "This is a sight to behold! Look at everyone. They are all so excited!"

Travis replied, "Yes. It is an amazing sight, but it's hard to say if everyone looks happy because I can't see many faces due to their masks. Why are they wearing those silly masks?"

Lydia said, "Oh, I thought everyone knew. When Europeans first came to America, they brought their Thanksgiving Day traditions. In 1605, a fellow named Guy Fawkes organized a group of men who plotted to blow up the Houses of Parliament and kill Great Britain's King James. They wanted to protest their government's opposition to Catholicism."

"The plan failed when a party of the king's men found thirty-six barrels of gunpowder and Guy Fawkes, with matches in his pocket, in a room beneath the Houses of Parliament. Fawkes and his co-conspirators were all found guilty of high treason and sentenced to death in January 1606."

She continued, "Many Londoners supported their king, his anti-Catholic beliefs, and the sovereignty of the established government. So, to celebrate the king's safety, they took to the streets and began lighting bonfires throughout the city. The next year, the Parliament designated November 5 as Guy Fawkes Day, an annual day of thanksgiving."

Lydia finished her history lesson by saying, "Many years later, supporters of Guy Fawkes, i.e., protestors of the established government, began wearing Guy Fawkes masks, such as you see here tonight. So, the burning bonfires symbolize government support, and the masks symbolize protest against the government. So I think it interesting that a single event can simultaneously show two opposing viewpoints."

Travis said, "Thanks for the explanation. Your story is interesting, but the fire is getting hot."

Lydia replied, "Yes. Look. Everyone is backing away from the bonfires. They've got their backs turned now. I'll stay here and watch out for you. Go. Now!"

Travis's heart leaped as he sprinted toward the Pallaton company office's front door. As expected, someone had locked the door. So, he quickly searched the area to see if Corey or Elena might have hidden a key in a conspicuous place. But, no such luck. Travis resorted to using the screwdriver he brought to jimmy the door.

Before entering, he glanced back to see Lydia standing guard. She was wearing her mask. If it weren't for the tense situation, he would have laughed at the sight of Lydia, a petite, pretty young woman wearing the hideous Guy Fawkes mask.

All other heads were turned away from the office and toward the bonfire. After a second surge of adrenaline, Travis was in the office, staring at Elena's desk. The bonfire illuminated the office, and Travis felt its heat radiating through the walls.

However, the room looked different than usual to Travis. It was filled with supplies for the mining operation. It was apparent that Corey had recently bought extra picks, shovels, food, and other equipment. He also saw two barrels of black powder next to the back wall. Travis thought, "Corey is following through on his plan to blast the mining site."

After he entered Corey's inner office, he found the top drawer unlocked. Travis was grateful for the small piece of luck because he knew that time was of the essence. He opened the drawer and thought, "Thank God. It's here."

Corey's office was well-lit by the bonfire's flame shining through a window. After unrolling the map on Corey's desk and a minute's review, all his deepest concerns came true. Corey had marked the map with an **O** for areas where his team had found gold and an **X** for those containing fool's gold. *Twenty-eight* spots were marked with an **X**, and only **two** were marked with an **O**. He could hardly believe it. The situation was far worse than Travis had imagined.

He was sweating profusely due to the room's intense heat and growing anger.

~~~~~

Meanwhile, Lydia was patiently standing guard when a young couple approached her. She didn't recognize them at first because they were also wearing masks. Brynn Dunham removed her mask as they neared and said, "Heh, Lydia. That's you. Right?"

Lydia was stunned when she saw Brynn and Jeremy standing next to her. They had seemingly appeared out of nowhere. She thought, "What can I say? *I must turn their attention away from the office.*"

She said, "Hi, Brynn. Hi, Jeremy. I'm surprised to see you. Isn't this the best celebration ever?"

Brynn replied, "Yes. I've never seen three bonfires here. In past years, it was always two."

Lydia pointed at the nearest bonfire and replied, "Yes, and this one is getting extremely hot because it's so close. Let's join the rest of the crowd. It will be cooler over there."

Brynn said, "Okay. Let's go."

Lydia's heart sank when she saw Jeremy remove his mask and look back directly at the office.

Jeremy said, "I saw you here with Travis a few minutes ago. Where is he now?"

Lydia pointed to the bonfires in the distance and said, "I believe he joined his parents at the other bonfire. Let's go find him."

Jeremy's face tightened, pushing Lydia aside, "You're lying! I see the office's door is open!"

Jeremy brushed Lydia aside, burst into the office, and instantly found Travis staring at the map. Jeremy yelled, "What the hell are you doing?"

Enraged, Travis glared at Jeremy and yelled, "You've been lying to us! You've only found gold in two places."

Jeremy pounced on Travis, throwing him to the floor. He pinned Travis to the floor and backhanded Travis's face several times before pounding his fists into his stomach. Travis gasped for air while Jeremy continued the onslaught. Jeremy's quick, agile body was too much for Travis's slow, uncoordinated, lumbering frame.

Jeremy momentarily stopped the beating and said, "You're right, Gimpy! There's not so much gold, but that's not your problem. Corey and I are dealing with it. You need to keep your mouth shut!"

By that time, Travis had regained his breath and his composure. Jeremy was faster than Travis but not larger or stronger. Travis reached up with his extra-long right arm and grabbed Jeremy's throat. His fingers closed in on his neck like a vice.

Keeping his grip tight, Travis stood up, shoved Jeremy next to the office's window, and said, "You will pay dearly for your lies and deception!"

Mayhem exploded as the words left his mouth. Glass shattered around them. Two of the office's windows broke, and a large portion of the roof caved in. Travis immediately released his grip and fell backward as a fiery barrel of terror flew into the office through the roof. Travis got up and hurried out of Corey's office. As he was about to leave the building, he turned and looked back in horror.

A fallen roof rafter pinned Jeremy to the floor. Travis saw a tarred, burning barrel of death from the bonfire lying next to one of Corey's barrels of black powder. Travis was hurt slightly, had difficulty breathing, and feared for his life. However, he did not hesitate because he knew the barrel of black powder could easily explode.

He ran back into the office to save Jeremy. Unfortunately, large ceiling remnants were piled on Jeremy's left forearm. His arm was burning out of control, and Travis smelled the stench of burning flesh. The weight was too much to bear for Jeremy alone, but with the help of Travis's giant body and enormous strength, he freed Jeremy from certain death.

Travis lifted Jeremy and dragged him toward the office's front door. By now, the heat was almost unbearable, and Travis could see sparks dancing on the top rim of the powder keg. Travis knew they only had a few moments before pending disaster. He was dazed, and the smoke was so thick that he had no sense of direction. Finally, he thought, "Where's the outside door?"

He heard Lydia and Brynn screaming, "Hurry, hurry. Get out of there!"

Led by the sound of their screams, Travis and his severely disabled cargo made it past the door's threshold. Travis breathed a sigh of relief when Lydia and Brynn helped him pull Jeremy from the fiery office.

After they made it to a safe distance, Brynn saw the gruesome damage done to Jeremy's body. The collapsed ceiling had crushed his left hand, and his left forearm was charred to a blackened crisp. It was clear to all that someone would have to amputate his left forearm below the elbow. Brynn knew that her and Jeremy's life would never again be the same.

She burst into tears and looked at Travis. She sobbed, "What have you done to him? You almost killed him. I hate you!"

Jeremy was barely conscious but glared a look of hatred at Travis.

Suddenly, all four heard and felt an enormous boom of thunder emanating from the office. Their ears were deafened, and they immediately distanced themselves even further from the office. An instant later, a second boom echoed through the air.

They were shocked when they looked in the direction of the office. The office no longer existed. Only an ominous rectangular-shaped area of scorched earth remained.

31: COMPANY MEETING
DOWNTOWN NORWICH
OTIS LIBRARY: UNION SQUARE
FRIDAY, DECEMBER 10, 1858

Norwich's first winter snow usually marked the end of a seemingly endless, back-breaking summer and fall of tending crops and animals. The Christmas season provided a much-needed period for locals to spend with their friends and families. Last night's storm left a beautiful four-inch blanket of snow throughout New London County.

However, the snow was yet another obstacle for Corey to overcome. He needed as many shareholders as possible to attend today's meeting. He would face them and try to settle their anxieties due to the fire. Corey and Elena were still reeling from losing their office on Hardscrabble Hill. They had been forced to cease all company operations because the reorganization effort had consumed all their time and energy.

Even the seemingly straightforward task of planning, organizing, and advertising a shareholder meeting became difficult. Elena had first tried to reserve a large meeting room in Lucas Hall for the meeting. The building, conveniently located in the heart of Norwich, would be an ideal meeting spot. But, the Independent Order of Odd Fellows, Lucas Lodge No. 11, had already booked the meeting room for every possible date on Elena's calendar. So she had to settle for the second floor of Otis Library. It was a smaller, less elegant venue, but it would suffice.

Deacon Joseph Otis, a retired Norwich merchant, erected the building and founded the library eight years earlier. He purchased its first books and provided a generous endowment in his will to continue its operation. The downstairs portion of the building housed the library, and the second floor provided a space for a vast, prestigious pastor's study. Today, Corey would use the pastor's study for his meeting. Otis had agreed to allow the use of his building for the price of one share of the gold mining company stock.

The morning snow would not deter wealthy local investors like General William Williams and his wife. However, most of the shareholders were farmers living on Norwich's outskirts. Four inches of snow would make it difficult for them to travel to the meeting. In addition, Corey knew he needed favorable public opinion within the ranks of the commoners. More than half of the private investors only owned a single share.

The meeting was set for 10:00. By 9:30, Elena, Jeremy, Bowie, and Crockett had the room prepared. Jeremy and his friends positioned the podium and placed two long tables next to the speaker's stand, a refreshment table, and sixty chairs. Jeremy knew the small space would force the audience to sit in tight quarters, but given the circumstances, it was the best he could do.

Elena set out coffee and an appealing array of baked goods in the front of the room. One of the bakeries in Norwich had recently learned how to make *balls of sweetened dough, fried in hog's fat* (a.k.a. doughnuts), as described in Washington Irving's book,

'A History of New York.' Elena thought the shareholders would enjoy the experience of eating a novel treat.

By 9:50, a broad cross-section of anxious investors occupied every chair in the room. Several stood in the overflow area near the back of the room. The sweet aroma of doughnuts helped calm the atmosphere within the room, but everyone still felt the tension.

As Corey surveyed the room, he marveled at the diversity of his shareholders. He saw farmers, local businessmen, bankers, and clergy. Reverend Hiram P. Arms, who represented the heart and soul of the First Congregational Church, sat in the front row, munching on a donut. And, of course, several of Norwich's elite civic and political leaders were scattered amongst the audience. Even the town's constable, the honorable Benjamin Durfey, and his lovely wife were settled in among his Pocawansett brethren in the back few rows of chairs.

Corey understood the stakes of today's meeting and expected that all would go well. Even though he sensed the audience's anxiety, he was personal friends with many attendees. He believed they would trust his words and judgment.

Several members of the Quinebaugan tribe sat in the front few rows. Corey thought it was fitting that he and his fellow Pocawansett tribesmen had sold shares of a gold mining company to present-day Quinebaugans on land previously occupied by their Quinebaugan ancestors. He spotted Travis Mathews sitting in the middle of several Quinebaugan investors. Corey knew that Travis was skeptical of the company's potential and hoped that he would keep his mouth shut and not cause any trouble.

Like everyone else, Travis was anxious to hear what Corey had to say. After the disastrous fire, Travis had privately met with the Quinebaugan investors. He shared his concerns about Corey's inability to find any substantial cache of gold, silver, or any other precious minerals. Although most Quinebaugan farmers only held one share each, Travis felt responsible for his fellow tribe members' investments. He'd personally shared the news of his discovery with them and did not want to lose their trust.

Upon Travis's advice, the Quinebaugan contingent attended the meeting today in hopes of finding a way to sell their shares back to the company. In addition, they wanted to minimize any future financial loss.

Travis disdained the idea of Corey misleading the public and held deep contempt for Jeremy. But he was proud that he had saved Jeremy's life and would do it again without hesitation. Travis hoped that Corey could see beyond their sharp differences. And on a personal, emotional level, he hoped Corey would publicly show appreciation for his heroic feat.

Brynn and her parents, who had invested heavily in the company, were seated in the third row. The Dunhams wanted to hear how the mining company planned to recover from the fire. Brynn's mother's concerns were comforted after she had spoken briefly with Elena earlier in the week.

Mary Dunham and her husband were working out how to pay for next fall's semester at Brynn's private school. They expected their shares in the mining company to cover the lion's share of the coming bill. John Dunham, a former mayor, was also worried about his reputation because many still looked to him for guidance in personal and financial matters.

Lydia and her parents were seated in the second row, just behind Travis and his family. Lydia had previously shared her concerns about the company's shortcomings with her family. Their financial stake in the company was small, but their family reputation, as with John Dunham, also mattered.

Most people in Norwich read and trusted the content of John and Lydia's newspaper. Over the past several months, they ran many advertisements and published encouraging news about the mining company. Townspeople relied on the Aurora for accurate and trustworthy information and opinions. Thus, Mr. Stedman and Lydia needed to listen carefully and observe how Corey Pallaton would publicly address investors today. If there were to be future exposés of the company, the descriptions would need to be accurate.

Jeremy sat at the front table alongside Elena and Corey. The office's burning rafters had consumed his left forearm and hand. The heat of the fire permanently disfigured his face and forced him to relearn how to accomplish simple, routine daily tasks. Setting up the podium, tables, and chairs using only one arm was difficult for him, and he hated that he had to rely on help from his friends. He would forever blame Travis Mathews for his disfigurement.

As Corey rose to address the assembly, Elena nervously collected and reorganized the reports she was about to present. She was the company's secretary, bookkeeper, treasurer, and accountant; however, Corey had supplied nearly all financial and gold inventory data.

Corey began, "Thank you for attending today's special shareholder meeting of the Wawecus Hill Gold, Silver, and Nickel Mining Company. I appreciate you making the journey through the snow and hope the trip was enjoyable. The first snow of the year is always beautiful, and I hope Mother Nature will bless us with a white Christmas."

He continued, "I know you have concerns about the well-being of your investments after the loss of our office. As you might expect, we are planning to rebuild. I've already contracted with an architect to design a new, more fitting office building for us. When owners like yourselves enter the new office this spring, you will be able to *feel* the profitability of our company through its luxurious accommodations. The initial plans that I've seen first-hand are remarkable."

"Now, I'd like to turn the meeting over to our secretary and treasurer, Mrs. Elena Pallaton. She will give you an update on the status of your company."

Elena stood and walked to the podium. She smiled coyly and wiped her brow with a dainty white lace handkerchief. The overcrowded room was heating up quickly because everyone held their overcoats, hats, and mittens on their laps.

She began, "Since the fire a couple of weeks ago, we have focused all our efforts on rebounding from this tragedy. I am happy to report that the company is in excellent financial condition, and I want to read the secretary and treasurer reports."

~~~~~

SECRETARY'S REPORT
(AS OF DECEMBER 10, 1858)

- Operations:
  - Discovered gold and began prospecting: 08/17/1858
  - Filed to become an investor-owned company: 08/29/1858
  - Began issuing company stock: 09/03/1858
  - Received a $5,000 loan for mining equipment and field office construction: 10/08/1858
  - Completed building field office: 10/25/1858
- Stock:
  - 500 shares of company stock were issued with a par value of $25.00 per share
  - 400 shares have been sold to a total of 40 investors
  - Only 100 shares remain available for purchase
  - Employees: president, vice president, secretary-treasurer, and 7 laborers

TREASURER'S REPORT
(AS OF DECEMBER 10, 1858)

- Assets:
  - Field office and furnishings
  - On-site mining equipment
  - 200 oz of gold, stored at a safe, off-site location
  - Checking account: $8,000.00
- Liabilities:
  - Bank loan balance: $2,000.00
  - Weekly payroll: Paid up

After reading the reports, Elena sat, and Corey rose to the podium.

He said, "We discovered gold on Wawecus Hill four months ago. During this short period of our company's existence, he hesitated. No, not our company, rather *our family* has experienced both jubilation and tragedy. I regard you, our company shareholders, as family members."

"I want to repeat one important detail Elena just reported. We have discovered and processed more than 200 ounces of gold. Our company is in excellent shape!"

He continued, "However, at this point, we have suspended all operations at the field site. The frozen ground and snow have made it unprofitable to continue prospecting for the remainder of this winter. We will renew our mining efforts early next spring."

"We're exploring different avenues for selling the gold we have on hand. At the moment, I'm working with two buyers in Boston who have shown great interest. The price of gold fluctuates daily, and my investment advisors are assessing when and to whom to sell our product. Once we've vetted the potential buyers and determined the optimal time to sell, we will reap the benefits of our labor. And, you will share in our profits via dividends."

He smiled and continued, "As Elena mentioned, we still have 100 publicly available shares for sale. Please remember that Christmas is just around the corner, and I might suggest that one share of stock in our company would make someone a generous gift."

"The Wawecus Hill Gold, Silver, and Nickel Mining Co. has a policy of supporting the local Pocawansett tribe. We currently support them by offering good-paying jobs. In the future, we plan to share a small portion of the profits to help pay for a low-income housing development on Wawecus Hill. Presently, all of our employees are members of the tribe. However, you, the shareholders, own the company, and you can feel proud that you are sharing a small portion of your profits with our tribe."

Corey spoke of the company's status for another half hour and then opened the floor for questions.

By the time he finished, the room was uncomfortably hot, and everyone wanted to leave as soon as possible. But they also wanted their questions answered. As the meeting lingered, the room's space seemingly became more confined, and a feeling of anxiety overcame most of the audience.

Finally, one of the Pocawansett tribesmen spoke up, "Mr. Pallaton, I believe you're doing a great job, and I'd like to commend you on a job well done. I believe a round of applause is in order."

With that, he began to clap his hands, and the whole room, except for Travis and the entire Quinebaugan contingent, joined in.

After the applause died down, one of the local businessmen asked, "What is the expected cost of the new office building, and how will it be paid for?"

Corey answered, "As many of you know, I previously worked as a home builder for Mr. Henry Bill. So, my team of craftsmen is experienced in the art of construction. My team will build the new office building once we review and approve the architect's plans. Then, we will build it at cost, with no profit for us."

The businessman asked, "Okay. That is generous of you. Did you have a fire insurance policy in place? Why must you build the elegant, up-scale office you described earlier? I believe an ordinary office would be in the best interests of the shareholders."

The hair on the back of Corey's neck bristled. He responded, "As I mentioned, the company is only four months old. We recently completed the process of assessing the value of the office building for insurance purposes. The policy was planned to go into effect on December 1, but unfortunately, the fire occurred several days before that date."

Brynn's father, John Dunham, stood and said. "I, too, appreciate your efforts, but I have a question. Due to unforeseen circumstances, I want to redeem my family's company shares. Could you explain the process of liquidating shares?"

Corey said, "As I mentioned earlier, I am currently vetting two potential markets in Boston. They are both interested in buying gold from us, but I want to ensure these men are financially sound and can maintain a steady, reliable source of income for the company in coming years."

"We've temporarily paused our stock buy-back program. Due to the freezing weather, I was forced to halt our mining operations. Also, the company will have to pay the cost of the new office building up front. We expect to reinstate the buy-back program in the fall of next year. At this point, our costs are high."

The room instantly warmed even more. Murmurs of discontent and grumbling broke out throughout the audience. Finally, after a long, uncomfortable minute, one of the Quinebaugan farmers stood, raised his voice, and said, "Two weeks ago, I used all my spare cash to buy one share from your little Pocawansett wife there. She told me that I could sell it back to you anytime and that it would be worth more than I paid."

The statement took Corey and Elena aback. They were well aware of the deep rift between the Quinebaugan and the Pocawansett, but the wariness between them had not been publicly displayed for many years. The chasm between the two tribes existed since the Great Swamp Massacre, almost 200 years earlier. Everyone sensed the feelings of mistrust and loathing between the two tribes.

Before Corey could reply, Travis stood and stated, "Mr. Pallaton, you could have purchased fire insurance several months ago. You failed to protect the company's assets. You have not secured an income stream for the company because you don't have any gold buyers under contract. When your wife informed prospective buyers of a guaranteed buy-back program, she lied to prospective buyers. You have not ...."

Elena's face flushed in embarrassment, and Corey was outraged. He pointed to the back of the room and yelled, "Bowie, Crockett, remove this man from the room immediately!"

Just as Travis was about to announce that Corey and his Pocawansett workers had not found any substantial amount of gold, Bowie and Crockett approached him. Travis also wanted to inform everyone that Corey lied when he proclaimed he had a store of 200 ounces of gold.

The heat in the room was now unbearable, but Travis felt an innate need to protect his fellow tribe members from Corey. He also wanted to ensure his tribe's trust in him.

Travis had brought several samples of the fool's gold that he and Lydia had found on his mineral plot on Wawecus Hill. He planned to put the iron pyrite on public display to expose Corey's deceit. As Travis reached into his pocket to retrieve one of the mineral samples, Crockett yelled, "He's got a knife! Everyone, look out! He's dangerous."

Pandemonium broke out. Everyone stood and looked to the single exit in the back of the room.

Bowie quickly drew his knife, put it to Travis's throat, and said, "If you say another word, Gimpy, you're a dead man."

Then, Crockett drew Travis's precious Damascus steel knife from Travis's sheath and handed it to Corey. Travis never had any thoughts of pulling his knife on anyone.

Corey stood up, waved his hands, and held Travis's knife above his head so everyone could see. Then, he commanded, "Everyone, relax. I've got his knife, and there's no more danger. Please sit."

After Crockett and Bowie hustled Travis out of the room, most of the audience sat. But the Quinebaugan and Pocawansett delegations continued to stand and glared intently at each other.

General William Williams stood when the Quinebaugan contingent and the Stedman family turned to make their way to the exit. He said, "Mr. and Mrs. Mathews, Mr. Stedman, all my Quinebaugan and Pocawansett friends, please calm down. We need to listen to what Mr. Pallaton has to say. I believe him to be a fair and honest man. He is working hard to help develop our community. Please do not allow the dispute between him and Travis Mathews to divide us."

The Stedmans, the Mathews, and the Quinebaugans admired and trusted General Williams. So, they sat down, giving Williams the benefit of the doubt.

The disgruntled Pocawansetts also sat.

However, Corey added more fuel to the fire moments later, saying, "I am sorry for this incident, but it doesn't surprise me. This man, Travis Mathews, used to work for our company. As a trusted employee, he knew where I kept a map showing where we had found gold. Unfortunately, he is also a greedy young man. On the evening of the fire, he broke into our Hardscrabble Hill office and attempted to steal our secret map. *He planned to rob me, our company, and you!*"

He pointed to Jeremy and said, "Everyone, please turn your attention to the front table. This man, Mr. Jeremy Pallawotuk, has been like a son to me. Unfortunately, he is now crippled for life due to the fire caused by Travis Mathews.

On Thanksgiving evening, Jeremy saw Mathews break into our office. He suspected Mathews was up to no good, so Jeremy bravely followed him into the office and caught him red-handed trying to steal the map."

"After Jeremy confronted him, Mathews dropped the map, set the building on fire, and fled. Seeing the office on fire, Jeremy tried to recover the map, but the burning roof fell on him and pinned his arm to the floor. Using his free hand, Jeremy was narrowly able to escape. He barely made it out of the burning office with his life."

He continued, "Everyone, please understand that everything Travis Mathews said earlier was untrue. He is an unscrupulous Quinebaugan liar. I'm sorry, but what I tell you is the truth."

The Mathews family and the entire Quinebaugan contingent were enraged. They had known Travis his entire lifetime and were sure he would never have acted as Corey outlined. Finally, they all stood in unison and left the meeting.

However, the Pocawansett contingent stood and applauded.

The farmers, local businessmen, and major shareholders wanted to trust Corey but didn't know who to believe or what to think. Of course, there was unanimous sorrow for Jeremy, and all the shareholders believed that Travis Mathews was a villain.

NORWICH GOLD

~~~~~

Bowie and Crockett shoved Travis down the stairs and out of the library. They neared the company's buckboard wagon, where Lightning patiently awaited on the snow-filled pathway.

Travis yelled out, "Okay, I've had enough. I'll wait here for my family."

Crockett replied, "You must be kidding, arsehole! It's time for you to pay the price for hurting Bear."

Travis saw the blackjack coming at his forehead, but it was too late. The blunt end of the lead-filled bludgeon grazed his eyebrow. As Travis touched his forehead, a steady stream of warm blood filled the palm of his hand.

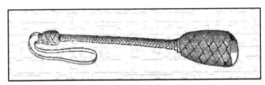

The next blow landed a direct hit on the back of his head, and Travis instantly blacked out.

Bowie told Crockett, "You lift his feet, and I'll lift the rest."

After positioning Travis's body onto the back of the buckboard wagon, they transported their limp, unconscious cargo down Bath Street.

Bowie studied his blackjack, smiled, and said to Crockett, "I guess there is a benefit to reading the newspaper. I read several articles about the Lincoln-Douglas debates in the Aurora a few months ago. Most people seem very interested in the candidate's political opinions, but I found the details of Mr. Lincoln's bodyguard much more fascinating. That guy is like a one-man army. One of the articles said that he carries two pistols, a pair of brass knuckles, a large Bowie knife, and a blackjack."

He continued, "I didn't know what a blackjack was, but I figured it must be a handy weapon. So, I bought this one a few weeks ago to find out."

He caressed the bludgeon for a full minute before saying, "Yes, I think it's pretty handy indeed."

After a three-minute ride through downtown Norwich, they arrived at a lightly wooded area near the banks of the Shetucket River.

~~~~~

Travis's head was pounding. A dense fog of slow-motion memories filled his brain. As he awoke from the deep abyss, he questioned, "Where am I? Why am I here? What happened?"

As the recent violent memories began to return, he tried to sit up but suddenly realized that both his hands were bound. A short length of rope was tied around his right wrist. The other end of the rope was firmly staked into a downward-sloping gravel bed.

His left hand was also bound with a rope. However, the other end of this rope was staked between two long, parallel steel rails. Terror filled Travis's entire being as the ground began to vibrate slowly. He couldn't break loose. The train would certainly sever his forearm and would possibly take his life. In an instant, Travis knew that Bowie and Crockett intended for Travis to pay for Jeremy's arm with his own.

~~~~~

John Stedman, his wife, and Lydia closed Otis Library's front door as they left the building. Lydia was anxious to speak with Travis. Deep within her soul, she appreciated the courage that he had shown. He had performed a noble and honorable act, and she wanted to wrap her arms around him.

She said to her parents, "Do you see Travis anywhere?"

They both shook their heads. They searched unsuccessfully along the northern side of Union Street, where the shareholders had tied carriages and horses. Then, as Lydia approached the head of Bath Street, her heart sank, and she cried out, "Father, Mother. Come! Quickly!"

Against the white four-inch blanket of snow, they saw a dark red pool of blood and a single set of wagon wheel tracks. Lydia began running down Bath Street. She knew they couldn't be too far because Bowie, Crockett, and Travis had left the meeting only minutes earlier. Her heart pounded as she followed the clearly defined wagon wheel tracks down the street.

She spotted Travis and the approaching train as she entered the slightly wooded area near the Norwich & Worcester Railroad tracks. She screamed. "Travis, get up! Get up quickly!"

She saw a massive puff of smoke puff belching from the locomotive's chimney and heard its whistle blaring. As she neared, Travis's situation was obvious. He needed immediate help. The slow-moving train applied its brakes as she began untying his wrist from the track. The metal wheels squealed against the rails, and the screech of pending doom made Travis and Lydia shudder.

In a flash, her nimble fingers freed him. After the train rumbled past them, Travis's broken and weary body took her into his arms and said, "Lydia Stedman, you are the most amazing woman I've ever known! I love you."

Tears welled up in Lydia's eyes as she was overcome with emotion. She said, "I love you too, Travis Mathews."

32: DEFAMATION
DOWNTOWN NORWICH
NORWICH CITY POST OFFICE
MONDAY, DECEMBER 20, 1858

In addition to publishing the Aurora, John W. Stedman had served as a postmaster in Norwich for the past five years. He loved the job because it brought the benefits of high social standing and community involvement.

There were two post offices in Norwich, one downtown at Chelsea Landing and the other on Norwichtown Green. The Chelsea Landing post office, first established in 1795, supported the thriving seaport at the headwaters of the Thames River. In November of 1827, the citizens of Norwich changed the name to 'Norwich City.' And later, in 1836, the downtown post office was renamed simply 'Norwich.'

The Town of Norwich post office, located on the Green, was led by its postmaster, Henry B. Tracy. But, the busier, more prestigious, modern Norwich City post office was located in the heart of Norwich, with John Stedman as its master.

However, today, Mr. Stedman was ill with the flu and could not fulfill his civic duty at the post office. But, he was close friends with John Dunham, the town's previous postmaster. Graciously, Mr. Dunham agreed to fill in for Stedman for the entire week of Christmas.

As usual, the office was humming with activity. Locals strode through the town to buy supplies, learn of current local events, and socialize. In addition, the Norwich City post office boasted an ornately carved bulletin board near the front door. Locals frequently posted announcements of upcoming public events and meetings on the board.

This morning, John noticed Jeremy Pallawotuk feverishly posting a flyer on the post office's bulletin board. John felt deep sorrow for Jeremy after last week's shareholder meeting. Seeing Jeremy's disfigured body upset John at a visceral level. He considered Jeremy a fine, hard-working young man and wished him the best.

Mr. Dunham knew his daughter, Brynn, to be finicky in her choice of suitors. She had her pick of eligible bachelors in Norwich and had chosen Jeremy. So when the subject of men arose, John trusted his daughter's opinion.

He rushed to Jeremy's side and said, "May I help you with that?"

Jeremy looked up from his task and replied, "Sure. My good arm is getting pretty tired. I've been working at this all morning."

As John pinned one of the flyers to the board, he was taken aback. He gasped and said, "Jeremy, these are pretty strong statements. Why are you posting them?"

Jeremy responded, "I saw you at the meeting, so you must know. Travis Mathews is trying to destroy Norwich's confidence in our company. He burned down our office, and he caused me to lose my hand and part of my arm. I want to stop his lies and restore our company's good reputation. Corey made these flyers and asked me to post them around town so people would know the truth."

John answered, "Yes, I saw and heard Mathews in action at the meeting. And I don't understand why he attacked Corey in such a savage manner. It looked like he was pulling a knife on Corey."

Jeremy said, "Yes. We want Travis Mathews and others like him out of town."

After posting the flyer, he said, "I'm going down to the Daily Courier's newspaper office next. We'll run an announcement of the company's quarterly earnings."

John answered, "That's a great idea. The Courier's publisher, Reverend Dorson Sykes, is a personal friend. I know him to be a God-fearing, righteous man. Please tell him hello for me. I'm sure that he will help you."

He continued, "Brynn tells me good things about you. I hope that you won't be too discouraged by your injury. Hopefully, your company can financially help you through your difficult adjustment."

Dunham was now ready to make his pitch. He said, "As you know, Brynn is planning to attend Miss Porter's School in Farmington this next fall. My wife and I have invested heavily in your company, and we plan to use the proceeds from our stock to pay her tuition. I asked Mr. Pallaton about cashing in a few shares during the meeting. However, his answer made it sound like there may be a problem."

Jeremy responded, "Well, we are not buying back shares at the moment. When would you need to pay the tuition?"

John answered, "We must pay it in late July or early August. So I'm hoping you could help Brynn and us with that."

Jeremy said, "Oh, by then, I'm sure you'll be able to share in the profits. There shouldn't be any problem."

Jeremy fervently prayed for a change in his luck because he remembered the scent of Brynn's lush body pressed against him. He didn't want to disappoint her. Perhaps he and his team would soon find a larger cache of gold.

Jeremy walked south to Franklin Square a few minutes later and entered the Daily Courier's office. He saw a portly man wearing thick spectacles sitting behind an oak desk and said, "You must be Reverend Sykes."

The man glanced up from his work and replied, "Yes. And whom do I have the pleasure of addressing?"

"I am Jeremy Pallawotuk. I'm the vice president of the Wawecus Hill Gold, Silver, and Nickel Mining Company and a friend of Mr. John Dunham."

Sykes stopped working, stood, and shook Jeremy's hand, "I'm pleased to meet you. Ahhh, yes. John and I go way back. He sold the Courier business to me several years back and helped start me on the right foot. What could I do for you?"

Jeremy said, "Well, I need two things. First, our company has recently compiled our fourth quarter 1858 business report, and we want to publish it in your newspaper."

After Jeremy handed the report to Sykes, he scanned it and said, "I have heard good things about your company, and after reading this, I'm impressed. Congratulations on your successful endeavor."

Sykes continued, "How many times would you like to publish it? I believe once this week and once next week would suffice."

Jeremy said, "We'd like you to run it twice weekly for the next month. A disgruntled former employee, who tried to rob us, is attempting to undermine our company's reputation. So, we want to quickly and effectively dispel his untrue allegations."

Jeremy continued, "That brings me to the second favor I want to ask. We're doing everything possible to let the public know how he has slandered our company's good name. We've made up a few flyers that I'm posting around town. Would you mind if I posted one outside your door?"

Reverend Sykes read the poster and replied, "Oh my son, it pains me that this man, Travis Mathews, has caused you such difficulty. May we pray together for a moment?"

Jeremy was surprised but deeply pleased. He knew he could use all the prayers the good Reverend would offer.

Sykes prayed aloud, "Father, I pray that your son, Jeremy, has a speedy recovery and that you will help him in all his endeavors. I know that Mr. Travis Mathews has wronged him and has sinned deeply. But, I pray that you show mercy on him after he suffers the wrath of your anger. Thank you, Dear Gracious Heavenly Father."

33: Disbelief
Downtown Norwich
C.C. Brand Whaling Gun Factory
Monday, December 20, 1858

Travis slowly squeezed the trigger of a freshly minted whaling gun, and an enormous *boom* thundered throughout the basement of Brand's factory. As usual, his shoulder suffered the insult of the blow from the gun's butt. But Travis was pleased.

He said, "Father, this recently designed rubber butt cushion works pretty well. The recoil still hurts, but not nearly as much as before. It needs to be just a bit softer."

Before he could finish speaking, Lydia burst down the stairs into the factory assembly room and announced, "Travis, you've got to see this. I can't believe it!"

She handed Travis one of the twenty flyers she held and said, "Take a look at this."

Travis's heart sank. He knew that Corey and Jeremy were scoundrels but didn't believe them capable of such a vile, deceitful act. He pointed at the flyer, saying, "Where did you get that?"

Lydia answered, "While working in our newspaper's office, someone came in and mentioned your name to me. They were surprised at what a rascal you've become. When I asked them why they believed that, they showed me a flyer."

She continued, "Someone has posted them all over town. They are disgusting, and it makes me sick to my stomach. On the way from the newspaper office to here, I peeled posters off storefronts and bulletin boards. They're everywhere."

As Lydia spoke, Travis simultaneously felt embarrassment, humiliation, shame, anger, and rage. The flyer's message crushed his emotional need for respect. His plan to expose Corey by taking the map from the company's office had failed miserably. Now, the thought of joining a whaling expedition was more appealing than he'd ever thought possible.

His father said, "We've got to pull ourselves together. Quickly now. Lydia. Let's you and I return to town and take down as many flyers as possible. You take the southern part of town."

He continued, "I'll do the same for the northern part of town. But, Travis, you've got to report this to the town's constable. Perhaps he can do something about it."

Travis thought for a moment and replied, "Okay. That sounds like a good plan."

Jonathan and Lydia scoured the town for the next hour, looking to remove the hideous flyers. Unfortunately, they found them posted on almost every corner of the city. Lydia spotted and removed posters from the front doors of Otis Library, Lucas Hall, the Norwich & Worcester Railroad passenger terminal, and Dr. Osgood's pharmacy. Someone had even posted flyers on several Norwich houses of worship.

As she gathered the papers, Lydia heard several whispers from passersby. They murmured, "Shameful. Simply shameful.

We should run that Travis Mathews out of town. You just can't trust those Quinebaugans."

It was the most humiliating experience of Lydia's entire life.

~~~~~

Travis made his way up the hill to the New London County Jail House on Cedar Street. He wasn't sure if the constable would be on duty, but he knew the jailers, who maintained the facility and inmates, could connect with the constable.

After he climbed the massive building's stairs leading to the front entrance, Travis was appalled. Someone had posted one of the flyers on the front door. He thought to himself, "How could this have happened? What the hell is going on here?"

He tore down the flyer, barged into the building, and saw Crockett sitting with his feet propped up on a large, old oak desk. He was wearing a badge that identified him as a deputy. Travis could hardly believe Crockett sat at the constable's desk.

Travis snarled at him, "What are you doing here? You're not the constable."

Crockett said, "Gimpy, you need to show more respect, or I'll throw your ass in a cell. You are right. I'm not the constable, but I am his Deputy. I'm filling in for my brother-in-law while he and my sister spend Christmas week with his family in Boston."

Travis was puzzled. He said, "What does your sister have to do with anything?"

Crockett grinned, "Oh, I guess I forgot to tell you. Her husband is the constable. You must have seen her at the company meeting because she sat between me and him. Her husband appointed me a deputy to watch the jail and handle any criminal activities in his absence."

He waited for Travis's reaction, smirked, and questioned, "What can I do for you?"

34: SOCIAL JUSTICE
NORWICHTOWN GREEN
FIRST CONGREGATIONAL CHURCH
FRIDAY, DECEMBER 24, 1858 – CHRISTMAS EVE

Lydia loved the Christmas Eve service at the First Congregational Church. She had never missed one in her entire life. The candlelit sanctuary, smiling faces of her fellow Congregational worshipers, and comforting words of wisdom from Reverend Hiram P. Arms always summoned a feeling of well-being. Additionally, the anticipation of spending more time with her family and Travis this Christmas season stirred a deep-seated sense of contentment within her.

Over the past few weeks, Lydia felt a growing connection to Travis. She was delighted he accepted her invitation to attend this evening's service. Even now, sitting next to him, she could feel a warm glow of energy while bathed in his pure aura. Lydia wanted to share a profound religious experience with Travis. She hoped this evening's message from the good reverend would begin to form a deeper, more spiritual connection with Travis.

This evening, the sanctuary felt entirely different from any typical Sunday morning. The flickering candles and crisp winter air created a nostalgic, soul-searching atmosphere. A feeling of fellowship helped bind the congregation on this special occasion.

Reverend Arms stood at the podium and began, "Welcome, everyone. I want to be the first to wish you a happy Christmas Eve, and I pray that your families are all in good health. As in past years, this evening's format is unique. It will differ from the normal Sunday morning service. I want to speak tonight about treating everyone with respect, kindness, and love."

"Fair and equal treatment for all must be blind to religious beliefs, gender, race, and ethnicity. Thus, we will review several social inequities that Jesus Christ experienced and how he rose above them."

Travis thought to himself, "*Oh no!* This sermon sounds like a repeat of the last one."

Reverend Arms continued, "When baby Jesus was born in Bethlehem, King Herod sent a group of Magi to search for him. Why? Herod announced that it was so he could personally worship the Messiah. But, in reality, his intentions were quite different."

"Herod targeted baby Jesus for cruel treatment based on his lineage. Herod threatened the existence of Jesus Christ and what his presence would stand for."

Reverend Arms continued, "Even today, in 1858, many people feel threatened by others unlike themselves. I've observed discrimination such as this in many forms."

He lifted a highly polished, silver chalice above his head so all could see and said, "Please, take a look at this beautiful communion cup. A woman named Sarah Kemble Knight donated it to this church more than 125 years ago. She was an adventurous, brave teacher and businesswoman who was a member of this congregation for many years."

"As Norwich's only businesswoman, she experienced the pain of discrimination. However, she rose above the transgressions.

The way she lived her life is a fine example of how one can overcome discrimination."

He continued, "In the late 1600s, Sarah conducted a writing school in Boston, where she was married to a much older man, Captain Richard Knight, a seasoned shipmaster. In addition to running the school, Sarah was engaged in various enterprises not usually associated with women of her time. For example, she often used her knowledge of settling estates and other semi-legal activities to help her friends."

"Shortly after her husband's death, Sarah was notified that one of her relatives in New Haven needed help settling her husband's estate. So Sarah set off for New Haven on horseback in the fall of 1704 to look into the issue. She was thirty-eight years old at the time, and much of the country she traveled was still unexplored and dangerous for any man, let alone a woman."

Reverend Arms continued, "Sarah kept a diary chronicling her perilous journey, dangerous encounters, and difficulties. Most of her challenges occurred solely because she was a woman."

"Several years later, Sarah Knight settled in Norwich and kept a shop and an inn. Her inn, the Knight Tavern, still stands directly across from us on the Norwichtown Green today."

"Unfortunately, Sarah also experienced another type of discrimination while in Norwich. She was a friend of the Quinebaugans. She traded with them and served them food and drink at her dual-purpose tavern/inn. Unfortunately, at that time, no taverns in the county were allowed to sell wine, liquors, cider, or any other strong drink to the Quinebaugan. When the town officials caught her selling liquor to Native Americans, they levied an exorbitant fine on her establishment. The fine was much greater than other fines imposed on male-operated taverns."

"He finished by saying, "Ladies and Gentlemen. We will drink from Sarah Knight's chalice tonight when we partake in Communion. While doing so, I ask you to contemplate two questions. Firstly, why weren't the Quinebaugans allowed to purchase alcohol, and secondly, why did Sarah Knight's willingness to do so result in such an excessive fine?"

"It is my belief there is a single answer to both questions. *Social Injustice.*"

Reverend Arms motioned to one of the deacons, held out the cup, and said, "Let us all celebrate the birth of baby Jesus and the examples he provided. Let us work together for social justice."

After Communion, the choir director, Aaron Stevens, stood at the pulpit. He nodded to Reverend Arms and said, "Thank you for your words of wisdom. I want to continue along the theme of social justice."

"This evening, I am overcome with pride and happiness. This past week, I received a letter from my son, Aaron Dwight Stevens. He is currently in Iowa, fighting for the rights of enslaved people. His letter informed me that he and several friends had recently freed an enslaved woman. He mentioned that local authorities are very angry with him, and he may face severe consequences. But, he is proud of his achievements, and so am I."

Stevens continued, "As you know, many of our fellow Americans in the southern states wield power over other humans to do their bidding. Unfortunately, a few people in Norwich still engage in this ungodly practice. But, I'm optimistic because there are hints of change in the air."

"Only a few months ago, the good Mr. Lincoln from Illinois clarified that slavery is a moral issue our nation needs to address. I've also noticed several of our newly published hymns contain calls to abolish slavery."

He continued, "Tonight, for the first time, we will sing a new Christmas hymn. It reminds us of the thrill of hope for a free world that fulfills Christ's birth promises. It was composed and written in France, but a man in Boston translated this beautiful hymn into English only three years ago. And I'm happy to say I learned of it last month."

"Please join me in singing 'O Holy Night.' And please pay particular attention to the third verse."

O HOLY NIGHT

O Holy Night! The stars are brightly shining.
It is the night of the dear Savior's birth.
Long lay the world in sin and error, pining
Till He appeared and the Spirit felt its worth.

A thrill of hope, the weary world rejoices.
For yonder breaks a new and glorious morn.
Fall on your knees! Oh, hear the angel voices!
O night divine, the night when Christ was born
O night, O Holy Night, O night divine!

Chains he shall break, for the slave is our brother
And in his name, all oppression shall cease.
Sweet hymns of joy in grateful chorus raise we
With all our hearts, we praise His holy name.

The words and music of the hymn touched Travis's heart. He placed his hand on Lydia's and smiled. Travis had been apprehensive about attending the service this evening because he still had unpleasant memories of the previous, uncomfortable experience here.

Reverend Arms rose and said, "Mr. Stevens. Thank you for discovering and sharing that beautiful hymn with us. And thank you for your words of wisdom about the issue of slavery. As I mentioned earlier, the theme of tonight's service is treating everyone (including women, other races, and people from other ethnic backgrounds) fairly."

"We are fortunate to have a small ethnic group here in Norwich, about a hundred souls, who should be honored and respected. The Quinebaugan were the first people in New London County. Their ancestors worked hand-in-hand with our European ancestors to form the basis of what we know today as Norwich. In September of next year, we'll all celebrate the 200th anniversary of the day that Quinebaugan Sachem Lucas conveyed the land upon which we now stand to Major John Mason."

He continued, "Over the years, we have helped the Quinebaugans assimilate in many ways. General William Williams has led our church's outreach program to them for the past several years. He teaches their Sunday school every week. General Williams. Thank you. Please stand to be recognized."

The General did not want to stand because he felt that Reverend Arms should have focused the Christmas address more on Christ's birth and less on social reform. But, finally, after his wife, Harriet, prodded him, he stood politely for a moment and nodded to Reverend Arms.

Reverend Arms continued, "I am proud that our congregation is open and available to all. We want to encourage everyone to learn of Christ's love and treat everyone equally. So, please, all women, daughters, and girls stand."

The females all felt slightly uncomfortable and a bit embarrassed. They didn't know what Reverend Arms had in mind. Finally, the entire choir and all the women stood. Reverend Arms said, "Ladies, we respect and appreciate you as humans. Thank you for your kindness and love."

Then, without further thought, Reverend Arms said, "If there are any African Americans, Native Americans, or people from any other ethnic cultures here, please stand and be recognized."

Travis's heartbeat quickened. He did not want to be the center of attention or be recognized. But he was proud to be a Quinebaugan and could not allow his personal feelings to shame his Quinebaugan heritage. Travis stood.

He was the lone person standing to represent any minority group.

Only last week, Reverend Arms attended Corey's shareholder meeting and witnessed the incident. He believed within his heart that he had seen Travis pull a knife on the mining company's president. He judged Travis guilty of intent to harm the honorable Corey Pallaton. So when he saw Travis standing, he was forced to think quickly.

After a moment, Arms said to Travis, "Please be seated."

Reverend Arms cleared his throat and continued, "I, and our esteemed choir director, have reminded everyone this evening of Christ's love and the diversity of many fine people in today's world."

He returned his attention to Travis and said, "But, I must also remind you there is evil in the world. There are wicked people and lazy, unproductive, dishonest people of all races. And, yes, some ruthless Quinebaugan thieves could be among us."

He stopped, glared at Travis for a moment, then continued, "So, treat everyone with respect, kindness, and love, but always remember there are those who would lie to you, rob you, and try to lead you astray."

Twelve joyful chimes rang out from the church's belfry, announcing that Christmas had arrived.

Reverend Hiram P. Arms concluded the service by saying, "Everyone. On this Christmas Day, I want you all to rejoice in Christ's birth and enjoy the warmth of your family's love."

~~~~~

Outside, on the church's front lawn, Travis and Lydia looked at one another in disbelief and bewilderment. Then, finally, Travis said, "Everyone thinks I'm a danger to society, a liar, a thief, and can't be trusted!"

Lydia placed her right hand on his left hand and said, "Travis, you're the most honorable man I've ever known. Someday, we'll find a way to expose Corey and Jeremy. Today, they are well respected throughout the community and wield many ill-founded positive public opinions. People want to believe them for their own selfish reasons."

Looking into his eyes, she remembered the primary reason for wanting to invite him to the service this evening. So she said, "Travis, would you like to pray with me?"

Tears filled his eyes, and Travis replied, "Yes, please."

Lydia prayed aloud, "Father, we thank you for Christ's birth, and we thank you for the life he led. But, Father, we also pray that you allow us to help the people of Norwich see the wicked ways of Corey Pallaton. We trust your judgment and know you will shine the light of truth on everyone someday."

Travis lightly kissed her cheek and trudged through the snow to his trustworthy steed, Moshup. He felt a deeper, more spiritual connection with Lydia and knew his God, *Munduyahweh*, had heard their prayers.

As Travis approached Moshup for the midnight ride home, he heard muffled footsteps approaching. He turned and saw General Williams marching through the snow toward him.

Williams said, "Travis. You've been honest and trustworthy for all the years I've known you. I, too, am wary of Mr. Corey Pallaton and his dealings. Unfortunately, public opinion is not in your favor, but I also know that the passage of time usually makes things right."

He continued, "Your employer at the map shop, Mr. Walling, told me you're the best apprentice he's ever taught. You've quickly mastered the art of taking and recording measurements. When you spoke with me last year, I was skeptical about employing you as a navigator. But, now you've proven yourself a worthy, capable young man."

"One of my cargo ships will sail to Marseilles this coming October, and I'd like you to sail with us. You'll be able to complete your training as a ship's navigator and, like your father before you, can live the abundant life of a sailor."

He concluded, "Leaving town for a while might do you some good."

After Williams returned to join his wife, Travis stroked Moshup's chin and whispered, "Decisions, decisions, decisions. I'd love to see Marseilles, London, and Sri Lanka."

35: JUBILEE PLANNING
NORWICHTOWN
TEEL HOUSE: BALLROOM
SATURDAY, APRIL 9, 1859

It had been a bleak, brutal winter in Norwich, and Lydia was happy for spring, milder temperatures, and the promise of new beginnings. The only fond memory of this past winter was when she and Travis went ice skating.

In mid-January, the Thames River froze near Chelsea Landing, and the entire town turned out for a respite from the dark winter nights. It was an impromptu gala event that featured horse-drawn sled races and young couples skating till dusk. She and Travis shared the day with an abundance of lively conversation, freshly made warm donuts, and hot chocolate. The silhouette of Travis's face against the late afternoon golden sunset was still etched in her memory.

Over the past several months, Lydia and her father barely had enough time to keep up with the demands of publishing the newspaper, creating wedding announcements and invitations for soon-to-be brides, and updating their journal for Norwich's upcoming 200th Jubilee.

Today, Lydia, her father, and other Norwich town leaders sat around the perimeter of a massive oak conference table in the

Teel House ballroom. General William Williams sat at the head of the assembly, where he presided as Chairman of the Jubilee Planning Committee. Today's meeting was the fifth such gathering.

As the ad hoc stenographer for the group, Lydia attended every meeting and carefully recorded every detail of the group's conversations and resolutions. She found the sessions to be fascinating, informative, and revealing. The meetings allowed her to learn how the leaders of Norwich governed the city.

As she looked around the room, Lydia noted many influential Norwich leaders. They included Mayor Amos Prentice, United States Senator Lafayette Foster, the publishers of two influential newspapers (her father and Mr. John Dunham), the owner of the Norwich & New London Steamboat Company, Mr. Henry B. Norton, and of course, Mr. Corey Pallaton.

General Williams opened, "Welcome, everyone. Thank you for taking time from your busy schedules to meet with us today. The goal for today's meeting is to share the status of your various committees and to ensure that we are on track for a successful Jubilee."

He continued, "First, I'd like to start with a report from the Invitation Committee. Who will be reporting for the committee today?"

Mr. Henry B. Norton stood and said, "I will. Although Governor Buckingham is the leader of this committee, he could not join us today. He asked me to give you an update. We have sent invitations to the governor of every state in the United States, the former President of the United States, Millard Fillmore, and more than 1,300 former residents of Norwich."

He continued, "I'm happy to say President Fillmore has agreed to attend. The president mentioned his ancestral ties and fond memories of Norwich in his acceptance letter. Additionally, he agreed to march alongside Governor Buckingham in the Grand Procession, which we'll hold on the first day of the Jubilee."

The entire room erupted in applause. When the applause subsided, Mr. Norton continued, "It has taken great effort to contact and invite all the governors and former residents. I want to take this opportunity to publicly acknowledge the fine work that my daughter, Emeline, and her friend, Miss Brynn Dunham, have accomplished. They've assisted me countless times these past few months, and we should thank them. Emeline and Brynn. Please stand and be recognized."

All heads turned as they rose from their seats near the back of the ballroom. Emeline was slightly embarrassed and nodded to her father. Brynn once again bathed in the light of attention. She flashed a pleasant smile to all the gentlemen in the room as she curtsied to Mr. Norton.

General Williams said, "Thank you to all. Please let us continue. As you know, one of the most important reasons for the Jubilee is to commemorate the founding of Norwich. We must respect our European forefathers and the Native Americans who occupied this land before us."

He continued, "In our last meeting, we tasked the Committee on Sentiments and Speeches to identify several individuals who could prepare discourses that address the rich history of Norwich. Mr. Stedman, I believe you represent that committee today. Please present your report."

John Stedman rose and said, "Yes, General. Our committee is pleased to report significant progress. Throughout the two-day event, various learned men will bestow speeches upon us. On the first day, we'll host a Grand Procession from Franklin Square to the Norwich Free Academy. Subsequently, Mr. Daniel Coit Gilman will address the entire Town and City of Norwich. He'll present a detailed account of the past 200 years of our distinguished history."

He continued, "We are fortunate to have him as a keynote speaker. Mr. Gilman is a Norwich native whose father once served as our mayor, and after graduating from Yale College, he became the college's librarian."

Once again, applause broke out throughout the room, and General Williams said, "Thank you, Mr. Stedman. You're doing a fine job."

Stedman, who had remained standing, said, "Thank you for allowing me to serve on this committee. I do, however, request your support on one issue. Mr. Gilman is quite familiar with our history from the European settler's point of view. But, he recognizes his inadequate knowledge of Norwich's history from the Quinebaugan point of view. Therefore, he earnestly desires to learn more about the Sachem Lucas, his people, their traditions, and how they worked together with our forefathers."

Williams and the other leaders looked around at one another and realized that Gilman had raised a significant issue. So Williams asked Stedman, "Do you have a remedy for this potential problem?"

Stedman said, "Yes, with your permission, I believe so. As you know, my daughter and I publish the Aurora newspaper. Over the past several years, we've run many articles and stories about our town's history. But, unfortunately, we've only published a few stories that mention the Quinebaugan way of life and their history."

"I run most of the business and operate the press. However, Lydia does most of the reporting, interviews, and fact-gathering. She researched and wrote all the stories we've published about the Quinebaugan."

Stedman nodded to Lydia and continued, "When I made her aware of Mr. Gilman's concerns, she enlightened me of the rumor that an old Quinebaugan hermit has extensive and profound knowledge of Quinebaugan history. He lives a few miles southwest of Norwich at an old Quinebaugan gathering spot. I believe it's called Kachina Rock."

He looked at Lydia and questioned, "Is that correct?"

Lydia cleared her throat and answered, "Yes. It is Kachina Rock. But, legend has it that the hermit is a *she*, not a *he*."

The audience chuckled. John smiled and replied, "I stand corrected. But, General, I suggest we research and find out if the rumor is true and, perhaps, ask this hermit to supply Mr. Gilman facts of the Quinebaugan tribe history."

General Williams said, "I believe that is a wonderful idea. We should vote on the issue. Will someone make a motion to that effect?"

John Stedman announced, "I make a motion that we appoint someone to find and speak with this hermit and invite her to address our body on the topic of Quinebaugan history."

John Breed, another former mayor of Norwich, seconded the motion.

General Williams said, "Would anyone like to add to the discussion before we vote?"

When Corey Pallaton stood to reply, Lydia's heart sank. She thought, "What could this man possibly have to add?"

He spoke, "Yes, sir. I've come here today to furnish you with the most current report of the Finance Committee, but at the moment, I stand before you as the Medicine Man of the Pocawansett tribe. Our people, too, have played an important role in Norwich's history. For example, we occupied land on Wawecus Hill and the area now known as Greeneville before the European white man appeared. Therefore, I believe someone from our tribe should also advise Mr. Gilman."

Williams's temperature bristled, and he fought to regain his composure. His distrust of Pallaton was growing by the minute. Finally, he said, "We must proceed on the motion at hand, and then we can address your issue, Mr. Pallaton. Is there any further discussion?"

No one else spoke, and General Williams said, "All in favor of Mr. Stedman's motion, please raise your right hand."

Everyone in the room except Corey raised their hand. Then, Williams said, "Is anyone opposed?"

Corey raised his hand.

Williams announced, "The motion passes."

He paused momentarily, looked directly at the Stedmans, and proclaimed, "Miss Stedman, you are tasked to seek out the woman you spoke of, learn what you can from her, and invite her to address our Jubilee."

Lydia was stunned and speechless at this development because she had only attended today's meeting to fulfill her roles of stenographer and reporter. When her father nodded, Lydia said, "Thank you for this honor. I will do my best to find and speak with her."

General Williams then said, "Thank you, Miss Stedman."

He continued, "On the other issue, Mr. Pallaton. The Pocawansetts are also a welcome part of our modern Norwich community. But, they were not friends of our forefathers or the native Quinebaugan. Nor did they play any productive role in the early development of Norwich."

Williams concluded, "Do I hear any further motions on the floor?"

Corey Pallaton sat down. He was seething but knew there was nothing more he could say or do.

General Williams said, "We must now turn our attention to planning the second day of the Jubilee. Mr. Breed, can you give us a report on the Formal Ball Committee progress?"

John Breed was the room's oldest and perhaps most well-respected person in Norwich.

Mr. Breed stood and said, "Yes. Thank you. My committee has made much progress. We'll host the Formal Ball in a huge tent that will house at least 2,500 people. Our staff will erect the tent across the street, in front of the Free Academy. It has been paid for and is being fabricated here in Norwich."

He paused for a moment and grinned sheepishly. Then, Mr. Breed said, "As I alluded to earlier, we expect a large number of participants. And, since I am not well-versed in the art of ballroom dancing or formal décor, I have asked my well-informed, delightful assistants to prepare a uniquely Norwich display of decorations to adorn the tent. My assistants certainly know how to throw a good party and are invaluable members of my committee. So, Miss Brynn Dunham and Miss Emeline Norton, please stand and be recognized."

They stood, and everyone applauded for a second time. They made a great team. Emeline efficiently performed most of the administrative and research tasks, and Brynn personally met with clients. It was difficult to say no whenever Brynn met someone in person and asked for a favor.

After they and Mr. Breed sat, General Williams resumed the meeting. He announced, "We need to hear from the Finance Committee. Mr. Pallaton, I believe you represent them today?"

Pallaton stood and said, "Yes, sir. The other two committee members, Mr. Mowry and Mr. Norton, are out of town on business pursuits and have asked me to deliver the report."

He began, "Our committee has created a budget for Jubilee, and we notified all committees of their allocations. Upon reviewing the expenditures presented to us thus far, I report that most committees have presented us with expenses and receipts that are well within budget. But, unfortunately, two committees have submitted several unreasonable and excessive expenses."

"Firstly, Mr. Stedman, the Chairman of the Committee of Sentiments and Speeches, has presented us with a bill for an extravagant purchase of mummy paper. Reading several flyers posted around town, I understand he plans to use our funds to publish a book using paper recovered from Egyptian mummies from 2,000 years ago. I have one of these flyers to show you."

Pallaton passed the flyer around the table. The flyer stated:

MUMMY PAPER

This paper is made by the Chelsea Manufacturing Company, Greeneville, Conn., the largest paper manufacturer in the world. The material of which it is made, was brought from Egypt. It was taken from ancient tombs where it had been used in embalming mummies.

Corey said, "I believe that Mr. Stedman should personally bear the cost for this exorbitantly expensive item and should not be allowed to pass the cost on to the good citizens of Norwich."

General Williams's eyebrows raised, and he looked at Stedman. Then, he said, "Mr. Stedman, is this accurate?"

John Stedman responded, "Yes, Sir, it is correct. The Chelsea Manufacturing Company is the largest paper producer in the world, and they will publish a book that will chronicle Norwich's 200th Jubilee for us. We'll use the profit from selling thousands of these books to pay all outstanding Jubilee bills."

He continued, "And, yes, we plan to use mummy paper *for one unique copy of the book*. That one special book will have a leather binding and be decorated with gold leaf. Everyone should understand that the book will be revered and cherished for generations. I hope Norwich will buy and keep the book on display for all, but if necessary, I will personally pay for it and keep it safe."

General Williams said, "Mr. Stedman. I can understand how many would consider the cost of your mummy paper book unreasonable. So, I believe it best for you to produce and purchase the book personally."

Williams motioned to Pallaton and said, "Please continue your report."

Corey reported, "Thank you, sir. Unfortunately, the Formal Ball Committee has also incurred several excessive expenses. I note that Miss Brynn Dunham has purchased many items for the ball that far exceed the budget."

General Williams looked to Brynn and said, "Miss Dunham. Are his statements accurate?"

Brynn angrily rose and strode to the head of the table. All eyes were on her as she spoke, "Yes, of course, they are accurate.

Gentlemen, the women of Norwich are also extremely proud of the past 200 years of our illustrious past. But please understand that we live in today's modern world. We, women, want to make our boyfriends and husbands happy. But, our comfort and feelings should also be an important consideration."

She continued, "So, yes, I'll listen to long-winded speeches and watch the Grand Procession parade through Franklin Square. But, you may rest assured that the most important Jubilee event, for most, if not all, the women in Norwich, will be the Formal Ball. It needs to be elegant and decorated beautifully."

She gave Corey a stern look and said, "I don't know which of you created the budget for the Ball, but I can tell that it needs to be doubled."

After a moment, she stood erect, placed her hands on her shapely hips, and said, "I make a motion that we double the budget for the Formal Ball Committee!"

General Williams was aghast but replied, "Do I hear a second?"

Brynn's father, John Dunham, the treasurer of the Chelsea Savings Bank, former mayor of Norwich, former publisher of the Courier, and former postmaster for the City of Norwich, proudly raised his hand and said, "I second the motion."

Williams's eyes opened widely as he said, "All in favor; please raise your right hand."

As before, everyone in the room except Corey Pallaton raised their right hand. He seethed at the audacity of the little bitch. Several months ago, she taunted him in his own home, and now, she had publicly humiliated him. Pallaton would never forget her impertinent behavior.

NORWICH GOLD

~~~~~

After the meeting adjourned, Emeline and Brynn pranced out the front door of the Teel House.

Brynn said, "That was fun, wasn't it?"

Emeline replied, "I'm not so sure about that. You may have just stirred up a hornet's nest."

Brynn replied, "Maybe so, but they deserved it. I need to speak with you about something else. I've been friends with Jeremy Pallawotuk for several months, and I like him because he is very handsome and quite confident. But, since he lost his hand during the accident, he's changed. He's much more aggressive toward everyone, including me. And I still remember when he kicked my poor little Dexter. So I'm thinking about breaking things off with Jeremy."

She continued, "Sometimes I think Jeremy is only a flunky for Corey Pallaton. Whenever I ask him about the mining company, he gives me an elusive answer. I pray they haven't been misleading everyone about their gold because my parents plan to sell their shares in the company to pay for my tuition for Miss Porter's School for Girls."

Emeline replied, "Yes. I, too, hope they haven't been lying. My parents have also bought into the company. Lydia's been saying all along that Jeremy hasn't been truthful. She may be right."

Brynn sighed and said, "Yes. Lydia used to be such a good friend. I do miss her friendship."

36: PESIKUTES RIDGE
DOWNTOWN NORWICH
LUCAS HALL: WATER STREET
FRIDAY, APRIL 22, 1859

Corey thoughtfully gazed out the window of his fourth-floor temporary company office. It was a comforting, peaceful site. He felt proud as he looked across the Thames River at the exquisite homes he had built on Laurel Hill. Corey had worked tirelessly to rise from near poverty to a now powerful force within the community. It gave him great pride to know that he was now well-positioned to help his Pocawansett brethren and gain an even stronger foothold in the circle of Norwich elite.

Corey saw scores of young men scurrying about Chelsea Landing. The port had become a landing pad for immigrants. But, he loathed the recent crop of poor European migrants in New London County. He was angered every time the thought of the migrant invasion came to mind. Unlike most in Norwich, Corey believed the foreigners arrived with few skills, begged for handouts, and hoarded the few available jobs that Pocawansetts had previously filled. Corey believed they flooded the city with broods of kids crying for food and free shelter. And it bothered him that many of these lazy outsiders were now intermarrying with the Pocawansett. The European customs and poor work ethics had begun to dilute his noble Pocawansett culture.

When Corey heard three gentle raps on the office door, he called out, "Enter."

A thin young woman with curly red hair entered and asked, "Hello, Mr. Pallaton. Do you have a few minutes to speak with me?"

Pallaton approached her and responded, "Hello, Maisie."

He touched her shoulder, led her into the office, and said, "Yes, please come in and have a seat."

She took the only seat, an overstuffed deep purple velvet upholstered couch.

She looked around the office and politely said, "Oh, thank you. My oh my. Crockett told me about your new office, but I never expected it to be decorated with so many unusual things."

Pallaton casually responded, "Yes. But this place is only our company's temporary office until we finish rebuilding the Hardscrabble Hill headquarters."

He continued, "This building, Lucas Hall, is a meeting place for several fraternal organizations in Norwich. The Independent Order of Odd Fellows routinely uses this particular room. The I.O.O.F. members call it Lucas Lodge No. 11. It's a wonderful organization that caters to underprivileged people throughout the United States. They aim to 'visit the sick, relieve the distressed, bury the dead, and educate the orphaned.' I immediately joined the group after learning of their benevolent work. They generously allowed me to rent the space."

Maisie looked about the room and responded, "I haven't heard of them, but they sure sound like an admirable group. But this room is a little creepy. Why are those mannequins dressed in purple robes, colorful aprons, sateen sashes filled with swords, and regal-looking helmets? Also, why are there red velvet curtains, so many small tables with oil lamps, and what do they use the stage for?"

Pallaton sniggered and said, "Young lady, you sure have a lot of questions. I am obliged not to tell you specific details of the I.O.O.F. I've been sworn to secrecy, but I will say that our monthly meetings here always include a modest dinner and private entertainment. It is usually a scintillating affair."

"We've helped many here in Norwich. What can I do for you?"

She responded, "As you know, Crockett and I were married last month, and we've been trying hard to make ends meet. He told me three families have already moved into your new homes on Pesikutes Ridge. The other wives tell me the homes are just the right size for couples like Crockett and me."

She continued, "The problem is that he and I have lived with his parents since our marriage. Their home is now overcrowded, and Crockett tells me he and I are the tenth family in line for a home in your housing development. He's worked so hard for you for many years, and we don't understand why we're so far down on the list."

Corey stood and began to stroll about the room. He'd only seen Maisie a few times before and strongly disapproved of her marriage to Crockett. His boys should marry good Pocawansett girls, not migrant harlots like Maisie. He asked her, "Maisie. Do you have a job?"

She answered, "Well. No. My mother and I came over from Scotland six months ago, and I haven't been able to find a decent job yet. I want to work in the Norwich Town House or a bank. On the voyage, my mother and father became sick with scurvy. Then, unfortunately, when my father died, our lives became a horrible nightmare. It was difficult after we arrived in Chelsea Harbor because my mother hadn't completely recovered physically or emotionally."

As she spoke, Corey became agitated. He'd heard this story many times before, and now the growing immigrant population's weaknesses were infecting Crockett and other members of his tribe. He could hardly listen to any more of her begging.

She continued, "So, after a month, my mother began working in the bleaching room at the Norwich Bleaching, Dyeing & Printing Company in Greeneville. She works twelve hours daily cleaning and preparing the cotton fabric for dyeing."

Corey became more anxious and angrily replied, "Yes. That sounds like a difficult situation, but why haven't *you* found a job?"

She answered, "Well, I tried to get a job at a bank but was not accepted because I have no experience. "

She paused momentarily, grimaced, and continued, "I'm a little ashamed, but I found a part-time position working nights at the Germania Lodge. I serve the men snacks and ale. In fact, that's how I met Crockett. He stopped by one evening after your prospecting team found gold out on the ridge. He was very kind to me, and I instantly fell in love with him."

She fluffed up the back of her long red hair, smiled at Corey, and said, "He tells me that I've got the most beautiful hair of any woman he's ever known."

Corey thought, "Just as I thought, she's just another harlot."

He said, "Yes. Your hair is beautiful. May I touch it?"

Maisie sat erect on the couch and said, "Oh, I don't mind. Sure."

Corey sat at his desk, opened its top drawer, and gently drew out a knife. It was an ornate bone-handled, Damascus steel-bladed knife. He showed her the knife and said, "I like beautiful things too. I was given this knife by a Quinebaugan boy who crossed my path once too often."

Maisie's heartbeat quickened, and she said, "Yes. That is a handsome knife. As you know, Crockett collects all sorts of guns. He's an excellent shot, too."

Corey rose and paced the room. Stopping behind her, he gently caressed her hair. Then, he commanded, "Sit still."

He grabbed the bottom six inches of her fluffy red hair and slashed it cleanly. Then, he walked around to face her and showed her the lock. Then, he said, "Now, that didn't hurt. Did it?"

She began to whimper nervously and said, "Why did you do that? I only want what's best for my husband."

He answered with a question, "How old are you?"

She said, "I turned nineteen on the day Crockett and I were married."

Corey said, "Maisie, you are correct. You and Crockett are currently tenth on the list for Pesikutes Ridge and will be able to move there by this time next year. But there are many ways for you to move up on the list. Have you ever wondered who prioritizes the list?"

As he moved closer, she sniveled lightly and replied, "Yes. I have wondered and don't understand why so many other families were placed before ours. That is why I came to see you today."

He stood directly in front of her, gently placed his hand on her back, and gently pulled her close.

Then, he announced, "I prioritize the list, and I would like nothing better than to place your name at the top."

Maisie felt she had no choice. As she loosened his belt buckle and settled on her knees beneath him, a tear began trickling down her freckled cheek.

Corey said, "That's better now. Be a good girl. I'll take good care of you."

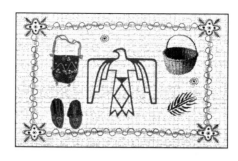

37: FAITH MATHEWS & RACHEL FLOWERS
LUCASVILLE
MATHEWS FAMILY RESIDENCE
SATURDAY, MAY 15, 1859

Travis, his mother, and Rachel Flowers sat in the Mathews family dining room eating breakfast when they heard a polite knock on the front door. Travis said, "It must be Lydia. I'll let her in."

He opened the door, hugged her, smiled, and said, "How was the trip?"

Lydia answered, "It was easy. It only took my carriage forty-five minutes to arrive from Norwichtown Green."

When she entered the living room, Lydia suddenly felt immersed in a familiar, comfortable time capsule. She said, "I love the feel of this room!"

Pointing to the walls, Travis replied, "Yes. My mother has spent years collecting these wampum-beaded sashes, feathers, headdresses, Quinebaugan-themed paintings, and baskets displaying Quinebaugan symbols. She has fused the collection to create a traditional Quinebaugan atmosphere."

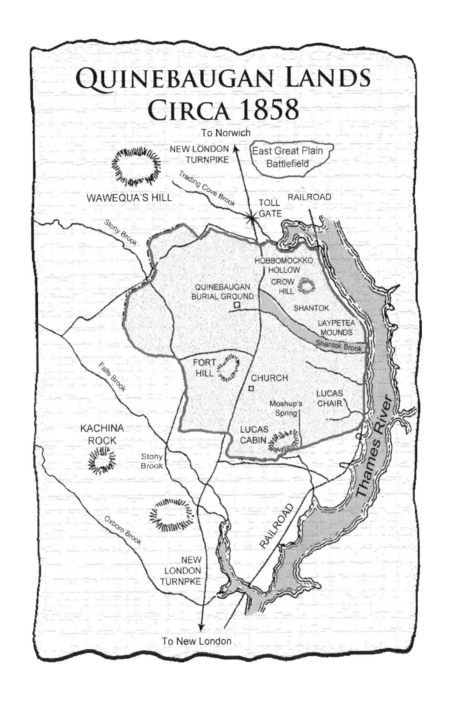

Lydia responded, "It certainly does. This room makes me feel at home because it's so cozy."

As they entered the dining room, Travis said, "Mother, do you remember Lydia from the Jubilee social mixer at General Williams's home?"

Faith rose, hugged Lydia politely, and responded, "Yes, of course. Lydia, it's so good to see you again. Travis has told me many good things about you over the past few months. Please allow me to introduce my dearest friend, Rachel Flowers. She's been my best friend since birth and is one of our tribe's most influential leaders."

When Rachel looked upon Lydia, she saw a brightly colored aura surrounding her. She stood and said, *"Yahtahay, sister."*

Lydia didn't fully comprehend the Quinebaugan word but felt Rachel's inviting presence and answered, *Yahtahay."*

A primal feeling of joy overcame Rachel as she greeted Lydia. She said, "I welcome you. It is good to finally meet you."

Lydia replied, "Thank you. The pleasure is all mine."

Travis's mother said, "Lydia, please sit and join us. We were just now enjoying a cup of coffee, and Rachel was about to serve us a batch of her freshly baked corn muffins."

Travis replied, "Thank you, Mother. I'll always say *yes* to Mrs. Flowers's muffins."

As they shared breakfast, Travis said, "Mrs. Flowers is our tribe's storyteller, one of our historians, and is well-versed in all details of our Quinebaugan heritage."

Lydia responded, "I am so happy to hear that because I want to learn everything I can about Quinebaugan culture."

Faith added, "We'll most certainly help you with that! Rachel recently created a group of women in the Quinebaugan Church called the 'Church Ladies Sewing Society.' She is the president of this close-knit group that frequently meets to discuss current events and other Quinebaugan issues. Perhaps you could join us?"

Rachel joined the conversation, saying, "Miss Stedman, I cannot begin to tell you how thrilled I am to see you again."

Lydia was perplexed. She thought, *"Why did she say again?"*

Rachel continued, "When you were a tiny baby, I held and rocked you in my arms. Of course, I was just a young girl at the time, but I still remember your sweet disposition."

Lydia was taken aback and responded, "Really? I'm sorry, but I don't remember."

After a moment, she smiled and continued, "Was I a good baby? What was the occasion?"

Rachel replied, "Lydia, you weren't just a good baby. You were an angel, a gift from *Munduyahweh*. I can see you've grown into a beautiful woman."

Rachel continued, "As you know, General Williams and his family have supported the Quinebaugan Church for many years. The General even taught Sunday school for us. But, it wasn't just the Williams family who supported our church. You remind me of another delightful young woman who once helped our tribe.

Several years ago, Sarah Lanman Huntington, from the Second Congregational Church in Norwich, worked with members of our tribe to help raise money to build the church. She and girls from our tribe traveled together, by horseback, to Quinebaugan and Norwich households to spread the news of our future church. They raised money by selling them hazelnuts."

Your parents also attended worship services there often. In addition, they became close friends with my parents and several other Quinebaugan families."

Lydia could hardly contain her curiosity. She replied, "That is very interesting. They never mentioned that. We've always attended services regularly at the First Congregational Church. However, I have faint memories of us visiting your church once or twice as a very young girl."

Faith spoke up, "So, Lydia. Travis told me that you've been given an assignment. Please tell us about it."

Lydia said, "Yes. The 200th Jubilee Committee charged Mr. Daniel Coit Gilman to prepare a discourse on Norwich's past 200 years of history. They want to tell the people of Norwich about the friendships between Sachem Lucas, the Quinebaugan tribe, and the Englishmen of Norwich in the 1660's timeframe. The gentleman is well versed in the English point-of-view of our history but desires to understand history from the Quinebaugan point-of-view better."

She turned to Travis's mother and continued, "Mr. Gilman asked me to learn as much about Quinebaugan's history as possible last month. He hopes I can uncover details of their history and pass them along to him. So when Travis told me that a woman named White Eagle knows the tribe's early history better than anyone, I immediately wanted to meet her."

Lydia continued, "I hope to speak with her about the Quinebaugan's history. So, Travis and I would like to visit her at Kachina Rock."

Faith and Rachel sat silently for a full, uncomfortable minute. Then, finally, Rachel said, "Two hundred years ago, our tribe flourished here in New London County. Lucas provided leadership and protection for hundreds of our fellow tribesmen. Our main village was here at Shantok, but we also thrived in several other small local communities at Wawequa's Hill,

Trading Cove, Massapeag, the banks of the Thames River, and Kachina Rock."

Rachel continued, "Today, our tribe has spread throughout New England, but our numbers have dramatically diminished. Fewer than fifty families remain in the Norwich area now. We need to regroup, reorganize, and bring our fellow tribe members closer together. We want to revitalize our traditions."

"Many years ago, when Faith and I were young, the tribe celebrated the Wigwam every autumn. The festival brought us together to celebrate the harvest, fellowship, and new beginnings. Our tribe hosted the festival at Kachina Rock for years. But, unfortunately, federal law outlawed Native American celebrations such as ours several years ago."

"Even today, the State of Connecticut plans to take ownership of all our homelands. They want to tax us on the land we have lived on for hundreds of years. However, we'll fight the annexation, and our noble tribe will become strong once again."

Turning to Lydia, Rachel continued, "Lydia. White Eagle is our most knowledgeable historian. As a young woman, she and her daughter lived among us here in Shantok. For a time, they occasionally attended the Quinebaugan Church. We were all friends with her and shared recipes, knowledge of herbs, and many other Quinebaugan traditions."

"But, later in life, she chose to live in solitude at Kachina Rock. White Eagle has lived many years and has experienced the full spectrum of human challenges. However, she has chosen to live there because she cherishes her privacy."

Rachel took a moment and carefully looked Lydia over. She finished by saying, "However, I am confident that she will accept you and Travis as honored guests. You will learn much from her."

Faith looked at her son and said, "Travis. Kachina Rock isn't hard to find. It's only a mile and a half from here. Continue south on the Norwich/New London Turnpike, then head west on Fort Hill for a mile. Moshup knows the way."

38: AQUILABLANCA
KACHINA ROCK
SATURDAY, MAY 15, 1859

Travis and Lydia were also anxious to learn more about the Quinebaugan artifacts they had found several months earlier. So, after receiving more detailed directions and advice from Faith, they packed the mortar, pestle, box of gold powder, tomahawk, and a picnic lunch.

Along the way, Lydia questioned, "Has your mother told you anything else about White Eagle?"

Travis smiled and said, "Well. Yes and no. Have you heard the story of Chahnameed?"

With a puzzled look, she answered, "I don't think so."

After Travis told Lydia the story of Chahnameed and his wife, he grinned from ear to ear and said, "Some people say that White Eagle knew Chahnameed, and some say she might have even been his wife! Yes, the one who speared him with a single strand of her enchanted hair."

Lydia looked at him and replied, "Come on. I know you're kidding. Isn't that just a myth? I was hoping you could tell me a little more about White Eagle. How did she get that name?"

Travis replied, "Well, my mother once told me that as a young woman, White Eagle almost had a full head of thick jet-black hair. I say *almost* because she also sported a shock of white hair on the crown of her head. The stark contrast of a white crown on her black hair reminded everyone of a bald eagle. However, the most interesting fact is that, as she got older, her black hair turned white, and her white crown turned black. No one can explain the transformation. I guess we'll see."

He continued, "Many people believe White Eagle is the last of the Laypetea, the Small Ones of the Woods. All I know for certain is that she knows more of Quinebaugan tradition than anyone."

~~~~~

After the twenty-minute ride from Travis's home, Moshup and the wagon slowed as Kachina Rock appeared. Travis's breath was taken away because it was even more imposing than he remembered.

He exclaimed, "There's something about this place that gives me peace. I still remember my family's picnics here years ago. We used a rickety, old wooden ladder to climb the rock. The ascent was scary, but we could look out over the entire Quinebaugan homeland once we were on top."

He continued, "Lucas held tribal meetings on Kachina Rock. The spot, of course, provided a stunning panorama, but it also granted protection. In the old days, Lucas was concerned about the possibility of attack from the Pocawansetts because he knew they had spies who knew when and where the Quinebaugan were planning to assemble. So, Lucas posted sentries around the perimeter of the rock during meetings."

Lydia responded, "Thank goodness we don't live in times like that now."

Travis said, "Yes. But Corey Pallaton and his crew are still pretty dangerous."

After hitching Moshup to a wooden post near a granite wall of coarse stones, they contemplated entering White Eagle's domain. A sapling fence enclosed a lush garden of squash seedlings, beans, young okra plants, Brussels sprouts, and wild mint. Several chickens scurried about, and Lydia noticed a bunny munching on one of the carrot sprouts.

When they saw a gigantic gray cat hissing and attacking the small rabbit, Lydia and Travis knew they were not alone. The cat was obviously someone's pet.

The four-foot-tall rock wall, overgrown with ivy and other vegetation, was a clear sign to Travis and Lydia that they were *not* welcome. The entrance to White Eagle's estate was guarded with a tall, thirty-inch wide, moss-covered, hinged wooden gate. It was just wide enough to allow one person at a time to enter.

As Travis pulled the gate open, its rusty hinges creaked loudly. A short, elderly woman suddenly appeared from the cave-like opening underneath Kachina Rock. She yelled out, "Get off my property!"

Travis and Lydia remained outside the gate, holding out their outstretched arms and hands for her to see. Then, finally, Travis said, "Please, we wish you no harm. I am Travis Mathews, son of Jonathan and Faith Mathews, and this is my friend Lydia Stedman. We hope to speak with you."

They stood frozen for what seemed an eternity as White Eagle scrutinized them. Then, finally, they were relieved when she spoke, "You may enter."

As they ambled toward her, Travis and Lydia felt her gaze. Lydia sensed White Eagle had noticed her short stature, slight limp, black hair, and single red feather adornment. Travis could see that White Eagle was also well aware of his extreme height, slight limp, and snake-shaped birthmark. They both felt exposed.

As they neared White Eagle, Travis was startled when his birthmark began to itch. It was the same burning feeling he had experienced after the rattlesnake had struck him when he stumbled on the Quinebaugan skeleton.

White Eagle gazed at Travis and said, "Your serpent has awakened."

Travis felt the urge to turn and run but sensed his destiny standing before him.

White Eagle guided them to a stone table situated beneath a giant oak tree. They noticed her demeanor change as she spoke. "I don't receive many visitors, but I am happy you came today."

She turned to Lydia and asked, "Why have you come?"

Lydia was surprised at White Eagle's sudden change in attitude. She answered, "Firstly, thank you for speaking with us. We've discussed visiting you for a long time and are happy to have finally found our way."

She continued, "This fall, the townspeople of Norwich will celebrate the 200th anniversary of the founding of Norwich. They plan to remind everyone of the friendship between the early Quinebaugans and English settlers. Today's Norwichians know that Lucas sold the land to the English in 1659 but have forgotten many aspects of the beneficial relationship. The event planners have asked me to find out what I can learn from you."

She concluded, "Travis has already told me several Quinebaugan stories he learned from his mother. After hearing the legends, I hunger for more. I am naturally curious, but somehow, your tribe's history touches me at a deep, visceral level. I would love to hear anything that you're willing to share."

White Eagle thought for a few moments and said, "Yes. The English have forgotten many of the favorable aspects of our long-standing friendship. We must discuss many things."

She asked Travis, "Did you say your mother's name is Faith Mathews, and your friend's name is Lydia Stedman?"

Travis responded, "Why, yes. That is correct."

White Eagle returned her attention to Lydia and said, "I met your parents many years ago at a Quinebaugan church service."

Lydia was taken aback and said, "You're the second person who told me that today. Mrs. Rachel Flowers said the same thing earlier this morning. I'm sorry, but I don't remember that."

"Well, of course not; you were only a baby. Rachel and Faith were close friends. They loved holding and rocking you to sleep. I also had the pleasure of holding you close. You always had a curious, bright spirit about you."

White Eagle continued, "I can see that you are ready for me to reveal the truth."

"My name is *Aquilablanca*, which translates to White Eagle in English. I was adventurous as a young girl. And, like you, I asked many questions. I lived with my parents in the Quinebaugan community of Shantok, where life was simple but filled with hard work."

"My family and the Quinebaugan tribe were content. However, my family was quite different from our fellow tribe members. For example, we often received private messages from *Munduyahweh* in our dreams and were physically different from everyone else. In addition, everyone in my family was very short in stature."

"*Munduyahweh* taught us how to grow corn, beans, squash, and a wide variety of healing herbs. We shared this knowledge with our brethren, but they feared us because we looked so different.

Eventually, my mother, father and I moved to the forest to live with the animals and birds. We learned to recognize the eagle's scream, the red-tailed hawk's screech, and the song of our friends, the cardinals."

White Eagle continued, "The Quinebaugan began calling us the Small Ones of the Woods because of our height and where we lived. The *Laypetea*, which literally means 'The Small Ones' in English, are shy little creatures who bring balance to our tribe. My family lived in harmony with them. I felt their spirit enter my body while I slept every night. They were a part of my family, and we were a part of theirs."

"After a while, the Quinebaugan believed we had completely transformed into Laypetea. The tribe treated us with great respect even though we lived separately from the Laypetea in the woods. The tribe brought us gifts of corn cakes, berries, and other treats. Eventually, they proclaimed us to be the last of the Laypetea."

White Eagle continued, "They were all wrong because our family was *not* Laypetea. But we didn't care what the others thought because we were at peace and harmony with everyone."

Lydia asserted, "Travis and I have heard of the Small Ones of the Woods. Thank you for sharing. Please tell us more."

White Eagle continued her story, "As a young girl, I enjoyed hunting for feathers, growing plants, making buckskin clothes, and wampum beads. Sometimes, when my father went fishing in the ocean for sea bass and tuna, I would journey with him. But I didn't fish with him. Rather, I remained on the beach, where I spent hours looking for purple quahog, conch shells, and seagull feathers."

NORWICH GOLD

She continued, "After we returned home, my mother and I made wampum beads from the shells, and I decorated my clothes with beads and bird feathers. My mother shared the beads with our fellow tribe members. The Quinebaugan used wampum to secure sacred bonds of honor, such as weddings, treaties, and other important agreements."

"One day, when I was a little older, I ventured to the beach alone and, by chance, met a handsome fisherman named Chahnameed. He was very charming, and I fell in love with him instantly. After that, we lived happily on a remote island."

"But, when I became pregnant, he left me alone for long periods and stranded me on the island. It was a terribly difficult period in my life. Chahnameed and I argued for many days. But, eventually, I escaped and returned to the Shantok community."

As White Eagle told her story, Travis and Lydia were both awestruck. The myth of Chahnameed was not simply a tale. It was a story of love and survival based on White Eagle's real-life experiences. But, neither of them had heard that Chahnameed's wife had ever been pregnant.

Finally, Lydia asked, "Did you give birth?"

White Eagle answered, "Yes. I gave birth to a beautiful girl. I named her *Plumaroja*, which means Red Feather in English. I named her this because I loved how the feathers made *me* feel. So, I placed red-tailed hawk feathers in her hair daily until she was old enough to do it herself."

She paused briefly and said, "I want to show you something."

She walked into the opening under the overhanging Kachina Rock and returned with what appeared to be an old wooden jewelry box. When she opened the box, Lydia and Travis saw a collection of feathers, beads, and other charms.

Lydia said, "These are exquisite. I've never seen such a beautiful collection. You're not going to believe this, but I, too, love feathers. I wear them in my hair, use them to pen newspaper articles, and make fans with them. When I wear them, I feel complete. They help make me feel beautiful. I especially love wearing the red-tailed hawk feathers."

White Eagle smiled and responded, "That does not surprise me. I need to finish my story."

"I raised Red Feather alone while living in Shantok. We attended the Quinebaugan Church, and yes, Red Feather was also a friend of Rachel Flowers. At a young age, Red Feather married a whaler. He and my daughter were a perfect match. Everyone treated us respectfully and recognized us as the last of the Laypetea. We were happy living in harmony with our tribe."

"Our tribal brothers and sisters were overjoyed when Red Feather became pregnant. They perceived her pregnancy as a sign that the Laypetea bloodline of the Quinebaugan tribe would continue. However, that joy was short-lived because, during a whaling expedition, a powerful hurricane claimed her husband's life. Their ship sunk, and search parties never found the ship or any sailor's bodies."

"I was sorrowful for Red Feather's loss but glad she and her unborn child were safe. Three weeks later, she gave birth to the most beautiful baby girl ever seen. The baby had a full head of jet-black hair and had the disposition of an angel. She was petite. She was so small that many thought she would not survive. But I knew she would survive because my daughter was also tiny when she was born. I knew the spirit of Laypetea was within her."

"I was overjoyed. However, the baby girl's body was not formed perfectly. Her left foot was far too small because it had not fully developed in Red Feather's womb. No one knew if she would ever walk properly because her foot was the size of a rabbit's. So her mother named her *Patadoe,* which means Rabbit's Foot in English."

Lydia began to tremble. A primal feeling of awakening began to stir.

White Eagle continued her story, "Everyone loved Patadoe. The size of her foot didn't matter to anyone. But, when Patadoe was only two weeks old, her mother passed away. The birthing process struck Red Feather with a severe infection. It was a tragedy of the worst kind."

"I took care of Patadoe for several months but did not have the resources or energy to give her the life she deserved. So when I learned that an English woman in town was barren and wanted to adopt, I spoke with her and her husband in the Quinebaugan Church."

White Eagle turned to Lydia, and with tears in her eyes, she said, "Patadoe, I see the red feather in your hair and your limp. *I see you.* Yes. The woman who adopted you, raised you, cared for you, and loved you was Mrs. Caroline Stedman. However, your birth mother was my daughter, and I am your grandmother."

Lydia's heart pounded wildly. She had always felt different from everyone around her. She now knew why. The spirit of the Laypetea was within her, and her native name was Patadoe. She rushed into Aquilablanca's open arms and felt the warm glow of familial love flowing throughout her entire being.

Lydia did not even try to stop the tears of joy streaming down her cheeks because she knew, without any doubt, that she had found her native home.

39: WAWEQUA
Kachina Rock
Saturday, May 15, 1859

White Eagle reminisced and shared fond stories about her daughter throughout the next hour. Lydia asked one question after another. Her curiosity was insatiable.

Lydia questioned, "Where was I born? What were my mother's favorite activities?"

White Eagle answered, "You were born while Red Feather and I lived in the Shantok community, and your mother loved birds. She could identify every species by their song or by their appearance. She especially felt an attachment to cardinals because she loved the sound of their song and their magnificent color. The spirit of the Laypetea was strong within her."

She continued, "We also enjoyed tending our vegetable and flower gardens. I liked planting and watching the vegetables grow. She especially loved the flower garden."

She pointed at a large, healthy plant near the fence and said, "Do you see that bush with the brightly colored red flowers?"

When Lydia and Travis nodded, White Eagle said, "That azalea bush was Red Feather's pride and joy. She loved red azaleas, red feathers, and red cardinals. When she was sixteen, a trader from Charleston, South Carolina, visited Shantok. He brought several unusual plants and vegetables that he wished to sell or trade."

"We had never seen flowers with such dazzling color. The trader told us that azalea bushes made their way to America from England only a year earlier, and this was his first time selling them in New England. We traded our hand-made wampum beads for several of his unique plants. He also sold me a collection of okra and Brussels sprout plants, and Red Feather traded for that azalea bush."

She continued, "After she passed away, I moved here to Kachina Rock and transplanted her precious plant. Its cheerful spring flowers remind me of my Red Feather, your sweet mother. Would you like to smell their scent?"

The three of them trekked to the magnificent azalea and examined it. The plant was in its full glory. They couldn't help but notice its healthy new leaves, many large red blooms, and a swarm of lively bees hovering around the flowers. The bees drank in the nectar.

White Eagle said, "Don't mind the bees because they won't sting unless provoked. They are my friends. I use their honey to sweeten tea and stay healthy. Would you care to join me for a tall, cool glass of meadow tea?"

When they returned to the stone table for tea, they saw a large, rotund, tabby cat perched upon it, occupying a third of its area. White Eagle waved her hand and said, "Shoo now! Shoo! I'll feed you later."

She smiled and added, "That's Jameson. He's just an old tom cat, but I love him dearly. He keeps me company and protects my garden from pesky rabbits."

She continued, "Travis, your mother, and her friends loved discussing the benefits of plants and herbs. Years ago, we learned from one another by sharing our experiences with various herbs, recipes, and medicinal remedies."

She smiled and added, "By the way, I use your mother's meadow tea recipe that calls for spearmint leaves and honey."

Travis smiled and replied, "This tea is delicious! My mother told me of your knowledge of our tribe's recipes, traditions, remedies, and herbs. She was right!"

Travis smiled at her and continued, "Lydia and I have brought you several gifts."

White Eagle answered, "Why, thank you. You're very kind."

Travis said, "A few months ago, while working on a survey crew on Wawequa's Hill, I found several unusual objects. My mother, Lydia, and I believe they are old Quinebaugan artifacts."

Travis pulled the small, golden-tipped tomahawk from his leather pouch and said, "I found this. I know it is a tomahawk, but I don't understand why it is so small."

He continued, "A couple of weeks later, our curiosity grew when I showed this to Lydia. So, we returned to the site to search for more and found several other fascinating objects."

Travis then handed White Eagle the stone box filled with gold flakes, the mortar, and the pestle. He said, "These are for you."

Travis and Lydia were surprised at White Eagle's response. First, she sat motionless with her eyes fixed on the objects. It appeared as though White Eagle had fallen into a trance. Then, after a full five minutes, she studied them carefully. Finally, she asked Travis, "Exactly where did you find these, and did you notice anything else out of the ordinary?"

Travis replied, "They were all buried at the base of Wawequa's Hill next to a small mound. We also found a skeleton, probably a male. When I uncovered the tomahawk, a rattlesnake bit me. Later, when Lydia joined me on the second expedition, she was also bitten. Both experiences were odd. But somehow, I felt the snakes' energy was connected to the skeleton and the artifacts."

White Eagle looked at him solemnly and questioned, "Was there anything else odd? Anything at all?"

Travis thought about the question momentarily and answered, "Well, yes, two other odd things happened, but I didn't think them important."

He touched the birthmark on his forehead and said, "On both occasions, my birthmark became hot. It burned. That doesn't happen often, but it catches me off guard when the burning sensation begins. I'm a little embarrassed, but it also happened today when I walked through your gate."

He continued, "The second thing that happened was also odd. After the snake bit Lydia, the skies suddenly darkened, and a powerful thunderstorm came upon us. However, the storm subsided quickly."

She gestured to his forehead and said, "You bear his mark."

White Eagle began another story, "Wawequa was Lucas's brother. He was a well-respected Quinebaugan who led a community of farmers and artisans near Wawequa's Hill. However, he lived in a turbulent period of the Quinebaugan tribe's history. Sixteen years before Lucas sold the land upon which Norwich lies, our tribe was under constant attack from the Pocawansetts of Rhode Island. They lusted for our land."

"The Pocawansetts murdered many Quinebaugan warriors, women, and children. However, one day in 1643, Lucas and our brave warriors defeated them soundly at the Battle of Sachem's Plain in Norwich. After our victory, Lucas delivered the Pocawansett leader, Pallatonomo, to an English court in Hartford for justice. And, after the authorities found him guilty, the English instructed Lucas to punish Pallatonomo in any way he saw fit."

"Lucas gave Wawequa the honor of carrying out the sentence because he knew the virtue and kindness in Wawequa's heart. His brother would proudly perform his duty because he knew the act would end hostilities between the tribes. It would restore balance, peace, and tranquility to the tribe. Lucas was well aware that Wawequa possessed the strength of a warrior and the fortitude to heal the wounds of our brethren."

She continued, "Legend has it that Wawequa used an enchanted tomahawk, crafted by his young son, Tantuk, to carry out the sentence. Wawequa's golden-tipped tomahawk later became a symbol of peace and harmony for our people."

"After Pallatonomo's death, leaders of our tribe displayed Wawequa's tomahawk at the Green Corn Festival every year. Our tribe's Storyteller told of Lucas's leadership and Wawequa's strength and bravery. The stories reminded everyone of our tribe's grand victory at Sachem's Plain. In those days, the festivals were held here at Kachina Rock."

"The Quinebaugan wanted peace and needed healing after Pallatonomo's execution. The tribe's women knew the serpent symbolized rebirth and healing. Folklore says they etched a snake tattoo on Wawequa's forehead to enhance his gift of healing. His son carved a snake's body into the handle of his famed tomahawk. Everyone believed the healing process began with virtues of Wawequa's heart."

"Wawequa's son, Tantuk, was a talented artisan who learned the finer points of making pottery, tools, and weapons from his mother. Tantuk, or perhaps his mother, crafted this mortar, pestle, and tomahawk."

White Eagle lifted the tomahawk and said, "I believe this is Tantuk's prototype for Wawequa's tomahawk. He probably assembled it before making his father's full-sized tomahawk. And, as an adult, I'm sure Tantuk treasured this object as a fond reminder of his youthful past. I suspect the skeleton you found was that of Tantuk, who took this relic to his grave."

She pointed to the mortar and said, "Look carefully at the base of this vessel. There are tiny specks of gold residue in its base. I also see residue on the head of the pestle. Perhaps Tantuk used these tools to grind gold-laden minerals into the golden flakes. Also, Tantuk very well could have used a few of the gold flakes in this box to gild the tomahawks. It is impossible to know what happened, but I'm sure this small tomahawk was *not* Wawequa's."

"Now look carefully at etchings on the mortar, and the tomahawk pictured is Wawequa's. The snake symbolizes his gift of healing, and the child-like figures are Small Ones of the Woods, the Laypetea, not merely children. As a young girl, my mother told me she and I had the honor of protecting our tribe's legacy and sacred artifacts. As the last of the Laypetea, it was our obligation. I didn't understand what she meant then, but the truth is now clear. My mother knew where Wawequa's tomahawk was stored."

White Eagle continued, "Unfortunately, Wawequa's sacred tomahawk is now lost."

After a long moment, White Eagle's voice cracked as she said, "She never got the chance to tell me where it is buried because she passed away while I was on the island with Chahnameed. I am ashamed because I should have never left Shantok."

She continued, "We must find the tomahawk."

After pulling herself together, White Eagle finished by saying, "Once again, our tribe lives in a time of significant change, and our tribe needs balance. Our numbers have dwindled, and many live scattered throughout New England. As a result, we forget our glorious traditions and heritage. I fervently believe we need to restore the Green Corn Festival. It will bring proper alignment and balance to the Quinebaugan tribe."

Lydia spoke up, "White Eagle, you're right. We must work to renew the strong bonds of our traditions. If we could find Wawequa's tomahawk, perhaps it could begin a reunification, healing process."

As Lydia spoke, White Eagle felt a long-lost glow of love return. Then, as her body quivered ever so slightly, she said, "Patadoe, my daughter, I want you to call me by my native name, Aquilablanca. Please say it."

Lydia felt deeply honored. After several tries, she finally pronounced her name correctly. Lydia said, "Aquilablanca. Your name is beautiful. Aquilablanca. It makes me feel complete just to say it. Thank you."

White Eagle replied, "I thank you. I haven't heard my native name spoken in many years."

She continued, "Travis. Another legend tells us that every male descendant of Wawequa is marked with the sign of a serpent. The snake's name is Caduceus, and her job is to watch, listen, wait, and help when needed. When called, a rush of energy fills her soul, and she summons the healer with whom she has bonded. She only calls Wawequa's son for help."

She looked at Travis and said, "Parents of almost everyone in our tribe give their children a middle name that honors a noble ancestor. My middle name, Kachina, honors one of my ancestors. The Quinebaugan named this rock in his honor. Travis, I knew your father and mother, but no one ever spoke of their middle names to me. Please tell me."

Travis replied, "My father's middle name is Hoscott. He told me our ancestors, the Hoscotts, were expert horsemen. And the word Hoscott originally meant *horse coat*."

White Eagle replied, "Yes, many early Quinebaugan loved horses. They used them mainly for farming and enjoyed a special bond. The horses were almost like another family member."

She questioned again, "And your mother?"

Tears slowly welled in Travis's eyes as he said, "My mother's middle name is *Wawequa*."

Aquilablanca replied, "Yes. The spirits of Wawequa and Caduceus are within you. I have prayed to our great spirit, *Munduyahweh*, for years for their return. I always knew that someday, our people would be reunited. So today, my heart sings with joy."

White Eagle stood, opened her arms and hands, and said, "Travis and Lydia. You've asked me to accept these artifacts on behalf of the tribe, but I must decline your request."

She continued, "There is still much work for you because the set of artifacts you've brought is incomplete. The most precious treasure of all, Wawequa's tomahawk, is missing, and I want the two of you to find it and bring it to me."

"I suspect you will find it buried along with Wawequa's skeleton. My mother surely knew the burial site's location but never got the opportunity to tell me. Therefore, I can only provide sketchy details. Perhaps he lies near my childhood home site, near the Laypetea mounds. Perhaps you could explore Lucas's Chair, Lucas's Cabin, Moshup's Spring, the Royal Quinebaugan burial ground, the Ashbow burial ground, Shantok burial grounds, Lucas's Fort, and maybe even Hobbomockko's Hollow."

"However, you must be careful when digging around the Hollow. It is dangerous because it is cursed with the spirit of a mighty Hoopanoag warrior. Your search will be difficult because Wawequa's bones and tomahawk could rest in any one of many places."

Travis responded, "Lydia and I searched for Quinebaugan objects near Lucas's cabin and Moshup's Spring already. We found the cabin's foundation and drank water from the spring. But, except for a few arrowheads, we didn't find anything out of the ordinary."

White Eagle looked to Lydia and said, "Patadoe, you must learn all our stories, traditions, and legends from Faith Mathews, Rachel Flowers, and me. Then, you must go to the organizers of Norwich's Jubilee and tell them of our glorious past."

"Travis, you and Patadoe must find the tomahawk. Follow your heart and listen to Wawequa's spirit. You will be guided."

40: LAYPETEA
NORWICHTOWN
STEDMAN FAMILY RESIDENCE
SATURDAY, JUNE 25, 1859

Lydia demanded, "Why didn't you tell me that Aquilablanca was my grandmother?"

Caroline Stedman answered, "Who is *Aquilablanca*? What are you asking?"

Lydia was furious. She responded, "You know good and well who she is. She's my biological grandmother, the sage who lives at Kachina Rock. Why didn't you tell me? Aquilablanca is her Quinebaugan name!"

Her mother replied, "I never heard the name Aquilablanca. I only know of White Eagle. I didn't tell you because your father and I were bound to secrecy until your eighteenth birthday. So we told you everything you needed to know a few months ago."

Lydia answered, "Yes. You told me that my grandmother cared for me after my biological parents died, but you didn't tell me I am Quinebaugan! And you didn't say anything about White Eagle either. I want to know why you failed to mention her."

Caroline had feared this day would come. She replied, "Yes. I knew she was your grandmother and planned to tell you someday. I only wanted to protect you as long as possible. Many people here in town fear her. Some think she may be a witch or possessed by some spirit. Years ago, the Quinebaugan tribe sent White Eagle and her family out to the woods because many believe their ancestors were dwarves or fairies. She was an outcast. Also, as a young woman, she made several terrible decisions which people believe resulted in the death of her daughter and son-in-law."

She continued, "Lydia, I only want the best for you. But, unfortunately, uneducated people here in town are sometimes cruel and callous."

Lydia responded, "Well. I am a woman now and no longer need that kind of protection from you. Did you know that my native name is Patadoe? It means Rabbit's Foot in Quinebaugan. I've always thought my limp was a curse, but now I am sure it is a blessing. It is a part of who I am and my heritage. So when Aquilablanca spoke my name, I instantly connected to my ancestors. So, how did you meet White Eagle?"

Caroline began, "As you know, your father and I have been close friends with General and Mrs. Williams for many years. One day, long ago, they invited us to join them for a Sunday picnic in Lucasville. We all loved exploring the countryside on Sunday afternoons after church."

"On that day, we attended church with the Williams family at the Quinebaugan Church, followed by a picnic. General Williams taught Sunday school there often and told us the tribe welcomed outsiders."

She continued, "He was right. Everyone welcomed us, and we were impressed with the pastor's sermon. He reminded us that our creator, *Munduyahweh,* loves and cares for everyone. He said we are all brothers and sisters, regardless of skin color."

Lydia's mother continued, "After the sermon, he fervently prayed for White Eagle and her granddaughter. He mentioned that the baby's father and mother had recently perished and needed prayer, comfort, and generosity."

"As we left the church, White Eagle held you in her arms, and the pastor introduced her to us. I instantly fell in love when she allowed me to hold you. You were the most beautiful baby I'd ever seen. You were so tiny, and I immediately felt the kind energy of your spirit."

"It was such a lovely day. While at the picnic, Mrs. Williams told us more about your parents. She said your father worked as a harpooner on one of her husband's whaling ships. He, like yourself, was short in stature but long in courage. There were stories of how he once saved the life of one of his fellow sailors. During a violent storm, the wind tossed one of his friends overboard, and your father instantly dove into the ocean and rescued him."

Caroline continued her story, "Unfortunately, just a few weeks before you were born, another of the General's ships was lost at sea while returning home from a successful whale hunt. A hurricane capsized the ship, and all aboard were lost. The entire community wept for your biological father and all the other sailors."

She continued, "Yes. Your father and I unsuccessfully tried to conceive a baby on our own for years. But I'm glad it didn't happen because we were destined to have you in our lives. Lydia, your father and I love you. And, yes, Patadoe, I am happy to learn your Quinebaugan name. You are indeed an extraordinary woman."

Lydia felt a renewed love and respect for her parents. She rushed into her mother's arms and said, "I love you and am glad to be your daughter. But I'm also happy to be Quinebaugan and want to learn more about their traditions."

Caroline said, "I'm happy for you, too. You'll learn many interesting things about your ancestors."

Lydia said, "White Eagle also told me my biological mother's name was Red Feather. It must be why I love feathers so much."

She paused and said, "Travis will arrive shortly, so I need to finish dressing. I'll return in a moment."

Two minutes later, Lydia reappeared in the room with a red feather prominently perched in her hair, smiled, and said, "Now I'm fully dressed. Travis likes my feathers too. Did I tell you that he keeps me fully supplied with swan feathers? He finds them near Trading Cove Brook and brings them to me at the newspaper office. So, since I use them to write my newspaper articles, I think of him often."

Caroline responded, "It sounds like you've become fond of him."

Lydia replied coyly, "Yes, you could say that. Today, Travis and I plan to visit a few places where the Small Ones of the Woods once lived. He wants to pinpoint their old homeland on the Jubilee map. Also, White Eagle told us she lived near the Laypetea mounds as a child. We're also hoping to find a few more Quinebaugan relics there."

They heard the sound of wagon wheels and the clippety-clop of Moshup's hooves upon the pavement. She smiled broadly and said, "Sounds like him now."

Lydia dashed to the front door to meet him and said, "I'm ready."

Travis stepped down from the wagon, gave her a quick peck on her cheek, and said, "Me too."

Lydia stowed the picnic lunch she and her mother had made behind the driver's bench and said, "It should be a good day for a picnic."

Travis held up a rolled map, smiled, and responded, "Yes. Picnic indeed. But don't forget that Mr. Walling is paying me to make this map. And I want it to be accurate."

Lydia pointed to the survey instruments and said, "I'm sure it will be. You've become very good at using those instruments."

She caressed her hair and said playfully, "You're good with your hands. I can vouch for that."

Travis's heart skipped a short beat, and he said, "Thank you, Miss Lydia. We need to get on our way."

~~~~~

Once aboard the wagon, Lydia asked, "So, what's our plan for today?"

Travis replied, "I've spoken more with my mother about the Small Ones of the Woods history and the folklore surrounding them. It seems as though different folks have different opinions of the Laypetea. She said that everyone believes they lived near the mounds, but, on occasion, a few of the village's young girls spotted them near Fort Hill while gathering berries. Fort Hill isn't too far from the mounds, so I'd like to investigate it first."

As the wagon neared the hill, Travis said, "My mother told me several things about Fort Hill. The *fort* in the name Fort Hill refers to Lucas's Fort. The sachem built it long before the fort at Shantok and used it as an inland stronghold. It is said to have rock walls on three sides and open to the east. He knew the Pocawansett would most likely attack from the east."

Travis added, "I once overheard Mrs. Flowers tell my mother that the Laypetea often used the area as a playground. While Lucas tended to tribal affairs, they scribbled etchings and drew pictographs on the fort's walls. Unfortunately, most, if not all, of the graffiti was lost when Connecticut built the Norwich/New London turnpike. So we need to keep an eye out because we might find residue of a pictograph."

After dismounting the wagon, Travis gathered the instruments, and they ascended the hill gradually. Travis had no difficulty lugging them due to his powerful physique. Then, however, he noticed that Lydia hadn't spoken for a few minutes.

Lydia thought about Travis's earlier words and said, "Travis, you know that I love exploring with you, but I'm a little concerned."

Puzzled, he glanced at her and said, "What could you possibly be worried about?"

She curled her lips and said, "Snakes. I also see ominous, dark-gray storm clouds in the northeast. And it has been hot all day. You just told me we're on our way to the top of a rocky hill. We both know that's where snakes love to sun themselves. And, if you remember last time …"

Travis replied, "Yes. I also thought about it, so we'll be extra careful. As a kid, I drank a small bottle of snake venom, which made me immune. So, maybe, since the last incident, you've become immune too."

Lydia answered, "I don't want to find out. But I would like to share something else with you. I've been considering and studying the significance of snakes throughout history. I know White Eagle told us snakes symbolize healing and rebirth, but I've recently learned that snakes are also considered guardians of valuable objects."

She continued, "Here's the story."

Jason and the Argonauts

Once, long ago, a winged ram flew through the air like an eagle. His golden wool symbolized authority throughout the land, and its citizens anointed anyone who possessed it as its ruler.

Unfortunately, someone stole the fleece from its rightful owner, King Pelias. So, the king enlisted a sailor named Jason and his crew to set out and retrieve it. If Jason could recover it, King Pelias promised Jason that he would become the rightful ruler of an area in modern-day Greece.

They sailed for many days on their ship, the Argo, and searched many islands. Finally, they found the fleece hanging in a tree, guarded by a serpent that never slept. After Jason hypnotized the snake, he grabbed the fleece and returned home a hero.

She finished by saying, "That snake was a guardian, and he was protecting a valuable, precious object. And I believe the Quinebaugans of Lucas's time viewed snakes as guardians and healers. We also know from experience that the rattlesnakes who bit you and me were guarding Quinebaugan artifacts. So, it can't be a simple coincidence."

Travis thought about her theory momentarily and said, "That makes a lot of sense. You may be right. I only hope that we don't run into any snakes today. I don't want to see you hurt again."

Lydia said, "I'm sorry, but I disagree with you. Since they are guardians, *we want to find them* because another serpent will probably guard the bones of Wawequa and his tomahawk."

Travis replied, "Of course, you are right again. But, we still need to be cautious."

Travis and Lydia could still see the nearby Quinebaugan Church in the distance when they reached the top. They easily found the remnants of the fort where someone had positioned several large boulders into a rectangular pattern. It was clear that the walls of the dilapidated fort had once been about six feet tall. Travis said, "Let's measure it and record it on the map."

Although the rocks were in disarray, they could estimate the original fort's dimensions. After they measured eighteen feet by twelve feet and marked it on the Jubilee map, Travis said, "Now for the fun part."

Travis pointed at a series of rocks aligned inside the fort and said, "These appear to have supported an interior wall. My mother told me to look for this room. She said we might find a kitchen or a pantry. It's where women cooked and stored food for those who sought refuge in the fort."

He continued, "She also said that the eastern face of the fort is completely open today, but it wasn't always that way. In Lucas's time, the Quinebaugan erected a wall of logs that faced potential attackers. So, Lucas's warriors could shoot arrows from small openings between the ends of the logs."

He set up Mr. Walling's sextant and chronometer. He noted the sun's exact position at exactly 1:00 p.m. Then, he told Lydia, "When we get back to Mr. Walling's office, I'll use his reference book and these notes to determine the exact latitude and longitude of this site."

Lydia was impressed. She said, "You've learned a lot from him. You should be proud of yourself."

Travis replied, "I do enjoy using the instruments and making maps. I wish the people of Norwich had a better opinion of me because I'd like to stay here. But, unfortunately, Corey Pallaton has got them thinking that I'm a crook and a liar. So I've lost everyone's respect."

She answered, "That's their loss. You're a fine man. Let's see if we can find Wawequa. Also, keep your eyes peeled for any pictographs on rocks. I'm hoping that a few of them have survived."

They carefully searched the area within a 100-foot radius of the fort for signs of a grave, mound, or etchings. But unfortunately, there was nothing out of the ordinary.

Lydia glanced at the sky and said, "A storm may be coming. We should eat."

Travis nodded, grinned, and said, "Okay. I've got a novel idea. Let's eat in the kitchen. Maybe we'll receive a message from the spirit of Wawequa."

Lydia chuckled and said, "Sure. That will be fun."

After laying out the tablecloth over the rubble where the kitchen had once been, Travis noticed a pile of built-up sticks, debris, and stones in the back corner of the kitchen. He said, "Lydia. Look over there. Those rocks appear to be concealing something."

Lydia looked and said, "I agree. They seem out of place, but I'm not touching them. Instead, find a stick, and you can poke at it."

Travis fetched a small branch from a maple tree outside the fort walls and began prodding at the pile. Within a minute, Lydia shrieked, "There! It's a snake."

A moment later, after the nine-inch long garter snake slithered harmlessly past them, they both laughed and began delving into the mound. Lydia and Travis worked side-by-side on all fours, gently excavating the pile with their hands and fingers. As they made their way deeper into the bank, Lydia felt a gently curving, almost flat, thin object with sharp edges.

She said, "Travis, look at this. It's amazing. It's a pottery shard that appears to have been a piece of a pot that stored vegetables or water."

Travis said, "Yes. I think you're right. It appears that the kitchen roof caved in, and the rocks smashed a pot below. Let's dig deeper."

They found scores of pottery fragments that had undoubtedly been a single, complete pot at one time. Lydia said, "This is a great find. I feel lucky today. Maybe we'll find something at the mounds. But, unfortunately, I don't think we'll find any skeletons here."

Travis replied, "Yes. We'll take these shards to my mother and Mrs. Flowers. It will be interesting to see what they say about them."

~~~~~

After gathering their things, descending the hill, and reloading the wagon, Travis and Lydia resumed their journey to the Laypetea mounds. He said, "I'm not exactly sure where we'll find the mounds, but my mother gave me a few hints."

He continued, "It's a wooded area very near the banks of the Thames River. The Small Ones of the Woods wanted to live in the forest yet still be near the river. In that area, they could easily find fish, nuts, berries, potatoes, squash, and corn to eat."

"Ten years ago, the New London, Willimantic & Palmer Railroad built their railroad upon the very spot of the Laypetea homeland. The mammoth locomotive that pulls the train from Norwich to New London, the *T.W. Williams,* is named for the company's president, Thomas W. Williams. He is General Williams's younger brother."

"The NLW&P Railroad is the only way passengers or cargo can complete an entire trip between the two cities using only rail. Since the Norwich & Worcester Railroad's southernmost stop ends at Allyn Point, passengers must board a steamship to New London."

Travis continued, "I was told the mounds are near an extremely sharp bend in the railroad tracks, about two miles south of Norwich. So the place shouldn't be too hard to find."

Lydia replied, "You just reminded me of an interesting magazine article about that area. Six years ago, the *T.W. Williams* pulled a load of timbers and other cargo from New London to Norwich. For some reason, the conductor forgot to slow down for the sharp bend in the tracks. It was a terrible accident."

"The train separated from the locomotive, jumped the rails, and barreled into a nearby house. The rail car injured, but did not kill, a woman inside the house. However, the accident made a huge mess, discouraging Norwichians from riding the train."

She continued, "Many rumors floated around saying the train conductor was distracted by three Laypetea dwarves. They stood on the tracks and pointed at him because they didn't like the loud sound of trains rumbling through their homeland."

Travis smiled and said, "Well. I'm not sure that story is entirely true. But who knows? Maybe."

Travis noticed deeper potholes in the hard-packed dirt road as they neared a densely overgrown, wooded area. Finally, when they came upon two downed trees blocking the road, he said, "Let's walk the rest of the way. I think we're pretty close now."

He hoisted the survey equipment on his broad shoulders again, and they strode down the narrow path eastward toward the Thames River. Lydia said, "There sure are a lot of birds here. I hear the call of cardinals all around us."

Travis responded, "Yes. I like their sound. It feels like they are trying to tell us something."

After a moment, he said, "Look, I see the train tracks. They're about 100 yards from here. The railroad company must have cut back the vegetation to make room for the train, making a clear view possible."

As they entered the clearing, Travis and Lydia were amazed at the charming panorama. In the background, they saw a majestic steamship filled with excited, spirited passengers sailing into Chelsea Harbor and several exquisite homes of Norwich's wealthy on Laurel Hill. The landscape before the railway was relatively flat but dotted with twenty or so oval-shaped mounds.

However, the view of Norwich was set against an unsettled sky. The crisp late afternoon sun in the southwest sky beat down upon the landscape, and black, ominous clouds hung low over the town in the north. Winds of a powerful Nor'easter were gathering momentum. The juxtaposition of light versus dark, calm versus unsettled, and dry versus wet created a sense of anxiety.

Travis said, "We need to take latitude and longitude readings before the storm arrives. I'll use the instruments to record the exact location at the sharp bend of the train track. We can use the curve as a reference point. Then we can use Mr. Walling's 100-foot measuring tape to pinpoint several mounds."

Lydia responded, "Okay. Let's do it quickly. We still have a few minutes before the storm hits."

After hurriedly recording the readings, Travis said, "Let's search the mounds."

Lydia said, "Okay. I've recorded the location of five of them in your book. But look at this one. It's different from the rest. It's more like a small cave."

Travis joined her and said, "You're right. It isn't an ordinary mound."

From a distance, the structure resembled a Laypetea mound. But upon closer inspection, Travis saw the *mound* was man-made. It was roughly in the shape of a square and had four walls made of small granite boulders. A two-foot opening in one of the walls looked somewhat like a door. Early Quinebaugans had built an underground structure into the side of a small hill.

Travis exclaimed proudly, "I know what this is. It's an *eagle's hole*."

Lydia replied with a puzzled look, "*A what?* I've heard of eagle nests but never eagle holes."

Travis said, "In Lucas's time, the Quinebaugan used these shelters to store food. Locating these enclosures partially underground made it easier to regulate the environment inside. The Quinebaugan women used them as cellars to store root vegetables and dried meats."

Lydia frowned and said, "Yes. But you didn't answer my question. Why is it called an eagle's hole?"

Travis laughed and replied, "Oh. Sorry. Eagles are the strongest, most courageous, and bravest of all birds. Several Native American cultures, including the Quinebaugan, consider eagles sacred because they fly close to the Creator. The Quinebaugan consider themselves the *Clan of the Eagle*. So, since the cellars belong to the Quinebaugan, they were Eagle's Holes."

He continued, "I saw an interesting mound near the bend. It appears the railroad builders left it undisturbed. It looks more like a burial site than any typical Laypetea mound. Let's see what we can find."

The sky was darkening, and the wind picked up. Lydia said, "Okay. We must hurry."

Travis grinned and replied, "Who's afraid of a little rain?"

Although they were anxious, they approached the small outcropping with great respect. First, Travis crouched down and removed the vegetation protecting the mound. Then, when they heard more rumblings of rolling thunder, they glanced northward to Norwich and saw slivers of heat-lightning hovering over the town.

Travis was concerned for Lydia's safety. He looked at her and nervously said, "Maybe we should return on a more pleasant afternoon."

Lydia pressed gently up to him and whispered in his ear, "No way Mr. Mathews. Let's dig!"

As the rain began, they scraped away several layers of roots, rocks, and pebbles. Then, six inches below the surface, they found a thick layer of pottery shards and a collection of small animal bones.

Travis said, "These are turkey, chicken, pork, and fish bones. This isn't a burial plot; it's an old garbage pit. Wawequa isn't here for sure. We gotta go."

By this time, the rain was violently blowing sideways, lightning had filled the sky, and the sound of thunder surrounded them. Travis grabbed the survey instruments and yelled, "We don't have time to return to the wagon. Let's go inside the eagle's hole."

She nodded, and they hurried to the small cave. Once inside the cramped quarters, Travis set the instruments down and looked at Lydia. She pulled the red-tailed hawk feather from her hair and said, "Looks like my feather got all wet."

He turned his full attention to her and saw the most beautiful woman in the world. The rain thoroughly drenched her thin summer dress. It clung to her tiny, firm body, and the look of love in her eyes melted Travis's heart. He said, "Let me help you with that."

He ran his fingers through her dripping wet, jet-black hair and pulled her close. As he did so, Lydia instinctively leaped into his arms and began to kiss the inside of his ear. Travis caressed the base of her back and pulled her even closer. The couple felt the call of the wild throughout their minds, body, and spirit.

They were unaware of any driving rain, fierce wind, lightning, or thunder. The only thunder they knew was the pounding of their hearts.

Nature's energy surrounded them, and the couple felt the earth tremble when lightning struck just outside the eagle's hole. It felt like the walls might collapse. Distracted by the thunder, Lydia nervously exclaimed, "What's going on?"

They felt a rhythmic, unnatural vibration intensifying about them. As the pulse increased, a primal instinct of fear possessed Travis. This moment reminded him of the day Corey's boys tied him to the Norwich & Worcester rail tracks. He looked to the railroad tracks and yelled, "Look, the train is coming. It's the *T.W. Williams!*"

Lydia responded, "Yes. It is. But look! Look at the rails near the bend."

They both clearly saw a small young boy standing a few feet from the tracks, pointing at the train.

Travis's eyes widened, and he exclaimed, "I can't believe it. I see one of the Small Ones of the Woods. Look. The conductor isn't slowing down. He's not paying attention because he's watching the boy."

The number and size of lightning strikes increased dramatically. Then, suddenly, a huge bolt struck the rail car just behind the locomotive when the train arrived at the bend. All the cars rocked sideways between the rails, and disaster appeared imminent.

Lydia's heart pumped violently. Scenes from her lifetime raced through her head, and she screamed, "It's going to jump the tracks and hit us!"

Thankfully, the train settled on the track a moment later and rumbled harmlessly past them. The storm diminished instantly, and no boys were to be seen.

They stared at one another in disbelief and questioned, "Was this a simple coincidence? Or perhaps, was *Munduyahweh* sending them a message?"

Lydia was relieved but deeply disturbed by the event. The train could have easily killed them, or a lightning bolt could have struck them directly.

She said, "I want to find Wawequa's tomahawk as much as you. Last time, a rattlesnake bit me; this time, we could have gotten crushed by a train. Yes, I'm adventurous, but I don't relish the idea of severe bodily harm!"

As she glared at Travis, another lightning bolt struck a nearby tree, and Travis instantly felt deep remorse. Once again, he had placed her life in danger. Travis knew he was responsible for her snake bite and today's close encounter with the train. And now, he had almost gotten her struck by lightning.

Travis felt the entire town of Norwich, except Lydia, wanted him gone, and now he had once again failed the woman of his dreams. However, he had fallen deeply in love with Lydia and could not bear the thought of bringing any harm or shame to her or her family.

He thought, "Lydia will be safer and happier if I leave town."

41: BURSTING BALLOONS
DOWNTOWN NORWICH
CHELSEA SAVINGS BANK: FRANKLIN SQUARE
MONDAY, AUGUST 1, 1859

Henry Bill, the vice president of Chelsea Savings Bank, politely ushered Mrs. Lucy Mathewson and her three-month-old baby into his second-floor office. He motioned her to a comfortable, over-stuffed leather chair and said, "Please sit and make yourself comfortable."

Lucy nervously replied, "Oh, thank you. I appreciate you seeing me today. Is it okay if I keep Martha with me?"

Mr. Bill smiled and said, "Of course it is. I love babies, especially adorable ones like Martha."

Lucy grinned and replied, "Well. I don't want to cause a problem, and my oldest daughter is downstairs waiting. I could leave Martha with her."

Bill replied, "No. That is unnecessary. But, please, what can I do for you?"

As Lucy peered out the tall window to Franklin Square below, she could only think of how wonderful her life had been before the recent challenging events. Today, she needed to protect her home and family. She said, "My husband and I bought a home from you on Laurel Hill almost five years ago. You must remember my husband, Wanton?"

Bill replied, "Yes, I remember Wanton and your home. If I remember correctly, my architect designed your home, my builder, Mr. Corey Pallaton, built it, and our bank gave your family a loan for the mortgage. Your husband is a leather merchant here in town. Right?"

Lucy responded, "Yes. He's operated the leather business for twenty years, making and selling boots, shoes, and saddles. However, things are changing for our family. Wanton is ill. The doctor tells us that his years of cleaning and tanning hides using the tannin-bearing bark of hemlock, sumac, and oak trees have caught up to him. Prolonged exposure to those chemicals has made him very sick. As a result, he doesn't have the strength to continue operating his business."

Bill responded, "I'm sorry to hear that, Mrs. Mathewson. What do you need?"

Lucy answered, "The final balloon payment for our mortgage is due next month. We made a 50% down payment when we took out the loan and have never missed a monthly payment. However, I am concerned because your bank recently foreclosed on one of my friend's homes when her family couldn't make the final payment."

She continued, "I foresaw this problem a year ago when I first noticed Wanton's declining health. So, I began working in the dye room at the Norwich Bleaching, Dyeing & Printing Company in Greeneville to help make ends meet. I haven't minded working at the Bleachery for ten hours a day and six days a week, but it has been hard on our family. It is hardest on my daughter, who waits for me downstairs."

Lucy paused for a long moment, wiped a tiny tear from the bottom corner of her eye, and said, "She's such a good girl. Mary is sixteen years old and tends to my husband and five children daily."

She said, "I'm hoping that you can help us. When I began working, it wasn't easy, but I was able to squirrel away a substantial rainy-day fund. So when I heard Mr. Corey Pallaton had struck gold out on Wawecus Hill last fall, I was thrilled! He and his wife convinced me that an investment in their company could help us pay the pending balloon payment."

"Last week, I asked Mrs. Pallaton if I could liquidate my shares to pay off our mortgage. I was delighted when she told me the shares were worth three times what I had paid because that is more than enough to pay our debt to you."

Lucy continued, "Elena said they would happily buy back the shares, but we must wait until next spring. Apparently, at the moment, the Pallatons are using most of their company's excess cash to rebuild their company office."

She finished by saying, "So, Mr. Bill, I'm hoping to pay the balloon payment using a new short-term loan from you. The term only needs to be for six months. Is that possible?"

Mr. Bill thought about her proposition and answered, "That depends. Our bank always requires some form of collateral for any loan. Your home is the collateral for your current primary loan, so we can't use that. What collateral could you offer for the new, short-term loan?"

Lucy smiled and answered, "Oh, that's easy. I offer you our Wawecus Hill Gold, Silver, and Nickel Mining Company shares. Luckily, the value of our shares far exceeds the amount I need to borrow."

NORWICH GOLD

He responded, "At the moment, the only answer I can give you is *perhaps*. I'll speak with Mr. Dunham, our bank's treasurer. Could you and I meet again next week?"

Lucy smiled and said, "Yes. Martha and I will stop by on Monday morning shortly before work. Thank you so much for your consideration."

As Lucy rose, Martha giggled and smiled at Mr. Bill.

Henry Bill shook baby Martha's tiny hand with his finger and said, "We'll see what we can do for you and your mother, Sweetie."

~~~~~

Mr. Bill showed Lucy out of his office and walked her down the stairs to the bank's outside door. As Lucy left for work, her eldest daughter cradled Martha for the journey home, and they all waved goodbye. Henry Bill deeply cared for the Mathewson family and hoped the bank could help them.

Henry Bill saw John Dunham and a well-dressed, graceful woman leaving the bank's foyer. Bill said, "John, I've got an issue I need to discuss with you."

Dunham replied, "That's good to know because I've got something to discuss with you also."

They both smiled, and Dunham said, "You go first."

After Henry related Lucy Mathewson's story and her request for a short-term loan, he said, "Has our bank ever accepted any shares of stock as collateral?"

With a perplexed look, John Dunham replied, "I don't think so, but that doesn't mean we shouldn't consider the idea. It is interesting that you should ask about this situation because I just had an enlightening conversation with Mrs. Fidelia Hyde."

Mr. Bill asked, "Was that her just now leaving?"

Dunham answered, "Yes, indeed. She, too, wants to use shares in the mining company for collateral. Her brother, our Connecticut Senator to the United States Congress, Lafayette S. Foster, will be running for reelection in a couple of months. She wants to make a substantial donation to help fund his campaign."

He continued, "And, quite frankly, I want to help her out because Senator Foster is a strong opponent of slavery and supporter of Abraham Lincoln. Foster's a good man and represents Norwich wisely. I know that funds from selling her twelve shares would go a long way in helping him."

Mr. Bill responded, "Yes. I agree. I don't understand why Corey Pallaton can't buy back a few of his company's shares. The newspaper articles I've read about his company are encouraging, but I'm starting to doubt its financial health."

As the conversation progressed, John Dunham's pulse and temperature increased. He, too, was planning to liquidate all of his company shares. He and his wife needed the money to pay for tuition at Brynn's finishing school. Finally, John said, "What are your concerns?"

Henry Bill replied, 'The Mathewson family story is similar to several situations that have become all too familiar. We may have a problem with Mr. Corey Pallaton."

"Five years ago, he built several homes for my clients on Laurel Hill. He is an excellent home builder, and I also know that Corey is dedicated to advancing his Pocawansett brethren's status. He's recently built a few houses on Wawecus Hill, near Goldmine Brook. He calls his affordable housing project Pesikutes Ridge."

NORWICH GOLD

Bill continued, "Well. Last week, two Pocawansett families living at the Ridge also requested a loan from us. They need the money to help pay the monthly installments on their mortgage. The fathers and sons of the families all work for Corey's mining company."

"They told me that Corey uses a cash/stock agreement for their wages. He pays their weekly wages, half in gold and half in stock shares. The gold is barely enough to meet their family's current needs, but he has assured them that the stock shares will be significantly more valuable in the future."

Bill continued, "When I asked them how they afforded the initial 50% mortgage down payment, they said that Corey donated it to their families. These gentlemen asked me if they could use their company shares as collateral for a loan that covers their monthly payments."

John Dunham interrupted him and questioned, "So. Did you give them the loan?"

Bill answered, "I haven't given them an answer yet because I wanted to do some research. I was also planning to ask your opinion before acting."

"I spoke with Lucius Carroll at the Norwich Savings Society this past Friday. He told me that Pallaton took out a substantial loan from his bank to start up the mining company last year. Unfortunately, Pallaton's recent deposits are substantially lower than before, and he hasn't paid his last two monthly payments."

"Lucius also told me he has temporarily frozen Pallaton's credit account at his building supply store downtown."

John's heart was now pounding. If he couldn't sell his shares, he wouldn't be able to pay for his daughter's education. Furthermore, a scandal like this would severely tarnish his family's reputation because he and his wife had been preaching the laurels of the Wawecus Hill Gold, Silver, and Nickel Mining Company to the entire community for months.

John finally said, "I'll speak to Corey in person. He's my neighbor and friend, and I'm sure there is a valid explanation."

42: LIQUIDATION
DOWNTOWN NORWICH
LUCAS HALL: WATER STREET
TUESDAY, AUGUST 2, 1859

When John Dunham hurriedly entered his office without knocking at the door, Corey Pallaton knew he was upset. Dunham carried a professional-looking leather messenger filled with business documents. At first, he thought Dunham's face was flushed from climbing the four flights of stairs, but upon closer inspection, his bulging eyes were a dead giveaway.

Dunham said, "Good afternoon, Corey. Do you have time for a quick meeting?"

Corey sensed Dunham's question was not a question at all. Instead, he recognized it as a demand. So Corey stood, sauntered to his temporary liquor cabinet, and said, "Hello, John. Please have a seat. May I pour you a glass of port?"

Dunham did not typically partake in libations during the afternoon, but today, he made an exception. He sat in front of Corey's desk and answered, "Sure. I would enjoy that."

Corey studied several of his many bottles of wine. After carefully selecting, opening, and pouring the drinks, he replied, "General Williams brought me several bottles of this sweet, red port wine from Portugal. He told me the vintners used raspberries, blackberries, caramel, and cinnamon for this particular batch."

He smiled and added, "I'm glad you've come for a visit because I've been looking forward to sharing it with someone."

After handing Dunham the wine glass, he raised his glass and said, "Here's to progress."

Dunham raised his glass and replied, "To Progress."

Pallaton said, "What can I do for you, John?"

Dunham measured his words and carefully replied, "I'm sorry, but this isn't a social visit. The vice president of the Chelsea Savings Bank has asked me to meet with you because several customers are requesting a new type of loan. Our bank officers are considering their requests but wanted to hear your opinion of the matter."

Pallaton fully understood where this conversation was headed and politely said, "Well, as you know, I'm always on the outlook for how I can help members of our community, but I fail to see why you seek my opinion. When it comes to making money, I know your officers are wise. So, *what is the matter* that you speak of?"

Dunham answered, "Two Pocawansett families have asked our bank for a short-term loan; by short-term, I mean six months. Presently, we only offer five-year mortgages. The terms are: 1) 50% down payment, 2) Monthly payments, 3) 20% balloon payment at the end of the five years, and 4) a physical home for collateral."

He continued, "The families all live in your housing development, Pesikutes Ridge, and the males all work for your mining company. I haven't seen the homes yet, but our bank's customers told me they are comfortable, well-made dwellings.

However, the Pocawansetts, who took out mortgages a few months ago, are now having difficulty making monthly payments. So they requested we give them an additional loan to help them make their payments."

"They've told us you pay their wages half in gold and half in mining company stock shares. However, they don't have enough cash to cover monthly expenses. You know these people much better than me. So how would you suggest that you and our bank can best serve them?"

Corey had known this day was coming for months. He said, "I always want what's best for my tribal brothers. So, I created the payment method you outlined to benefit them the most. The shares of stock they've earned are worth far more than any liquid cash. I know they and all other shareholders will lead a wealthy, comfortable life in future years."

Dunham responded, "Yes, but at the moment, they are struggling and need available cash. Would it be possible for you to change the ratio of 50% cash and 50% shares to perhaps 80% cash and 20% shares?"

Corey deflected, "Everyone should plan for the long term. Unfortunately, short-term considerations often lead to foolish decisions. So, please tell me why it is a problem for your bank to provide them with short-term loans."

Dunham answered, "The only thing of value that your workers can offer as collateral is their company stock. And the problem is that our bank has never used company stock as collateral. So, although the bank wants to help, we're unsure how to proceed."

Corey answered, "Well, we all live in changing times. Your bank would do well to use the shares as collateral. They've tripled in value in the past year. I'd also like to let you in on a secret. We found another large vein of gold in the hillside only last week, and it's the largest one yet. Please keep this to yourself."

He continued, "I have considered changing the payment ratio, as you suggested. But, candidly, our company has a minor, temporary cash flow issue. You and I are meeting today in this office here at Franklin Square because of that hooligan troublemaker Travis Mathews. So I've been forced to outlay a large portion of our profits to pay construction costs for a new office building."

He continued, "The severe deep freeze temperatures and incessant snow Norwich experienced last winter caused another financial difficulty. I had to shut down mining operations for four months."

Dunham sorely wanted to trust Corey's words. He replied, "I can only imagine the cost of the new building and making payroll. I know it's been a challenging set of circumstances for your company. If you remember, I attended your company meeting just after the tragedy. I thought you explained the situation quite professionally."

Dunham was now ready to make his ploy. He said, "Thank you for the wine. It has an exquisite texture and taste. And you have convinced me that it is in my bank's best interest to allow our customers to use your company stock as collateral."

He opened his messenger bag and pulled out his stock certificates. He said, "In return, I'm hoping you can do one thing for me. Caroline and I bought many shares almost a year ago."

He showed the certificates to Corey and said, "If you remember, back in December, you said you could repurchase them from me after a year. I am pleased they are worth three times what I paid, and now I'd like to cash them in."

Corey scowled and responded, "John, I'd like nothing better than repurchasing them from you because I know they will soon be worth even more. As I said earlier, we uncovered a huge gold deposit last week. Unfortunately, it will take a few weeks to blast it out, process it, and sell it to our Boston-based buyers. So I need you to wait for just a few more months. I'm sure we'll be in a better position by the end of this year."

Dunham answered, "Corey, I'm sorry. But I need the cash now. Brynn plans to begin at Miss Porter's School for Girls next month. So I've got to pay her tuition next week."

Every time Corey heard Brynn's name, he bristled. She publicly embarrassed him, and he detested how she pranced around town like royalty with that pesky little, yapping dog. He had seen how Brynn endlessly teased Jeremy and kept him eternally frustrated. Now, the little twit wanted to be *finished* so she could find herself a wealthy white man. Corey could barely stand the thought of her.

After controlling his contempt for Dunham's daughter, Pallaton responded, "John, I am truly sorry. Unfortunately, I cannot help you at the moment. I suggest you use your shares as collateral to obtain a six-month loan. Then, you and the other shareholders you mentioned could also benefit from owning a part of our mining company."

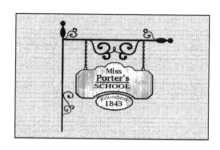

43: Goodbye, Miss Porter
Norwichtown
Dunham Family Residence: Washington Street
Wednesday, August 3, 1859

Mary and John Dunham were nervous. The day they had feared for quite some time was now upon them. Mary called out, "John, Brynn, breakfast is ready! It's on the table."

Recently, Brynn loved to sleep late into the morning. After all, it was summertime, and she was enjoying the utopian, almost perfect, period between high school and finishing school. Life was good, and Brynn was happy with her comfortable lifestyle. She chirped, "I'll be down in a minute."

John entered the dining area and smiled apprehensively at his wife. Then, he said, "I love you, Mary."

Mary looked at him and replied, "Yes. I know. We'll get through it. This, too, will pass."

Mary called out again, "Brynn. Your eggs are getting cold."

Brynn lumbered into the dining room and sat down at the table. She said, "Why do you make me get up so early? It's not even 10:00 yet."

After a mundane discussion of their day's scheduled events, John stood and announced, "I'm going to make pancakes. Would anyone care for a stack?"

Mary smiled and replied, "Sure. That sounds good to me."

Brynn was awake by now and said, "Yes. I'll have a couple. But only if we've got molasses."

Mary piped up, "We do. I bought a pint just last week. The merchant told me they imported it directly from the West Indies."

Brynn asked, "Where are Alvina and Mary?"

John replied, "I've given them the day off. I allowed them to spend the day with their mother at the Almshouse. They told me that she hasn't been doing well lately."

Brynn suspected something was amiss. Alvina hadn't mentioned anything wrong with her mother, and her father only made pancakes when he was about to deliver bad news. Brynn's mother also appeared far too chirpy. Brynn looked at her mother and said, "Okay, what's the matter?"

Mary deferred to her husband. She nodded to him. She knew Brynn's fury was about to erupt.

John began, "Brynn, unique circumstances often change our lives. Sometimes, obstacles that loom in our pathway appear insurmountable. But, through many years of experience, I've found that solving difficult problems always strengthens one."

Brynn was perplexed. She said, "Father, I don't understand a word you just said. What are you trying to tell me?"

John dropped the bomb, "We need to postpone your entrance to Miss Porter's school."

Brynn's jaw dropped. She looked incredulously at her father and said, "What? That cannot be true!"

Mary said, "Brynn. It isn't forever. We only need a few more months for our finances to improve."

Brynn shot back, saying, "How is that possible? You've told me for months that the mining company shares will pay the tuition. Are you going to use my money for something else? Why are you doing this to me?"

Mary replied, "Brynn. Please understand. We're not doing anything to you, and we're not using the shares for anything else. Your welfare and happiness are more important to us than anything."

Brynn angrily said, "It isn't fair. Emeline Norton has been going there for two years now. Her parents don't seem to have a problem with finances. The school can't be that expensive."

John interrupted her, saying, "We can't cash in the shares at the moment. The mining company cannot redeem our shares because the fire forced them to fund the reconstruction of their office building."

He continued, "However, there is a bit of good news. Corey Pallaton told me that the company's miners discovered a large vein of gold and silver last week. He assured me he'd buy our shares in a few months, and then you'll still be able to attend school. You'll simply have to wait one more semester."

Brynn couldn't control her anger and shouted, "I'll have none of this! You've got to do something!"

Mary replied, "Honey. We've done all we can."

As John and Mary's weak explanations continued, Brynn's body shook with utter disappointment. She started crying and sobbed, "I can't bear this. What will my friends think? Emeline and I were going to be roommates. She's already got it set up. She's also working on getting me into her sorority."

Mary replied, "Brynn. As we said before, it's not forever. It's only a one-semester delay."

Brynn defiantly replied, "I don't believe you. That school is vital to me. Even homely, Emeline has two men interested in her now. This is so embarrassing to me!"

Her parents bowed their heads slightly, and John said, "Brynn. We're truly sorry."

Brynn looked her father in the eye and replied, "I'm going to speak with Jeremy. I know that he'll redeem the shares. He is the vice president, and I'm sure he has a lot to say about what happens within company business."

As she stormed to her room, Brynn yelled back at her parents, "I'll fix this!"

Five minutes later, Brynn returned to the dining room. Her appearance had totally transformed. She wore a low-cut, tight-fitting dress and a large floppy hat.

She stood at the outside doorway, turned to her parents, and said, "I'm going to pay a visit to Jeremy. He works at the company's office on Wednesdays, and I know he will listen and help me."

~~~~~

Brynn regrouped her composure during the fifteen-minute carriage ride to downtown Norwich. There was no way she would allow others' failings and mistakes to dictate the terms of her life. In her heart, Brynn knew that Jeremy was infatuated with her and would solve her problem.

As she hitched her family's carriage in front of Lucas Hall, Brynn noticed the Wawecus Hill Gold, Silver, and Nickel Mining Company's wagon nearby. She was shocked to see a well-muscled young stallion hitched to it. Brynn thought him a magnificent animal, fit for royalty, and wondered where Lightning could be.

After entering the building and climbing the four flights of stairs, she opened the door to the company's temporary office in the Independent Order of Odd Fellows' space. Brynn broadly smiled at Jeremy and said, "Hi, Jeremy. I'm so happy to see you."

Jeremy rose from behind Corey's desk, hugged her, and kissed her politely on the cheek. Then, he said, "Well, I'm happy to see you too. I certainly didn't expect to see you here today."

She handed him a small bouquet of pink roses and said, "Well, I thought I'd come for a visit and try to brighten your day. Every time I've visited this office, it's been so dreary. So, I thought I would cheer it up with a few roses. I picked these just before I came here."

Jeremy replied, "Thank you. And, by the way, I agree with you. This office is a little dingy. How are you? You seem happy."

Brynn knew she was anything but happy but that perhaps her luck was about to change. She said, "I am feeling optimistic. I noticed your wagon outside with a handsome young stallion. Where's Lightning?"

Jeremy said, "Well, I'm sorry to inform you that Lightning is no longer with us. He was old and had too much trouble pulling the company wagon. The new horse is powerful and fast, too. Unfortunately, I'm unable to race anymore, but Crockett will enter the harness race at next month's county fair. He's a good driver, and we have a good chance at winning now."

Brynn again remembered how cruelly Jeremy had treated Lightning in last year's race. She said, "But what did you do with Lightning? Did you find a good home for him?"

Jeremy squinted and said, "Well. That's not quite how it works. Corey needed money to help pay for Zeus, and he sold him to a dog food production company."

Brynn was appalled. She scolded Jeremy by saying, "You named your new horse Zeus? You could have donated Lightning to a needy family here in Norwich."

She continued, "You've told me how well your company is doing. I don't understand why you wouldn't have enough money to purchase a fine horse like Zeus."

Jeremy responded, "Well, things have been slowing down for us lately, and we've had to cut back on a few of our expenses."

He added, "By the way. You look lovely today."

She swung her hips ever so slightly as she approached him, smiled, and said, "Thank you. You've been so kind to me."

She began, "I know the accident has been physically demanding for you, and I've been thinking of a future for you and me that will make life easier for us. As you know, I plan to begin studying at Miss Porter's School for Girls next month. I will learn everything I can about cultivating, growing, and selling flowers. Then, after I graduate, I'll open a thriving florist shop."

She continued, "I'd like for you to be my partner. You could manage the finances and run the daily operations, and I'd furnish the flowers and tend to customers. What do you think?"

Brynn's ideas for Jeremy's future angered him. He was a proud Pocawansett, and there was no way he would play second fiddle in a florist shop. He said, "Brynn. I want to spend my life with you, but I'm not excited about your idea. I'll have to mull it over."

She said, "Well. That's my plan, and I hope that you will join me. However, for today, I do need your help."

He was relieved because he knew she was about to give him a way to redeem their relationship.

She said, "My parents need to sell their company shares to help pay for my tuition. But yesterday, Corey told my father he couldn't cash them in. I don't understand why not. We've owned the shares for over a year, and Elena told us we could sell them back to you after a year."

Jeremy scowled and said, "It isn't that simple. The cost of rebuilding the company office has been exorbitant, and the company is currently short on cash."

Brynn stood erect and said, "Yes, I've heard that, but I also know that Corey has bought a new, expensive racehorse, has paid for all the materials to build five houses on Wawecus Hill, and that your miners have discovered a large vein of gold in the mine. So, why can't my family redeem a few shares? We only need enough for my school. So, it shouldn't be that difficult for you."

Jeremy squirmed and replied, "As I said earlier. The issue isn't that straightforward. I'm not so sure that Corey can afford it."

Brynn flashed her anger and said, "Jeremy. You're the vice president of this operation, and you've told me for months that the company is going great guns. Have you been lying to me?"

Jeremy couldn't believe she accused him of lying. His anger began to build, and he replied, "No, I haven't lied. It's just that the company isn't doing as well as we had hoped."

She stood her ground, pointed at him angrily, and demanded, "Just how badly is the company doing? May I see the map showing where you've found gold and silver? Corey told my father that the recent discovery was promising. First, however, I want to see the proof with my own eyes."

Jeremy would not continue to take the verbal abuse, saying, "The map isn't here. It's in Corey's safe at his home. But looking at the map won't help you because there was *no discovery*. In fact, the map doesn't show much of anything. Corey misled your father about the existence of a new find to keep him quiet!"

Brynn glared at him.

Jeremy thought for a moment as he collected his thoughts. He was angry, but his fear of losing Brynn forever trumped everything. Then, finally, he said, "There is one possible way for you to cash in the shares. But you'll need to be careful."

Brynn placed her hands on her hips, faced him, and said, "Okay. Let's hear it."

Jeremy said, "Elena doesn't know how poorly the company is doing or the meager amount of gold we've actually found. She believes all is well. Also, I know that Elena likes you and only wants the best for your future."

He continued, "Although we're low on cash, there might be enough to liquidate your shares. So, if you ask Elena privately for a favor, I believe she'll accommodate you. She always tries to help the women of our community."

Brynn lightened up and responded, "That sounds like a good idea. But, how could I meet with her alone?"

Jeremy answered, "Well. You're in luck. A young Pocawansett woman living in the new housing development is expecting a baby any day, so Elena is throwing her a baby shower tomorrow afternoon. You could stop by her home to speak with her before the shower. I know you live just across the street from the Pallatons. It should be easy to meet her privately because Corey plans to work here, in this office, tomorrow. He wants to avoid the baby shower."

Jeremy added, "But be careful not to say anything to your parents or Corey before you meet with her. Corey isn't fond of you and would probably prevent the transaction."

Brynn was satisfied with the solution but was still angry with Jeremy.

She turned to him and said, "Jeremy. Thank you for giving me this idea."

As Brynn left the office, she felt an array of mixed emotions. She was angry that Jeremy couldn't liquidate her family's shares and saddened that she could never trust him again. He had lied and hidden the truth from her one time too many.

44: Pixie, Dixie, and Velvet
Norwichtown
Pallaton Residence
Thursday, August 4, 1859

Brynn had recovered from yesterday's shock of the awful news. Now, she was looking forward to meeting with Elena. She had come to respect Elena as a dedicated business administrator and a devoted wife. Brynn had witnessed first-hand how Elena supported the mining company as a secretary, treasurer, and salesperson. She thought it shameful that Corey had deceived Elena. Without any doubt, Brynn knew she would never marry a man she couldn't trust.

Today, Brynn's strategy was simple: appeal to Elena's maternal instincts, sense of style, and social standing. She would impress Elena with her fashionable dress and remind her how vital Miss Porter's finishing school was to her future.

Since it was a hot, humid August afternoon, Brynn wanted to be cool and comfortable yet maintain a sophisticated appearance. The family's new sewing machine sparked an interest in French fashion design. So, she and Alvina recently designed and fabricated a floral-themed summer dress that incorporated her love of roses and buttons. She knew the dress would impress Elena with her keen sense of style and fashion.

Perhaps it would help persuade Elena to redeem the shares of stock.

As she gazed into her full-length bedroom mirror, Brynn smiled at her creation. The freely flowing, thin cotton cream dress was a work of art. It featured dark red-colored, cloth-covered buttons running the length of both arms. At first glance, the buttons looked like authentic, tiny rose buds. However, the most striking aspect of the dress was the two vertical rows of larger red buttons. Alvina had arranged them as two columns rising from her ankles, over her knees, along the front of her rib cage, and finally skirting the perimeter of her breasts.

She chuckled to herself, "Those skinny Parisian models don't hold a candle to us American girls."

She knew that Elena would approve.

Brynn filled a small, ornately decorated silk purse with a dozen fancy, distinctively unique buttons as she left her bedroom. She thought, "A small gift is always appreciated."

Brynn called out, "Mother, Father. I'm leaving now. I'll return later this afternoon."

When they didn't answer, Brynn realized that her parents weren't home. However, Dexter responded with enthusiasm. He barked playfully and blocked her path just as she approached the door to leave. She thought, "I don't want to leave him alone."

After remembering that Elena was fond of Dexter, she decided to take him along. She found his leash and collar and said, "Dexter. How would you like to visit Elena? I know that she'd love to see you."

A moment later, she smiled and added, "I'm going to dress you so that our outfits match." Brynn found a tiny rosebud and attached it to Dexter's collar.

She said to him, "Now. That's better. You're so handsome!"

Moments later, they crossed the street and strutted to Elena's front door. She thought to herself, "This should be easy."

She banged the heavy brass door knocker, and the door opened promptly. Brynn was *shocked* to see Corey standing in the doorway. She curtly said, "Hello. I'm here to see Mrs. Pallaton."

Dexter barked several times before Brynn calmed him.

Corey stepped back to avoid Dexter's fury and looked Brynn over thoroughly. He thought to himself, "Nice dress. Nice rosebud buttons. Nice hair."

He replied, "She isn't here."

She thought quickly, held up the silk purse, and said, "Oh. Yesterday, Jeremy told me that your wife was hosting a baby shower here today, and I just wanted to offer my congratulations."

As Brynn spoke, the hair behind Corey's neck bristled. He didn't like the dog, and he sensed Brynn's nervousness. Corey knew she was hiding something, and he needed to learn the real purpose of this unexpected visit.

He knew that Elena would be away for hours, but he lied, saying, "Please. Come in. Elena will be returning home shortly. She postponed this afternoon's baby shower because the expectant mother went into labor this morning. So all our tribe's women are now attending to her at Pesikutes Ridge. We're all hoping for a healthy boy."

Brynn followed him into the front foyer of his magnificent home. When they passed through the doorway to Corey's study, she couldn't help but notice the two snake tanks. As in earlier visits, the snakes rattled her. Brynn tried to show courage by saying, "So. How are Mutt, Jeff, Ginger, and Spice doing? They look well fed and happy."

Corey chuckled politely and answered, "They're doing fine."

He sensed Brynn's trepidation and wanted to build on it. He despised everything Brynn stood for and wanted to see her squirm. He said, "Have you ever wondered why I keep these snakes here, near the doors to my office?"

She answered, "Elena told me you use them as part of some Pocawansett ritual."

He replied, "Yes. That is true. But there is more to that explanation. I also keep them here to protect my office."

Corey pointed to an intricate system of cords, pulleys, and gears attached to each glass tank, which he'd also connected to the office door. He said, "The snakes are my guardians. I'm sure Jeremy told you the safe contents are valuable, and someone must protect them while Elena and I are away. So, I created this unique security system."

Brynn fidgeted and said, "I don't understand how that contraption could guard your drawing room."

Corey had hoped for that exact response. So, he said, "Okay. I'll show you. Please stand right here next to the end of Mutt & Jeff's tank."

As she neared the tank and studied the snakes, Corey pulled one of the cords downward and said, "If an intruder opens the office door, the cord pulls the tank's door open."

Then, he demonstrated by slowly opening one of the drawing room's two doors. As he did so, the glass pane on one end of the snake's tank lifted, and Brynn could see that the snakes had a clear path to freedom.

Brynn screeched and instinctively jumped back. She yelled, "Stop it! They'll get out."

When Dexter saw Brynn's reaction, he barked at the top of his lungs and yanked his leash so violently that she lost her grip. Dexter began running around the study, but Corey grabbed the leash before he could do any damage. Corey pointed at the chair before his desk and commanded, "Tie him to that chair."

After Brynn secured Dexter to the chair, Corey closed the door slowly, and the glass pane lowered itself back into the closed position. He sheepishly grinned and said, "You have nothing to worry about because they're sleeping."

Brynn's nervous energy began changing to anger. She knew her charm and beauty had little value in this setting and was aware of Corey's suspicions. So, she quickly decided to take a direct approach.

She said, "I believe my father spoke with you a few days ago concerning our family's shares in your company."

Corey nodded and replied, "Yes. So you must also know that I can't repurchase your shares today."

Brynn's ire was in full blossom. She said, "Yes. So *you must know* that we've owned the shares for over a year and that if you don't repurchase them, you'll be in breach of your contract with us."

Corey calmly studied her. He wondered how a lovely girl like Brynn had developed such disdain and a lack of respect for her elders. Finally, he quipped, "Could you show me the clause in our contract referencing the one-year period?"

Brynn lashed out, "You know that no one wrote it into the contract. Elena verbally promised it to my family and all the others who bought shares."

He responded, "Yes. So, there you have it. There is no breach of any contract. And, as I told your father, you'll have to wait a few more months before we buy the shares from you."

She frowned at him and commanded, "I need the money now, and you're going to pay it. Jeremy told me several things that I'd like to share with you. Firstly, I know that your company is on the verge of bankruptcy, that you've been lying to everyone about a recent discovery of gold, and that you're not even paying your employees their full salary. I also know you have misled your wife about this state of affairs. I will tell Elena everything if you don't repurchase our shares today. Right here! Right now!"

Corey sat at his desk, glaring at her, deciding how to proceed, when Brynn added, "I know you don't have enough money to pay off everyone right at this moment, but Jeremy also told me that you have plenty in the safe to pay for *my* tuition."

He rose and began to pace around the room slowly. Then, finally, he said, "You may have wondered how our new housing development got its name."

Brynn fumed and thought to herself, "No. Not really. I hadn't given it a thought."

However, she remained silent as he continued. Finally, he said, "After the Quinebaugan killer, Wawequa, murdered our Pocawansett Sachem Pallatonomo, his nephew Pesikutes reorganized the Pocawansett warriors and tried to avenge his death. However, they failed. In retaliation, the Quinebaugans and English decimated my tribe. The few surviving women and children had no choice but to scatter throughout New London County."

"A few months after Prince Philip's War, the town of Norwich gifted land on Wawequa's Hill to sixty-five homeless Pocawansett women and children. However, at that point in time, the land was so overgrown and far away from town services that the women could not survive. So, they moved into Norwich and became indentured to their masters."

He looked at Brynn and asked, "Have you ever asked your servants, Alvina and Mary, how their mother ended up at the Almshouse? Are you aware of their ancestors? You have enslaved two of my Pocawansett tribe and should be ashamed!"

Brynn responded, "That isn't true. Alvina is my friend. We care for her and Mary, and they enjoy working for us. My parents pay them fair wages."

He bellowed, "They have no other choice!"

By now, Brynn could no longer contain her anger. She said, "You need to set aside the past and grow up. You are so afraid of white people that you cannot see the truth, even if it stares you in the face. Look around this room. You've filled it with handguns, rifles, and even a whaling gun. Are you expecting a whale to attack you? I don't understand why you are so afraid. I think you're a coward, and I will tell everyone of your deceit!"

He would take no more of her insults. *Corey knew what he had to do.*

He sat back slowly and announced, "Okay, you win. Can we agree to settle our differences and declare a truce?"

Brynn's regrouped her composure, calmed down, and replied, "Okay. I only need enough cash for my father to pay one semester's tuition today. You can pay the rest later."

After Brynn sat, Corey opened the top drawer of his desk and pulled out a small, brightly colored package labeled "Fry's Five Boys Milk Chocolate."

He said, "One of my fellow tribesmen recently sailed on one of General Williams's commercial product trips to London. He hit upon this delightful delicacy while gift shopping for his wife in a local market. A few years back, Mr. Joseph S. Fry and his partner John Vaughan patented a chocolate refining process that transformed the world. They discovered how to convert the chocolate beverage we enjoy drinking so much during the winter into a solid form. The J.S. Fry & Sons Company now produces these chocolate bars in England and has begun to export them to the United States. Have you ever tasted one?"

After she shook her head and showed little interest, she replied, "No. This is the first I've heard of a chocolate bar."

He unwrapped the package, showed her the bar, and broke off one of its squares. After taking a bite, Corey said, "Oh my God! This really tastes good. It's no wonder why Elena loves these. As a peace offering, I'd like to share this with you."

After breaking the bar in half, he rose from his desk and handed it to her.

Brynn did not want to accept any gift from him, but her curiosity overcame her as she smelled its aroma. When she took the first bite, she was shocked! The candy was sweet, creamy, smooth, and melted in her mouth. She had never tasted anything so delightful. Without thinking, she blurted, "This is delicious."

Corey walked to the safe and said, "I have something else for you that you deserve."

Brynn watched as he reached beneath the largest tom-tom drum, proudly displayed on a table behind his desk. He retrieved the safe's machined brass key and showed it to her. He said, "I'll show you."

Corey inserted and turned the key to open his massive company safe. It appeared to Brynn that the safe was empty. However, it wasn't. Corey opened one of many steel drawers and removed a small, shiny silver box. He handed it to Brynn and said, "Go ahead, open it. Tell me what you think of it."

NORWICH GOLD

She didn't want Corey to think she was too eager. So, Brynn put the box down and took another bite of the chocolate bar. After slowly settling back into Corey's massive leather chair, broke off a large square of the remaining bar and said, "This candy is so good. I want to share it with my little buddy here. He loves everything I share with him."

She turned to Dexter and said, "Here, boy. Have a nice piece of chocolate. You'll love it!"

She had no idea what to expect or what Corey had in mind. After retrieving and opening the box, she saw three sets of twelve-inch-long ropes of braided human hair. One was black, one was brunette, and one was red. At the end of each braid was a tiny black leather belt. The belt was about three inches long and a half inch wide, with a miniature silver buckle."

She focused intently on the hair. Then, finally, she gasped and thought, "What the hell is this? What could anyone use it for?"

Suddenly, Brynn felt Corey's powerful hands grab her wrists. He was crouched behind the chair, and before she had time to react, he tied both her wrists tightly to the arms of the massive chair. She screamed and fought to stand but couldn't free herself.

Then Corey positioned himself before her in a flash and bound her ankles to the chair's front legs.

He glared at her and said, "You won't tell anyone anything!"

Brynn was defiant. She blurted out, "You don't scare me. My father will ruin you!"

Corey strolled around the chair several times and said, "So, what do you think of my little collection?"

Brynn responded, "I have no idea why you keep the hair and don't really care. I think that you're sick in the head."

Corey replied, "Okay, I'll show you."

He reached into the top drawer of his desk and removed a hairbrush, a red rubber band, and a knife. Then, showing Brynn the knife, he said, "This weapon is truly a work of art. I imagine some Persian artisan toiled for many hours carving its handle and honing its fine Damascus steel blade."

After brandishing it before her, he continued, "Yes. This is the knife your friend, Travis Mathews, pulled on me during our quarterly report. You must remember it?"

Brynn's confidence dwindled and was replaced with fear. She thought, "I may have underestimated him."

Corey showed her the rubber band and said, "You've probably never seen one of these. A fellow in London invented these several years ago, and I was lucky enough to have purchased a handful. Most people use them for gathering mail into bundles, but I've found several more interesting uses."

Corey walked behind the chair and began brushing her silky, long blonde hair. He said, "You do have beautiful hair. I'll give you that."

Brynn unsuccessfully tried to wiggle free and shrieked, "Stop it. Don't touch me!"

Corey ignored her pleas and said, "I know many girls like their hair brushed and styled. So today, let's see how you look with a new style. Say, perhaps a ponytail?"

After brushing her hair and using the rubber band to form a tight blonde ponytail, he said, "Oh yes. That's much better."

Then he showed her the knife again and said, "But I think your hair is much too long. Do you agree?"

Brynn trembled and said, *"Please. No. Don't do it."*

He ignored her plea again and cut a handful of her long hair. After showing her the fruit of his labor, he walked to his desk and sat down. He said, "That wasn't too bad. Was it? I only need a few strands; you still have almost all your hair. No one will probably even notice."

Thinking the worst of his abuse was over, Brynn gathered her courage and said, "You'll never get away with this. I swear I'll tell everyone and the good people of Norwich will run you out of town."

Corey replied, "No. I don't think you'll be talking to anyone. Oh, by the way, did you know chocolate is poisonous to dogs? It first makes them vomit, then gives them diarrhea, and sometimes even kills them. I wonder how hardy your little mutt is? He'll probably last at least another day."

Brynn's heart sank. She screamed, and tears began flowing down her rosy red cheek. She cried, "No. Let me go."

Corey sat comfortably at his desk. He slowly and deliberately began braiding Brynn's lock of hair into a string-like rope. He said, "Thank you for helping complete my collection. Now I've got red, black, brunette, and blonde leashes. My friends will also thank you."

She looked at him incredulously and said, "You are sick. You've got what you wanted. Let me go."

He scowled at her and replied, "No. I need you to promise me that you'll never speak with anyone about my company or today's little encounter."

She thought momentarily and defiantly replied, "You have no control over what I do or say. If you let me go now, I promise only to tell Elena. No one else will know."

Saying nothing, Corey thought to himself, "*Who does this little bitch think she is?*"

He replied, "Brynn, I know you're interested in flowers and botany. Well. I'm interested in mammals and reptiles. As you probably know, snakes are reptiles that enjoy eating small mammals. Say, for instance, mice. All my snakes, Mutt & Jeff and Ginger & Spice, love mice. So to keep them happy and healthy, I also maintain several families of mice."

He stood and walked to the back of the room, where Brynn saw a cage containing three mice. He said, "I'd like to introduce you to Pixie & Dixie and their baby, Velvet."

He brought the cage near Brynn's face and said, "I'm sorry that I'll have to say goodbye to them soon, but Mutt & Jeff are famished. I'm a good custodian for these little rodents, and I feed them regularly and keep them happy until the day they depart this world."

He continued, "I see that you've adorned your dog's collar with a small rosebud. I think it's cute and believe Velvet would like his collar decorated, too. He would be honored to wear one of those dainty little buttons from your dress. Don't you agree?"

Her stomach churned, and Brynn nearly threw up when Corey approached her again, leaned in close, and cut one of the tiny, rose-like buttons from her dress.

Next, he sat back at his desk, reached into a drawer, and pulled out a handful of sunflower seeds. He said, "Velvet is a curious little mouse. Even though he is a finicky eater, he loves these seeds. Today's meal will be his last, but I plan to give him a sumptuous feast today."

After spreading several seeds on the desktop, Corey lifted the braided rope of red hair from the silver box and said, "You see. I've made a leash and collar for Velvet. He tends to run off when I'm trying to feed him, and I don't want that to happen. If he escapes today, Mutt & Jeff would become very angry."

After adding the button to the rodent's collar and tightening it around his neck, he lifted Velvet from the cage and put him on the desk. As Velvet devoured the seeds, Brynn thought, "I don't think he's ever fed that mouse. Why is he showing me this?"

Brynn's heart pumped wildly when Corey lifted the tiny mouse from the desk and tied the end of its leash to her ankle. After Corey placed a large handful of sunflower seeds on the floor before Brynn's chair, Velvet began an eating frenzy. When Brynn felt Velvet's soft, furry body and long whiskers brush her ankle and climb onto her foot, a primal, uncontrollable fear filled her entire body. Brynn's bladder released, and her urine puddled beneath the chair.

Brynn cried out and screamed, "I promise. I'll never tell anyone. Get the mouse away from me. Now!"

Corey yanked Velvet's leash back and returned him to the cage. As he untied Brynn's restraints, he warned, "If you ever speak to anyone about the health of my company or our little discussion today, you will regret it. And, unfortunately, much worse things could happen to you."

He added, "You can also tell Travis Mathews to watch his back. I've heard the lies that he's been spreading. Tell him that if he continues, I'll be coming for him."

Brynn grabbed Dexter and ran out of the office, thinking, "We'll see about that."

As she left the Pallaton home, she placed the silk purse containing Elena's gift on a side table next to the front door and thought, "Elena and I are still going to have that conversation."

45: Lucas's Chair
Lucasville
Friday, August 5, 1859

Travis and Lydia were optimistic as they sat atop the Mathews family carriage on their way to Lucas's Chair.

Lydia announced, "We have a good chance of finding Wawequa's tomahawk today."

Travis wiped the sweat from his brow and responded, "Why do you think that?"

She answered, "Firstly, I believe the Quinebaugan would most likely bury Wawequa's tomahawk with his remains. They probably thought he would need it for protection in his afterlife. Secondly, the area surrounding Lucas's Chair is an ideal burial spot for Quinebaugan royalty. The area is somewhat secluded and commemorates where a glorious, historical event occurred."

Travis said, "I agree with you. Wawequa may be buried here. Has anyone told you the entire Lucas's Chair story?"

Lydia smiled and replied, "I've heard bits and pieces but would love to hear your rendition."

Travis said, "It's not *my rendition*. It's a story that our tribe's storytellers have passed down over the past 200 years. It's a tale of patience, persistence, friendship, and triumph."

He began, "Two years after Lucas and Wawequa levied justice to the Pocawansett Sachem Pallatonomo, his tribe sought revenge. Upon Pallatonomo's death, his younger brother Pesikutes and his uncle became Pocawansett co-sachems. After many months of planning, they decided that Pesikutes would lead an attack on the entire Quinebaugan settlement at Shantok. Ruthlessly, during the siege, the Pocawansett did not discriminate. Their warriors attacked the fort, filled with innocent men, women, and children."

Lydia commented, "So that's why Corey Pallaton named his development Pesikutes Ridge. It was to honor one of his royal ancestors."

He continued, "That's right. Even though the Pocawansetts greatly outnumbered the Quinebaugans, Lucas and his braves defended Shantok for many days. When Pesikutes realized that instant victory was beyond his grasp, he developed a new strategy. The marauding intruders surrounded the Quinebaugan Shantok, preventing anyone from entering or leaving the community. The plan was to starve the Quinebaugans into submission."

Travis continued, "Fortunately, Lucas had befriended Thomas Leffingwell several years before the siege. Leffingwell taught Lucas to speak English, and Lucas shared his knowledge of his tribal customs with Leffingwell."

"Since Lucas knew Leffingwell routinely paddled his canoe from Fort Saybrook to a river bank near Shantok, he crafted a plan to find him and seek his support. While under siege, Lucas escaped Shantok via a secret passageway through the Pocawansett warriors. He ventured eastward to a huge outcropping overlooking the Thames River. Today, we call the natural structure Lucas's Chair."

Travis continued, "Lucas remained there, without sleeping, for three days before he connected with Leffingwell. When Leffingwell learned the dire news, he immediately returned to Fort Saybrook, paddling thirteen miles. After he gathered meat, corn, and peas from his personal stores, Leffingwell returned to Lucas's Chair and rescued the Quinebaugans. At dawn the following morning, Lucas elevated a huge chunk of beef up a pole in Shantok. When Pesikutes saw the fresh provisions, he knew it useless to continue the siege."

Lydia responded, "That story reminds me of how important it is to work together. We all need a helping hand at some point in our lives."

The three-mile carriage ride from the Norwich/Lucasville border followed along the New London, Willimantic & Palmer Railroad tracks and paralleled the Thames River. Due to thickly forested overgrowth, the dirt road was barely passable. However, as they neared where they believed they would find Lucas's Chair, Travis announced, "I think we're almost there."

They hitched Moshup and the carriage to a nearby red maple tree. The flat area near the train tracks led to a steep, craggy hillside. Travis said, "Let's record our current location. Then, when we find Lucas's Chair, we'll use it as a reference point on the map."

Travis and Lydia climbed the hill after they posted their location in Mr. Walling's survey book. After cresting the ridge, they stopped and took a long swig from Travis's canteen. Lydia said, "This is truly a magnificent view. I can easily see Chelsea Landing and Laurel Hill across the river."

Travis added, "Yes. The scene is rustic and beautiful. But, the view to the south is more important. Lucas surely chose this spot so that he could watch river traffic arriving from the south. This spot offers an outstanding view down the river."

After a two-minute search of the area, Lydia pointed to a partially overgrown rock formation and said, "That might be it."

As they approached the mound with excitement and reverence, Travis felt it. His snake-shaped birthmark began to warm. His heart pumped wildly, and he exclaimed, "We're here. This is it. I feel it."

Lydia exclaimed, "Oh my God, White Eagle was right. *Munduyahweh* blessed you with a wonderful gift. I can see your birthmark changing color."

She added, "Let's explore the chair."

At first, it didn't look much like a chair. Instead, it more closely resembled a rock ledge covered in bramble. After they cleared most of the vegetation, a flat, four-foot-wide, horizontal surface, backed by a tall, vertical ledge, emerged. Travis reiterated, "This is definitely Lucas's Chair. Let's map it."

After recording the location and referencing it to the previously registered point, Lydia said, "Okay, now that business is out of the way, we can begin the fun part."

Travis nodded. The land near the chair was rocky and uneven. And Travis said, "We've got to be extra careful of snakes. As you know, they love curling up next to rocks like these."

Lydia pursed her lips, looked at him, and said, "Yes. I was thinking the same."

Travis scurried around the area and said, "This place is all rock. No one would choose this area as a burial ground. We should leave."

Lydia turned to Travis and said, "We're just getting started. Slow down. Let's check things more carefully."

Travis had an odd look on his face. Then, holding up a large rock, he said, "Lydia. There's nothing here, and besides that, the area is dangerous. You could easily get bitten by another snake or turn your ankle on one of these rocks."

Lydia glanced at him and said, "This isn't like you. Why do you seem so worried about my well-being? Is there something else on your mind?"

Travis replied, "Is it that obvious?"

They sat, and Travis began, "As you know, these past few months have been frustrating and difficult for me. Every day, someone in Norwich accosts me and asks why I continue to spread lies about Corey's company. I want it all to stop."

Lydia replied, "Yes. It will cease after we expose Corey. We only need to find a way to get Corey's map."

He replied, "Yes, I know, but there's more. General Williams has offered me a job as an assistant navigator on one of his ships. It's the chance of a lifetime, and I've wanted to see the world for several years."

Lydia answered, "Travis, you know I want only the best for you, but you and I have a wonderful life together here. You've learned so much from Mr. Walling and could easily work as a professional map maker in Norwich. Also, we haven't finished making the commemorative map for the Jubilee. I still believe we'll find Wawequa's tomahawk someday. But we must do it together."

Travis replied, "Yes, I've thought about that too. Over the past nine months, I've been responsible for a rattlesnake biting you and a lightning bolt almost striking you. I've also wasted much of your time on wild goose chases like this. I don't want to put you in danger, hurt you, or waste any more of your time."

He continued, "Lydia, I love you and want to be here for you. But I also want to see the world and sail the seven seas. General Williams's boat leaves in October for Marseilles, and I'm seriously considering joining him."

Lydia was deeply disheartened. She reluctantly said, "This news deeply saddens me because I love you too. I hope that someday we can even become closer. We've shared so many wonderful experiences in such a short period. Nonetheless, I do understand your yearning for adventure and want you to be happy."

Travis replied, "I've been curious my entire life and enjoyed our search for our ancestor's golden tomahawk. When we find it, I genuinely believe our tribe will rally together. However, the scorn I've felt during these past few weeks has made me miserable, and for the time being, I think it best that we focus our efforts elsewhere. Therefore, I want us to put a hold on our search for Wawequa's tomahawk."

The return carriage ride to Norwich felt empty. The only sound heard was that of Moshup's hooves striking the path before them. Their uncertain future disturbed them both at a gut level.

46: FINAL PLANNING
DOWNTOWN NORWICH
WAUREGAN HOUSE: BROADWAY
SATURDAY, AUGUST 13, 1859 - 2:00 PM

The town was bustling with activity in anticipation of the upcoming celebration. Everyone knew the 200th Jubilee would become an epoch event in Norwich's rich history. So, with only three weeks left before the opening ceremonies, citizens gathered to finalize plans.

The meeting planners converted the Wauregan House dining room into a meeting hall. The room was filled with more than 100 people from all walks of life: farmers, industrialists, printers, politicians, teachers, and, of course, chairmen of the many Jubilee planning committees.

General William Williams stood at the head of the room and announced, "Welcome, everyone. Please take your seats."

After a moment, he motioned to Reverend Hiram P. Arms and said, "Could you please lead us in a moment of prayer?"

The room fell silent as Reverend Arms stood and reverently prayed aloud, "Lord, we give thanks to thee for this opportunity to celebrate the history of our most esteemed town. We ask for your wisdom and guidance to complete the planning of this historic event."

General Williams said, "Okay. Let's get right to it. The first day of our Jubilee will feature a grand procession from Franklin Square to William's Park in front of the Free Academy. Mr. Birge, would you please update us on your committee's progress?"

Mr. Henry W. Birge was honored to represent this all-important committee. As Connecticut Governor William A. Buckingham's nephew, Birge had direct access to hundreds of potential parade participants, and everyone respected his ability to make friends and influence others.

Mr. Birge stood and said, "Thank you, General. We've received an overwhelming number of positive responses from local and regional dignitaries. I plan for the community, state, and federal officials to lead the procession from Franklin Square to Williams Park. Twenty or so military units and marching bands will follow them through the streets of Norwich."

He continued, "We've engaged local business leaders to display their wares on horse-drawn carts. As a result, we've received encouraging feedback from more than twenty-five local vendors. Additionally, several manufacturers have informed us they will enter floats. They include Mowry's Manufactory, Chelsea Manufacturing Company, Bacon Manufacturing Company, the Shetucket Company, and the C.B. Rogers & Company. Unfortunately, I still have a short list of candidates I haven't received a response from."

Birge paused momentarily and asked, "Are there any among us that can now affirm their participation?"

John Stedman, his wife, and daughter Lydia sat at a table near the front. John stood and said, "Yes, Mr. Birge. I'm happy to say that the Aurora newspaper will enter a float. I apologize for my delay in replying to your query. We weren't sure if there was a safe method of loading our printing press on a cart."

As he sat, he smiled and added, "I *think* we've got it figured out now."

The congregation chuckled politely, and Stedman loudly asked Lydia, "You have it figured out. Right?"

Lydia laughed and replied, "We'll talk later."

After Birge completed his report, he sat, and General Williams addressed the group, "Thank you, Mr. Birge. May I hear from the Arches Committee?"

J. Lloyd Greene, the son of former mayor and industrialist William P. Greene, stood and said, "Yes. General Williams. We've completed the design and procured all the materials needed to build several impressive arches. First, we'll build a magnificent arch in Franklin Square, where the parade will commence. Then, at the end of the parade route, we'll also erect an arch at the entrance to Williams Park. We'll position the arch near the dinner tent."

Mr. Greene sat, and General Williams continued to call for more committee reports. Then, finally, he said, "Ahh, yes, that brings us to the dinner."

Williams quickly scanned the room for Mr. C.C. Brand, the chairman of the Dinner Committee. When he couldn't find Brand quickly, he said, "Is Mr. Brand here today?"

C.C. Brand, Travis, and his father sat at a table near the back of the room. Mr. Brand requested they be seated near the back door of the Wauregan House dining room because Travis continued to suffer public scorn due to the powerful, negative influences of Corey Pallaton.

Mr. Brand waved his arm, rose, and said, "Yes. Yes. Yes. I'm back here. The Dinner Committee has also made great strides. We've procured a tent accommodating 2,500 diners, and I've ordered enough food for everyone."

He continued, "We've also contracted for a smaller tent that keynote speakers will use to deliver their addresses. We'll hold the dinner and formal ball inside the larger tent."

When Brand sat, General Williams rose again and said, "Thank you, Mr. Brand. That brings us to the formal ball. Mr. Breed. Would you please give us an update?"

John Breed, the elder statesman in the room, was respected and loved by all. His pleasant, fatherly manner attracted even the most pessimistic and gloomy individuals. Today, he reveled in his role as the Chairman of the Formal Ball Committee and was joined by Brynn Dunham, Emeline Norton, and the Jubilee's music director, Mr. Aaron Stevens.

Breed rose and said, "I'm pleased to inform you that Mr. Stevens and the ladies of Norwich have heartily embraced this momentous, unfolding event."

He continued, "Mr. Stevens has used his charm and clever wit to convince Miss Frances Manwaring Caulkins and Mrs. Lydia Huntley Sigourney to write new hymns specifically for the Jubilee. We are blessed to have such exquisite talent among us. Arrangements for the ball's music are complete."

Stevens sat, and John Breed continued, "I'm also happy to inform you that Miss Dunham and Miss Norton have ordered a unique collection of beautiful decorations for the ball. In addition, they've chosen a theme for the ball showcasing Norwich's wide variety of roses."

He nodded to Brynn and Emeline, smiled, and added, "I am certain they'll create an air of beauty and awe everyone will appreciate."

General Williams continued down the long list of committee reports before adjourning the meeting.

Finally, he said, "Thank you all for coming today and for your hard work. Future generations of Norwich citizens will never forget the elegance and wonder of our 200th Jubilee."

~~~~~

As Travis was about to exit the back door, Lydia approached his table. She tapped his shoulder, smiled, and said, "Hi, Travis."

He turned, smiled sheepishly, and said, "I'm happy to see you."

She replied, "I'm looking forward to the Jubilee. It should be a lot of fun."

Travis was relieved that Lydia seemed to have recovered from the news of his desire to leave town. He cared deeply for her and wanted to maintain their relationship. He grimaced slightly and replied, "Well. It will be enjoyable for most people but not so much for me."

She tilted her head and said, "I understand. I know that many townspeople have been rude to you."

Travis replied, "They have been more than rude to me. Many have been downright contemptuous. Last week, a guy I'd never seen before stopped me in the street and spat on my boots. He told me to quit spreading lies."

Lydia smiled reassuringly before he could say any more, saying, "Well. I think you're the most respectable, handsome man in town."

She paused and continued, "I've got a job for you."

Travis perked up and replied, "What could that be?"

Lydia replied, "My father is extremely busy preparing for the Jubilee and has given me the task of building Aurora's float. Our parade float will feature Aurora's printing press, loaded on our horse-drawn cart. My father, mother, and I will ride on the cart and hand out flyers."

Travis said, "That sounds fun and interesting. I believe it will be good for everyone to see what a real printing press looks like."

She replied, "Yes. But, there is a minor problem. I can't figure out how to load the press on our cart. Could you look at it and help me develop a plan?"

Travis chuckled and replied, "Of course. It's always my pleasure to rescue my lovely damsel in distress."

By this time, the dining room was all but empty. But then, Travis and Lydia heard a voice call out from the other side of the room. Lydia.

They turned and were surprised when they saw Brynn striding toward them. It profoundly saddened Lydia that she and Brynn had been at odds for the past few months. They had shared a cherished, mutual friendship before the office fire incident.

Brynn looked about the empty room and asked, "Do the two of you have a few minutes to speak with me?"

Lydia sensed a marked change in Brynn's demeanor. She had been distant and cold lately but appeared in need of a friend today. Lydia replied, "Brynn, we've always got time for you. Are you okay?"

Brynn shook her head and answered, "No. I'm not okay. Lydia, Travis. I am so embarrassed. I've been so mean to you and so wrong in my thinking about you. Can you ever forgive me? Please. I am so sorry."

Brynn waited for a response as tiny tears welled in the bottom corners of her eyes. Lydia stepped forward, hugged Brynn, and said, "Of course I forgive you. Before this Jeremy thing, you were always like a sister to me. I love you."

Brynn's tears now gushed down her cheeks as they sat in the empty dining room. Finally, Lydia questioned, "What has happened?"

Brynn responded, "You've been right all along. Jeremy has lied to me for months, and Corey Pallaton is a bastard!"

Travis and Lydia listened intently as Brynn relayed the details of how Corey had humiliated her.

She finished by saying, "Corey Pallaton is a twisted, sick man who has inflicted much harm on me and everyone else in Norwich. We've got to stop him."

Travis said, "I agree. But it ended in disaster when we tried to expose him last year."

Brynn replied, "That is true. But, now, without a doubt, I know that Corey stores all the company's documentation and processed gold in his safe."

She continued, "Jeremy told me that the receipts for the gold Corey sold in Boston are also there. The receipts can prove that Corey's sales are only a tiny fraction of the amount he has lied about publicly. He's only sold a few ounces of gold and hasn't found, processed, or sold silver or nickel."

Brynn finished by saying, "When Norwich learns of Corey's lies and deceit, he'll be finished!"

Then, Travis said, "Okay. But the receipts alone will not be enough. We'll need to convince everyone that Corey has lied for the past year and the map showing how much gold Corey's miners have actually found. Did Jeremy or Corey mention the map?"

Brynn smiled wryly and answered, "Yes. Corey waved it in my face and taunted me with it. I didn't get a good look at it, but, at first glance, the number and size of their discoveries appeared minimal."

She added, "Oh. I almost forgot to tell you. Corey keeps the key to the safe beneath the largest drum, right next to the safe in his office."

Lydia and Travis turned to one another and briefly gazed into each other's eyes. Then, Lydia said, "Let's do it!"

They proposed, evaluated, and discussed several schemes for the next hour, finally agreeing on a simple, fool-proof plan. Travis, Lydia, and Brynn would need to work together as an effective, seasoned team to be successful. And this time, they were convinced nothing could go wrong.

47: JUBILEE PROCESSION
DOWNTOWN NORWICH
AURORA NEWSPAPER OFFICE: WATER STREET
WEDNESDAY, SEPTEMBER 7, 1859 – DAWN

This morning began Norwich's third century, and Norwich's sixty-two-man Artillery Company A stood at the ready. The battery commander ordered them to commemorate the moment at precisely 5:23 a.m. So when the sun's first light peeked over the Rose of New England at dawn, the battery commander, Captain Tannar, shouted three times, "Ready. Aim. Fire!"

The almost deafening sounds: *Boom! Boom! Boom!* abruptly awakened John, Caroline, and Lydia Stedman. However, they weren't concerned or surprised. Instead, they were anxious to greet what they expected to be one of the most exciting days of their lives. It was the first day of their beloved city's 200th Jubilee, and the Stedmans would play an essential role in making it memorable.

After gathering in the dining room, Caroline questioned, "Would anyone care for sausage and eggs?"

John answered quickly, "No. We need to get going as soon as possible to finalize the float. So please grab a couple of apples and pears for us, and we'll be on our way."

Lydia heard church bells ringing throughout the city as they rode to the Aurora newspaper's printing office atop the Stedman family carriage. She remarked, "The bells are so inviting. It's as if they are calling to us."

Caroline replied, "Yes. I like the church bells much better than the *booms* that woke me up. John, do you know where the explosions came from?"

John chuckled, "Of course I do. It was a cannon salute from the Third Regiment Connecticut Militia, Artillery Company A. Governor Buckingham asked them to serve as the harbinger for the Jubilee. By the way, you can expect more than 300 militiamen marching in the parade today."

He continued, "The Jubilee planners also asked every church in town to ring their bells during the hour after dawn. That's why you hear so many bells."

By 7:00 a.m., they arrived at their newspaper print shop, and Lydia called out, "Good morning, Travis. You're here early."

Standing beside Moshup, Travis smiled and yelled back, "No. You're late."

He kissed her lightly and said, "Aww, just kidding. I'm happy to see you."

John looked at his wife and Lydia and asked, "Could you bring the booklets to the cart? Travis and I need to load the press."

As Caroline and Lydia left to begin their task, John and Travis turned their attention to the job of loading the printing press on the Aurora's float. Travis and Lydia had transformed the ordinary horse-cart into a float using signs and banners the day before. The most prominent sign read, "The Way to Wealth."

Travis said to John, "Here's the plan. We'll use these two jacks to lift one end of the press and then ask Moshup to pull it onto the float. He can slide it into place using these ropes. Then, you and I only need to guide the press. We'll use the two railroad ties I positioned on the cart's baseboard. So, it should be easy."

John's eyebrows lifted, and he remarked, "That's a clever plan. Let's see if it works."

After ten minutes of jockeying and jostling, they settled the printing press safely into its new, temporary home. John approached Travis, slapped him on the back, and said, "Thank you! I've worried about getting it safely in place for days."

By this time, Caroline and Lydia had loaded 1,000 eight-page booklets on the cart, and Travis had hitched Moshup up with the Stedman family horse. Finally, the Aurora float was ready for its glorious debut. Their journey to Franklin Square began with John at the reins, Travis riding shotgun, and the gaily dressed girls in the back seat.

As the Stedmans neared downtown Norwich, they were awestruck. Lydia shouted to her father over the sounds of the boisterous crowd, "Where did all these people come from?"

Although the route from their Water Street office to Franklin Square was only a four-block trip, they became trapped in a traffic jam. John, Caroline, Lydia, and Travis saw more than 1,000 people gathered in the downtown area.

John replied to Lydia, saying, "The Jubilee planners told me to expect 1,500 people to march in today's procession. So they organized the parade into ten divisions, and we'll be in the sixth division. We'll follow the C.B. Rogers & Co. woodworking machinery float. Please look around and see if you can find his display."

It was 8:00 a.m., and John knew they still had time to find their place in the lineup. They slowly made their way forward as they passed by the tenth division. It was a grand cavalcade of horsemen who carried brightly colored banners.

Subsequently, they passed the ninth and eighth divisions. These groups included members of the Somerset Lodge No. 34 of Free and Accepted Masons, the Columbian Encampment No. 4 of Knights Templar, and teachers and pupils of the Norwich Free Academy.

Lydia made a mental note of the scene that she would later relate in an article for the Aurora. She contemplated the juxtaposition of plainly dressed, ordinary school children marching alongside members of fraternal organizations dressed in full regalia. It seemed to her that the children should wear costumes like these instead of grown men.

As they passed Governor William A. Buckingham's home on Main Street, they finally found where other business-themed floats were congregating. Travis surveyed Franklin Square and saw more than two dozen other floats sponsored by local manufacturers and merchants. He was most interested in the Bacon Manufacturing Company float. It featured twelve men machining, assembling, and cleaning pistols. Travis thought the pistols to be finely crafted, precise weapons. They were significantly different from the blunderbuss-like whaling guns he made and tested.

Lydia pointed to the Chelsea Manufacturing Company float and said, "Father, look. They've got large sheets of paper, a paper-cutting machine, and a press on display."

For the second time today, John raised his eyebrow and replied, "That looks like a complex operation. They are making something. I wonder what it is."

Lydia responded, "I expect nothing less than awesome from them. It is only fitting that the largest paper manufacturer in the world presents an extraordinary float. I want to see what they're doing."

She descended from their cart and approached the paper company's float. After several minutes, Lydia returned and announced, "They are cutting the paper to size, printing music sheets, and distributing them to bystanders.

Lydia showed her mother one of the flyers and continued, "Look. It's the hymn that Mrs. Lydia Huntley Sigourney composed for our Jubilee. And it's printed on mummy paper!"

Looking perplexed, Travis asked, "What on earth is mummy paper?"

Lydia answered, "One of the company's adventurous, imaginative employees took a trip to Cairo, Egypt, last year. While visiting the Egyptian National Museum, she saw an interactive display where Egyptologists were dissecting a mummy. Their goal was to learn how ancient Egyptians made mummies."

She continued, "When Chelsea's employee saw the researchers discarding the rags from the mummies, she conceived a novel idea. She brought the rags home to Norwich and used them to create paper from the mummy rags."

At 10:00 a.m., everyone heard a thunderous boom that echoed throughout Franklin Square. Another of Colonel Kingsley's cannons signaled the precise moment for the parade to begin. Travis looked ahead through a sea of people and caught a glimpse of his father, mother, and other tribal elders.

He nudged Lydia's elbow and said, "Look, there's my parents, our tribal council, and elders. The Jubilee planners have assigned them to march in a place of honor in one the most prestigious divisions."

Lydia agreed, "Yes. I see the Quinebaugan elders alongside Norwich's clergy and distinguished educators. It pleases me to see them honored in such a grand manner."

As the procession moved forward, Lydia saw the former president of the United States, Millard Fillmore, standing beside the Norwich Jubilee President of the Day, Governor William A. Buckingham. She felt honored to have the opportunity to see President Fillmore in person.

John, Caroline, Lydia, and Travis saw hundreds of cheering spectators surrounding them as the Aurora float passed under a mammoth arch bearing the words:

A HEARTY GREETING 1659-1859 BI-CENTENNIAL

John and Travis waved to the crowd while Caroline and Lydia passed out the fruits of their labor.

Several days earlier, Lydia had printed eight-page pamphlets containing dozens of common-sense advice from Ben Franklin's 1758 "Poor Richard's Almanac." The booklet included Franklin's essay "The Way to Wealth."

When the parade spectators opened their gift from the Stedman family, they found a treasure trove of helpful advice:

THE WAY TO WEALTH

Early to bed and early to rise
makes a man healthy, wealthy, and wise.
There are no gains without pains.
One today is worth two tomorrows.
Have you somewhat to do tomorrow, do it today.

Lydia and Caroline enjoyed distributing the pamphlets throughout the two-and-a-half-mile parade route from Franklin Square to Williams Park. However, Lydia's favorite moment along the parade route came when they arrived at Little Plain on Broadway Street. As they passed underneath an elegant arch with a banner bearing the words:

NORWICH, THE ROSE OF NEW ENGLAND

Everyone saw and heard an adorable group of children standing at the Central Grammar School, singing a hymn that praised the mighty deeds that God teaches children.

The children's voices touched Lydia's heart. She secretly yearned for the day she and Travis might have children of their own.

The final legs of the parade snaked westward through Mill Lane, Sachem Street, and Yantic Falls. Hundreds more eager spectators gazed admiringly from their home windows and porches as they passed.

The most spectacular parade in the history of Norwich ended as its participants passed underneath another mammoth arch. The arch at the entrance to Williams Park read:

NORWICH WELCOMES HOME HER CHILDREN

When the Aurora float entered the park at 1:00 p.m., Travis suddenly realized he was famished. As he eyed the colossal dinner tent situated in the center of the park, he thought, "With such a gigantic tent, I'm sure I'll have no problem finding plenty to eat."

48: JUBILEE DINNER
NORWICHTOWN
WILLIAMS PARK: INSIDE THE DINNER TENT
WEDNESDAY, SEPTEMBER 7, 1859 - AFTERNOON

The grand procession ended for the Stedman family as hundreds of people greeted their arrival at Williams Park. Unfortunately, parking was a problem for the Stedmans. John drove their cart around the complete perimeter of the park in search of a suitable spot. They passed by the Free Academy and the homes of Henry P. Norton, John Dunham, Corey Pallaton, and General Williams. Finally, they secured a spot to hitch the cart on Sachem Street, only two blocks from the park.

Travis hopped off the float and said to Lydia, "This has been great fun, but can we talk later? I need to help Mr. Walling finish setting up the head table inside the dinner tent."

As he left, Lydia waved and replied, "Sure. We'll talk later."

When Travis entered the massive 200-foot by 80-foot dinner tent, he saw Henry Walling scurrying about the front of the dining area. Walling said, "What's taken you so long? I expected you here a half hour ago."

Travis replied, "It took us that long to park. I'm sorry. It couldn't be helped. What can I do?"

Walling, holding up the end of a twelve-foot, narrow wooden table, replied, "Grab the other end of this table and help me move it into place."

Travis replied, "Where does it go?"

Walling looked at him wryly and said, "This is the head table. Where would you expect to place it?"

Travis winced and replied, "Okay. I get it. Truly, I'm sorry I was so late."

Walling replied, "I forgive you. Could you find a tablecloth? I believe you'll be able to find one in the tent near the kitchen area."

Travis strode through the spacious tent and entered a slightly smaller tent adjacent to the main dining area. He thought, "This is the largest kitchen I've ever seen. There are at least 200 chefs and their assistant cooks."

He hailed a young man carrying a tall stack of white linens from the kitchen to the dinner tent and asked, "Excuse me. I'm looking for tablecloths for the head table. Could you help me?"

The young man hurriedly replied, "Yes. I'll bring them right out."

Travis returned to the head table and helped Mr. Walling set up chairs for the dignitaries. When they finished, Walling said, "Okay, Travis, we need to set up our display quickly."

Walling pointed and said, "The maps and easels are behind the music stands in the band area."

After Travis retrieved the maps, he asked, "What band will be playing?"

Walling said, "It's a distinguished military band that only plays for very important people. Say, for example, the President of the United States. They are the Brooklyn Navy Yard Marine Band.

They play drums, trumpets, and cymbals to honor dignitaries. We need to hurry because the band and everyone else will arrive shortly."

Travis looked around the room and saw hundreds of dinner tables and benches. People were pouring into the tent from every direction, and he felt a sense of anticipation in the air. Finally, he asked Walling, "Do you need anything else?"

Mr. Henry F. Walling smiled at Travis and said, "Nothing more to prepare, but I would like to speak with you on a different matter."

Travis was puzzled. He replied, "What's on your mind?"

Walling answered, "You've been the best apprentice I've ever trained. And, the Quinebaugan map you and Lydia made is one of the most accurate, beautiful examples of fine cartography I've ever seen."

Travis smiled and said, "Thank you. It's truly been a pleasure making it. I've learned so much preparing it, and admit that I'm sad that the adventure we had creating it is over."

Walling said, "I wanted to speak with you about that. I've signed a new contract with city planners in New York City, and they've asked me to map a new section on the outskirts of Brooklyn. So, next month I'll be closing the office here in Norwich. Several people have offered to buy it, but I want to give you the right of first refusal. Would you be interested in becoming its owner and operator?"

Travis was overwhelmed by the offer and replied, "Well. I'll have to think it over carefully. But, quite frankly, I've been offered a job as an assistant navigator on one of General Williams's ships. I've considered taking him up on the offer but haven't decided yet."

Travis's thoughts immediately turned to Lydia. He thought, "I could stay here in town."

Travis replied, "Thank you for your offer. It's very appealing, and I'm interested. However, I'm not sure how I could work out the finances. May I give you an answer next week?"

Walling said, "As I mentioned earlier, there are several interested parties. Could we meet on Monday afternoon?"

Travis replied, "But that's only five days from now."

After a long, one-minute silence, Travis added, "Okay. Monday afternoon will be fine. I'll let you know then."

Walling nodded, winked, and said, "I'm sure you'll make the right decision."

~~~~~

The tent was now bursting at its seams. Over 2,000 people sat at the dinner tables, and the twenty-four-piece Brooklyn Navy Yard Band was ready to play. Ushers had directed the Stedman family, many Norwich businessmen, and other distinguished guests to tables near the front of the tent. Travis, his family, and many Quinebaugan tribal members sat in the middle section. The event organizers designated a small area near the rear of the tent for the Pallatons and a small contingent of other Pocawansett tribal members.

In addition to partaking in a fine dinner, Lydia also needed to take copious notes for the book chronicling the 200th Jubilee she and her father were compiling.

The tent's decorations made Lydia proud to be an American and a Norwichian. She saw United States flags, patriotic banners, and other historically-based Norwich paraphernalia throughout the dining area. She had never seen such a display of pomp and circumstance.

Everyone in the tent heard a loud voice announce, "Ladies and Gentlemen. May I have your attention?"

A moment later, he declared, "Please stand. The President of the United States!"

The band triumphantly played "Hail to the Chief" as the former president of the United States, Millard Fillmore, strode from the kitchen tent to the front table. Everyone cheered wildly and applauded with gusto. Moments later, the Jubilee's President of the Day, Governor William A. Buckingham, followed President Fillmore.

Buckingham bowed to Fillmore and the audience, then stood by his seat. Next, Connecticut's U.S. Senator Lafayette Foster, Reverend Hiram P. Arms, and the honorable Daniel C. Gilman followed Buckingham into the tent.

Buckingham said, "Please be seated. I greet you with a cordial welcome on behalf of the Committee of Arrangements. As many of you gathered here today, I am not a lineal descendant of Norwich's first settlers. We have arrived from all parts of the country and all walks of life. However, we join together as one to celebrate this momentous occasion. I thank you, native Norwichians, for accepting us into your fold of kindness and generosity."

He continued, "In the name of all our citizens, past and present, I bid you welcome."

Governor Buckingham stood and said, "This afternoon, we are blessed with the presence of Mrs. Lydia Huntley Sigourney. Many call her the 'Sweet Singer of Hartford,' but we all know her to be a native of Norwich. *We call her brilliant.*"

1859 Hymn by Lydia Huntley Sigourney

We praise the God who guides our feet,
Back to this sacred spot of earth,
With filial gratitude to greet,
Our mother, on her day of birth.

We praise Him for these cultured glades,
Redeem'd from thorns and savage sway,
For rock, and stream, and woven shades,
That charm'd our childhood's cloudless day.

We praise Him for the happy homes,
The prosperous marts that thronging rise,
The peaceful academic domes,
The church spires pointing to the skies.

We praise Him for the righteous dead,
Who have their course so nobly spent,
And o'er their race rich luster shed,
When through Heaven's open gate they went.

We praise Him for the wondrous change,
The last two hundred years have wrought,
For His blest gospel's glorious range,
Of faith and hope and holy thought.

And as the past with joy is bright,
So may the unborn future prove,
And wrap thee in new robes of light.
Sweet land! The mother of our love.

Sung to the tune "Old Hundredth"

He continued, "I'm happy to inform you that she has written a hymn specifically for today's meeting. Many of you received a copy of the lyrics from the Chelsea Paper Company float this morning. So please, everyone, stand and join our choir in singing Mrs. Sigourney's hymn."

Everyone rose and joyfully sang the new hymn, praising God for the simple things of life, loving families, and peaceful homes. As Lydia sang along, she nearly cried because the lyrics stirred a deep desire for strong, loving familial bonds.

After the congregation sat, 200 wait staff marched into the tent, eager to satisfy the desires of their patrons. Caroline Stedman smiled at her husband and said, "Well, John. What will you order this afternoon, roast lamb or boiled tongue?"

John smiled and replied, "As the polite gentleman you know I am, I'll not hoard the boiled tongue. So I've decided to try the roast beef, pickles, and berry pie."

Caroline and Lydia both laughed and ordered their dinner. Lydia decided on roast turkey, succotash, Indian pudding, and pears. She said, "I've never eaten Indian pudding but want to try it."

Caroline smiled and said, "Lydia, I am pleased to see you embracing your Quinebaugan heritage."

During dinner, Governor Buckingham rose from his chair and said, "I hope everyone is enjoying their dinner."

He held up a large wooden bowl filled with food and continued, "I'd like to share this with you. The Quinebaugan Sachem Lucas gave us this bowl as a token of friendship almost 200 years ago. The bowl was filled with a gift of Indian corn and

BILL OF FARE

MEATS

BEEF ALAMODE	ROAST BEEF
ROAST LAMB	ROAST MUTTON
ROAST CHICKEN	VEAL FILLET
LEG OF MUTTON	PRESSED BEEF
BROWNED HAM	CORNED BEEF
ROAST TURKEY	BOILED HAM
BOILED TONGUE	JELLIED TONGUE

SIDE DISHES

CHICKEN CURRY	RICE CURRY
PICKLED BEETS	CHICKEN SALAD
PIKLES	LOBSTERS
SUCCOTASH	FRIED OYSTERS
TOMATO	PORK AND BEANS

DESSERTS

PEACH PIE	APPLE PIE
CUSTARD PIE	BERRY PIE
BLANCH PUDDING	RICE PUDDING
CONNECTICUT PUDDING	INDIAN PUDDING
PUMPKIN PIE	ICE CREAM

FRUITS

PEACHES	PEARS
APPLES	ORANGES
WATERMELONS	CANTELOPES
BREAD ROLLS	RAISINS

FANCY CAKE

today, members of our local Quinebaugan tribe have once again offered their blessing. The Quinebaugan cooks roasted, pounded, and cooked this corn, especially for us today. The friendship between our two groups has weathered the test of time and is even more vital now than 200 years ago."

He motioned to the Quinebaugan contingent and continued, "We are joined today by many of our Quinebaugan friends. Would you all please stand and be recognized?"

The Mathews family, the Flowers family, and all the Quinebaugans inside stood to a rousing round of applause. Travis said to his mother as they sat, "That felt good. I am so proud to be a part of this community."

Faith nodded and replied, "So am I."

Corey Pallaton nudged his wife and whispered, "Get ready to stand. They'll be calling on us next to be introduced."

However, that did not happen. Instead, Governor Buckingham applauded the Quinebaugan contingent, smiled broadly at the audience, and sat.

Corey thought, "I can't believe he's forgotten to recognize the Pocawansett. Perhaps I should wave to him as a reminder."

He decided against attracting Buckingham's attention because he thought the governor had a more appropriate time in mind to recognize his tribe.

Travis turned to his mother and said, "I have some news to announce. Mr. Walling will open an office in New York City and will leave Norwich in the coming months."

His mother replied, "That is interesting. I'm happy for him but sad for you. I know that you've enjoyed learning and working for him."

Travis continued, "Yes. That is true, but there's more news. He's offered to sell me his Norwich business. I'm considering taking him up on the offer, but there is a problem. I'd have to take out a sizable loan because I don't have enough money even to make the down payment."

Faith replied, "Your father and I will help if we can afford it. We'll have to discuss the matter later. But, I am excited for you about the opportunity."

Governor Buckingham stood again and said, "I hope everyone has enjoyed this scrumptious dinner. Thanks go out to the organizers and cooks. Please, a round of applause for them."

After polite applause, Buckingham continued, "I take pleasure in introducing you to our keynote speaker. He is the son of one of our former mayors, a graduate of Yale College, and he serves today as the Librarian of Yale College. I give you another of the sons of Norwich, Mr. Daniel C. Gilman."

Gilman rose, acknowledged thunderous applause, and began, "We are here to review the record of 200 years in one brief hour. The task assigned to me was difficult, and I ask your pardon for the incompleteness of the story I shall tell."

"On June 6, 1659, the Quinebaugan Sachem Lucas conveyed a nine-mile square tract of land that contains present-day Norwich to our European forefathers. The following spring, members of a Puritan congregation in Saybrook and several farmers from New London pulled up their roots and settled the very spot we stand today."

"While preparing for today's discourse, I questioned why these thirty-five men had been attracted to Norwich. What was it that so charmed the farmers of Saybrook to embark on such an adventure? The new life would undoubtedly require sacrifice and many unknown dangers. Why would they be willing to abandon the improvements they had long labored to obtain in Saybrook?"

Gilman continued, "After much research, I have not found a definitive answer to this burning question. However, one reasonable historian proffered a plausible, interesting theory. In a word, he contends it was the *birds*."

He continued, "Mrs. Frances Manwaring Caulkins related his idea in her published book several years ago. She wrote:

WHY SETTLERS MOVED FROM SAYBROOK TO NORWICH

"It has been said that the Norwich settlers, being for the most part farmers, were driven from Saybrook by the crows and blackbirds. This story is at least suggestive of a great nuisance in the early days of our country. It is well known that clouds of the gormandizing fowls, darkening the sky and filling the air with clamor, would come down upon the newly planted maize in late May or June when the young shoots could be easily torn up and, in a few days, leave the fields of a whole district in ruin. These cormorants were peculiarly troublesome upon corn fields, near the sea, or large rivers, obliging the farmer to plant and replant and sometimes destroying prematurely the whole harvest."

Gilman waited momentarily, smiled, and said, "Ladies and Gentlemen. *We do not have a bird problem in Norwich today!*"

Everyone laughed, and Gilman continued, "Of course, there are several other explanations for why our founders settled in Norwich, but I prefer the bird story."

Mr. Gilman refocused his discourse by saying, "I know many of you here today grew up in towns surrounding Norwich. Today's Norwich comprises twenty-nine square miles, and the original nine-mile square land that Lucas conveyed to our ancestors encompassed more than eighty square miles."

He walked to the end of the head table and pointed to a large, colorful map of New London County. He said, "This map shows the locations of the original nine-mile square and today's boundary of Norwich. After dinner, I welcome you all to examine it more closely."

He continued, "So, I must question you. To where did fifty-one of the original eighty square miles disappear? Of course, the answer is that the land became the birthplace and home of many of you here today."

He pointed to the map and said, "Franklin, North Franklin, Bozrah, Baltic, Lisbon, Jewett City, Preston, Lebanon, Griswold, Ledyard, and Lucasville. They are all part of our family. So, likewise, *You* are all part of Norwich's family."

He announced, "Anyone here today who was born or lived in any of the towns I just mentioned, please stand."

Approximately 800 of the 2,000-member audience stood, and Mr. Gilman said, "Today, we are reunited again. We are all brothers and sisters. Thank you. You may be seated."

Next, Gilman approached Travis and Lydia's map of ancient Quinebaugan sites and said, "We must also pay tribute and respect to our Quinebaugan partners. Without their friendship and help, we would not be here today."

Gilman pointed at the map and said, "This map shows precise locations of the original Quinebaugan homeland and their sacred spots. I am grateful to Mrs. Rachel Flowers, the tribe's historian, for guiding Mr. Henry Walling and his young, adventurous map makers. Thank you for creating this enduring treasure for us."

Mr. Gilman presented a comprehensive narrative of the first two hundred years of Norwich's history for the next forty-five minutes. At its completion, everyone was proud to be associated with Norwich and happy they had been able to attend this historic event.

Governor Buckingham rose, thanked Mr. Gilman, and said, "Mr. Gilman has just expounded upon Norwich's proud, prestigious past. But we shouldn't neglect the topic of our bright future."

He continued, "Gold was discovered within our city limits several months ago, and I'm proud to say that one of our local companies is leading an effort to mine the site. I'm convinced its profits will boost our local economy for many years. In addition, the profits will help many of you who own shares in the company. I'm happy to inform you that the company's president, Mr. Corey Pallaton, is with us tonight. Corey, could you please stand and be recognized?"

Corey had wanted Buckingham to praise the many contributions that the Pocawansett tribe had made to Norwich over the years. However, he was nervous because he did *not* wish Buckingham to highlight his *company's successes*. Corey's team hadn't found *any* gold for the past few months. He didn't know how to respond to Buckingham's comment about the company's profitability.

Corey stood, bowed gracefully to the audience, and said, "Thank you, everyone."

Governor Buckingham closed the evening's activity by raising a glass of wine and toasting, "To Norwich's bright future."

49: JUBILEE BALL
NORWICHTOWN
WILLIAMS PARK: INSIDE THE JUBILEE TENT
THURSDAY, SEPTEMBER 8, 1859

The final day of Norwich's 200th Jubilee was capped off with a magnificent Victorian-era formal ball. The Jubilee staff and helpers had transformed yesterday's dinner tent venue into a vast, elegant ballroom. The military band was replaced with an orchestra of violins, cellos, violas, and double basses, and yesterday's patriotic display was replaced with garlands, festive ribbons, and a multitude of floral arrangements. As a result, the air was now filled with anticipation and excitement on this clear, serene, late-summer evening.

Tonight's head table was occupied by Mayor Amos Prentice, his wife Hannah, John Breed, his wife Amie, Norwich businessman Henry B. Norton, and his wife, Emeline. Mayor Prentice stood and announced, "I bid welcome to everyone and thank you for joining us at this most exquisite ball. I'm sure it will become a cherished memory."

He smiled and continued, "Although he needs no introduction, I'd like to introduce you to the Chairman of our Formal Ball Committee. This fine gentleman taught me the virtues of hard work as a boy and how to run a hardware store when I came of age. I owe much of my success to his wisdom and guidance. This man is a pillar of our community and one of our former mayors. I give you Mr. John Breed. A round of applause. Please."

John Breed rose slowly, smiled, and addressed the audience. He said, "Thank you, Mayor Prentice, and thanks to everyone here for joining us this evening. I am thrilled to have played a small part in organizing Norwich's Jubilee. The past two days of our celebration have recalled countless fond memories of Norwich and her people. The Jubilee has given me time to reflect on how many things have changed, and others have remained constant."

He paused, smiled, and continued, "Fifty years ago, it would have been difficult for me to see your smiling faces at this event because we only had candles and oil lamps for lighting. I am told that the illumination of our tent this evening is made possible by several thousand small gas jets. This new technology is safer, easier to ignite and control, and best of all …"

He paused, chuckled, and continued, "Prevents candle wax from dripping on everyone."

Everyone laughed, and he continued, "And ladies, years ago, I would not have been able to take in the beauty and elegance of your lovely dresses. So I am grateful for that, too."

The audience applauded, and he continued, "I'm happy to say that even with my old, tired eyes, this new-fangled lighting allows me to clearly see many old friends, such as General Williams and his lovely wife, Harriet. Next to them, I recognize many new acquaintances, such as Corey Pallaton and his wife, Elena. So thank you, Norwich Gas Light Company, for your ingenuity and expertise!"

He finished by saying, "I'll take no more of your precious time. I pray everyone has an enjoyable evening, and now I relinquish the floor to my colleague who has worked to make this Formal Ball possible. He planned, organized, and coordinated every detail. So, ladies and gentlemen, I give you Mr. Henry B. Norton."

Mr. Norton stood, bowed politely, smiled, and said, "Thank you, Mr. Breed, for the kind, overly generous introduction. Indeed, I have assisted in the planning of this ball. However, the design, creation, and assembly of all the decorations you see here tonight were made possible by my lovely daughter, Emeline, and her friend, Miss Brynn Dunham. My sincere thanks go to them."

He continued, "These young ladies hung the banners and ribbons and designed all the rose-themed floral arrangements and garlands. All the roses were grown in my family's greenhouse and the Dunham family's greenhouse. My daughter and Miss Dunham bred, fed, and nurtured the thousands of roses you see this evening."

He continued, "This evening's ball is the last planned activity of our Jubilee, and I am its final speaker. Therefore, I want to add one final tidbit I believe is of historical interest to all."

"Yesterday's procession was the most extraordinary display in our 200-year history. I was impressed with the pomp and circumstance, the patriotic and the Norwich-themed banners along the parade route."

Mr. Norton continued, "As the parade passed underneath the majestic arch we erected near Mrs. Lydia Sigourney's home on Broadway, you may have noticed the words:

NORWICH, THE ROSE OF NEW ENGLAND

Yes, our lovely town truly is the 'Rose of New England,' I want to share the origin of our well-deserved nickname."

THE ROSE OF NEW ENGLAND

The authorship of this well-deserved, honorable title has been attributed to my friend, Mr. Henry Ward Beecher. But unfortunately, the words, Rose of New England *do not appear in any of his published writings. Nor can the words be found in his famous* Norwich Star Paper, *which after many years is still as perfect a picture of the old town as if he had written it only yesterday.*

When the Committee on Decorations for this Jubilee met a few months ago, it was considering an appropriate designation for the town when the chairman, James Lloyd Greene, said, "Well, she is a rose, anyway!"

Mr. Edward T. Clapp responded, **"Why yes, Norwich is the Rose of New England!"**

The suggestion was accepted, and our newly minted nickname was inscribed on the arch under which the procession marched on Broadway. This account of the origin of our sobriquet remains undisputed and must be accepted as veritable history.

Henry B. Norton finished by saying, "So. With that in mind, I wish you a wonderful evening."

Norton turned to the orchestra's conductor and said, "Maestro, you have the floor."

As they played a bright Viennese waltz composed by Johann Strauss, the atmosphere within the tent sparked to life.

Hundreds of couples began whirling and twirling about the makeshift dance floor. The men's freshly waxed handlebar mustaches made for a handsome sight, and the ladies' jewelry sparkled in the lights of a thousand tiny gas jets.

The muddled scent of various perfumes and roses filled the air. Everyone felt the highly charged ambiance created by the combination of sights, sounds, and fragrances. It was an experience that no one would ever forget.

~~~~~

Travis's emotions also ran high. During last evening's sleepless night, he'd made a difficult career decision and was now ready to announce it to everyone. He was anxious to enlighten Lydia and Mr. Walling. After searching the room for several minutes, Travis finally spied Mr. Walling speaking with Lydia and her parents. He thought, "Mr. Walling must be congratulating Lydia on her fine work on the Quinebaugan map."

As he headed toward Lydia and Walling, Travis noticed General Williams had just broken free from his wife and their dinner companions, Corey and Elena Pallaton. So Travis cornered the General at the wine bar and said, "Good evening, General Williams."

Williams turned to him and replied, "Good evening to you also. How are you and your parents?"

Travis replied, "Thank you for asking. All is well with us. I know you must hurry to return to your companions, but I wanted to speak with you privately for a moment."

Williams replied, "What can I do for you?"

Travis said, "Thank you for your kind job offer. As you know, I've always wanted to sail on one of your ships and see the world. But I've recently developed a love for cartography and making maps. I've learned that Mr. Walling will leave town soon because he has decided to acquire and run a new business in New York. So, after much deliberation, I've decided to purchase his business. I'm sorry to say that I must respectfully refuse your offer."

General Williams replied, "Well, Travis, that doesn't surprise me. I've seen the product of your map-making skills, and I've also seen the way you look at your friend, Miss Lydia Stedman. So it appears that you have more than one good reason for wanting to stay here in town."

Travis blushed slightly and replied, "Yes. I believe your observations are in order. I appreciate your understanding."

Williams replied, "That is all good and well, but I still need a reliable supply of your sturdy whaling guns. Will you and your father continue to make and test them?"

Travis smiled and said, "Oh yes. I'll keep working for Mr. Brand until my new business can financially support me. Anyway, I enjoy firing the whaling guns."

Travis could hardly wait to tell Lydia. He looked around the room and saw that she was now speaking with President Millard Fillmore. Travis didn't want to barge into their conversation. But, he also relished the thought of conversing personally with a former president of the United States. So finally, Travis thought, "I'll just position myself near them and see what happens."

As he did so, Lydia caught notice of Travis and motioned to him. She said, "President Fillmore, this is Travis Mathews. He's the man who led the Quinebaugan map-making effort I told you about."

President Fillmore said, "I'm happy to make your acquaintance, Mr. Mathews. I told your friend here how impressed I am with the Quinebaugan map. You've done an outstanding job identifying the location of many Quinebaugan traditional spots."

Lydia continued, "Travis, I'm interviewing President Fillmore for an article I'm writing for the Aurora. He was just now telling me of his connection to Norwich. So, President Fillmore, please continue."

Fillmore said, "Yes. Thank you. My bloodlines run deep in Norwich. My grandfather, Lieutenant Nathan Fillmore, was born in Franklin. The town was called Norwich West Farms then but is named Franklin today. He, his brother, and their large families were successful farmers in Franklin for many years. In fact, one of your Jubilee organizing committee members, Reverend Comfort Day Fillmore, is one of his descendants. The good Methodist minister, Comfort, is my cousin."

Lydia responded, "Thank you for sharing that. Our readers will be interested. Did your grandfather stay in Franklin?"

President Fillmore scowled and said, "Well. That is a sad story that ends with several pieces of advice."

Lydia answered, "If you're willing to share, we'd love to hear it."

Fillmore began his story, "My grandfather and his brother loved Franklin, but a real estate developer in western New York offered to sell them a huge, successful, fertile farm at an attractive price. They were both hard-working, enterprising men who desired an even better lot in life. So they took him up on his offer."

Fillmore continued, "They collected all their money, bought the farm, and removed to New York. Unfortunately, after a year or so, local government officials determined their deed to the

New York farm was illegitimate. The so-called real estate developer was, in fact, a shyster, and my grandfather and his brother became penniless farmers. They lost everything they believed they owned and were at the mercy of the proper land owners."

Lydia said, "That is horrible! But, somehow, you became president of the United States. How did your grandfather go from penniless farmer to grandfather of the president of the United States of America?"

Fillmore smiled and said, "That's easy. The answer is hard work; lots and lots of hard work. My grandfather taught my father the value of hard work. And my father instilled a solid work ethic in me at a very young age."

He continued, "I have two messages that I'd like you to share with your readers. Firstly, we live in the United States of America, and almost any difficulty can be overcome with hard work and dedication. And secondly, be careful of people who lie to you, want to cheat you, and lure you into schemes that take your money. It can take years to recover from the actions of such vile people."

Lydia responded, "Thank you so much for sharing. I'm sure our readers will take your story to heart. I truly appreciate the time you've given us."

President Fillmore smiled and said, "It has been my pleasure."

When they were out of earshot, Travis told Lydia, "I think it interesting how an unethical land developer duped his grandfather. Unfortunately, we've got the same problem here today. So I guess that history truly does repeat itself."

~~~~~

Moments later, Travis and Lydia froze and locked eye contact. And without saying a word, he took her by the hand and guided her to the dance floor, where they began an awkward waltz. And as before, they found the task of gliding gracefully across a dance floor challenging. But their somewhat awkward movement did not matter to either of them.

Travis said, "I can't believe you just interviewed the former president of the United States. You're amazing!"

Travis wanted Lydia to be his dance partner, business partner, best friend, and partner for life. He recognized her as his true soul mate. Travis wanted to experience all the joys of love and life with her, and he knew tonight would be a turning point for their relationship.

As the waltz ended, he said, "I have some news I'd like to share. Yesterday, Mr. Walling told me he's leaving town and has offered to sell me his business."

He continued, "I know I told you earlier that I'd planned to work for General Williams on one of his ships, but if I buy Mr. Walling's cartography office, I could stay in Norwich. So I informed the General I won't go to sea with him."

Lydia's heart soared, and she piped up, "That's wonderful news! I've got something to tell you."

Travis interrupted her, "No, wait. Please let me finish. Everything is not completely set in stone yet. First, there is the problem of finance. As you know, I've been saving money at the whaling gun factory and have also saved a small amount while working for Corey Pallaton. But, I'm still working out the details of gathering enough money for a down payment on the business."

Lydia smiled and said, "Okay, Mr. Mathews. I hear you. Now, it's my turn to speak. First, I'd like to say that I've loved working with you while making the Quinebaugan map. I enjoyed decorating the maps and now know how to print and market them."

She continued, "Mr. Walling has also offered to *sell me* his business. My parents think it is a wonderful idea, and so do I. But I have the same problem as you. I can almost make the finances work alone, but not quite."

Tears began to well into Travis's eyes, and he said, "You're thinking what I'm thinking, aren't you?"

Lydia leaped into his arms and kissed him, saying, "You know I am, Partner!"

~~~~~

After several minutes of discussing their bright future as a team of map makers, Travis said, "It's time."

Lydia nodded and said, "Yes. It is time. Let's find Brynn."

A moment later, they saw Brynn and Emeline Norton surrounded by an army of eligible young bachelors. Lydia was ecstatic to see that Brynn had broken her ties to Jeremy and was now free to socialize with everyone.

They approached Brynn and signaled to her from a distance. Brynn nodded back in acknowledgment. The plan was set into action.

Travis and Lydia ambled to the tent's rear exit door and unceremoniously stepped out of the gaily-lit ballroom into the dark of night.

After five minutes of idle conversation, Brynn searched the tent for Corey and Elena Pallaton. She saw Corey and Lucius Carroll ordering drinks at the bar. Then Brynn spied their wives and Jeremy on the opposite side of the ballroom, conversing with General and Harriet Williams. She thought, "This is a perfect opportunity. I'll join the wives and keep them talking for hours."

Brynn told Emeline, "All this gossip and talk of flower gardens has made me thirsty. Would you excuse me for a moment? I want to find a fresh glass of lemonade."

Emeline smiled and said, "Are you sure you want to leave me alone with all these fine gentlemen?"

Brynn replied, "Why, certainly. I'm sure they would like to hear of your boat tours to Westerly, Rhode Island."

One of the young men piped up, "Yes. Emmy, please tell us about your sailboat endeavors."

Brynn made her way over to the women and Jeremy.

~~~~~

Lucius Carroll, who served as Corey's banker and mining equipment supplier, said, "Corey, I don't like conducting business at social events, but I have been planning to pay you a visit."

With a perplexed facial expression, Corey questioned, "What's on your mind?"

Carroll replied, "Our bank's treasurer, Mr. Francis Perkins, approached me last week because he's concerned that you haven't paid your loan for the last two months. I also noticed that you've only repaid a small portion of the credit line I gave you at my store. Is your company having problems?"

Corey had hoped to avoid this conversation, but Carroll had cornered him. Corey knew that he had to provide Carroll with a plausible explanation. So he replied with a lie, "My field team and gold processors have been bustling. Last week, we used the barrels of gunpowder you sold me to blast into the side of Wawecus Hill. We're now in the process of digging a mine shaft. The explosion uncovered a huge gold-rich vein. But, unfortunately, we haven't had enough time to process all the gold."

He continued, "Since then, we've been working overtime, and because I'm now paying them time and a half, the extra payroll costs have caused a temporary cash flow problem. I haven't had time to travel to Boston, where my buyers reside."

Mr. Carroll replied, "Okay. But I need you to continue your payments very soon. Mr. Perkins requires payment from our borrowers so we can provide loans to others."

As they approached their wives, Corey said, "You mustn't be alarmed. I'll resume the payments shortly."

When they reached Harriet, Elena, Charlotte, and Jeremy, Corey heard Harriet Williams say to Elena, "Oh. I'm thrilled your company has found that new gold in the hillside. You must be excited."

Elena responded, "I haven't seen it personally, but … "

When Brynn politely elbowed her way into the group, Elena and Corey were taken aback as she nestled into Jeremy's side.

Elena knew that Brynn and Jeremy had recently broken off their relationship. But she wasn't sure if it was public knowledge. Perhaps they were back together? Elena was unsure.

So, she said, "Oh. Hello Brynn. It's nice to see you."

Corey and Jeremy were stunned to see Brynn. They both thought, "What the hell is she doing here?"

Brynn glanced at Corey and said, "Thank you, Elena. It's so nice to see all of you. I just wanted to stop by and say hello."

Brynn questioned, "Did I hear you say something of a recently discovered gold vein?"

Mrs. Harriet Williams repeated herself, saying, "Oh yes. They've found more gold in the side of Wawecus Hill. I'm happy for them because I'll be able to share the wealth with my future girls' school in New London."

Brynn responded, "That is so generous of you, Mrs. Williams. I do hope that your plan is successful."

Brynn turned to Elena and said, "I wanted to congratulate the new arrival to your Pocawansett tribe personally. Corey told me how your planned baby shower turned into a live birth situation."

Everyone noticed as Brynn smiled and winked at Corey. Elena began to feel a bit uncomfortable and quietly said, "Oh. Corey hadn't mentioned your visit. But, yes, the baby and new mother are both healthy."

Brynn continued, "Oh, yes. When I stopped by to visit you the other day, he told me about the new baby. After Corey and I spoke privately for several hours, I left you a little present. It was a silk purse filled with brightly colored buttons. I know he is attracted to my buttons, so I thought I might share a few of mine with you. Perhaps he would be interested in you wearing a few of my buttons."

Corey was livid. He motioned to Jeremy to get rid of her.

Brynn felt the tension and thought, "I can't hold them any longer."

As Jeremy moved toward her, Brynn said, "Ahh. I see the orchestra is taking a break, and I wanted to request a special melody. It's been nice speaking with you."

Everyone heard a distant, piercing scream cut through the night air as Brynn left to approach the orchestra's conductor.

Corey and the rest of their group raced outside the tent. When they heard a second scream, Elena shrieked, "That is coming from across the street. It's in the direction of our home."

When they turned their attention to the Pallaton home, everyone saw a single light flickering inside the house. Elena said, "I'm sure we didn't leave any candles burning! Someone's in our home!"

Corey, General Williams, Lucius Carroll, and Jeremy raced toward the home while Mrs. Williams, Mrs. Carroll, and Elena, dressed in their lush ball gowns, did their best to follow.

50: REVELATION
NORWICHTOWN
PALLATON RESIDENCE: WASHINGTON STREET
THURSDAY, SEPTEMBER 8, 1859

The bright, cheerful sounds of the orchestra and the tiny lights from a thousand gas jets faded as Travis and Lydia strode past Williams Park on their way to the Pallaton residence. Lydia asked Travis, "Do you think anyone noticed us leaving?"

He glanced back over his right shoulder and replied, "No. Everyone is focused on the ball; even if someone looked in our direction, they couldn't see us in the darkness."

They came prepared for both the ball and tonight's planned extracurricular affair. Travis was dressed in a black suit and carried a four-inch-long candle, a book of matches, and a metal file. Lydia had also dressed appropriately. She wore her dark maroon dress and limited her jewelry to a single strand of deep-red garnets and her favorite red-tailed hawk feather in her hair.

Travis's heart pounded as they neared the front door, and he said, "No one is around, so let's first try the front door. If it's locked, we'll use a window."

Lydia stepped in front of Travis and slowly turned the ornate brass knob on one of the two front doors to the Pallaton home.

They heard a faint click, and to their amazement, it opened smoothly. She looked at Travis and whispered, "Perhaps this is a sign of greater things to come."

Once inside the foyer, they could barely see anything. The faint light from the ball, 140 yards away, wasn't enough for them to see the floor leading to Corey's study. Travis removed the candle from his pocket and handed it to Lydia. He said, "Hold this."

He reached into the pocket of his left pants and searched for the book of matches. It wasn't there. So, he searched his right pants pocket. It wasn't there either. His heart beat even faster than before. Finally, he said, "I can't find the matches. They must have fallen out while dancing."

Lydia calmly said, "Have you checked your coat pocket?"

Travis yanked the matches out from inside his left breast pocket a moment later. Unfortunately, the matches flew from his hand when Travis's arm struck one of the legs of Corey's entry table. He said, "Damn! Where did they fall? We've got to hurry."

Lydia knelt on one knee and passed her hand over the oak floor. She said, "Here they are. Calm down. We've got this, but we do need to hurry. Brynn won't be able to distract them much longer."

Travis lit the candle and hurried past the front window and down the hallway. They burst into the study and began surveying the room's furnishings. Then, holding the candle at arm's length, Lydia said, "Okay. Brynn said that Corey keeps the key to the safe under the largest drum, nearest the safe."

Across the room, they saw Corey's collection of seven tribal drums. Together, they knelt near the largest drum. Lydia held the candle as Travis reached down to tilt the drum on its side.

Lydia screamed at the top of her lungs! Two rattlesnakes were slithering toward them.

Her scream frightened the snakes, so they stopped and coiled themselves in a position ready to strike.

When Lydia screamed a second time, Travis calmly said, "Easy now. Take it easy. Step backward very slowly."

He carefully positioned himself between Lydia and the snakes. His birthmark warmed, and on this occasion, he understood its significance. He needed to connect with the snakes' energy.

So he moved closer to them while maintaining eye contact. Travis could see that Mutt & Jeff were afraid, and he wanted to calm their fears. He thought, "I don't want to hurt them."

Travis gently lifted both snakes just behind their heads when he was within arm's length. He was fearless as he held one in his left hand and the other in his right hand.

Lydia laughed nervously, and her pulse slowed as she said, "We forgot about Brynn's warning of the snakes."

Travis rolled his eyes and said, "Yeah. You can say that again."

Travis rose and walked to the snake tanks. He momentarily studied how Corey's alarm system worked and thought, "Corey is an arse, but the design of his security system is ingenious."

He gently lowered the two snakes into the tank containing the other two rattlers. Next, he closed the door through which they had entered the office. Then, he jokingly said, "They can guard *us* now. If anyone else enters, *our* four buddies will greet *them*."

Lydia replied, "We need to hurry."

They returned to the drum display and once again tilted the largest one on its side. Travis said, "Move the candle closer. I don't see the key."

Together, they knelt, drew themselves next to the drum's base, and saw no key. But, in a flash, the candle set fire to one of the eagle feathers that adorned the drum. The single flame quickly leapt into the menagerie of ribbon decorations.

Travis removed his jacket and feverishly worked to quell the quickly growing fire. Finally, after a thirty-second effort, he controlled and smothered the flames.

They set Corey's smoldering drum aside and searched feverishly for the key. Finally, after another minute, Travis calmly exclaimed, "It's not here. I'll use my file to pick the lock."

He grabbed his file, ran to the front of the safe, and said, "Please, hold the candle closer."

Travis tried to insert the file into the lock's tumbler. Then, he exclaimed, "The file is too large. I can't get it in the hole."

At that precise moment, they heard angry voices outside the front door.

Travis and Lydia heard Corey bellow to his companions, "Someone's in my home! General Williams and Jeremy, you stay here. I'm going in!"

Travis's heart sank when he heard Corey's voice. He knew there was nothing more he could do. He had failed again.

Suddenly, his snake-shaped birthmark sparked to life. This time, it wasn't simply a warm glow. His forehead burned as if it were on fire. Travis felt guided to look upward. The only thing he saw was Corey Pallaton's prominently displayed whaling gun. Travis grabbed it, took aim, and yelled, "Lydia, stand back and cover your ears!"

In a flash, a loud blast was felt and heard throughout the house and all of Williams Park. The bomb-lance easily pierced the safe, and its doors limply dangled from its hinges.

Travis and Lydia were momentarily stunned by the explosion but were thrilled to see the safe and its contents open for display.

Corey Pallaton barged into his office. The sight before him enraged him. He couldn't believe Travis Mathews and Lydia Stedman had broken into *his* home!

As Corey rushed to attack them, Travis and Lydia witnessed an incredible sight. Mutt, Jeff, Ginger, and Spice were slithering toward Corey. He had unknowingly freed the guardians when he entered the room.

However, Corey never saw the snakes coming at him. For a moment, Corey thought his leg stung from stumbling on the corner of the desk. But after Mutt & Jeff struck his calf muscles, Corey's legs were paralyzed, and he fell instantly. He watched helplessly in horror as Ginger and Spice slithered up his leg inside his pants legs. Moments later, when they bit into his family jewels, all feeling was fully restored.

Corey screamed in agony when Mutt struck his carotid artery, and Jeff landed on his vocal cords. Ginger and Spice then chose Corey's eyeballs as their next target. They mercilessly struck him, time and time again.

Corey's writhing screams turned to whimpers as Travis and Lydia witnessed the most gruesome sight of their lives.

By the time General Williams, Lucius Carroll, and Jeremy entered the room, Corey's lifeless body lay on the floor. General Williams was on the verge of attacking Travis when he yelled, "What the hell is going on?"

Travis's commanding voice answered, "Corey's snakes attacked him. Please stand back, and I'll take care of the snakes."

Elena and Harriet now appeared at the office doors and waited in astonishment when they saw Corey lying on the floor.

They shuttered in fear when they saw Travis grab the snakes and carefully place them safely back into their glass tank.

Elena burst into tears. She rushed to Corey's side, lifted his head, and said, "Is he going to be okay?"

However, as she touched his limp, lifeless body, she knew the answer. She was sure he was gone, and her life would never again be the same. Elena crumpled to the floor in agony alongside her husband. Seeing her blood-soaked, baby-blue, ruffled ballroom dress that enveloped Corey's body was a sight that the Williams' would never forget. General Williams looked at Travis and demanded, "What have you done?"

Travis stood erect, looked him in the eye, and replied, "I have done nothing! Corey Pallaton has been deceiving you and the rest of Norwich as well. He has stolen your money and lied to you. Lydia and I tried to tell everyone months ago, but no one listened because we had no proof. *Now, we have proof.* Let's take a look at the contents of the safe."

Lydia sifted through scores of signed stock certificates and quickly found the highly sought-after map. She held it up and exclaimed, "Ahh, here it is."

Lydia handed the map to Travis, and he announced, "This map shows the location of all the precious minerals that the Wawecus Hill Gold, Silver, and Nickel Mining Company has found over the past year. Look. *The map shows no silver, no nickel, and only a smidgen of gold deposits.* There is *no* mention of any large, promising new vein of gold. I'm sorry, but Corey has conned everyone."

Travis glared at Jeremy and said, "*You* made this map and gave it to Corey. How long have you known there is *no gold?*"

Jeremy was stunned, dumbfounded, and speechless. Finally, he said, "Corey threatened me and forced me to keep quiet. We found a few rocks that contained gold, just not nearly as much as Corey told everyone. We kept hoping that we might find a large deposit."

Lydia stood next to the safe. She said, "Look here, inside the safe, there are *no stashes of gold-bearing minerals or gold dust.* However, I do see a few gold coins. These are probably the remnants of money used by customers to buy shares of Corey's worthless company."

Elena was in shock. She said, "But, he told me we were sitting on a fortune. I trusted him."

Mrs. Harriet Williams winced and said, "Yes. But, I'm afraid it wasn't *your* fortune he held. *It was ours!*"

Elena tried to defend her husband, "I am truly sorry for the loss of your money, but Corey did fund the construction of several homes out on Pesikutes Ridge. And, for the past year, he has provided jobs for many of our tribe members. Corey loved and tried to protect the Pocawansetts here in Norwich."

No one in the room wanted to argue with Corey's grieving widow. Instead, they felt great sorrow, knowing that Corey had also lied to her. They knew the walls of her life were tumbling down around her.

General Williams concluded, "Mrs. Pallaton, we are sorry for your loss, but many of our friends' and neighbors' finances will be devastated. In addition, his lies will affect Harriet and me personally, and the reputation of Norwich will be tarnished forever."

Lucius Carroll took General Williams aside and said, "We need an investigation into everything associated with Corey's company. Hundreds of Norwich citizens will be sorely affected, and Corey has also hoodwinked several financial institutions."

General Williams replied, "You are right. We need to get the sheriff here to investigate before any leaves."

Carroll replied, "I agree. I saw him at the ball. I'll fetch him."

After Lucius Carroll left, General Williams looked sternly at Travis and said, "I don't know whether to hold you in contempt or to congratulate you. But a man is dead due to your reckless actions, and you have acted like a common burglar."

Travis replied, "Yes, Sir. I understand. But I tried every legitimate way possible to show everyone that Corey Pallaton was damaging people's lives here in Norwich. So I had to stop him."

He continued, "I didn't cause his death. Corey brought the snakes into this room and accidentally set them free himself. So his death is the consequence of his own careless actions."

General Williams replied, "Well. I partly agree with you, but we'll have to see what the sheriff concludes."

After the sheriff and Mr. Carroll arrived, the sheriff grilled Travis and Lydia for over an hour. Finally, the sheriff ended the evening's investigation by saying, "I need the two of you to promise me that you will meet in my office tomorrow afternoon. We'll have your statements drawn up by then, and I may have a few more questions."

Travis and Lydia nodded in agreement.

As Lucius Carroll left the Pallaton home, he told Jeremy, "I want you in my office at the bank tomorrow morning. You've got some explaining to do."

THE NORWICH AURORA

51: RECOVERY
DOWNTOWN NORWICH
NORWICH AURORA OFFICE: WATER STREET
FRIDAY, SEPTEMBER 16, 1859

The bell attached to the Aurora's office front door dinged as Travis entered. John Stedman glanced up from his desk and said, "Good afternoon. Please, come in."

Travis replied, "Thank you, Sir."

He raised his voice slightly, waved, and said, "Hello, Lydia."

She looked up, smiled, and said, "Hi, Travis. I'll be with you in a moment. But, first, I need to finish this article."

John said, "Travis, I haven't had the chance to tell you how much I appreciate what you and my daughter have accomplished recently. I've always believed in the two of you and knew you were always right about the mining company. It was obvious that Corey was misleading many honest, hard-working people in Norwich."

He continued, "However, it was wrong of you to break into someone's home. But, *sometimes,* a fair result justifies the means for such a questionable deed. I know it took great courage for you and Lydia to stick to your beliefs. But, please, keep things within legal limits next time."

Travis replied, "Thank you. I will. Lydia and I met with Norwich's sheriff after he completed a thorough investigation at the Pallaton home and interviewed Mrs. Pallaton. She told him that Lydia and I were not responsible for Corey's death, and she did not press charges for us breaking into her home. So, I'm grateful for that."

John replied, "Yes, Lydia told me those things, and I feel sorry for Elena Pallaton. She is now an impoverished widow with our entire town angry at her late husband."

Travis replied, "Yes, it's a sad situation. Unfortunately, several Pocawansett families occupying homes on Pesikutes Ridge are now in dire straits. Many are unemployed and have no means to repay their mortgages."

Lydia stepped forward and joined in the conversation. She said, "It is heartbreaking. However, I have an idea that may help. Let's contact several local establishments and find out if they have any job openings. Then, perhaps, we could organize and advertise a job fair for the unemployed Pocawansetts. I believe many local businesses would gladly participate."

John replied, "That's a grand idea. Could you and Travis follow up on it?"

They nodded, and Travis said, "We'd be pleased to lead the effort."

John's face turned solemn, and he said, "Many people have been adversely affected by Corey's scheme. Senator Lafayette Foster's sister owns many shares in the company and wants to know if there is any way to recover her loss. The Norwich Savings Society, the Chelsea Savings Bank, and Lucius Carroll's wholesale store have also suffered enormously. There's a rumor around town that Senator Foster's office will open a civil investigation into the matter."

Travis replied, "It is amazing how one scoundrel can severely affect so many people's lives. However, I want to share one positive development resulting from our escapade."

He turned to Lydia and continued, "Lydia, your article in last week's Aurora describing the downfall of the Wawecus Hill Gold, Silver, and Nickel Mining Company and the demise of Corey Pallaton has sparked a great deal of interest. Many are now reviewing their investments and their home safety. After people read how I blasted Corey's safe open with the whaling gun, several people stopped by our factory and asked to learn more about the gun. They wanted to know how to use it to defend their homes."

He continued, "So in only two days, my father and Mr. Brand developed a new type of cartridge that the whaling gun can shoot. The new round contains a collection of buckshot, copper-plated discs, and dozens of BBs. People's concerns for financial and personal safety have dramatically increased recently, and I think those are both good things."

John replied, "Well, Travis, you've just described a sad state of affairs in our town. But, now that you mention it, I, too, have been significantly more concerned for my family's safety."

Lydia added, "I just finished writing the article for the Aurora about President Fillmore. It tells readers how an unscrupulous crook cheated the president's grandfather. As a result, his family was left destitute. But, the story's point is to show that he and his father worked hard and overcame their hardship. They never gave up trying to better themselves, and eventually, Mr. Fillmore became president of the United States. It's a story of hard work and diligence overcoming extreme adversity."

John Stedman replied, "Lydia, I can hardly wait to read and edit your article. I am so proud of you. At this point in time, many of our readers need an uplifting article that provides hope for a brighter future."

Travis said, "I want to read it too, but we must get moving. Brynn and her parents are waiting for us at the picnic."

Lydia nodded, smiled, and quickly gathered things. They stepped outside and climbed aboard Travis's carriage that waited outside the Aurora's office.

52: Dunham Family Picnic
Norwichtown
Dunham Family Residence: Washington Street
Friday, September 16, 1859

Brynn and Dexter bounded from the Dunham front porch to meet Lydia and Travis. Dexter had suffered horrible diarrhea after eating Corey's chocolate bar but was now fully recovered. Brynn vowed never to eat chocolate again.

Brynn chirped, "Hi, Lydia. Hi, Travis. It's great to see you. Let's join my parents in the backyard."

Lydia descended from the carriage, hugged Brynn, smiled, and said, "Thank you for inviting us."

After Travis tied Moshup securely to one of the Dunham's hitching posts, he removed a burlap bag from the carriage. He gingerly lifted the gunny sack and followed Brynn to the backyard. Dexter barked for attention, tugged playfully at Travis's foot, and sniffed the bag.

Travis smiled and said, "This little guy sure is curious."

Brynn added, "Yeah. He is quite the pup. He loves greeting our visitors."

As they neared the family's backyard gazebo, John Dunham approached Travis and said, "Can I help you with that?"

Travis grinned broadly and replied, "Oh no. I've got it. I only need a safe spot to put it."

John replied, "Right over here, next to the table inside the pavilion, will be fine. What have you got there?"

Travis replied, "It's for our afternoon entertainment pleasure. It's a mystery that I hope we can solve together."

Brynn's mother, Mary, jumped into the conversation, saying, "I love a good mystery. So that will be fun."

She added, "Please, everyone, have a seat. May I bring you drinks?"

Everyone nodded, and Travis said, "Mr. Dunham, your yard and gardens are stunning. It must take a lot of work to keep them so healthy."

John replied, "Yes, but I'm happy to inform you that Brynn does most of the gardening and upkeep."

Lydia said, "Brynn, did you design the wisteria arrangement on the gazebo's latticework?"

Brynn nodded and replied, "Why yes. My first thought was to cover it with roses, but I changed my mind after our family vacation to New York City. When we took a carriage ride through Central Park, I saw a gorgeous display of purple wisteria trees on a pergola. So when I noticed that, I knew we needed to replicate it here in Norwich."

Lydia responded, "Well, it's beautiful. That's not to say your hostas, azaleas, and roses aren't as lovely. Your entire backyard has an inviting, wonderful feel about it."

Mary returned to the table inside the pavilion with a serving tray bearing a pitcher of freshly made iced lemonade infused with several springs of spearmint. She said, "I hope everyone likes lemonade. It is one of Brynn's favorites, especially after I've muddled in spearmint."

After Brynn's mother served the drinks, her father stood and made a toast, "I'd like to propose a toast to the past 200 years of

Norwich. And I pray that the next 200 will be as good as the last."

Everyone raised their glass and said, "Here, here."

John continued, "Lydia, I read your articles in last week's newspaper. First, I want to congratulate you on doing a fine job describing the parade, the dinner, and the ball. How is your booklet describing the Jubilee events coming along?"

Lydia replied, "Yes. My father and I are just now getting started compiling detailed descriptions of all the speeches and events. It is a huge job and will likely take us six months to complete. We'll donate the money we earn from its sales to help pay the expenses incurred by the Jubilee activities."

John replied, "The entire town will benefit from your efforts. Thank you."

John paused momentarily and turned his attention to a subject near and dear to his heart. He looked at Lydia and asked, "Will you include a description of the *extracurricular activities* after the ball?"

Lydia blushed, and Travis came to her rescue. He answered, "No, sir. There won't be any mention of Mr. Corey Pallaton or his treacherous deeds."

John replied, "Travis, I know you worked for Corey Pallaton as Jeremy's survey team member. Brynn once told me that you personally found a substantial amount of gold on Wawecus Hill."

Travis replied, "Yes. I worked for Corey, and I did find a handful of gold-bearing rocks. *But it was only a handful.* I suspected Corey's smokescreen after his survey team and I thoroughly scoured the Goldmine Brook area. It turned out that we found a lot of fool's gold. I want to reiterate we only found several handfuls of real gold-laced minerals."

Travis knew that Brynn's father wanted to hear more of Jeremy's involvement and continued, "I'm not sure what part Jeremy played in the scheme, but I know that at some point, he was fully aware of the deception."

John replied, "We trusted Jeremy because he seemed honest and hard-working. Also, Mary and I knew Brynn was attracted to him. So, we felt comfortable buying into the mining company. As you probably know, we planned to pay for Brynn's school tuition using profits from our shares."

He continued, "This past December, I was angry at you when we witnessed the incident during the company's quarterly report. I thought you were jealous of Jeremy's successes. But, as time passed and as I tried to cash in our shares, I began to suspect that you and Lydia were right. So, with all those events now in the past, I must say I apologize for any ill thoughts I might have held toward you."

Since last week's incident, several people had approached Travis with gratitude and thanks. However, when Travis heard John Dunham say it publicly, he was deeply grateful.

Travis said, "Mr. Dunham. Thank you for saying that. It means more to me than I have words to explain."

John stood again and made a second toast, "A toast to Travis Mathews and Lydia Stedman."

After everyone acknowledged the toast, John raised his glass again and said, "I know these past few months have been emotionally difficult for my daughter. However, she has endured the experiences with grace and elegance. A toast also to my delightful daughter, Brynn!"

Brynn said, "Thank you, Father. I'm not so sure how *delightful* I've been lately. I want to apologize for how I've acted recently. I was utterly disappointed because I so wanted to attend Miss Porter's School. But, as you pointed out earlier, I can wait until next year."

John sat and announced, "I have news on that front. Miss Porter, a connoisseur of fashion and style, attended the formal ball last week. Before all the commotion, your mother and I had an enjoyable conversation with her."

He paused, grinned broadly, and continued, "I must admit that Miss Porter has a wonderful sense of humor and a congenial manner about her. But I don't want to let that divert my attention now. So, anyway, she was impressed with how you and Emeline decorated the tent. She noticed and remarked that Emeline had incorporated several design concepts she learned from her into the banners and ribbons. Miss Porter was pleased that the good people of Norwich could see the results of her training efforts and influence."

John continued, "She was surprised when we told her you designed and made all the rose-based floral arrangements. She could hardly believe that you've had no formal training. So, when she learned of your innate talent for working with flowers, she instantly wanted to help develop your skills. So, I'm happy to announce that she has offered you a scholarship. She will waive your first semester's tuition, and you can start school next Monday."

Brynn bolted from her seat and hugged her parents. She said, "I've wanted this for so long. Thank you. Thank you!"

After a short back-to-school discussion, Brynn's mother said, "I want you to know how sorry I am that we allowed Corey

Pallaton to swindle us. We thought we could trust him, and we're sorry for the pain it caused you."

Brynn bristled and said, "Thank you for saying that, Mother, but it wasn't your fault. I was also tricked. But Travis, Lydia, and I took care of him. I pray that God doesn't punish me, but I've got to say I'm glad to see Corey Pallaton gone."

Lydia joined in, saying, "Well, he got what he deserved. He should have never kept a group of rattlesnakes as pets. When they attacked him, it looked like they were taking revenge. I don't think he fed them enough."

Brynn cringed and said, "Well, I know that he sometimes fed them mice, but, as far as I'm concerned, he shouldn't have kept a family of mice as pets either."

Mary questioned, "So Brynn, you, Lydia, and Travis apparently planned to expose Corey. What was it?"

Brynn replied, "It wasn't very complicated. My job was to stall Corey and Elena while Travis and Lydia found the map. But, when I heard Lydia scream, the plan fell apart."

Brynn questioned Lydia, "Why did you scream?"

Lydia responded, "I'm a bit embarrassed about that. Travis and I were excited when we entered the house and forgot that you had warned us of Corey's *security system*. So, I was startled after his snakes got loose and encountered them face-to-face."

She turned to Travis, smiled, and said, "But Travis took care of the situation. Thank you."

After providing a detailed account of how they opened the safe and seized the map, Travis said, "Lydia and I also have an announcement."

Lydia sat tall in her chair, and the Dunham family's attention was aroused as they awaited the news.

Finally, Travis said, "As you all know, many here in the town have scorned me over the past several months due to Corey Pallaton's lies. That, coupled with my strong desire to explore the world as a ship's navigator, coaxed me into making a decision. I had planned to leave Norwich."

He glanced at Lydia and continued, "But, as you also know, Lydia and I worked together for Mr. Henry Walling to create the Quinebaugan map you saw at the Jubilee dinner. We learned a great deal about Quinebaugan culture and tradition throughout the process. And we also honed our skills in land-surveying, map making, decorating, publishing, and printing maps."

He continued, "Last week, Mr. Walling told us that he is leaving Norwich for a new project in New York City and will sell his business here in Norwich. So, after working out the financial details, Lydia and I will purchase his business. We will become Norwich's premier map producer."

Mr. Dunham clapped Travis on the back and said, "Congratulations. Greeneville and Norwich's west side are growing at a lightning pace and will need many new maps."

He looked at Lydia and added, "I know the two of you will be successful, and I'm very happy for you."

Lydia replied, "Thank you. We're excited and looking forward to it. I'm sure it will be enjoyable and profitable. It's still in the planning stages, but we're confident we can build our business together here in Norwich."

Travis lifted his burlap bag and said, "Ahh. So that brings us to the subject of today's entertainment."

Everyone chuckled, and Brynn questioned, "Okay. So what's in the bag?"

Travis carefully removed the Quinebaugan mortar and pestle.

He said, "Several months ago, Lydia and I found this mortar and pestle near Goldmine Brook on the side of Wawecus Hill. We know for certain that someone used it to grind precious minerals and extract gold powder. But, we believe there is more to the story."

Travis then pulled out the small tomahawk they had found. He continued, "In the same mound where we found the mortar and pestle, we also recovered this small tomahawk and the skeleton of one of our ancestors. Everyone, please examine the tomahawk, mortar, and pestle closely."

He passed the items around, and finally, Travis said, "Lydia and I were especially impressed with the etchings on the mortar. It seemed to us that they were more than ordinary decorations. We thought them to be clues for a hidden message. So, we took them to an old Quinebaugan sage who lives at Kachina Rock. She agreed with us. She noticed that the artisan had carved two tomahawks into the mortar. One was very small, like this one."

He held up the tomahawk and said, "The other one depicted is substantially larger. She believes Wawequa used the large tomahawk shown to render justice to the Pocawansett Sachem Pallatonomo. And she believes the decorations on the mortar are clues to where we may find Wawequa's tomahawk."

He continued, "So, we searched for it for the past few months while mapping the Quinebaugan sites. Unfortunately, we were unsuccessful and gave up the hunt. Do any of you have any ideas?"

John Dunham was mesmerized and excited. Then, he said, "I want to tell you a story."

He pointed to the Dunham home and began, "I grew up in this house, on this land. My father bought it many years ago from Major Ebenezer Whiting, a Revolutionary War officer.

After his service, Major Whiting bought the land because he owned and operated a distillery at nearby Yantic Falls."

He pointed in a southwest direction and said, "Since the Falls are only several hundred yards from here, the Major and his wife, Annabella Fitch Whiting, chose this ideal location for their homestead."

Dunham stood and said, "Here's where the story gets interesting. The Whiting family knew the rear portion of their sixteen-acre lot was home to an ancient Quinebaugan burial ground, but unfortunately, there were no marked graves at the time. However, when Whiting dug the foundation for our house, he found a huge Native American skeleton, many arrowheads, and a collection of crude stone tools."

Lydia questioned, "Did your father provide more details?"

John replied, "Yes, he did. He told me several interesting things. For example, after Major Whiting and his family abruptly moved out and put up the house for sale, several neighbors warned him the house was haunted. They said Whiting's wife, Annabella, complained of hearing the thumping of drums and cries of someone screaming out in an unknown language."

He continued, "Major Whiting died only weeks after leaving Norwich for Massachusetts. Many believed that spirits forced him out of the house, eventually driving him insane. So, the house sat empty for over a year before my father bought it."

Travis said, "Didn't those fears concern you?"

John replied, "Oh no, not at all. I was just a kid. As I said earlier, my parents moved in right after my older sister was born, and then five years later, I was born in this very house."

John continued, "I have always respected the Quinebaugan people and their traditions. Twenty-six years ago, the mayor of

Norwich and members of the Quinebaugan tribe approached me. They told me that the sachem, Lucas, was buried on my property and wanted to erect a statue in his honor. I agreed, and you can see the monument over there by the rose garden."

Lydia turned to Brynn and said, "Brynn, have you ever heard any drums or other odd sounds?"

Brynn replied, "No, I haven't. You should know that I love our home and our garden. But, I must admit, I never go near the back corner of our lot because it's overgrown, and the contour of the land slopes steeply downward toward Yantic Falls."

She continued, "A couple of years ago, I went back there thinking I could clear the bramble and perhaps enlarge our vegetable garden. But, there was a host of rattlesnakes sunning themselves on the rocks. The entire area felt creepy to me."

Lydia said, "I've walked by the Lucas monument a thousand times but didn't know other Quinebaugans who may have been buried here. Perhaps Lucas's brother, Wawequa, is also buried nearby? Did you see any mounds or outcroppings back there?"

Brynn answered, "Yes, there are several. But I stay away because I've seen so many rattlesnakes there. Dexter doesn't even go there. It's too dangerous."

Travis rose and questioned Mr. Dunham, "Do you mind if we take a quick look? Perhaps we can find Wawequa's burial plot."

Dunham replied, "I don't mind. I think you may be on to something."

Brynn said, "This isn't a good idea. Someone will get bitten."

They all stood and began walking toward the area. Dexter hopped up, barked, and ran to Brynn's side. She said, "Hold on, Dexter. Take it easy."

Dexter ignored her and trotted forward. However, he stopped when he encountered the first clump of the bramble.

Without thinking, Travis politely commanded, "Everyone, stand back."

Travis pushed several small tree branches aside and tried to see through the brush.

Lydia stepped beside him and announced, "Travis, I can see four mounds that may be burial plots, but I also see several snakes surrounding them. So I don't think this is a good idea."

Travis ignored her, turned to Brynn's father, and said, "Mr. Dunham, do you have any garden tools I could use to clear a path to the mound?"

John disappeared into his greenhouse and proffered a scythe. He said, "I know this isn't the ideal tool for the job, but it's the best I've got."

Travis accepted the tool and said, "Thanks. I only need to get past the first few feet. It's mostly clear after that."

After he whacked away the first few vines and bramble, he saw scores of timber rattlesnakes slithering amongst the warm rocks. He thought momentarily and said, "Brynn and Lydia, you are correct. There are too many snakes here, and it's too dangerous. We'll have to return on a cooler day later this fall."

As he turned to leave, Travis felt his birthmark begin to warm. His pulse quickened, and he sensed something incredible was about to take place.

Dexter joined Travis at the edge of the clearing, and they saw all the snakes turn away in unison. Then, like a school of fleeing fish, the snakes retreated and slithered down the hillside toward Yantic Falls. Travis had never seen anything like it before. He felt as if he was Moses and the Red Sea had just parted before him.

Travis and Dexter stepped over several rocks and reached one of the four mounds. As Travis began to sift through the dirt and debris covering the stones, Dexter started to yelp and bark incessantly.

When Travis looked up to see what caused the excitement, he saw six snakes perched on one of the mounds. He was surprised to see *any* remaining snakes.

Suddenly, the snakes snapped to attention and stood erect in line. They looked like a family of lemur statues staring at Travis. Then, as he and Dexter approached the area, Travis's birthmark burned more intently, and the snakes suddenly laid down and slithered away.

Dexter pounced on the mound and feverishly began digging. His front paws excavated the mound as if there were no tomorrow.

By now, Lydia and the entire Dunham family had joined Travis, and they watched Dexter unearth what appeared to be the end of a small tree branch. Seconds later, however, everyone could see the full-sized tomahawk emerge.

Travis knelt and carefully removed the remaining dirt and debris from the gravesite. Finally, he freed the ancient relic and showed it to Lydia and the Dunham family. He said, "Ladies and Gentlemen, I present you Wawequa's tomahawk."

Lydia and Travis examined it together. Although much of the curved wooden handle was decayed, they saw remnants of a snake carving along its length and a large smooth granite head with traces of embedded gold.

Finally, Travis said, "I can hardly wait to give this to Mrs. Flowers. She and the other tribal leaders will be happy to see that we've found it. They will know what to do with it."

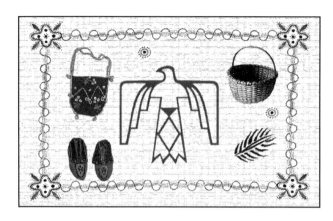

53: Green Corn Festival
Lucasville
Quinebaugan Church
Friday, September 30, 1859

Lydia Stedman called out, "Mother, could you help me?"

When Caroline entered the room, she saw her daughter as a beautiful Quinebaugan princess for the first time. Caroline thought, "She is breathtaking."

Lydia wore a fitted buckskin dress decorated with hundreds of tiny handmade silver bells and a single feather in her hair. Caroline almost cried when she saw the brightly colored bead necklace she had given Lydia the day before. And her heart skipped a beat when she noticed the golden glow of energy surrounding Lydia.

Caroline beamed with pride and replied, "Yes. It would be my pleasure. What do you need?"

Lydia replied, "Could you fasten the corsage to my wrist?"

Brynn had designed, made, and given Lydia a Quinebaugan-themed corsage of tiny red, pink, and white roses. The arrangement reminded Caroline of a sacred Quinebaugan tribal symbol.

As her mother completed the job, Lydia said, "I can hardly wait for today's Green Corn Festival, and I don't quite know what to expect."

Caroline responded, "Well, don't think for a moment that you're the only one. The Quinebaugans haven't held one during our lifetime, so everyone is curious. It will be lots of fun."

The Stedmans boarded their carriage a few minutes later and began their journey to Quinebaugan Hill. When they reached the base of the hill, they looked up and saw the Quinebaugan Church perched on its crown. Lydia asked her father, "You've attended this church before, haven't you?"

John said, "Yes, your mother and I visited the church several times when you were just a baby. However, I worshipped at the First Congregational church throughout my childhood."

He continued, "I have fond memories of the Quinebaugan Church. As a young man, several members of our congregation and I wanted to proclaim the gospel of our Lord and Savior, Jesus Christ, to our Quinebaugan neighbors. So we, along with the good people of Norwich and members of the Quinebaugan tribe, joined in unison to build the church building. Since then, the Quinebaugans have used it as their Congregationalist Meeting House."

Caroline added, "The Quinebaugan Church is the Quinebaugan's primary social and religious gathering spot. Lydia, you'll fit it with them perfectly. They are your biological sisters and brothers."

Lydia said, "Yes. I'm excited about that and know I'm beginning a new chapter in my life."

Her mother replied, "I believe you are too."

After securing their carriage, the Stedman family stepped onto the Quinebaugan Church green. They were greeted by a large banner spanning two ten-foot tall poles bearing the word **YAHTAHAY**. Lydia said, "Travis's mother told me to watch for that banner. She told me the Quinebaugan word, *Yahtahay*, means 'Welcome' in English."

As they walked behind the church, Lydia said, "Do you mind if I leave you to find Travis?"

Her mother replied, "Of course not. We want to look around and speak with several of our friends."

Twenty wooden benches carved from local chestnut trees were scattered around the green. Lydia saw dozens of tribe members and visitors milling around while socializing and eating. When she spotted a young boy take a bite of a fried turkey leg, she smiled and thought, "I know exactly where I'll find Travis."

She turned her attention to a twenty-foot-wide by a thirty-foot-long arbor in the middle of the green and saw a host of tables surrounding its perimeter. The entire area was festive and bursting with activity. But, at the moment, Lydia only needed to follow her nose to find Travis. She found him at the buffet table situated adjacent to the arbor.

Lydia quietly approached Travis from behind, poked at his side playfully, and cried out, "Boo!"

Travis spun around and almost spilled his bowl of clam chowder on her. Then, after laughing, he kissed her carefully to avoid spilling any food. Then he warned her, "You'd better watch out because you may end up wearing my lunch next time."

She laughed and replied, "My parents and I just got here. What are you eating?"

He replied, "At the moment, it's a bowl of clam chowder, but this is the second course. I started with a plate of succotash, beans, and corn on the cob. They've got a lot of tasty food here. Are you hungry?"

She replied, "Yes, but I want to look around first. I know the Quinebaugan Ladies' Sewing Society has several items for sale. I heard they made a few unique, Quinebaugan-themed items specifically for this event. I want to shop around before someone else buys all the best ones."

Travis said, "Okay. Let's check it out together. Oh, by the way, you look great!"

They strolled around the outer perimeter of the all-natural arbor and found the Quinebaugan Ladies' Sewing Society display tables. They saw Travis's mother standing behind one, answering questions from a potential customer.

When they were within earshot, they heard her say, "We're hosting two tables today. The ladies of our church group made everything you see on this table. It's all for sale. I want to draw your attention to these beautiful aprons I sewed for this occasion."

Gesturing to the other table, Faith continued, "This second table displays items from our Quinebaugan past. The items are not for purchase, but my colleague, Rachel Flowers, would love to describe their historical significance."

After the customer left, Travis said, "Hello, Mother."

Faith turned to them and gasped, "Lydia, you look fabulous! Come over here and give me a big hug."

Lydia was slightly embarrassed at Faith's reaction but was relieved to know her regalia was acceptable. They hugged, and Lydia said, "Thank you. I love this festival. It's so good to see everyone together and see all the interesting things. Besides the aprons, what are you selling?"

Faith waved her hand over the table and replied, "We're offering beaded leather bags and wampum shell necklaces for ladies and stout leather pouches for gentlemen. One of the church women also donated several baskets woven with birch bark. She decorated the baskets bearing the symbol of our tribe."

Lydia pointed to one of the items and said, "I especially like that beaded leather bag. It matches my regalia perfectly."

Before Lydia could buy it, Travis whispered something in his mother's ear. Faith said, "Oh, Lydia, I'm so sorry. Travis just reminded me we promised that bag to Rachel's daughter. I accidentally put it out for sale."

Faith placed the bag under the table, pulled out a similar purse, and asked, "Are you interested in this one?"

Lydia scowled and said, "No, it is the wrong color, but thank you. I really liked the other one. But I still want to walk around and see what else is available."

As Travis and Lydia moved on to the next table, Faith winked at Travis, and he smiled.

Rachel Flowers stood behind a collection of Quinebaugan treasures. As Travis and Lydia stood before them, Rachel looked at them and said, "Welcome. I'm happy to see you two. I want to tell you how proud I am of you. You've done our tribe a great service."

Travis responded, "Thank you, Mrs. Flowers. It is we who are indebted to you. Thank you for planning and organizing this event."

He pointed at one of the items on the table and questioned, "What is the significance of this old bracelet?"

Rachel smiled and said, "It is one of our most precious gifts. This bracelet was made using only the finest wampum beads and was owned and worn by our original Sachem Lucas. It is one of very few of his surviving personal items."

Travis said, "I feel honored just to be in the presence of such a treasure."

Rachel pointed to several beaded pendants and baskets and continued, "Our female ancestors passed these down to their daughters for several generations. They are uniquely Quinebaugan, and we are blessed to have them."

Lydia marveled at them and replied, "They are beautiful."

It was nearly noon, and Travis saw several kids licking ice cream cones. He said to Lydia, "Let's get some dessert."

After they reached the dessert station, they saw a six-and-a-half-foot tall, muscular man dressed in full Quinebaugan garb selling ice cream. Travis noticed something unusual about the dessert. He told the vendor, "I see everyone eating vanilla ice cream with an odd topping that looks like ground peanuts. What is it?"

The Quinebaugan man smiled broadly and replied, "Everyone asks me that question. Next year, I'll bring my son to answer it. But, for today, I'll explain again, for the one-hundredth time."

He said, "For generations, indigenous people used dried food for sustenance during long journeys. Many tribes dried venison and beef to make jerky. Our Quinebaugan ancestors ground large kernels of dried flint corn into powder and called it *yokeag*. They carried it in small leather pouches, added water, and cooked it when hungry."

The man smiled again and continued, "Well, it turns out yokeag has a pleasant, nutty flavor that makes for an excellent topping on ice cream. Would you like to try a cone?"

Lydia turned to the Quinebaugan, laughed loudly, and replied, "Of course he would. He'll eat almost any dessert. I'll pay."

As Travis bit into his tasty delight, he and Lydia heard the booming sound of a kettle-sized Quinebaugan drum begin to beat. It was exactly noon, and everyone knew it was time for the Green Corn Festival ceremonies to begin.

All ceremonies would take place inside the arbor. Travis's father and several other tribesmen had erected the imposing structure only days before. They used a group of twelve-inch diameter chestnut logs as support columns. Each log was crotched at the top and supported an array of smaller birch saplings. The roof and walls, fashioned of birch branches, formed a comfortable, intimate setting for a ceremonial meeting place. Each arbor wall faced a cardinal direction, but everyone only entered from the East.

The Quinebaugan and their visitors filed into the arbor as Travis's father and three other tribesmen beat the kettle drum in unison. Everyone saw three chairs and a large burlap bag displayed in the center of the open meeting area.

Travis held Lydia's hand tightly as they passed through the eastern portal. They immediately felt a sense of reverence and pride when they saw Rachel Flowers standing in the middle of the ceremonial area. She stood beside an oak chair, her head slightly bowed, hands crossed below her waist. Rachel wore a beautifully decorated beaded belt bearing the Quinebaugan symbol around her waist.

The drum stopped after everyone settled into their seats, and she announced, "Everyone, please be seated."

She waited a moment and began, "Welcome, everyone. Welcome, Aquilas. Yes, we are Aquilas. We are *Munduyahweh's* Tribe of the Eagle!"

Rachel energized the audience when she threw back her head and belted out a series of whoops and hollers. The drums beat wildly, and everyone joined her with enthusiastic howling and clamor.

Rachel smiled and, after a minute, resumed, "Ninety years ago, our last Sachem, Isaiah Lucas, passed from this world into the next. Unfortunately, the tribe was not allowed to appoint a new sachem due to laws in this country. But we, the Quinebaugan, are still here. We have been here hundreds of years and will remain hundreds more."

She continued, "Our goal today is to remember the past, enjoy the present, and contemplate the future. When several other members of our tribe and I marched in Norwich's 200th Jubilee parade a couple of weeks ago, we honored our ancestors, our heritage, and our traditions."

Rachel continued, "Our Quinebaugan Church Ladies' Sewing Society decided to host today's Green Corn Festival to renew a nearly forgotten celebration of our heritage. Our ancestors held the last festival on this very spot many years ago. Unfortunately, far too much time has passed since we last celebrated the harvest. From this day forward, I propose we host the Green Corn Festival annually."

"Our tribal stories and traditions form the backbone of our heritage, and we must also respect and honor our land and sacred places. As a part of Norwich's 200th Jubilee, two of our youth explored and mapped many of our ancestral sites."

Rachel reached into the tube next to the burlap bag and unrolled a map. She said, "This beautiful map is the result of their efforts, and we'll display it publicly later this afternoon. When I first saw the map, I remembered our forefathers' brave and noble acts. I hope it does the same for you."

She surveyed the audience and said, "Now, I'd like to honor the young man and woman who created this treasure. Mr. Travis Mathews and Miss Lydia Stedman, would you please join me?"

Rachel hugged Travis and Lydia and said, "Thank you for all your efforts. We are grateful for your contributions to our tribe. Would you like to say a few words?"

Travis nodded, faced the audience, and said, "Yes. As most of you know, Lydia and I spent months exploring old Quinebaugan sites and preparing this map. However, the map isn't the most precious fruit of our efforts."

He nodded to Lydia, and she removed all the Quinebaugan relics they had found from the burlap bag.

They held out the mortar, pestle, stone box filled with gold powder, and the small tomahawk for everyone to see. He said, "While surveying the areas, we found these artifacts. They are all a part of our tradition, and we now return them to you, the Aquilas, the Tribe of the Eagle."

After they handed the objects to Rachel, Travis held up the full-sized tomahawk. He brandished it, shook it vigorously over his head, and said, "This is Wawequa's tomahawk. Two hundred years ago, he used it to silence our adversaries and ensure the well-being of our tribe. That day marked the beginning of a peaceful epoch for our people. Today, we wish to reaffirm our unity and solidarity."

He began chanting, "Aquilas. Aquilas. We are the Aquilas. Aquilas. Aquilas. We are the Aquilas!"

The crowd gleefully joined in his cry for unity and sat after Travis presented the tomahawk to Rachel Flowers.

Travis and Lydia returned to their seats, and Rachel said, "Thank you again. We also want to share a few stories with you this afternoon. There are several tribal leaders here with us. Some of them are known to you, and some are not. Our storyteller's name is *Aquilablanca*. In English, her name translates to White Eagle, and I'd like to introduce her to you."

Rachel continued, "Many years ago, Aquilablanca lived in Shantok with her daughter Plumaroja, which means Red Feather in English. They were active community members and often joined us at the Quinebaugan Church. However, White Eagle left Shantok and moved to our most sacred Quinebaugan site, Kachina Rock, after her beloved daughter died unexpectedly. Today, White Eagle enjoys a quiet, solitary life there. She has been, for many years, and still is, our tribe's storyteller. I'm happy she is with us today and wants to share her wisdom."

Rachel looked to the audience, spotted White Eagle, and said, "Aquilablanca, the floor is yours."

White Eagle rose slowly and ambled her way to Rachel's side. She sat in the middle chair and said, "Thank you. I am humbled to join you today, and yes, it has been many years since I've had the opportunity to share our stories with you. Today's story focuses on the virtues of balance and harmony."

White Eagle smiled coyly, gestured to the audience, and said, "Before I begin, I'd like to ask Mr. Travis Mathews to stand."

Travis's heart skipped a beat. And thinking he hadn't heard her request correctly, he froze. However, when everyone turned to him and looked at him with anticipation, Travis stood.

She continued, "Travis, please come stand next to me."

As Travis made his way to the center, he turned to face the audience and felt a hundred sets of eyes upon him. His six-foot, four-inch frame towered over the diminutive figure of White Eagle.

She looked up at him and began, "Moshup was a gentle giant who sometimes lived near Shantok, sometimes in the sea east of Massachusetts, and sometimes on Martha's Vineyard. He walked among us as a respected builder most of the time, but since Moshup could shapeshift, he sometimes preferred to assume the body of a whale so that he could swim with his friends beneath the sea. Moshup, with his kind and gentle spirit, bridged the gap between man and beast and between land and sea."

White Eagle pointed to the chair beside her and said, "You may be seated."

White Eagle faced the audience, smiled again, and said, "Miss Lydia Stedman, please stand."

Lydia's heart raced because she could only imagine what White Eagle might say or do next.

She continued, "Please join us here."

Lydia made her way to White Eagle's side and stood, facing the audience, in front of the remaining empty chair. Like Travis before, Lydia felt everyone's attention bearing upon her.

White Eagle said, "Squannit was the leader of the Small Ones of the Woods, the Laypetea. She was tiny in stature but possessed great wisdom. She also had magical powers that could affect the forces of nature. Squannit taught our ancestors many secrets of herbal medicine and how to cultivate corn, beans, and squash."

White Eagle pointed to the chair, said, "You may be seated," and began her story.

SQUANNIT AND MOSHUP

Squannit and Moshup were very different from one another. He was tall, and she was short. He had a gentle, calm disposition, and she was very emotional. He enjoyed swimming and fishing in the ocean and, in many ways, ruled the sea, while Squannit loved cultivating vegetables and herbs on land. She was the Queen of the Small Ones of the Woods, the Laypetea.

Soon after they met, Moshup and Squannit fell in love, married, and raised twelve daughters and twelve sons. Each balanced their partner's unique, individual traits and backgrounds. However, they sometimes argued due to their extreme differences.

Many years before the birth of Lucas, the Quinebaugan and the Hoopanoag tribes lived in harmony. The Quinebaugan, who loved to hunt, settled at Fort Shantok, and many of the Hoopanoag, who loved to fish, settled on Martha's Vineyard.

One day, the tribes asked Moshup to erect a bridge between Shantok and Martha's Vineyard so they could visit one another more easily. Moshup worked day and night for many weeks to build the bridge. He was so intent on erecting the bridge that he worked day and night without rest. Many complained because every time Moshup stepped into the sea, he caused huge waves that capsized their fishing boats.

To make things even worse, Squannit felt neglected while Moshup was away. So, one day, she shouted out to him with all her might. Moshup was at sea, still building the bridge, and did not hear her, but suddenly, the skies around him darkened, and an enormous thunderstorm erupted.

It destroyed a portion of Moshup's bridge, and Moshup KNEW that Squannit had spoken. She wanted him home.

Moshup learned that he needed to lead a more balanced life. As a result, he changed his neglectful ways and eventually finished the bridge. All the Quinebaugan and Hoopanoag learned the virtues of balance and harmony from the example that Moshup and Squannit set forth.

She gestured to the audience and said, "To be one with our great spirit, *Munduyahweh*, we must all live in harmony and lead a balanced life."

After pausing, White Eagle said, "There is one more story I want to share with you. As a young girl, my parents and I lived amongst the Laypetea. Their storyteller told me of Moshup and Squannit's many adventures. She told me how they brought balance to the world."

"Moshup and Squannit passed from this worldly domain after two hundred happy years together. But, after their death, a legend spread that their spirit would return if our tribe ever became out-of-balance."

She continued, "I sense our world *is becoming more out-of-balance every day*. I was deeply disappointed when Rachel Flowers told me that Connecticut now wants to seize our native homeland and force us to pay them taxes. An action of that magnitude would completely throw our tribe out of balance. We need the spirits of Moshup and Squannit to return."

After White Eagle finished the story, she said, "I want to thank Rachel for asking me to join you today and for her cordial introduction. Now, I'd like to tell you more about *my past*."

She continued, "While living with my daughter, Red Feather, in Shantok, I loved sharing our tribe's stories with her. The leaders of our tribe and I planned for Red Feather to become our next Storyteller. Unfortunately, my heart was broken when she died while giving birth to her daughter."

"Red Feather may not physically be with us here today. But, the light of her spirit burns brightly within her daughter. Her daughter – my granddaughter, is here with us today, and her name is Patadoe, which means Rabbit's Foot in Quinebaugan. Patadoe, would you please stand and be recognized?"

Lydia trembled, and tears welled into her eyes as she stood. The drummers beat the kettle drum, and everyone inside the arbor applauded.

White Eagle reached down into the burlap bag and retrieved a gift. She held up a tiny pair of brightly beaded slippers, turned to Lydia, and said, "May you always walk in the footsteps of our ancestors."

She turned to the audience and announced, "The spirit of the Laypetea is within Patadoe, and it is my deepest desire that she will become our next Storyteller. I promise to teach her all our stories and legends."

White Eagle reached into her bag again. This time, she removed an ornately decorated basket. She turned to Travis and said, "I present you with this basket. Our artisans decorated it with Quinebaugan symbols to remind us of our heritage and traditions. I want you to use this basket to collect the sum of our tribe's wisdom and knowledge. And when needed, you can share its medicine with our people."

After Travis gratefully accepted the basket, White Eagle said, "I hope this young man will someday become our tribe's Medicine Man, and I ask for everyone's support."

White Eagle circled Travis and Lydia. She said, "Would the two of you please stand, hold one another's hand, and face the crowd?"

Travis and Lydia could only imagine what White Eagle would say next. Their hearts beat wildly in unison as they stood and reached out to each other.

White Eagle tapped Travis's shoulder, then tapped Lydia's shoulder, and proclaimed, "The spirits of Moshup, Squannit, and the Laypetea are here among us today! They will provide balance and guidance to us in the days ahead."

Everyone jumped to their feet and clapped so loudly that *Munduyahweh* smiled in heaven.

Rachel Flowers joined White Eagle, Lydia, and Travis and announced, "Thank you, White Eagle! We will now celebrate our bountiful harvest."

Travis's father and the other three drummers began beating a new, lively rhythm, and Rachel Flowers said, "Ladies. Please join me in the first Green Corn Dance we've danced in over fifty years."

All the women rose, assembled in the center of the arbor, and swayed in unison. They danced in a circular pattern as the drum began to sound its rhythmic beat. Their hearts beat wildly because it was their first Green Corn Dance.

The women had learned and practiced the pattern only two weeks earlier but had never felt the thrill and excitement of dancing alongside their sisters while dressed in full Quinebaugan regalia.

At that precise moment, the past was forgotten, and the future was irrelevant. The women were all one with their sisters.

Travis sat in the audience, watching the bonds between his mother, White Eagle, and Lydia deepen as they danced. The stories he heard today, along with the food he shared with his fellow tribal members and observing the Green Corn Dance, all made him proud to be a Quinebaugan.

When Travis focused on Lydia, he was transported to a different time, place, and dimension as she danced alongside her sisters. He could not take his eyes off the red-tailed hawk feather in her hair, the tiny beaded slippers she wore on her feet, or her fitted buckskin dress.

He thought, "She is the most beautiful woman I've ever known, and I love her with all my heart. Together, we'll serve our tribe and the people of Norwich in countless ways."

Travis felt the spirit of his Quinebaugan ancestors strengthen deep within his soul because he knew he was among the right people at the right place and time. He was excited about their future because he knew that *Munduyahweh* had called him and Lydia to bring the community of Quinebaugan, Pocawansett, and Norwichians together as one.

He understood that everyone deserved fair opportunities, respect, honor, and a chance for a life filled with happiness. Every individual's beliefs and values are only a tiny piece of the greater whole, and after he and Lydia would remind everyone, he was confident the balance would be restored.

The future was bright and optimistic for a reunited, more balanced community!

Afterward

The Wawecus Hill Gold, Silver, and Nickel Mining Company, formed in the early 1850s, was based on the supposition that rocks in the area contained gold, silver, and nickel. The owners obtained a 100-year mineral lease for a land area of approximately 100 acres adjacent to Wawecus Hill.

The company's 1868 annual report is available at the Connecticut Historical Society in Hartford, Connecticut. It shows thirty-seven investors owning shares of stock. Each of the 20,000 shares had a par value of $25 ($538 in 2023 dollars). Seven investors held more than 1,000 shares each. In 2023 dollars, 1,000 shares would cost approximately $215,000. The report lists the market value of one share as *unknown*.

Norwich's Lafayette S. Foster became the acting vice president of the United States after Abraham Lincoln was assassinated. Foster was undoubtedly well aware of the company because his brother-in-law Augustus Hyde owned approximately $10,000 (2023 dollars) in shares.

The Wawecus Hill Gold, Silver, and Nickel Mining Company operated for at least 20 years. John Stedman's "1870 Stedman's Directory of the City and Town of Norwich" contains the last known reference to the company.

I've diligently searched for company records discussing profitability, operating practices, and net worth. I haven't found any. I believe the company never found gold, silver, or nickel in Norwich or anywhere else.

Bob Dees

About the Author

Mr. Dees and his wife have resided in Norwich for many years and love sharing stories of Norwich history with everyone. Bob is a historical fiction author, Norwich history enthusiast, and website developer. He designed, developed, built, and maintains the IconicNorwich.org website, chronicling 300 years of Norwich's history. The site is a not-for-profit resource used by students, history buffs, and researchers.

REFERENCES

1. "History of Norwich, Connecticut: From Its Possession by the Indians to the Year 1866," (1866), by Frances Manwaring Caulkins
2. "300 Years of Norwich History: IconicNorwich.org"
3. "The Norwich Jubilee. A Report of the Celebration at Norwich, Connecticut, on the Two Hundredth Anniversary of the Settlement of the Town. September 7th and 8th 1859," (1859), by John W. Stedman
4. "Old Houses of the Ancient Town of Norwich, 1600-1800," (1895), by Mary Elizabeth Perkins
5. "A Pequot-Mohegan Witchcraft Tale," (1903), by Frank G. Speck
6. "Squannit and Moshup," (2017), by Kara Newcastle
7. "Decorative Art of Indian Tribes of Connecticut," (1915), by Frank G. Speck

ILLUSTRATION ACKNOWLEDGEMENTS

ShutterStock, Open ClipArt, CanStock, GoGraph, Frank Speck

Made in the USA
Middletown, DE
03 January 2024